KNOCKOUT QUEEN

THE HEIGHTS CREW
BOOK FOUR

By

E. M. MOORE

Edited by Heather Long

Cover by 2nd Life Designs

Huge thanks to my beta readers: Bibi, Ashton, Lisa, Jorden, Summer, Jennifer, and Angie!

Saint Clary's University

Those Heartless Boys

The Heights Crew Series

Uppercut Princess

Arm Candy Warrior

Beautiful Soldier

Knockout Queen

The Ballers of Rockport High Series

Game On

Foul Line

At the Buzzer

Rockstars of Hollywood Hill

Rock On

Spring Hill Blue Series

Free Fall

Catch Me

Ravana Clan Vampires Series

Chosen By Darkness

Into the Darkness

Falling For Darkness

Surrender To Darkness

Ravana Clan Legacy Series

A New Genesis

Tracking Fate

Cursed Gift

Veiled History

Fractured Vision

Chosen Destiny

Order of the Akasha Series

Stripped (Prequel)

Summoned By Magic

Tempted By Magic

Ravished By Magic

Indulged By Magic

Enraged By Magic

Her Alien Scouts Series

Kain Encounters

Kain Seduction

Rise of the Morphlings Series

Of Blood and Twisted Roots

Safe Haven Academy Series

A Sky So Dark

A Dawn So Quiet

Chronicles of Cas Series

Reawakened

Hidden

Power

Severed

Rogue

The Adams' Witch Series

Bound In Blood

Cursed In Love

Witchy Librarian Cozy Mystery Series

Wicked Witchcraft

One Wicked Sister

Wicked Cool

Wicked Wiccans

Brawler hasn't let me go.

He thinks I'll unravel, I bet. He thinks I'll melt into the street at our feet. Just become one with the pavement. An inanimate object with no feelings. Especially not love or fear.

It's always love or fear, isn't it? The two types of emotions that have the strength to bring you to your knees. Right now, both of them rise inside me until each one wraps me up in a never-ending tornado of feelings. Dueling cyclones of worry turn me inside out until thinking clearly is like trying to look through distorted glass. Johnny's gone, and Oscar?

Where the fuck is Oscar?

Brawler and Magnum talk beside me. They've scared

the EMT's away. Neither one of them will be going to the hospital via ambulance, and neither will I. There's no reason for it. Our injuries are internal of the non-physical variety. It's our hearts that hurt. Maybe I'll rip mine out of my chest and put it on one of the stretchers. If the medical professionals are good at their jobs, they'll know what to do. They'll speed it to the nearest Emergency Room. Resuscitate it. Perform some sort of fancy, life-saving procedure and clap their colleagues' backs at the end of the day for a job well done.

But no. Heights Crew shit can't be fixed like that. That would be too damn easy.

Johnny is missing. Gone. Taken by another depraved group, much like the one I've tied myself to. I can't go to the police. Or the firemen. Or anyone with morals. None of the so-called heroes I grew up believing would be the ones to save me if I was ever in danger can help me now. Call 9-1-1, right? That's what we're told?

I chuckle at the lies we're handed down. At the complete farce I find myself in. Fear roots itself to my veins, tangling up in everything until I'm choking on it just like I was choking on the thick, black smoke that filled The Ring.

Brawler pulls me away at arm's length, brows furrowing as he inspects the completely delirious gaze that must be showing on the outside just as much as I'm feeling it on the inside.

I'm going mad. That's what this is. The Heights has finally taken my sanity from me. It was bound to happen sooner or later, if I'm honest. I should've prepared better for my inevitable stint in the psych ward.

"Kyla?" he murmurs, clearly worried.

I peer up at him. All six-foot sooty inches of broad shoulders and muscular planes. His chiseled chest plastered with ash as if that's what he's made of. Just skin and dying embers and turquoise eyes that desperately seek me in the hell I'm in.

Johnny and Oscar. Oscar and Johnny.

We know what happened to Johnny, so there's nothing we can do about that right now. "Oscar," I croak out, flicking my gaze between Mag and Brawler. "Did you guys see him when we were in there? Anywhere?" My mind catapults between different scenes. Mag pulling me away from the fight... The first gunshots... Hiding under the bleachers...

No Oscar.

Neither of them answer, and I should've known they wouldn't. Brawler was fighting, and Magnum was watching over me.

Who watches over them though?

"We need to find him," I say, my voice steeling inside me, hardening now that I have something to focus on other than the complete and utter despair that our enemy has Johnny and Oscar is God-knows-where.

I wiggle out of Brawler's grip and head for the burning building. I don't know where to start searching for him, but that seems like the most logical choice considering that's where we saw him last.

"He was in the crowd," Magnum says, coming up to walk beside me. "Right on the perimeter while you were fighting. When Jiko jumped into the ring, I pulled you out. I didn't see him after that, but I wasn't looking either."

Brawler tries to hold back on my hand from behind, but I yank out of his grip. "Kyla, what are you doing?" he growls. "You can't go in there."

The steel door Magnum and I came out of looms just a little further ahead. No one has come out of it since we did. No one went back in either.

I ignore him and keep moving toward the door until he catches my wrist and turns me to face him. "He wouldn't want you to go back in there. Come on." He gestures toward the roof of the building where the flames leap out. The firemen point their hoses at the fire to try to wrangle it under control.

"I'd go back for any of you," I say, voice eerily calm, a complete contradiction to the rapid beat of my heart. Oscar and Johnny's faces filter through my brain. Half of me is missing. Literally half. I clamp down on my jaw and focus on what's right in front of me. "I'm going in, Brawler."

I turn away from him and walk right into a black-clad fireman. He tips his yellow hat up to gaze down at me past his blackened nose. "You can't be this close. Get back. Let us do our jobs."

"One of my friends is still in there," I tell him, pointing back at the burning building, not even knowing if it's true. If he's not in there, where the hell is he? He would've been trying to find us already if he was okay.

The fireman takes my shoulders in a firm grip. "I'm sorry, Miss, but you have to get back. We'll do our best to save anyone who's still in there, but we can't go in until the fire is under control."

A groaning sound comes from the building. The fireman whirls around, hands spread out, blocking us as he simultaneously moves us back. The roof nearest to us collapses into itself. A volcano of ash and flames lick toward the sky until it rains down white, snow-like cinders.

"Oscar!" I scream, but the sound I make is only eaten up by the void. My heart squeezes painfully. The thought of Oscar inside, trapped under the burning roof almost brings me to my knees. The fireman runs forward, leaving us there and dodging people and police. He yells at everyone to "Get back!"

Brawler wraps his hands around me from behind, dragging me backward a few feet. "We just have to wait."

"Fuck that," I snarl. Desperation triggers my muscles to move. I push away from Brawler, heading in the opposite direction the fireman went. I scan the building, looking for another door, looking for Oscar, for anything. All the while,

Johnny's pained expression stays forefront in my mind. If there's a chance we can save Oscar, I'm going to do it. Then, I'm going to kill whoever took Johnny, make them suffer like I know he's suffering right now.

Magnum and Brawler flank me as we make our way around the side of the building. A cop stands in front of a barricade that leads down the alleyway between this building and the next. He straightens when he sees us moving toward him. We must look like a sight. Brawler and I in fight gear, but looking like we took a bath in char. Then, there's Mag, the ever-steady sentinel whose usual calm demeanor is marred by the sweat and fallen embers that litter his clothes.

"You can't go back there," he says. "It's been deemed unsafe."

"We're looking for our friend. He was in there," I say again. Panic has taken control over my voice until I barely recognize it. It's high and squeaky, riddled with heartache.

The cop's lips thin. He gives me a pitying look that does nothing but anger me. "Listen, you're better off heading back the way you came and then give his name to—"

I don't give him a chance to finish his sentence. I fake him out, squeezing past him and ducking under the white and orange roadblock that acted as a barrier. My feet slap the uneven pavement as I take off at a run. No doubt I'll have cuts and scrapes on the bottom of my feet, but I don't feel anything right now, other than the determination to find Oscar no matter where he is.

Luckily, the other end of the alleyway isn't manned yet. I turn the corner, scanning the wall for a different entrance. This side of the building isn't quite so chaotic with people, so hope blooms inside me. If I could just find a door. Something. Anything.

Except for blown-out windows, the fire hasn't even reached this side of the building. I skip over the glass as best I can until a scream pierces the air.

I spin on my heel. Further down the block, a gang of guys spill out of an alleyway. Hands shove a dark-haired boy to his knees and aim a gun at his head. Fear crawls its way up my throat. That's Oscar. "No!"

I run toward them. They've angled themselves away from the building, so I can't see what's happening, but I don't stop. The burning in my lungs increases, but my gaze narrows ahead with laser focus. I leap toward the taut shoulder of the asshole holding a gun to my boyfriend, tackling him with the force of my body. We go down hard, and the gun slips from his hand and skids across the concrete.

Hands grab for me, but I posture up and bring my fist down on the back of the guy's head. His head cracks against the sidewalk in front of us. Knocked out from the impact, he doesn't move, but that's not good enough for me. Rage fuels my movements. I pick his head up and slam it into the concrete again and again. Blood rushes over my fingers and pools on the concrete below us.

"I'd stop if I were you," a voice says.

I throw the lifeless head back to the ground and gaze up into a barrel of a gun. The same gun that skidded over the concrete. I don't dare look away from it, not to even peek two feet to my right where Oscar should be to make sure he's okay. Instead, I stare down the abrupt end to my life.

2

A gunshot cracks through the air, and I wince, waiting for the explosion of pain to hit. It never comes.

I open my eyes. The guy who was holding the gun is now face-down in front of me. A second shot rings out. I jump, but a lifeless hand lands to my left seconds later. A stampede of footfalls barrel toward me. I blink, finding Magnum and Brawler running this way, Magnum shoving his gun back into the waistband of his pants.

I breathe out a sigh of relief. That crack shot of a man. Hallelujah. They never made it around the policeman like I did but thank fuck they're here.

I scramble off the guy I'm still towering over. He moans, but he won't be going anywhere for a while, so I crawl toward Oscar. *One Kyle and Anna. Two Kyle and Anna.*

He's okay, he's okay, he's okay, I tell myself. The sidewalk bruises my knees, but that's a pain I can handle. The one that screams in my brain, wondering if something is seriously wrong with Oscar? That one I can't.

Brawler gets to Oscar first. He lays his fingers on his neck and closes his eyes. Within a moment, he breathes out an easy breath.

A sob works its way out of me. He *is* okay.

When I get to him, we turn Oscar over. His lids flutter open. Cuts and bruises litter his face, and red marks mar his perfectly tan skin. His mouth opens, and then he winces before saying, "Princesa?"

I wrap my hand around his, biting my lip at this variation of my nickname. Emotion threatens to barrel right out of me. "I'm right here," I tell him.

He smirks. "I came to save you." His bloodied, cracked lips are still so perfect I could kiss him.

I chuckle, the deliriousness coming back. "Nice try, Drego, but it looks like it was my turn to save you."

He tries to get up and groans, hugging his free hand to his stomach. "Why do they always go for the ribs? Fucking assholes."

Tears threaten my eyes, but a joking Oscar is a living Oscar, and that's all I want.

He surveys our group, looking to see who's here and who's not. Looking for the one person we're missing. He tilts his head to the side. "Um, Princess?"

A lump the size of my frail heart lodges in my throat. I blink away the tears as I inspect him. He's clean. Other than the fact that he looks like he got the shit kicked out of him, it doesn't appear as if he was in the fire or the explosions or anything. He's certainly not as dirty as the rest of us. "You're okay?" I ask, doubtful and not totally trusting what I see. There must be something wrong with him. Internally, perhaps? I continue to scan him, but he only nods. It's too much. I throw myself at him. A half sob-half crazed laugh escapes my throat. "I'm so happy."

He pulls his hand through my hair. "You don't sound happy, Princess," he whispers, pulling me close and cupping the back of my head as I let the warmth of his skin melt into mine. For a brief moment, it's like heaven. Then, he asks the question all of us want to know. "Where's Johnny?"

Magnum speaks up, ignoring Oscar's question. None of us want to face that head-on right now. "We need to get out of here." He darts his gaze around the back alley. Like usual, he's always looking for the next threat. We pull Oscar to his feet, and I hold onto him as people start walking our way, avoiding our gazes and pointedly not looking at the two bodies at our feet.

Everyone in the Heights has come out for this. The call of destruction just too much for them to ignore.

I turn my head, my mouth finding Oscar's ear as we follow Magnum. "They took him," I whisper, answering his earlier question and only letting half the words I want to say break free because I still don't want to believe he's gone. Was this all a stunt just to get Johnny?

He was shot in The Ring's box. The last time I saw him, he was half-unconscious. Are his kidnappers going to take care of him? Are they going to use him as leverage? Or are they just going to kill him and be done with it?

My throat catches, and I grip Oscar so tight I know it must hurt. He darts his gaze around the growing crowd. "We need to get out of here," he echoes.

We come around the back of the building, and Magnum pulls up short. Ahead of us, the police are on the scene, setting up more roadblocks. "Fuck. The car is blocked in." He hesitates for a moment before he leads us down the next block devoid of people. He stops beside a car before taking his gun and breaking the driver's side window. With all the surrounding chaos, no one's here to notice. He unlocks the vehicle, and we all get inside, Oscar gingerly getting into the backseat first before I slide in next to him.

Magnum does something to the car, and it springs to life. We're a mere few blocks away from the chaos when he explains why we're sitting in a stolen vehicle, "The cops have The Ring surrounded." He presses his lips together. "I didn't want to explain to them what we're doing at a place that just got shot up and bombed...especially since Kyla is with us. Everyone from the Crew who escaped will be getting their asses out of there as soon as possible."

Or if you're Big Daddy K, you're already gone because

you're a piece of fucking shit who couldn't care less about his son.

It's true though. The police are not my biggest fans right now. I can't be caught at the scene where a bombing, a shootout, and a fire occurred. If the police don't know about the dead bodies with bullets in them yet, they will. If I'm found near that shit, that sounds like probable cause to take me in given my recent history. With Johnny in a hostage type of situation, the last place I need to be is behind bars. Or back at Greenlawn.

I shiver at the thought. I don't want to be away from the guys ever again, especially not for something I'm guiltless of.

I lean closer to Oscar for comfort, careful not to jostle him too much. From an outsider's perspective, I'm sure we look pretty fucked up. Magnum, Brawler, and I look like we've been to hell and back. Oscar's the only one who could pass as human at the moment, except when you look at his face.

Wind whips through the car as Magnum steers us out onto the highway. Oscar takes a moment to shrug his hoodie off, so he can wrap it around me. I know I should be asking what we're doing and how we're going to get Johnny back, but I don't want to admit that I'm in way over my head this time. Whoever took Johnny is the enemy I didn't even know I was making. The enemy I never could've prepared for when I came to the Heights.

After a silent forty minutes, Magnum pulls down a dirt

road. The bumps bouncing the car make me look up, and a familiar view greets me. We're at the cabin. Johnny's cabin.

"Where are we?" Brawler asks from the front.

Magnum parks. We're deep in the woods here, so we don't have to worry about ditching the stolen piece of property yet. As far as I know, no one else knows about this place, so we can be fairly certain the authorities won't find us or the car here. They'd have to know this place existed to check it out, and the Crew is smarter than that.

"This is..." Magnum peeks over at Brawler, a shadow falling over his face. "This used to be a training area for the Crew, but right now, it's a safe house."

I lean forward. "This is where they took me after the tower was bombed."

Magnum pushes the door open, and the rest of us follow his lead and get out of the car. I help Oscar to his feet and hover close, snaking my arm around his back. His movements aren't too restrained, but he keeps his arm around his midsection, shielding his ribs.

The porch steps loom in front of me. It doesn't feel right to be here without Johnny. A brick settles in my gut, and the same slice of determination that first hit me rears its beautiful head again. I have to figure out what happened to him. I have to save him. I can't think about what they might do to him. I can't think that they'll hurt him even more than he already is—or worse...kill him.

I pull my shoulders back and lead Oscar toward the

front entrance. Our lives are about to go to shit again. No doubt the police will be all over our asses. Big Daddy K will be on the warpath. No matter what he does to his son, in his head, he still loves him. I bet he could even justify why he left him at The Ring. He'll probably blame what happened to Johnny on someone else instead of realizing his part in all this.

Magnum opens the front door with a key and then flicks on the lights. "Swanky," Oscar whistles as the interior is illuminated.

"You should see the hot tub upstairs."

"There are bathrooms attached to every bedroom," Magnum says, his security guard persona on already. "Let's get cleaned up and then report back here, so we can figure out what to do."

Oscar and Brawler nod and start for the steps, but Magnum's jaw clenches in an odd way, so I stay where I am.

"Ready, Princess?" Oscar asks.

"I'll be right up," I tell him, keeping my eyes on Magnum. The thud of footsteps up the stairs is a steady drum in my ears as Brawler tries to help Oscar, but Oscar only ends up shoving his hands away. "The master bedroom is mine," I call out just as they hit the top.

As soon as they're out of earshot, Magnum peeks at me. His hazel-green eyes are dead, drowning in darkness. He swallows. "I was supposed to keep him safe. Johnny's my responsibility."

I tilt my head. "I thought I was your responsibility..."

"Before you, I was assigned to Johnny," Mag explains. "When you guys met, he told me to stick by you because he didn't want anything to happen. What happened is my fault."

I take his hand in mine. Magnum and Johnny go way back. "We're going to find him," I promise. "We're going to find him and get him back and—"

"K's going to be pissed," Mag says, interrupting me.

I grit my jaw. "Maybe he shouldn't have left him in the fucking box then."

Magnum reaches out for me, and I step into his embrace. He presses a kiss to my forehead, lips moving over my skin when he says, "Just get cleaned up. We'll meet back here."

"Do you want company?" I ask, biting my lip in apprehension. I'm not sure he should be alone right now, even though he's not giving off any needy vibes. In fact, it's the exact opposite. I have a feeling he just wanted to get that off his chest, but what he really wants is to be alone.

He shakes his head. "I'll be fine. I just need a minute."

He gives my forehead one last kiss and then spins, taking off through the kitchen to the lone bedroom on the first floor. When I was here alone, I did some snooping, so I know for a fact there's a small bedroom just past the kitchen pantry. He disappears, and I stand there for a minute, still watching the empty space where he was.

Eventually though, I turn and head up the stairs. As

directed, Oscar and Brawler left me the master bedroom with the kickass shower. I peel my fight sports bra and shorts off. The areas my clothes covered look ghostly white in comparison to the ash and soot discarded all over my body.

I take the braid out of my hair, running my fingers through the mess as I watch myself in the mirror. I should be freaking out more than I am. Putting my mind to something has always worked wonders for me though. When I have a goal, I can work toward it. It's when my life is in upheaval that I can't ever seem to find my footing.

Yes, Johnny is gone, but we're going to find him. We're going to bring him back to us where he belongs, and then hopefully, we can get the fuck out of the Heights for good.

I'm seriously getting sick of this place. At this point, if my guys weren't tethered here, I'd think about giving up the whole revenge on Big Daddy K thing and just leave.

I laugh to myself. No, I wouldn't. I'm too fucking stubborn for that.

Once my hair is untangled as good as it's going to get, I turn on the shower, holding my fingers under the rain fall showerhead to gauge the temperature. Once it's this side of scalding, I step in. Immediately, the water turns a murky gray at my feet. Standing under the spray, I can almost wash off everything that happened today. The fire. The bombs. The evidence disappearing right this very second. The only thing that can never get washed away is the internal scarring. The cut when I realized Johnny had been shot. The incision when Brawler and Johnny disappeared behind a wall of fire when the floor cracked between us. The gash when Brawler told me Johnny was gone. That he'd been taken. And the complete loss when I realized we didn't know where Oscar was.

I use the shampoo and conditioner that are already in the shower. The smell reminds me of Johnny, and I breathe in deep, allowing his essence to fill me. Johnny might be the strongest person I know. To have grown up in such a hideous excuse for a childhood, but to come out with integrity and principles. Sure, he's not perfect. He wouldn't admit to being an angel either, but against all odds, he is decent. He's caring. And he's learned how to love when I'm not sure his father even knows what the word means.

K uses his love as manipulation. As fear. As an iron fist to follow orders.

Johnny's better than that.

I let the water cascade down the crown of my head for a few minutes, clearing my head to make sure I'm ready for the brainstorming session that's about to go down. Then, I shut the water off, grab a towel from under the sink, and walk out into the bedroom.

Brawler's sitting on the edge of the bed. His dirty fight shorts are gone, and in its place, a pair of dark gray joggers hug his hips with no shirt. His muscles bunch as he looks up at me. As soon as he sees my face, he pales.

My mouth parts. "What?"

He swallows. "Your face."

I bring my fingertips to my cheek. "What is it?"

He shakes his head and looks away. "I hurt you."

I close my eyes and breathe out, understanding filtering through me. I fought Brawler just hours ago. Barely any time at all, even though it seems as if a week has gone by since then. My face must be bruised and swollen. I knew he'd have this reaction. I walk toward him, putting my fingers underneath his chin and making him look me in the eyes.

He grimaces.

"Hey," I say, waiting until I have his full attention. "It had to be this way. Besides, if it makes you feel any better, I can't even feel it."

He rolls his eyes. "It doesn't make me feel any better. You know I never wanted to hurt you, Kyla. I would never—"

"—under normal circumstances? Of course, I know that." I lean over to press what's supposed to be just a soft kiss to his lips, but Brawler's hunger takes over. His fingers sink into my heated flesh as he pries my mouth open with his tongue, forcing his way through like he expected a barrier.

He groans and moves to his feet, wrapping his arms around me and holding me so tightly as if he's scared I might run away. "I need to make this better."

In his words are the undercurrent of the real problem. He needs to feel close again. He needs reassurance.

He takes my hands, stretches them above my head and then backs me up to the bedroom wall. Somewhere along the way, my towel drops. He presses into my bare skin, and the length of his cock brushes my hip. "I don't know what I can do to show you. That wasn't me. I don't do things like that." He looks at me, his turquoise eyes filled with regret. His large muscles stand out, straining as if he's holding a lot in. "Can you forgive me?"

"There's nothing to forgive," I try to tell him. "We're only doing what we have to." I stare at his swollen lips, and my body vibrates with the tension between us.

He steps closer, and his cock nudges the apex of my thighs. I swallow, heat enveloping me like a rabid wildfire.

He takes my hands in one of his and then brings his other down to brush his fingers beneath my eye, hovering just over the painful parts. "I put these marks on you." He shakes his head. "It's unforgivable."

"These marks..." I tell him, voice raspy. "They're just skin-deep. They don't change anything between us. Nothing will change what's between us, Brawler. Nothing."

He groans, succumbing to his tightly wound urges. He moves forward, dropping his head so he can suck on my neck while he lifts his hips into me.

I spread my legs, welcoming his touch. "We can prove it to each other."

Brawler pushes his joggers down, freeing his cock. He aligns the head with my opening, and I suck in a breath at feeling him so close. I meet him at the same time he presses forward, angling my hips toward him. We both make mutual sounds of satisfaction when he pushes inside. For a moment, we stay that way, taking deep breaths and enjoying the feeling of being together.

"I'll never hurt you again," Brawler promises. He starts to move, grinding his pelvis against mine. "You're my everything." He punctuates each word with a thrust of his hips.

He won't listen, so I need to show him how I've already forgotten what happened. I wiggle out of his grip and sink my fingers into his ass. "I need more," I tell him, already heady with sex. Brawler broke through the barriers I put up when I first came to the Heights. He put a sledgehammer through the concrete blocks despite the danger he was putting himself in with Johnny and the Crew. I owe him everything.

I start to climb his body, and he easily lifts me to wrap my legs around his bare, muscular ass. Pinning me against the wall, he thrusts inside me over and over, each movement of his hips teasing my clit.

My moans spur his movements, and he stays there, working my body over until it tightens. Deep spasms rock me, and I ride out an amazing orgasm that curls my toes.

"Beautiful..." He cups my ass and turns. His steady footsteps take us to the bed, and he holds me to his chest until I'm safely pinned between him and the mattress.

Despite the shitty day we've had, the fact that my

energy is spent, and my lungs still burn a little, I want nothing more than for Brawler to forget about the stupid bruising on my face or the fact that we fought in a ring for other people's pleasure. We're so much more than that. We can't let one event define us. "Can I ride you?"

He flips us in an instant, gripping my hips to steady me. I find purchase with my palms on his killer chest to slide up and down his cock. With each stroke, I'm telling him what happened doesn't matter. I'm telling him the bruising is temporary, but what's permanent is our feelings for each other. When his exterior cracks, my pleasure heightens. I grind down over him until an orgasm hits me so hard I cry out, doubling over him, hands fisting the sheets on the bed.

"Fuck, Kyla," he groans, taking a nipple into his mouth and sucking it, spurring on another round of spasms over his cock. He jerks inside me, and then sits up, holding me on his lap as he works his hips up and pulls me down at the same time. He watches how we come together, his hips thrusting upward in this sexual dance between the two of us. "Come again. For me?" He slips his hand between us, rubbing my nub. It's too much. I bring the whole house down with my scream as my climax basically attacks me.

Brawler tries to ride it out, a fierce expression of determination on his face, but he can't. He gives in, jerking inside me as he unloads his hot cum with a possessive roar. It's almost unlike him, but I understand that need to be a part of something, especially when you think something is threatening to take it away.

I wrap my arms around him as the last of his tremors subside. He pulls me down, our legs tangled as we kiss, sealing the moment with a soft embrace of lips.

"You understand now, right?" I ask.

"What I understand is that your capacity to love, Kyla, is undeniable." He brings his fingers up to trace under my eyes again. It stings, but I don't pull back. There's no sense in making him feel worse than he already does. "You're still beautiful," he says. "Even when you're sad about Johnny. Even when I put these terrible bruises on your face."

I press my palm against the white angel wing covering his neck. It's always had a look of devastation to me. Beautiful yet sorrowful at the same time.

I'm all for the sad angel. Sometimes, grief can be the best motivator.

"We'll find him," Brawler promises, sensing the change in my thoughts. He pulls me to him and presses a kiss to my lips that's more of a valiant pledge than anything else.

Whoever took Johnny Rocket better watch the fuck out.

3

————

*B*rawler and I walk out of the master bedroom hand-in-hand. Oscar meets us at the top of the stairs, hair slicked back and dark eyes like shadows in the night. He catches my hand before I walk downstairs, gaze focusing on my face. He takes a deep breath while scrutinizing the area around my eyes. Eventually, he just squeezes my hand and lets us go downstairs.

I move ahead of them now that I'm on a mission. When I hit the bottom, I turn to find Oscar clapping Brawler on the back in a reassuring gesture. Brawler's heart is on his sleeve. He's obviously affected by the bruising on my face, and I get it. I totally do. There are some marks on his face that aren't sitting well in my gut either, but at least I can tell myself that maybe Jiko did those.

I gasp. Shit. "Jiko..."

Brawler shrugs. "I didn't see what happened to him."

"Me either," Oscar sneers.

Everything happened in an instant, so I didn't get time to think too much into it, but Jiko fought Brawler. Why?

I sneak a glance at Brawler, but he's already shrugging and rubbing the back of his neck.

Oscar grunts. "The guy's an asshole. Who cares?"

I don't disagree with him, but he grew up like Johnny. Everything he does is for a reason. Johnny wasn't mad at him for turning him in. Why? Because Jiko was playing the game. The game their fathers set up for them when they were only kids. Since Jiko jumped into the ring, this was just another move on the board. I bite my lip, mulling it over in my head, but I didn't see everything because I was kind of passed out for a bit. Not that I'm bringing that up right now. "What happened?" I ask. "After..." I trail off, not wanting to drag Brawler even further down the rabbit hole of hurting me. He doesn't need to hear he knocked me out cold, and I'd rather not re-live it either.

"Brawler knocked you down and was about to end the fight when Jiko just rushed him. He tackled him to the ground and started whaling on him."

"I wouldn't say he whaled on me," Brawler corrects. "He got in some good shots until I recovered from the surprise attack." The lines in his forehead deepen. "You think he did that for you?"

I shake my head. "I don't know. I guess it makes sense he

would try to make up for what he did to Johnny. I don't think he did it because he was mad you were beating me." I nod, my thoughts forming to the only logical conclusion. "He did it to get back in Johnny's good graces. By him stepping into our fight, neither one of us actually lost. You still won, technically, but also, I didn't lose. Therefore, we both got to save face."

"So…" Oscar says, rolling his hand forward.

"So, I'm saying he did it to show Johnny they're still friends. Johnny was worried about me losing the fight, even knowing that Brawler had to win because he's a recruit. This way, I didn't technically lose because Jiko stepped in at the exact right time."

Oscar nods slowly. "The crowd loved it, too. They were torn about who to root for when you were fighting each other, but as soon as Jiko came in, they wanted his blood."

"Good. K will be happy then. Hopefully," I add because who even knows what makes that fucker happy other than bloodshed. "I wonder if he made it out okay."

"Fuck him," Oscar deadpans. I smile because Oscar is as bad as me in the retribution department. I don't let shit go, and apparently, neither does he.

"I just meant that he would be a good ally to have in getting Johnny back. He's in the gang business, so he knows how these things operate. Also, I think he actually cares for Johnny."

"Yeah, well, I'm in the Crew too, so I know how things

operate. Then of course, there's Magnum who's been in it a hell of a lot longer." He peeks around the kitchen. "Where is he, anyway?"

I turn to find the hallway to the other bedroom clear. The door to the bedroom is even slightly ajar, but I don't hear anything coming from inside. I swallow and sidestep Brawler to go look for him. I slip down the dark hallway and peek inside the room. Nothing is amiss. Everything is dark like Magnum just slipped inside to turn around and leave again. There's not even the heavy coating of steam in the air like he'd just gotten out of the shower.

"Princess," Oscar calls out. "You're going to want to see this."

My heart thuds as I make my way back into the kitchen. Oscar picks up a piece of white paper on the kitchen counter and holds it out to me. "I'll be back," he says, repeating the neat scrawl on the note. "Who does he think he is? The Terminator?"

I snatch the paper from Oscar's hand. "Seriously?" I close my eyes. Of course. He just waited for me to go upstairs. I asked him if he wanted company, and he said no because he already knew he'd be leaving the house. I scan the note again, but there are only three words on the damn thing. No clue as to where he was going or why. "Does anyone have their phone on them?" I ask, glancing between Oscar and Brawler. My phone is still at The Ring. Though, who knows if it's still even working or if it's melted by now. I drop my head back at that thought. If it's intact, the police will find it as soon as they start putting the puzzle pieces together, so they're going to know I was there.

Fear rips through me. I turn to Brawler. "The phone. *My* phone." My *real* phone. The one with my aunt and uncle's number inside it. The only clue to my other life. I clench my stomach.

Brawler shoots his hand out and grabs my wrist. "It's okay. It's safe. It's at my house. I didn't take it to The Ring."

Relief floods me. "Thank God. Fuck."

"But your other phone is still there. So is Brawler's." Oscar shakes his head. "The police are going to know we were there anyway. Unless that's why Magnum stepped out."

Stepped out? I want to argue with him about his choice of words, but he pulls his phone out, so I don't. I can argue with the guy I'm really mad at.

I try to take it from his hands, but he pulls it out of reach. "Not a good idea, Princess. If we're connected to what happened at The Ring, they'll trace our phones. I turned mine off before we left the Heights."

Fuck, fuck, fuck. He has a point. I eye a phone on the wall and move toward it. "I don't suppose you guys know Mag's cell number off the top of your head, do you?"

They both just stare back at me with blank faces. Of course not. Who remembers numbers nowadays? That's it.

We're going to memorize everyone's number after this, in case we're ever in a situation like this again.

I smile. "So, if the police could track us here and know where we are, couldn't they do the same with Johnny's phone? He probably had it on him when he was taken. Unless it fell out of his pocket. But we can trace him that way, can't we?"

Brawler hauls himself onto the stool at the kitchen island. He's moving slower than normal, so I can tell he's sore. "That means the police can track Johnny, but we can't."

"K has an in with someone on the police force," I say, thinking back to the cop who patted Magnum on the back when we exited out the back staircase. Maybe he's their dirty cop? They seemed too chummy for being on the opposite ends of the good guy-bad guy spectrum.

Oscar starts rummaging through the kitchen cabinets. He pulls out several bags of chips and places them on the island before leaning against it to catch his breath. I start to go to him, but he waves my worry away. "K has an in. We have nothing."

"Well, K's going to want to save Johnny."

"If he even knows he's missing," Brawler points out. "That asshole took off with one of his security guys before we got caught in the room and separated. He knew Johnny was shot, but just fucking left. He probably has no idea what happened after that."

Oscar raises his brows into his hairline as he opens one of the bags. "Really? What the fuck? I didn't think he'd do that to Johnny."

"He did," I say, reliving that moment in my head, still praying Johnny was awake enough to see it for himself. His father fucking left him there, injured. "He's a fucking asshole, but he might be a useful fucking asshole in this one instance."

"What happened to you, anyway?" Brawler asks, spinning the chips Oscar opened so he can take a handful for himself.

Oscar's fists clench. "The crowd fucking panicked. I got swept away with them toward the exit. I tried to turn to get back to you guys, but it was fucking impossible. I would've been trampled. Then, as soon as I got outside, two guys jumped me and hauled me away."

I move closer and reach across the island to slide my hand over his tense knuckles. "They were probably the same ones who came in shooting, recognized you, and..." I trail off because I'm pretty sure they're intention was to kill him, but I can't let myself think that. "Did they say anything?"

He shakes his head. "Not a damn thing. Just kicked the shit out of me."

After a while, Oscar asks exactly what happened while we were inside, and I give him the play-by-play, starting with Magnum pulling me to my feet while Brawler and Jiko were still fighting and ending with us moving down the back stairwell. I don't tell them the exchange I witnessed in the hallway between Magnum and the cop. I still don't know what to think of it, or even whether it's important at all. For all I know, they could've gone to school together. And honestly, none of that matters right now anyway because the only thing that does is getting Johnny back. If he's the dirty cop, I'll ask him to trace Johnny's phone myself.

"Any thoughts on who took Johnny?" Brawler asks, shrugging. "We don't have access to phone tracers or anything else right now, so we have to go on what we know."

I take some chips and place them in a pile next to Brawler and then pull myself up onto the barstool. "The problem is we don't know all that much. Johnny was investigating who killed Farmingham and the other guy, but if they found more evidence, he didn't say anything to me about it."

"That's because you were getting ready for the fight," Oscar says. "My vote's on Gregory. He killed Farmingham and Turner. We know he did because he left the dumbass candy as his calling card. He wanted K to know it was him."

"Sounds risky," I say. "Taking K's son?"

"Exactly," Oscar agrees. "Which means he thinks too much of himself. Or," he pauses. "He actually has good reason to think too much of himself. Maybe he's got a bigger group than we know about."

"Do we really think he's responsible for bombing the tower though? He didn't leave candy there if he did. I know

Johnny inspected the bomb..." I run my fingers through my hair. "I don't know what he found out. Fuck."

"It's not your fault," Brawler says. "Johnny didn't tell you anything because he wanted you to focus on the fight. We can only work on one problem at a time."

"Except the problems are coming from all directions." I shove a chip into my mouth and chew slowly.

"There's that other guy who showed up, too," Brawler says. "Mag's cousin. He didn't seem like he was a part of Gregory's guys, but we were leaning toward the idea he had an affiliation with another group since he was excommunicated."

"Right. Mag was thinking he was part of a group called the Dragons. We don't know anything about them though." I peek up at Oscar hoping he's going to prove me wrong, but he just shrugs in answer, so I'm guessing we really don't know anything about this group called the Dragons either. And we especially don't know if they have anything to do with Johnny. "If I had to guess, I'm thinking Gregory took Johnny. Seems like a ballsy move. Even worse than killing the lower-level guys." It pains me to say that because a life is a life, but in the Crew scheme of things, Johnny has a lot more power. A lot more sway. K was pissed that Gregory killed the two low-level guys, but when he finds out Johnny is gone, he's going to be furious.

"So, how do we find Gregory?" Brawler asks.

"He's always found us before." He tried to take me right

before my first attempt at fighting in The Ring. Now this. "I wish we could identify the shooters at The Ring. Then we would know for sure."

"Either way," Oscar says. "If Gregory doesn't have him, he might know who does. You ever heard of 'The enemy of my enemy is my friend'? If he doesn't have Johnny, he knows who does. It wouldn't surprise me if the Crew had more than one group trying to take them down. Let's not forget K killed Roza Fonz a couple of months ago. Gangs don't take the killing of other leaders lightly."

I breathe out. We really need Magnum here to have this talk, which is why I'm so pissed he left without saying where he was going and without having a way to get in contact with him. He knows the major players better than we do. We're just talking into the air, not sure anything will stick.

Stepping down from the stool, I head toward the refrigerator. The chips taste good, but they're not dampening the hunger starting to squeeze my stomach. I find a few single-serve frozen pizzas in the freezer and throw them in the microwave. After we've chowed down on that, we take the chips and some bottles of water, and move toward the living room. I start the fireplace like I learned the last time we were here, so we can have a nice, cozy fire after this shitty day.

The flames reflect on Brawler's face and torso. "I hope Magnum gets back soon. I need to make sure my mom is okay..." He licks his lips. "And you guys realize it's almost Christmas, right?"

My eyes widen. Shit. I hadn't even realized. Back home, my aunt and uncle's neighbors would've started decorating before Thanksgiving. Well, damn. That means I spent Thanksgiving at Greenlawn Reformatory and didn't even know it. There's nothing in the Heights that says we're in the happiest time of the year. No decorations. No volunteers ringing bells asking for donations. Nothing. "I take it the Heights doesn't celebrate."

"With what money, Princess?"

I snuggle into Oscar carefully, hating the way these guys grew up. Brawler, at least, looks as if he'd miss Christmas if he didn't get it.

Car lights filter through the windows and light up the wall. Each of us sit up. Oscar stands from the couch and heads toward the window to peer outside, still with a protective hand over his midsection. "It's Mag. He's got someone with him."

My heart leaps in my throat. All three of us funnel outside. I ignore the biting of the pebbles under my feet as I wish with everything in me that Magnum somehow found Johnny. Instead, Magnum shoves a blindfolded guy forward. He presses his finger to his lips, so we all step aside as Magnum drags him up the steps and into the house.

One thing is clear, it's not Johnny. Every hope I'd conjured in the last fifteen seconds drops in an instant, leaving me whiplashed and cold.

We follow the strange pair, and Magnum forces the guy

to sit on the coffee table. He ties the guy's hands behind his back with zip ties that he pulls from his pocket. "Shit," the guy growls. "That fucking hurts."

I try to place the voice, but I don't have much time to figure it out before Magnum unmasks him.

It's Cole.

Magnum sits casually on the couch opposite him and crosses his legs, glaring at his cousin. "This is where you start fucking talking. Where is Johnny Rocket?"

4

___

Cole pulls at his wrists, scowling at the way he's tied up. "Is this any way to treat family? I've done nothing but try to help you, brother."

"Is that what you're doing?" Magnum asks casually. "Because the way I see it, every time something bad happens, you're around. You show up at the murder scene of one of our guys and then you call me right before The Ring gets shot up." I chew on my lip. I'd forgotten he'd received a call right before shit went down.

Cole's gaze travels to Brawler, Oscar, and I, lingering on my messed up face for a blip. "Jesus. What happened to you?"

"I'm fine," I snarl. I can feel Brawler's heated, apologetic gaze on me, but I ignore it. "Answer his fucking question."

"I don't know. It sounds like I'm helping to me. I told you about Gregory. I warned you about the shootout."

"It sounds like you know about the trouble, which is why you're going to tell me where Johnny Rocket is."

The cousins match each other gaze for gaze, a challenge in each of them. There aren't any outward similarities between the two of them that I can see. Magnum has a head of copper hair while Cole's is a brown fauxhawk. Cole is smaller than Jacob, too. His frame on the slim side, kind of lanky. Then again, I prefer my guys with a bit of muscle.

After the stare off to end all stare offs, Cole eventually gets bored and looks around. He inspects the cabin first, gazing at the finishes, craning his neck to see as much as he can. Magnum seems as if he's content to wait this out. He knows his cousin better than I do, so whatever. Eventually, the guys and I take seats around the living room. It would be almost peaceful with the fireplace still going if it wasn't for the guy tied up, blocking the view. I have a sneaking suspicion this isn't how Magnum usually interrogates, but he's most likely giving his cousin the benefit of the doubt.

"I know what you're thinking, Jacob," Cole finally says. "But I'm on your side. You don't have to tie me up and disorient me before bringing me here. I would never hurt you. Or your friends."

"Who are you associated with now? What gang?"

Cole swallows.

"See?" Mag asks. "This is why I don't trust you. It's a

simple question. You know I'm still part of the Crew. You also know I should've killed you when I saw you, and I didn't. I'm asking you one simple thing. You say we're family and that you're trying to help? I'm actually asking you for help right now. Who are you associated with?"

"It's not that simple," Cole growls.

My stomach squeezes. "Hey," I say, waiting until Cole looks at me. "I really need to find Johnny, so if you know anything, *anything*," I plead. "I would be forever grateful."

Cole sighs. "It's not that easy." He turns his gaze to Jacob. "You know it's not easy." He pauses for a moment before he looks at all of us. "I've been trying to help you guys from the beginning. I told you I wanted to help, but you know what happens to people who snitch, Jacob."

Mag leans forward, placing his elbows on his knees and cupping his scruff in his palm. "Who is it you're working for now? Let's just start there. It won't go outside this room. You can trust these guys."

Cole gives us all one last lingering look and then hangs his head. "The Dragons."

Well, at least we guessed his affiliation correctly. "How did you end up with them?"

"I had to get the hell out of the Heights, and quick. I'm not good for anything else. Mag knows that. I finally met up with these guys who were more than eager to take an ex-Crew member in. They thought I could give them info about how the Crew is run, but that didn't happen."

"Did the Dragons take Johnny?"

Cole drops his head back. "Fuck, Jacob. You're killing me, man. You're fucking actually killing me. You know that, right?"

Mag scoots forward on the couch cushion. "You must care because you came to me in the first place, man."

"You know how much I care about family," his cousin says through clenched teeth. "It killed me to leave everyone here. You, Mom, Dad, Colleen. Christ."

"Maybe you could come back..." I offer.

Jacob places his hand on my leg, giving me a short squeeze that silences me.

Cole focuses on that spot while Oscar laughs. "Yeah. No. He defected, so he'll never be welcome back into the Crew or the Heights. Unless he wants to die."

Whatever the reasoning was for Cole defecting, he lost everything. That's what the four of them are in for when we finally leave. Mag doesn't speak to his mom, a relationship he might be able to salvage only if he isn't involved in the Crew. But the others? Unless they're coming with us, Oscar and Brawler will have to leave their moms. Oscar might not be able to control what his mother does, but I don't see Brawler leaving his mom, ever.

I place my hand on Mag's, which is stretched over my knee. "Is there a secure phone Brawler can use? He has to check in at home."

Cole perks up. "How's your mom doing, Mack?"

Brawler rubs the back of his neck. His skin is blotchy red, embarrassment creeping up. His mom is a sore spot for him, but also a sense of responsibility and love. "Living off depression medication."

Cole slumps forward a little, a different light in his eyes as he stares at nothing. It sounds as if Brawler's brother, Manning and Cole were pretty close friends once upon a time. So much so that Brawler remembers Cole.

"That phone in the kitchen is safe," Mag says, looking past me to Brawler. "Let me know if she needs anything."

Without Johnny, Mag flows easily into the leadership position. It's as if we're our own Crew here, and he's the one getting shit done.

Brawler gets up, and Oscar takes his place next to me on the sofa. As the night progresses, he seems to be getting stronger and stronger. Cole's gaze bounces between us. He furrows his brows like he's trying to make out what's going on. He knows I'm Johnny's girlfriend, so I bet he's probably wondering why Magnum is freely touching me and why Oscar is sitting about as close as he can get.

It's probably not the smartest idea to do this in front of him, but there's just something about this cabin that makes the other world feel like a lifetime away.

My heart skips a beat in my chest. Johnny should be here. "Listen," I say, eyeing Cole and leaning forward. "I get you're putting your life on the line by being straight with us. You've helped us in the past, and I appreciate that. I need to know what happened to Johnny. I need to find him. I need to know if he's alive, what the plans are for him. I need to get him back." My voice cracks, and I clear it and look away. Oscar sneaks his arm around my back for support. "I know you're not a bad guy, you're just scared. We are, too, because our friend is gone, and we need him back."

"I wish I could help you," Cole says after a moment. The first time we met him, he was kind of cocky. He had the total gang vibe going on. The earrings in his ears, the badass attitude. Now, though, he looks like a lost soul, not knowing what to do. "I don't know where Johnny is, and if I did, I would tell you. Johnny's my brother. He always will be, even though I doubt he'd say the same for me."

"You'd be surprised," I say, thinking of how far he's come. "He was injured. Shot," I clarify. "Do you at least know if he's okay?"

"I don't know anything about him. At all." He stares straight at me. "I swear I would tell you if I did."

"I'll get you out of the Heights," I tell him. "I'll give you some money to get away. You can move to the East Coast and start over again. I—"

"I really don't know," Cole says, interrupting me.

"But you know something," Mag says. "You knew The Ring was about to get shot up, which means you know who did it. Was it the Dragons? Or was it Gregory's guys? And how do you know so much about Gregory if you're a part of a different gang?"

Cole drops his head. His shoulders slump forward as if he's been carrying on a bravado he can't quite keep up anymore, which is saying something, because he didn't look like he'd been carrying anything. Behind us, Brawler walks up to the back of the couch as Cole starts talking. "I'm not high enough up to know anything useful. I was only brought here because I'm from the Heights. The Dragons don't care about me. I'm low-level scum." He gazes at his cousin. "If they cared, you know they wouldn't bring me back here to potentially get murdered by my old crew."

I get his scared, lost look now. This poor guy has nothing. He's affiliated with people who don't give a shit about him. I move across to sit next to him on the coffee table. Mag sighs when I grab Oscar's knife and cut through the zip ties around Cole's wrists. "If you hurt her, I'll kill you," Mag seethes.

Cole ignores his cousin's harsh words, pulling his hands in front of him and rubbing the bright red lines that are criss-crossing over them. I slide back onto the couch.

"Thanks," Cole says. He runs his now free hand through his closely shorn hair. "What I do know is that Gregory has it out for Big Daddy K. He asked the Dragons for help and somehow got them on his side. I don't know the particulars, but I wouldn't be surprised if Gregory is making a play for the Crew and has told the Dragons they can have some of the territory. That's the only way I see our guys getting involved, but either way, we're here."

"Did the Dragons take Johnny?"

Cole shrugs. "I don't know anything. I wish I did. Everything I heard was second-hand or said in passing. I'm here for one reason only, and that's as backup in case they need to know something about the Heights that I might know. I found out about your recruit by accident. I figured you'd be the one to look the scene over, so that's why I showed up." Cole fixes Mag with a stare that says so much more than words. He misses his cousin. I get it. His whole family may as well be dead to him because when he defected, he lost everything here. Hell, it might even be worse than what I went through. At least my parents *were* dead. They weren't physically here to see me and vice versa. But knowing the people you love are still here, but you just can't get to them? That has to be another level of grief. Of loneliness.

And trust me, I know about being lonely.

"What about tonight?" Mag asks.

Damn. He's like a dog with a bone. He's not giving his cousin an inch.

"There was a lot of activity, so I knew something was going down. You know me, I kind of lingered in a bunch of places to hear what I could hear. I knew it had to be big, and I was worried you might be mixed up in it. As soon as I found out what the plan was, I called you. Did you get out in time?"

Mag shakes his head. "No, dude. We were caught in the middle of it."

Cole's lips thin. "I tried."

"We know," I tell him. "We appreciate it. It all happened too fast. There was just no way."

Cole gives me a small smile. I don't know what the others think about him right now, but I feel for him. He sits up straighter. "I know you're worried about Johnny. If I had to guess, they won't kill him. They'd use him as a bartering tool. Johnny's a big target, but ultimately..." He swings his gaze back over to Magnum. "...You know it's Big Daddy K that they really want. If they kill Johnny, they still have to kill K anyway. Maybe they're trying to get him out of hiding. Maybe they're trying to shake him up, get him to make a stupid mistake."

"He doesn't make stupid mistakes," Mag says.

Cole shrugs. "Those are just my guesses."

"Could you find out?" I ask. As soon as the idea filters through my tired, scared brain, I grip onto it with everything I have. "If you go back to wherever the Dragons are, could you find out where Johnny is?"

Cole's leg jumps up and down. He runs his fingers through his brown faux-hawk a few times, blowing out a breath that's making me nervous even just looking at him.

"I'll help you," I tell him. "I mean it. I have money put away. It's not the Crew's, it's not anybody's but mine. I'll buy you the first fucking plane ticket out of this place if you help us with this."

"I see why he likes you," Cole says, gaze locking on

Magnum's. He shakes his head. "I didn't think you'd ever find a girl that lived up to your expectations, man."

Magnum stiffens, but I bump his shoulder with mine. "He just had to look a little younger, that's all."

Cole smiles. It lights up his face, making him look more handsome than I've seen him yet. "Does Johnny know?"

I nod and lean back. "About all of them."

He laughs now. "Jesus. He probably hates the fuck out of every single one of you."

Oscar shrugs. "Pretty much."

Cole frowns, sadness creeping back into his face like wild ivy. "I would help you guys anyway, but I don't know about the ticket out of here. What I really want is to have my life back."

Magnum's jaw ticks. "The Crew?"

Cole shakes his head. "Nah, man. I just want my family back, you know? You, and everyone..."

"I can't promise you that," Mag says.

"We can if we take K out."

Cole's gaze widens. Oscar slumps back into the sofa. "Oh, Jesus. You had to go and say it out loud."

"What?" I ask.

"Kyla, we don't know anything about him," Oscar says, clearly frustrated that I let the cat out of the bag.

"You don't, but I do," Mag says. He leans over, holding his hand out to Cole. "You with us?"

Cole's jaw tenses. He gazes at his cousin's hand before

he places his own in it. Mag pulls him forward until they give each other a bro hug, clapping one another on the back.

They both settle back onto their seats, and I can't help but smile. Finding Johnny just got a little easier.

Maybe. Hopefully.

"So, let me get this straight." Lines form between Cole's eyes when he looks at me. "You want to kill Big Daddy K? The most powerful leader the Crew has ever seen?"

I shrug like it's not a big deal.

Honestly, this has only solidified my goal from the beginning. Cole missed out on years with his family. This is just another piece of evidence in the "I'm doing the right thing" category. And if I can save Cole along the way, even better.

5

Because I'm nice like that, I heat up two more single-serve pizzas in the microwave for the newly reunited Magnum and Cole. Things are still a little tense between them. Maybe it's the years of being apart. I don't understand the reasoning why a gang would tear families apart like this. It doesn't seem like something Magnum would let happen. Though, once you're in the Crew, you're a victim of their policies. He couldn't be Cole's cousin even if he wanted to be.

The two guys accept their heated dinners with soft smiles. Magnum's does funny things to my insides. I don't know all of his past, but I know the Crew has been his only family for too long. Maybe this could be the start of a new beginning for him. Cole said he doesn't want to leave the

Heights, he wants the Heights back, but maybe he'd leave if everyone he loved could come with him.

Or maybe we just need to take the threat out of the Heights. Big Daddy K is the root. The weed spreading and infiltrating. If we take him out, maybe everything else would get better. Though, some people wouldn't like that at all. The way residents talk, the Crew is the best thing that happened to the Heights. Some would argue K was the best thing that happened to the Heights because he grew the Crew to the size it is now. It's a freaking powerhouse.

"What's with the frown, Princess?"

I sink back into Oscar, keeping the ice pack Brawler insisted I use on my face. "Just thinking about K, wondering if it's enough to take him out? Or if someone else will take his place and continue his shitty ways?"

"By that time, it won't be our problem," Brawler says. He's looked pensive since Cole got here. He got to talk to his mom, so I don't think that's it. I think it's Cole himself. He probably sees him as a connection to his brother, which always puts him in a funk.

"Let's worry about one problem at a time," Mag says. His hard gaze reminds me of when he said he wouldn't help me kill K. I get it, but the overall decision isn't his to make. I've already made it. He doesn't have to help if he doesn't want to. There is wisdom to his words though. The big picture can seem almost impossible to pull off. Right now, we need to worry about getting to Johnny.

"Here's what I'm thinking," Cole says. Now that he's more animated, his eyes are similar to Magnum's. They don't have the hint of green, but they're a hazel color and the same almond shape. "Take me back to the Heights. I'll continue on as normal in the Dragons, keeping my eyes and ears open. The second I hear anything Johnny-related, I'll let you guys know."

"You'll need a way to contact us."

"I've got Mag's number. That should be fine. I check my phone daily for bugs, and if I know my cousin, he does the same."

Jesus. These guys are like two peas in a pod. It makes sense that they think similarly. They were brought up together. My sheltered ass is not going to complain that I don't think to worry about my phone being bugged.

"That's another thing, too," Oscar says, tracing lines over my back. "We have to think about going back ourselves. They'll expect us."

I growl at the thought. I am in no mood to face K. The coward left his son there to get taken. What kind of spine-less, dickless asshole fucking does that?

"You really don't like him..." Cole says. His gaze is suspicious. I suppose he has every right to be. For all he's aware of, I came to the Heights and started dating Johnny.

"I have reasons," I say, switching the ice pack to the other side of my face.

He shrugs and sticks the last of his pizza in his mouth,

setting the plate down next to him on the coffee table. "It's all good," he says around a mouthful. "Just curious."

He can stay curious. I'm not saying I don't trust him. I obviously do...to a certain extent. But not everyone needs to know about my background.

"I think if we stay here for the night, we'll be fine," Magnum says. "I'll take Cole back tonight, then come back. In the morning, the rest of us can go back to the Heights."

Oscar pulls me into his side like he didn't just get jumped hours ago. Before the fight, I was staying at his place. I'm assuming that's still what's happening. Staying in the tower with Johnny gone doesn't seem like a good idea. I'm sure my standing hasn't improved in K's eyes, though I don't think he can fault me for what happened at the fight, so that's the only positive that came out of today... Wait, yesterday? What time is it even? Exhaustion is starting to creep up on me. That's all I know.

Mag stands. He takes his cousin's plate and places it under his own before walking into the kitchen to deposit them in the sink. "You ready?" he asks, staring at Cole.

Cole gets to his feet. He starts toward the door but turns back to us. "I really am sorry about Johnny. He's like a brother to me. I'll do everything I can."

I give him a small nod. I'm putting a lot of faith in this rival gang member, but I'm desperate.

Mag steps toward the door, but freezes. He tilts his head, and then curses. "Fuck."

Instantly, we're all on alert. Oscar stops his trail of fingers over my back. He swivels his neck and then follows Magnum's line of sight. A car is pulling up the drive, bouncing along the same ruts as we did when we drove up a few hours ago. "It's got to be the Crew," Oscar says.

"Shit," Mag says, confirming Oscar's suspicions.

Cole is like a deer caught in the headlights. He's frozen mid-step, skin gone pale.

"This way," Magnum orders, jerking his head toward the kitchen. He runs past the island with Cole hot on his heels. They disappear down the hall while the car comes to a stop. Oscar, Brawler, and I stand, watching the Magnum look-alikes pour out of the vehicle, guns drawn.

They race up toward the house while my heart flip-flops in my chest, tumbling over itself.

"Act cool," Oscar says. "We're allowed to be here."

Easy for him to say. He's not the one who saw K leave his son at The Ring. Do they know about Johnny? K could be pissed we haven't checked in and decide to just kill us all right now. What's stopping him? Nothing. Absolutely nothing stops him from doing exactly what he wants to do when he wants to do it.

The door careens open, bouncing against the cabinets on the opposite side. The black-clad security personnel spread out in the room.

"Hey, hey," Oscar demands, lifting a cocky eyebrow at all of them. "What the hell is this?"

Once again, I'm taken aback by the bravado he can exude when he needs to. He has this bold, brave authority about him that probably served him well on the football field and in the Heights.

Yet, here we are. Again. Guns pulled on us when Oscar should be riding out the rest of his days as an elite athlete, colleges all lined up. Brawler should be in the gym, downing protein like it's candy, searching for amateur fights. Me? I just want a place big enough to fit all the guys. No threats. No hair-raising activities other than training...and a whole lot of sexing.

I inspect the newcomers, and the only guard I recognize is Trey. I don't know how many we lost at The Ring earlier, but at least he knows who we are. Magnum comes out of the back with a towel around his hips, his chiseled chest on full display. I'm happy to see Cole isn't with him. Hopefully, he's hiding in the woods by now. It's not ideal, but it's better than the Crew seeing him. They wouldn't ask questions. They wouldn't think. They'd just kill. "Guys, what the fuck?"

Trey lowers his weapon. "K's ordered you to come back to the tower."

"What do you think we were just about to do? We came here to get cleaned up and wait for the dust to settle, and then we were heading back. We have news K won't like." Mag glares at the other security guys who haven't lowered their guns. "Are you seriously going to keep those raised at

Rocket's girlfriend, a recruit, and a member? I think we have outside threats we need to be worried about, not members of our own fucking team."

The guys lower their guns right away, holstering them. Not surprising. Magnum is not only stoically demanding around his security guys, he's badass.

"We know about Johnny," Trey says. "K wants to know what you know."

It's itching at the end of my tongue to tell everyone that K might know if he'd stuck around long enough to find out.

Magnum's stomach flexes as he breathes. He looks calm, but I can only imagine what he's feeling under that exterior. "Let me just get dressed."

Trey assesses the situation, gaze catching on everyone in the room. "We'll take Kyla and Drego. You can follow with the initiate."

Magnum's muscles bunch, but it's gone within a fraction of a second. "You might want to take the initiate instead. He was with Johnny when he was taken, so he'll be able to provide more details than they could."

Trey nods. "Fine. We'll take Kyla and the initiate." He gestures us forward. I glance over at Mag, and he gives me a slight nod. I don't want to head into the lion's den without all of them. Nothing good has ever happened in K's suite, but it would be suspicious to make demands to ride with each other.

Fuck it. I move forward, Brawler trailing behind me.

Tossing my ice pack to Oscar, I give him a sly wink that tells him not to worry though I doubt it will do any good. I walk past the Crew's guards and to the door, and they follow. When we get out into the chilled night air, Trey orders us into the back of the SUV. There's a third row of seats that Brawler and I occupy while the four guards sit toward the front.

Brawler and I link hands out of view of the rest of them and await the journey back to the Heights. It seems as if all roads lead me back here. I hope that's not a sign. A fate-filled compass that's supposed to tell me something. My plan has always been to get away from the Heights. Not get stuck here.

The guys make small talk in the vehicle, mostly talking about this one or that one who didn't make it. They make guesses as to where Gregory is hiding out like the pussy that he is. They don't bother talking to us, and we don't bother inserting ourselves into their conversation either.

The longer the drive takes, the sooner I know we'll be getting back to the tower, and that scares the shit out of me. Without Johnny there, I'm nothing to the man. At least with Johnny's presence, his dad might think twice about killing me because of what it will do to his son—maybe. But without him there—and hyped up because of what happened—he's probably a loose cannon.

Forest turns into dilapidated houses. We enter the Heights like slamming head first into a bad idea. My stomach knots, but I play it as cool as I can. Mag will be here shortly. Brawler's with me right now, and this is exactly the reason why he joined the Crew. To protect me. To make sure he could be there when shit went south.

The guard in the security booth waves us on. There's another on the other side, peering in the windows as Trey drives slowly into the underground parking lot. I hadn't realized how much of a relief it had been to be away from here after what happened the last time I set foot in this place.

We file out of the car and head toward the elevator. Having K on our side with this will help. He'll want Johnny back no matter what. I'm sure of it. It can't hurt to have Cole working on the inside and the entire Crew's focus on getting Johnny back and taking out the people who did this. He just better be okay.

No one talks as we exit the elevator and go to the familiar door on the right. For a moment, I let my gaze linger on the left-side door. A part of me hopes that this has all just been a misunderstanding and that Johnny could be waiting for me in his suite, worried sick about me, and wondering where I am.

When I walk into K's suite, all of that hope disintegrates. A familiar cry of pain shatters the room. I take off, searching for him. It was in this very same space the last time I heard him cry out like that, and I swear to God, I will not fucking let anyone hurt him like that again.

I burst into the living area, finding K standing in front of a TV, a thin black remote in his hand. He steps out of the way, revealing his son.

My knees tremble as I watch the screen. He's awake now. Barely. Blood is everywhere, similar to how I saw him when his father tied him to a chair in the middle of this damn room, but this is different. This time, he doesn't have friends around. He doesn't have a father who's "teaching him a lesson", he has enemies who are making him suffer.

A man in a black mask shoves his fingers into Johnny's hip. Blood pours from his gunshot wound as a cry ricochets through the room they have him in. I fall to my knees and cover my mouth with my hands. Tears prick my eyes.

They're torturing him. They're torturing my Johnny Rocket.

6

Big Daddy K looks over his shoulder. He traces his gaze down to find me still on my knees, staring at the now paused screen. Moving forward, he reaches his hand out. I loathe this guy. Every time I touch him, I want to stick my hand in bleach to erase the feeling, but I stick my hand out anyway. He helps pull me to my feet.

His nostrils flare. "They're doing that to my son."

I can't keep from staring at the screen. Johnny's jaw is clenched tightly. Blood from his nose stains his teeth. "They sent that to you?"

K releases my fingers, drawn to the screen as well. "I was sent this an hour ago."

"What do they want?"

"No demands yet."

Brawler edges up beside me, and at least I have his strength to pull from. His formidable body still uncovered except for the joggers around his hips. "I was there, sir," he starts. "When Johnny was taken."

K whips his head around, glaring at Brawler. He inspects him, his beady pupils rounding ever so slightly. He gazes around the room, finding Trey as if looking for corroboration. "Magnum's coming. He confirmed the story though," the guard informs him.

K turns back to Brawler. I replay him leaving The Ring again in my head. First, seeing him run off like a pussy with his one remaining guard. Part of the anger he feels better be directed at himself. He fucking ran while his son was shot. "After we got down from the box," I say, starting to relay the story. I don't like the way he's looking at Brawler right now. "...a crack opened up in the foundation of the building. Flames shot up through the center, and it threw Mag and I one way and Johnny and Brawler another. Whoever has Johnny accosted them when they were trying to escape out a separate fire exit."

"I tried, sir," Brawler says. "They flanked us, knocking me out." He looks up at the bulge on his forehead. "I didn't see their faces. I didn't even see how they got away. By the time I came to, they were long gone."

K starts to pace, still strangling the remote in his hand.

The words to call him out for his actions are on the tip of my tongue. If he didn't leave with the other guard, maybe Johnny would be here. Maybe if we fled together, they would've ended up on Brawler and Johnny's side, and with two more people, those bastards would've had a harder struggle to take Johnny.

"Is it Gregory?" I ask. K doesn't know everything we know, but he received the footage somehow. He must have an idea of who sent it.

"No confirmation, but that's our best guess," K says, voice even despite his haggard appearance. At least he has the decency to look like shit. Unlike all of us, he hasn't showered. Small pebbles dust his hair. He got away before the fire, but not before the bombs started going off.

Bombs? Seriously? That's twice now. Who fucking does that shit besides Johnny? This is getting too close to World War status, except the fighting only takes place in the Heights.

"Where would he get access to the firepower, the men, or the explosives?" I ask, thinking aloud. Gregory went from Crew businessman, running Candy's, to the larger threat he is now. Either they underestimated him, or the Dragons have done wonders for his power and reach.

K lifts his gaze to mine. He narrows his eyes, inspecting me. "That's exactly what I'd like to figure out."

"I want to help in any way I can," I tell K, letting the

truth bleed straight through me. I don't like Big Daddy K, and I certainly don't want to work with him, but we have the same goal right now: to save Johnny, and he most certainly has the power to do that.

"I think you've done enough," he bites out.

We lock gazes, neither one of us backing down. I don't want him to see my fear, or maybe I'm well past that. I don't have fear for myself. I have fear for what's happening to Johnny. "We have the same goal," I tell him, lifting my chin just slightly. I don't want to defy him, I want him to see how motivated I am.

"If it weren't for you," K starts, falling back onto the leather couch with pressed lips. "Johnny wouldn't have let his work slip. The Johnny before you would've already found Gregory and had him dealt with by now. You're making him weak."

Fire singes my veins. He's wrong about that. So, so wrong, but arguing about this with him would be fruitless. I'm giving Johnny a life, not taking it away. The only thing he cares about is that he doesn't have his errand boy at his beck and call anymore.

Also, the only person K should be blaming for all this is himself. That's probably why he's lashing out. He fucked up. He knows it. But a big man like him will never admit when he's wrong.

"He never shared the information he'd been able to get on Gregory, so I can't speak to that."

"Because there wasn't anything," K roars. He throws the remote. It shatters against the wall beside the TV that still shows Johnny's anguished face. The veins pop out on K's arms as he breathes heavily. He lifts his gaze to us again, but locks on Brawler. "And you, you were there, and you didn't save him? In the Crew, your elders are your priority. You either save them or die trying. Since you're not dead, I'd say you didn't do your job."

I clench my hands to fists. There's no way he's blaming this on Brawler. He's not even a part of the damn Crew yet.

Footsteps thud into the room. Big Daddy K moves his gaze that way. "You..."

I glance over my shoulder to find Magnum. Oscar is nowhere to be seen.

The black-clad, copper-haired bodyguard moves in close. He stands in front of K. "It's my fault. I was tasked with keeping Johnny safe."

"You're damn right you were."

K leans forward. I don't immediately see what he's doing until his hand is in front of him. Pressed into his palm is a small, black gun. He aims it at Magnum's hip.

"You know what happens," K says.

Mag nods.

I step forward, but Brawler catches my arms and holds me back. The bang that reverberates through the room rings in my ears until a tinny sound is the only thing I hear. Magnum grits his teeth, immediately placing his hand over his hip. The fabric under his hand turns shiny with blood.

"Now, get out of my face. All of you." K tosses the gun to the coffee table and sits back, staring at the screen with dead eyes.

Brawler pushes past me to wrap Magnum's arm around his neck. He helps him hobble toward the door. I make my feet move because the alternative is staying in the same damn room as K, and the only time I want to do that is when I'm the one pulling the trigger.

As soon as my brain catches up with my physical body, I run toward Mag. My hearing returns in stages. Mag's even yet harsh breaths fill the hallway as we move toward the elevator. The guards in the hall look away, giving Mag the respect he deserves, but not in any way shocked about what just happened. It's as if they all expected it. Did fucking Mag know this was going to happen? Getting shot because Johnny got taken?

I ask myself this all the time, but what kind of fucking world is this?

"You didn't have to do that," Brawler says when we get in the elevator.

"He was going to do it to me anyway," Mag says, leaning half on Brawler and half against the back wall.

"You knew?" I ask, confirming my suspicions. He just walked in. Hell, he returned to the tower, even when he knew that was going to happen. The balls on this guy. Fuck.

"That's how things work," Mag says.

"In a fucking crazy world."

"Shh," he chastises, then sucks in a breath when the elevators open.

We go straight for Mag's apartment. Out of the choice between mine and his, his is the best bet on actually having what's needed to deal with this new wound.

We take him in and set him on the couch. For being shot, he's being surprisingly calm, gritting through what must be pain to put on a brave face for us.

"First-aid kit?" Brawler asks.

"On top of the fridge."

Brawler retreats while I drop to my knees in front of him. I help him unclasp the buttons on his pants and maneuver them carefully down, revealing the small wound still leaking dark crimson blood.

Mag peeks down and sighs. "Through and through. He barely got me."

"This is insane," I say, heart pumping loudly in my chest as I watch the blood seep through his fingers. This reminds me so much of the night of the shootout when he was hit in the arm. He was casual about that, too, bandaging himself. He's done this to himself too many times.

Brawler returns with the first-aid kit and within minutes, the entry and exit points are cleaned and bandaged. Magnum pops a couple of pills and lies back.

"Why the fuck would he do that?" I seethe, still staring at Magnum's wound, not understanding.

"To teach me, and everyone else, a lesson. Not doing your job has consequences." Brawler sits back on the coffee table. I reach out for Magnum's hand, and he squeezes mine. He looks over at Brawler. "I know you have to get home, man. Go check on your Mom. I'm good. Kyla can take care of me."

I squeeze his hands a little tighter while Brawler hesitates.

"Seriously," Mag says again. "I dropped Oscar home, so he wouldn't be involved. It's best if you lie low for a bit. Get everything better at home, and we'll all talk soon."

Brawler leans over, pressing a kiss to the side of my head. He runs his hand down my arm before getting to his feet and heading toward the door. "Lock this behind me," he says.

He leaves, and I get to my feet, doing exactly as he said before returning to the couch. "Can you get me an ice pack from the freezer?"

I nod, grabbing the pack and returning to find Mag stretched out on the couch lengthwise. He reaches for the ice pack, and I place it in his hand. He lifts his shirt and places the gel pack on the bandages before pulling his shirt back down to cover it.

I bite my lip. "You're sure you're going to be okay? Doesn't the Crew have a doctor we can go see?"

"It'll be fine, Kyla. The doc won't be able to do any more for it than I just did. Just come here." He motions me toward him and scoots to the edge of the sofa, leaving me room between his body and the couch. I carefully maneuver myself there, placing my head at the junction of his arm and torso. I reach my hand over his chest, feeling his strong heartbeat under his shirt. The longer we lie there, the more exhaustion tries to yank me under. Mag runs his fingers through my hair. "Don't fight it, beautiful. We can't do anything more right now." Even as he says it, he brings his phone out of his pocket and pulls up an app. His screen pulls up a feed of us right now. He rewinds the time-stamped video and then watches it on fast forward.

"What are you doing?"

"Making sure no one came into my room while we were gone."

"Bugs?" I guess. If K doesn't trust us right now, it wouldn't surprise me if he decided to watch over us.

He shifts on the sofa and lets out a long breath. "I should've looked as soon as we came in."

"Are you kidding me? You're shot. I could've done it."

"Remember when I said people should be taking care of you now."

I gaze up at him. "Yeah, that was before K shot you."

He smirks, and little-by-little, he starts to relax. I don't know if it's the painkillers kicking in or if lying with me is calming him down. Hopefully, it's a bit of both. "I can't believe I had to get shot for you to lay with me like this."

I smile into his side. "I'll lay with you whenever you want."

He tucks his phone near his thigh after watching the footage and shifts toward me. He lowers his lips to mine, kissing me softly for a couple of beats before resting his head back against the throw pillow he shoved under his neck.

"Did you get Cole back to the Heights, too?"

Mag nods. "He'll call when he hears something."

"K isn't going to just sit back."

"All the better," Mag says. "Both sides working on it means we'll find something sooner rather than later."

"They're torturing him," I say, trying not to think about the video replay I saw but failing.

"I saw." His voice cracks, and he clears his throat.

"K won't trust any of us anymore."

"This is the gang life, Kyla. He issued his punishment to me, which means it's done. It's not you he's mad at, technically. It's what you're doing to Johnny. He's afraid. He's acting out. He'll get his shit together, and tomorrow, everyone will be on deck to do whatever we can to find Johnny."

"Except he shot you."

He squeezes my arm. "He knew what he was doing. The wound is superficial at best. It's just a reminder of the stakes for everyone."

No one needs reminding. Not when we just lived through what we did, only to have the people who are supposedly on our side turn on us, too. I'm no gang expert, but I can't imagine this kind of ruthless tyranny will last forever.

Instead of fighting against Gregory, maybe we need to be working with him.

7

Something stirs my hair, and I blink awake. It takes me all of a half second to remember where I am and what happened.

I peek up to find Magnum staring at me, a soft smile curving his lips.

"You're awake?"

He nods, then reaches up to run his fingers through my hair,

"Why didn't you wake me? I'm supposed to be watching over you."

"We can agree to disagree," he says. His hazel green eyes are laser focused, sharp. His intense stare awakens my nerve endings.

"Are you okay? Do you need anything?"

I start to sit up, but he pulls me back down. "I just need you. Here."

My lips buzz. I peek at his mouth and then move back to his eyes. He certainly looks like he's fine. He's not grimacing in pain anymore. I lift his shirt, revealing his tight abs and flexed muscles. He's kicked his pants all the way off, and his boxer briefs are dangerously low and tight over the bulge of his cock.

I tear my gaze away from all the fun stuff and glance at his bandage. There's a blotch of darker coloring from the red underneath, but it's only the size of a nickel. Maybe what he said earlier is right. K knew what he was doing, and he only shot him for attention, not to really hurt him.

"It's fine," Mag says. He places his finger under my chin and lifts my face to peer into my eyes again. He frowns as his gaze snags on the area just below. "I don't want you worrying about me." He brushes his fingers along the edges of what must be the bruising on my face. It stings a little. We must be a sight. I look like I got my ass kicked—because I did—and Mag's been shot.

I delve my fingers under his shirt and into his coarse chest hair. The copper trail leading from his belly button to his chest stands out in contrast to his pale skin.

His eyelids flutter closed at the contact.

"How long was I out?"

"A couple of hours," he answers.

"Were you awake the whole time?"

He shakes his head and opens his eyes once more. "I was in and out. I wanted to stay up and watch you sleep, but exhaustion pulled me under more than once."

Fluttery butterflies spread through my chest. He wanted to watch me sleep... I love that we can find moments like this in the midst of the shitstorm. It makes it all worth it.

"I think we gave your cousin a shock," I smile, remembering when I told him I was with all of them. Not just Johnny and not just Johnny and Magnum.

Mag cracks a smile. "That was kind of fun." He drags his gaze down my front while he licks his lips. I'm not even sure he realizes he's doing it, but it makes me feel powerful. Like I'm delectable to him.

Not things I should be thinking considering he's down with a bullet wound.

"Remember when you told me your secret?"

I nod, searching his gaze.

"I have one," he breathes.

I freeze. My pulse kicks up, knocking my heart into my ribs.

"Everyone has secrets in the Heights," he continues in a low voice while trailing his finger up my arm. "You asked me to trust you even though you weren't going to tell me yours at first."

"I remember," I tell him, mouth suddenly dry, like now that I know I'm missing something, I want it. I don't want just the surface-level of any of these guys. I want them all, right down to their very core.

"I have a secret I can't tell anyone," he says again. "It's driving a wedge between us. A wedge you're not even aware of, and one I want so badly to close." His voice turns heady, and his gaze fills with want, dousing me in lust. A more potent feeling than when I was with him in K's suite during our forced sexual experience. If this is what it feels like to be on the other side of Magnum's needy gaze, I don't want to leave. Ever. "Tell me it's okay for you not to know right now. Tell me you trust that I'll tell you when the time is right."

We've all had secrets. Especially me. Ones I felt like I couldn't share, and ones that didn't affect the way I feel about all of them. Even Johnny has his own secrets still. He told Mag about K killing his mom, but he hasn't told me yet, and I can't forget about the one secret I'm still keeping from Johnny....

Sometimes secrets are better left for when the person is ready. I know that better than anyone.

"What's the wedge?" I ask, watching his full lips.

"I want to have all of you, Kyla Samson. I've had blue balls for months. I've pushed and pulled with you, letting you into my life little by little, so that you understand when I finally tell you, but I don't want to wait anymore."

My lips part. "Jacob..."

He groans, the sound straight from his heart, like it's dug its way out of his chest just to lay itself before me. "When you call me that, I fucking lose it. I want to be me around you. I want you to be you around me. The Heights is a gap we can't bridge right now though."

"We will eventually."

He traces his finger over my collarbone and down before pausing in the middle of my chest. "If you're ready, I want to remove another barrier." He makes his proposition clear when he drags his finger down my torso to the apex of my thighs.

I squirm under his scrutiny and light touch. "You know my answer already."

I'm not sure which one of us moves first. Whether I'm the one who grabs his wrist and forces his fingers to my throbbing core or if my hand just comes along for the ride. He circles over my clit, right through my joggers. Our eye contact never wavers, like we're living in each other's minds for the moment. Lost there with just one another.

Jacob retreats only to push under my joggers, finding me with nothing on underneath. A muscle jumps, and I jerk toward him at the first touch of skin on skin.

"Are you sure?" I ask.

"I've wanted this for so long," he breathes.

The pads of his fingers swirl along my clit. "Your w-wound," I say, biting down on my lip to keep from crying out. "You'll be okay?"

"You might have to take charge," he says, "but I'm more than okay with that."

Mag shifts so he has both hands free. I help him pull my shirt off, nipples already at attention.

"I'm so fucking hard for you." He strokes his fingers down one nipple, and I hold my breath as sensations throb straight to my core. He pushes a finger inside my pussy again. Thankfully, his joggers are kicked off, so all I need to do is cup his cock to prove his statement. His hips jerk forward, stroking right into my palm.

I take my hand away only to pull his shirt over his head and then our hands are back on one another's bodies, igniting the embers between us. His thumb plays over my peaked nipple until I'm riding over his hand. I free his cock from his boxer briefs. Wrapping my fingers around the base, I stroke him.

"I blocked out what happened between us in K's suite because I wanted this, Kyla. Only this. What can I do to make you come right now?"

My fingers tighten over his cock. Oh Jesus. "Your tongue on my clit," I breathe. Magnum's silent, raw possession between my legs sounds like heaven right now.

He doesn't waste time after I've made my request. He maneuvers down the couch, moving my leg around his body until he's poised in front of me. He works his finger inside, locks gazes with me, and then darts his tongue out to an explosion of pleasure. I rock into his face. His scruff teases my pussy, and I don't look away from the friction between us.

"I just wanted this one moment," he breathes before moving back in, the tip of his tongue parting my folds until he teases my nub over and over.

"Jacob." My toes curl, a warning that I'm so close.

He removes his finger, gripping my hips and pulling me toward him. The strokes of his tongue are relentless, working me up expertly until I hit the pleasure threshold and crack right through it.

I cry out, my fingers gripping the leather couch as I come into his mouth.

He pulls away, his hazel-green eyes almost predatory. He gets to his feet and then scoops me in his arms. The movement takes my breath away, but then I remember what we've been through in the last day. "Jacob! You were shot!"

He takes me to his room, edging the door open with his foot. He lays me down on the bed and pulls my joggers all the way off before removing his boxers fully. The bandage is a stark reminder of what he went through earlier, but it doesn't stop him. He crawls over me, parting my legs before sliding his cock into my folds right to the hilt.

Pausing once inside, he breathes through his nose. "How did I ever stop the first time? Fuck, Kyla."

"Don't stop this time," I beg, reaching for his hips to pull him closer. I avoid his bandage, sliding my fingers around to his ass instead. He pumps inside me with slow, sure strokes. His chest muscles ripple in my face until I'm practically hypnotized.

This feels different than last time. Nothing is rushed or hurried. I'm not worrying about Johnny or racing to my orgasm. I'm enjoying being in his strong arms, watching the different emotions play all over his face. He once told me he hadn't been with a woman in a while, but I wouldn't know it. He hasn't lost a step in this department. Or maybe when it's right, it's just right. The chemistry and tension we've worked up together over these past months finally coming to a desperate stop.

He lowers himself to sweep his tongue inside my mouth. I taste myself on him, burying my fingers at the nape of his neck, not allowing him to move. I've had the least amount of time with Jacob, and we have some serious making up to do.

"I'm not going to be able to get enough now," he moans. "I'll be like a love-sick teenager."

"Why do I think teenage Jacob is exactly like mature Jacob?"

He grins and slams inside me. My mouth opens in a silent scream. He continues his assault, knowing exactly where to touch me. "Experience is a good thing."

"Experience...and a big dick," I pant, noticing the way he's stretching me.

He pulls partly out, leaving the head inside while he teases me. "This cock right here? You want it?"

I groan a yes, and he slams inside me again. The bed knocks against the wall behind our heads.

Pulling out again, he gives me teasing strokes that fire

me up. He does it until I'm begging him to plunge deep inside. When he finally gives it to me, I wrap my legs around his waist so he can't get away again.

He smirks. "You fight dirty."

"You're a tease," I tell him before pulling him down to kiss me. Our tongues and lips tangle in heady moans before he's pumping inside me with intent. A cute look of concentration crosses his face, which I only notice for a moment until he starts grinding against my core. Heat swamps me like a raging fire, tightening my insides. "Oh, Jacob."

He drops his forehead to mine, keeping the same rhythm. Perspiration dots his brow.

"Are you okay?" I ask, worried that we've taken it too far.

"Just come with me," he says, straining against me. "I want to feel you at the same time."

I move my hips in time with his. If the trembling of his body is evidence, he's holding back for me. Meeting him stroke for stroke, I chase another orgasm at the hands of Magnum, but this time with his cock instead of his tongue. It's not difficult to find the moment of bliss where you know nothing's going to stop you from toppling over the edge. I sink my nails into his ass as I start to shake. "Mmm, yes, Jacob."

"Again," he says through clenched teeth.

"Jacob, yes," I tell him. Our movements frantic now. He's sliding inside me in furious strokes until I come apart, my name on his lips.

As soon as Jacob passes my lips, he jerks inside me, spilling his cum into my core. Tremors rake his body as he leans over me, pressing our chests together as he rides out our joint ecstasy.

He presses a soft kiss to my lips. "That was perfect, angel." He shivers and all but collapses on top of me, his arms and legs giving out before shifting to his side, pulling out of me.

The first thing I do is check his bandage. There's fresh blood there, almost encapsulating the entire bandage, but he yanks me back into his arms. "None of that matters. I just want to lie with the girl I've fallen for."

I settle onto his chest, smiling. Dipping my fingers into his chest hair again, I say, "I hope your usage of the word girl isn't another tease about my age."

He moans. "Trust me. I know you're a woman."

Entwining his fingers with mine, he holds my hand on his chest where his heart beats just beneath his skin. I slip back into sleep, feeling content in more ways than one.

8

When I wake, Magnum's not next to me. I move my hand over his cool sheets and then flip onto my back. I strain my ears, but don't hear anything until the door cracks open. Expecting to see Magnum, I'm a little taken aback when Oscar ducks his head into the room. Despite some bruising around his eyes, he looks fine. He's even walking normally, too.

He assesses me, the sheets just pulled up over my breasts. "You look thoroughly fucked. Great, now I'm hard *and* insecure. You know he got shot yesterday, right? Maybe fucking wasn't the best idea."

I bite my lip to keep my smile at bay, but it doesn't work. I crook my finger at him until he swaggers inside Magnum's bedroom. "Do I detect jealousy, Oscar Drego?"

"Nope. Just a healthy dose of failing to measure up."

As soon as he's within reach, I pull him down next to me. "Let me guess, you're on babysitting duty."

"We don't call it babysitting duty, Princess. We call it watching over the most precious thing we've ever seen."

"Well, now you're just trying to get into my pants."

He raises his eyebrow. "I'll be surprised if you're wearing pants under there, and yes, I think I've been trying to get into your pants since day one," he says unapologetically.

It's a crime to have all these guys around and not want to fuck them, right? That seems like a waste.

"You need to stop looking at me like that," Oscar groans.

"Or?" I push the covers down and straddle him, resting my core just over where he's hardening in his pants.

"Or I'm going to find myself inside you so quickly I'll probably embarrass myself."

"Where's Magnum?" I ask, turning to peek out the bedroom door.

"K requested his presence to talk about Johnny, so he called me in to watch over you."

"Brawler?"

"With his mom still. She had an episode, and he's pulling her out of it. Christmas is a hard time for them."

That pulls me up short. "What the fuck day is it?"

Oscar's hands creep over my hips, settling on my ribs where he encourages me to rock over him. "It's Christmas Eve, Princess." He frowns. "I didn't get you anything."

"You're about to," I tell him. I shift back to undo the button on his jeans. Once the fly is open, I pull his pants and boxers down until he reaches inside and frees his cock.

"It'll have to be a quickie," he warns, stroking himself.

Oscar is a fucking masterpiece in front of me. Even with his shirt on, there's a peek of his taut abs. His tanned hand gripping his cock is like pure crack. Magnum must have unleashed something inside me last night because I'm more than ready to climb on top of Oscar.

"What are you waiting for?" he asks, pumping his hips into the air.

"Watching you do that is like the best porn."

He grips himself tighter, making exaggerated strokes until I can't stand it anymore. I push his hands away and hover over him before dropping down onto his hard cock.

"Fuck," he groans. "Fuck me hard and fast, Princess. I can't wait."

I move over him until I find the angle and rhythm I like and then do exactly as he says. I ride him hard and fast, his stiff cock sending pleasure through my nerve endings with each stroke.

Oscar places a hand on my chest and pushes, leading me to a seated position. "This is my favorite porn."

He's changed the angle, but I'm so powerful up here. Freeing. I hover my fingers over his abs and lower over top of him again and again. He moans in encouragement. Words pass his lips that make me feel so beautiful and wanted that before long, I'm grinding over him before coming so hard my vision goes out briefly.

Oscar takes control of my hips slamming me down over him two more times before he comes apart, too. He's still jerking inside me when I lean forward. He wraps his arms around me, bringing us close and pressing brief kisses over the curve of my neck. "Every time we do that," he says, vulnerability peeking through his taxed breathing. "My confidence grows. I don't think you can fake what you just did."

I move my mouth to his ear, taking his lobe between my lips and biting teasingly before saying, "I'm not faking anything with you, Drego. When we get out of this, I'm going to be on the sidelines of your football games. I'll wear your school colors. Maybe even your practice jersey. I'll be yelling and clapping for you the whole time."

His dick twitches inside me. "I can picture it, but it sounds like a dream."

"That doesn't mean it can't come true."

He groans and tips his hips up. "I'm fucking hard again, Kyla."

Yes, he fucking is. He test pumps into me with a grimace, and then flips me over, landing on top, pumping his hardening cock into me again.

"I don't want to stop."

I reach up to cup his face, watching the different emotions play across his features. "Are you okay?"

"I'm so hard it fucking hurts."

I spread my knees wider. "Then take me."

He confiscates my hands and holds them above my head. His test pumps turn more pronounced. He groans. "Jesus fuck, Princess. I don't know what you're doing to me."

Sweat dots his hairline and upper lip. He shakes as he works his cock in and out of me. The way his body reacts to mine invigorates me. I move my body in tune with his as best I can considering he's not giving my hands up. I meet him stroke for stroke. Long minutes pass. He's uttered every swear word in the book, some in Spanish. He's called me every pet name imaginable in between moans as he coaxes his orgasm out. When he finally does come, his climax is so pronounced he actually roars in relief before collapsing on top of me.

"Fucking hell, Kyla. You've ruined me. No one will ever be able to measure up to you."

I smirk. "You're not seriously talking about other girls when you're balls deep inside me, are you?"

He groans at my teasing. "There are no other girls. I'd share you with ten more guys." He lifts off me to give me a stern look. "Don't get any ideas."

I pull him down to give him a chaste kiss on the lips. "I'm not interested in any other guys. This is not a case of the more the merrier. It's us five. There's just something about it. It's so right. Don't you think?"

He sinks on to me again, nodding into the crook of my neck. "Family," he says, and that word means as much to him as it does to me. My family was taken from me too quickly. Each of the guys don't have a real family to speak of, only us. Besides my parents, this is the tightest bond I've ever felt. He gives me one more kiss to the neck before lifting off me. "We need to wash up and get ready for when Mag returns because as soon as he gets back, hopefully we'll have some new information about Johnny and can go from there."

"Don't tell me you're getting a soft spot for Johnny," I say, remembering how they wrestled on the floor a couple of weeks ago.

"He grows on you. Like fungus. Or mold. Or—"

I laugh and playfully kick him out of the bed.

For a moment, I almost forget we're in Mag's apartment. It so closely resembles my own that I don't even think about it until I get in the shower and don't see my usual shower stuff inside. Using Magnum's shampoo and conditioner, I wash up and then change. I swear I'm always wearing t-shirts and joggers that are too big for me, but if it's a look, I'm totally rocking it.

When I pad out into the living room, Oscar is already there. "He has cereal. Hope that's okay."

I shrug. Anything sounds good at this point. I've worked myself up an appetite.

He places a bowl of Honey Nut Cheerios in front of me.

"Oh, by the way, I heard from Jax and Finn. Well, Finn, actually. He wanted to know if we were okay."

I peek up. "You didn't tell him everything, did you?"

He shakes his head. "I told him you were fine, but that you didn't know what happened to your phone. Brawler, too. I did not tell him about Johnny."

"Good," I say, relief flooding me. "I don't want them anywhere near this mess."

"Finn has a soft spot for you, I think," Oscar says, digging into his own bowl of cereal.

"He's a good guy. They both are," I say, hating to leave Jax out. Sure, he's a little abrasive around the edges, but he's just trying to look out for his brother. I respect that more than anything. "I'm so glad they stayed away from The Ring. Who knows how many people—just spectators," I say. "...died." It's like my parents' story all over again. People, minding their own business, not doing anything to bother anyone, but wind up dead because of gang shit.

"Hey," Oscar says, reaching over the island to put his hand on top of mine. "I know. Let's just focus on what we can do, okay?"

While I nod in answer, the door to the apartment opens, and Magnum steps through, pocketing a set of keys. I set my spoon down and go to him, wrapping my arms around his waist. I forget about his injury at first, but he doesn't shy away when I accidentally touch him there. He only pulls me tighter. I swear I could dig my finger right into his wound and he wouldn't react because he only wants me next to him.

Mag stealthily locks the door behind him. Leaning over, he sniffs my hair, and I imagine he's smelling his scent on me. His fingers clench tighter to my skin for a brief moment before he lets me go.

"What did you learn?" Oscar asks.

Magnum breathes in deep and then lets it out. He leads me to the kitchen island so I can continue eating while he reaches into the fridge and takes out a strawberry protein shake. "K used his connection at the force to get the names of the dead shooters. Old Crew guys."

Oscar lifts a brow. "Defectors?"

"Some," he says. "Some were our guys until...now."

"Gregory," Oscar guesses, voice hard.

"He won them over somehow," Mag says. He drinks his protein shake with one hand while keeping his other around my back.

"I bet he's fucking furious."

"Livid," Mag answers.

"He didn't hurt you again, did he?"

Mag shakes his head. "He needs me right now, Kyla. I'm the least of his worries. You're the least of his worries. He's chomping at the bit to get Johnny back. You'd think he actually cared."

He probably does, in his own way. I can't help but think that. Psychos don't know they're psychos, right?

I'm almost afraid to ask, but I gaze up at Magnum after pushing my cereal bowl away. "Anything else?"

"Twenty-seven dead, including the shooters."

"The police must be all over this," Oscar says. He moves his wary gaze to me.

"They are," Magnum agrees. "There's only so much K can hide. There's no secreting away twenty-seven dead bodies and explosions and a fire that probably half the Heights heard or saw."

"Is he getting heat from the cops?"

"Right now, they can't tie him there. He'll probably get pulled in for questioning, like the rest of us if we get tied to the scene."

"It wasn't a secret who was fighting that night," I say, already worried I'm going to get sent back to the reformatory or worse. This would be the worst possible time because Johnny needs me right now.

"We'll have to stay under their radar for as long as we can," Mag says.

"So, what's the plan?"

I recognize the tightness in Mag's shoulders and the flexing of his limbs. He looks like a tiger ready to pounce. He's itching to do something, and I'm sure it's not discuss the night with us over and over.

He swings an apologetic gaze to Oscar. "I had an idea."

Oscar drops his head, flicking his now empty bowl further away from him.

"I'm sorry, man," Mag says. "I said nothing to K. I would never say anything to him, but your mom might know where Gregory is. If she can get us to Gregory, Johnny might be there."

Oscar lifts his shoulders. "I thought the same. I called all the usual places this morning, and no luck." He lifts his palms off the island. "I have no idea where she is."

Magnum nods. "I know it won't be easy, but she hasn't been around for a while, right? It wouldn't surprise me if she's wherever he is. He would've kept his girls." Mag cringes when he says that, but Oscar makes no reaction to his words at all. I reach across the table and thread my fingers through his. Magnum clears his throat. "K's got the guys he trusts going to the families of the guys who used to be one of us."

I suck in a breath. "He's not hurting them, is he?"

"Not yet," Magnum says. "I have a wife to talk to and report back, but I thought that your mom might get us there even quicker. We're looking for places they might have been frequenting lately. That might lead us to their home base."

"It has to be in the Heights or close to it," Oscar adds. "We don't stray far."

"Especially since a few of the guys were double-crossing Big Daddy K. They were working for him and listening to Gregory at the same time. The place has to be close."

"And we think Johnny's there?"

"It's what we have to go on for now. Cole's still working

his angle, so if the Dragons have him, we'll get it through him. Right now, we have to work on Gregory."

I squeeze Oscar's hand. "Let's do it," I say.

Mag glances away. "We'll have to split up. I've been instructed to take Brawler to talk with our ex-guy's wife. You guys can go look for Mama Drego."

Oscar tightens his grip on me. "Looks like it's you and me, Princess."

9

Magnum, Oscar, and I leave the tower at the same time. Magnum takes the car to pick up Brawler while Oscar and I hop on his bike. He's quiet while we get ready to leave, pensive and thoughtful. I don't have time to ask him about it before he hands me a bike helmet and helps me onto the back.

Wind flutters my hair as Oscar deftly maneuvers around the streets of the Heights. I recognize a few of the places from when I went looking for his mom with him the first time. Dirty back alleyways. Sleeping bags rolled up next to dumpsters with cardboard box huts turned into houses. Oscar's stomach tenses under my arms, but all I can do is hold him close.

I wonder what happens to someone like Oscar's mom.

She raised a good kid. A football star by any right. She got out of the Heights, even. Out of the place that led her down this path, if only for a short while. Now, she's caught up in a hell few could understand.

It makes my heart hurt just thinking about it. Oscar and his mom could've thrived outside the Heights. When they came back, Oscar's entire world shifted. His mom got back with the wrong people and started doing drugs. He had to join the Crew to help fend for himself. To think all of it could've been avoided. Maybe. If someone actually gave a crap about them.

Oscar slows the motorcycle. He pulls it up next to a curb and kills the engine. He helps me get off, but signals for me to keep the helmet on until he pulls me into an alley I don't think I've been in yet. Once we're secluded in the long, narrow brick-lined walk, he helps remove my helmet. He gives me a small smile. "I wanted you to keep it on in case the cops are doing rounds. You stick out on these shabby streets."

He holds the helmet under his arm and then takes my hand in his as we walk the length. He peers at the crumbling walls of the two buildings that face each other. "My mom's been known to frequent here. There's a dealer in this old building." He cocks his head to the right. "He basically squats here."

Much like the rest of the older buildings in the Heights,

the one to our right is abandoned. When Rawley Heights started to die out, industries moved elsewhere, leaving all of these buildings to decay, like worms festering in the heart of the Heights. I've often wondered what the tower looked like before the Crew got their hands on it. I can't imagine it would've looked any nicer than this shithole.

"Let me do the talking," Oscar says as we walk farther down the alley. Our steps echo around us. A cockroach skitters in our path, and I do my best not to scream, but Oscar can tell I'm skeeved out. He squeezes my fingers, just a tiny amount of pressure that lets me know he's here for me.

To distract myself, I think about the future. About a time when we won't have to worry about cockroaches or how to ask a dealer if he knows where Oscar's mom is. Hopefully, that means Oscar's mom will be straight and alive and not prostituting. "Um, so," I say, still staring at our surroundings. "I was serious when I said we should get some of your footage and send it to colleges."

His steps falter briefly, but he continues on. Albeit, silently.

Probably not the best time to talk about this, but Oscar needs something to look forward to. To let him know that his life won't always be what it is right this very second. I tug back a little on his arm. "Hey, did I say something wrong?"

He shakes his head. "I'm just amazed you think we're actually going to get out of here." He's not being mean. In fact, he smiles a little. A coy one that warms me. "Nothing you've seen yet has thwarted these plans you have for us in the future. Can you imagine Johnny going to college?" He laughs now, a full belly one that ricochets around the buildings. "He'd probably blow up the science lab...again."

I smile at the imagery. That's not the first time I heard that Johnny blew up the science lab. "Johnny doesn't have to go to college. Neither does Brawler. I want all of us to do what we want to do, but you, Oscar Drego, are going to college. That's the only way you'll play football, and I know that's what you want. That's everything you've ever wanted, right?"

He stops and turns in the alley. His dark gaze sharp when he looks at me. "Look around you, Kyla. Do you see where we are? I'm about to head into a drug den to ask where my mom fucking is. I don't think I'll be going to college, let alone playing football again. Ever again," he says, shaking his head.

"Just humor me, okay?" I ask, trying to evade the argument I feel coming on. He doesn't like talking about this, and I don't blame him. How many times can you wish for something, not get it, but still keep on wishing? At some point, it has to feel like a fool's errand.

Fuck that.

"Listen, all you have to do is get me the tape. I'll send it out to the colleges in the area. It would help if you tell me what colleges you'd actually like to go to though. What's the poster you have in the room? There's a big S..."

"State," Oscar says automatically. His cheeks burn afterward, and he looks away.

I smile. "State. Good. I'll send it there. Do I have to talk to the coach at the school? Do you have footage in your room? Where can I find the highlights of your career?"

He grinds his teeth together but answers me anyway. "My mom has some from Spring Hill. I can find that. I guess. Even though it's dumb. It's pointless."

I make a mental note to get in contact with the Rawley High football coach, too. Oscar not playing football would be a travesty.

"It's a waste of time," he says again, trying to drive the point home.

"Don't care," I tell him with a quick smile. "I have time."

He raises his brows. "Oh, you have time? In between finding your one boyfriend who was kidnapped, staying out of the way of the police, and K and—"

I press my finger to his lips to stop him from talking. "I always have time for you, and this is important."

He takes a deep breath, his solid shoulders moving under his shirt. It always amazes me how lithe and muscular he looks even under regular clothes. I'm glad I went to my old suite and put on some actual clothes rather than the joggers I've been living in. Sure, I'm wearing a belly shirt under a pair of overalls with a jacket over all of it, definitely not clothes I'm used to or comfortable wearing, but it doesn't matter. Oscar uses his free hand to thread through my hair at the nape of my neck. He tugs a little, just enough to let me know he has a fistful. "I love that you care, but I have a hard time believing anything good is going to come out of all of this." He swallows then glances away like he's ashamed. "Can we go in there and ask this prick about my mom now?"

I push up on my tiptoes and give Oscar a solid kiss on the mouth. His grip tightens once more until I step back. "Yes, we can go find your mom now."

He starts to walk toward a rusted door on the side of the building but stops again. Without turning around, he says, "I'm worried about what you might see if we find my mom. If she's like before..."

I can read the apprehension in his tight shoulders. "Your mom needs help. That's all."

"She wasn't always like this."

"I know," I tell him, swallowing the serious lump in my throat that's now forming. "It doesn't matter what we find. I'm here."

Oscar hesitates for only another fraction of a second before leading me toward the door again. The hinges creak when he opens the solid metal. The sound echoes through the vast room. Shadows shift, and it takes a second for my eyes to adjust before I realize there are people inside. They're squinting into the light the open door provides. The inhabitants are disheveled. Dirty. Lost.

I hold onto Oscar's hand tighter.

He scans the room. "I'm looking for Cynthia Drego. Anyone seen her? I'm her son."

A bunch of grumbles accompany his question, but it doesn't deter him. We move further into the old building that looks like it used to be a factory. Metal beams are still shoved horizontally into one corner that people are using as a flat surface to play cards on.

"Cynthia Drego?" Oscar calls out again. "I'm her son."

People glance up disinterestedly then return right back to what they were doing. Some are just staring aimlessly, only shifting their gaze to watch us briefly before returning to stare off into the distance.

He calls out a few more times before we get to the back of the big room. Plastic flaps fall over a cement door-shaped hole in the wall. Oscar brushes them aside and moves in. A guy in his mid-twenties with loose, curly hair to his ears glances up and stops what he's doing. "Dealing? Or personal?"

"Neither," Oscar says.

The guy's brows sharpen as he inspects us even closer. He lingers on the bruising on my face. "What is it then?"

"Looking for my mom." Oscar lets go of my hand and crosses his arms. "Cynthia Drego. She's about five foot four. Brown hair. Kind of frail looking. Probably high. My coloring."

The guy shrugs. "Don't know. She buy direct?"

"Listen," Oscar says. "I'm just her son. I want to make sure she's eating and shit. I'm not looking for anything else."

"Still don't know," the guy says, shrugging like he couldn't care less. It's obvious he wants to blow us off. "Did you check her usual places?"

Oscar nods stiffly beside me.

"What about the corners? The hot spots? The places where johns take their girls?"

It takes me until the last part of that sentence to figure out he's already insinuated that Oscar's mom is prostituting. I reach out and squeeze Oscar's hand. I don't know if it's to help support him or to remind me why I shouldn't kick this guy's ass right fucking now. He's supplying the drugs to all these helpless people. He's giving them their Achilles' heel. What could these people in the other rooms do if they weren't hooked on whatever this asshole is cooking up?

"How about a guy named Gregory?" Oscar asks. "You heard of him? You know where he is? Last I knew, he had my mom." His voice gets even more strained the longer he talks. Hard, coldness creeps into his questions until I can tell he's barely holding it together. At this point, it will be me holding Oscar back from kicking this guy's ass, and I'm not even sure I want to do that.

Aww, morality. So blurry sometimes.

"Listen, I don't know where she is. If you're not buying or dealing, you should leave. I've got shit to do."

"Lives to ruin, you mean."

The guy has the audacity to smirk. "Aren't you in the Crew? Looks like I'm peering in a mirror, brother. You might want to step off that high horse. You're in the first circle of hell like the rest of us."

I hold back on Oscar's arm as he attempts to step forward. The guy isn't even worth it. If he does know where Gregory or Oscar's mom is, he won't say anything. I doubt many would. Not without incentive, and because we're keeping this from the Crew, we can't use K's name to get what we want. "Fuck him," I whisper to Oscar.

He finally turns, and we walk back out. Oscar switches on his phone flashlight and shines it everywhere. We get pissed off remarks, but they're all too high or tired or just plain fucking killing themselves slowly that they don't even have the energy to do anything other than grunt in annoyance.

We exit out the rusty door, the groaning hinge greeting us to the outside world. The sun is bright as it shines overhead between the two buildings. Then again, anything would be brighter than what we just saw in there.

Oscar marches back toward his bike, the helmet in his hand swinging by his side. "I fucking hate going to places like that. All I think is I can't believe she would willingly do that to herself. Does she never wake up sober and realize what a shitshow her life has turned out to be? Does she never wonder what I'm doing? Does she never think that there's a nice bed and food in our fucking apartment?"

I run after him to catch up. I still his swinging hand. The truth is, I have nothing to say to him. Everything he said is right. I thought the same thing when we were inside, but the truth is, neither of us have had a drug problem. I don't know what it's like. I can guess. I can theorize. I can wonder just like him, but it doesn't do us any good. "When we find your mom," I say, "...we should get her out of the Heights."

"I feel like we'll always be stuck here. *I'll* always be stuck here," he says finally. "Do you think I can go to college with my mom being pimped out on the streets? I can't go live in a dorm not knowing if she's living in one of these damn boxes." Oscar gestures toward the home someone made for themselves. "I can't fucking do that, Princess. Fuck. What kind of person would that make me?"

I press my palm to his cheek. "Then we'll get her out. If that's what you need to feel like you can leave, we'll get her far away from here. We'll figure it out."

"I tried," he finally says. "I fucking tried. I did it. I got us out of here." He shakes his head. "All roads lead back to the Heights. That asshole was right. We're in the first level of hell. Nothing is going to change that."

He sits the helmet on my head and helps me arrange it before clicking the chin strap, effectively ending the conversation. I could keep talking to him. I could keep telling him there's a chance, but Oscar's not in that space right now. Hell, we can't even find his mom, so anything I say will just be background noise.

What Oscar needs—what all these people need—is actual action.

My to-do list is getting lengthy, but I wouldn't have it any other way. I care about these guys too much not to help them in any way I can.

10

Oscar and I stop at a small corner shop. I swing my leg off the bike, looking around at where we are while taking the helmet off. I'm sure I run my fingers through my hair to get rid of the helmet hair, but Oscar doesn't seem to mind. He takes the helmet from me and kisses my temple before threading his fingers through mine.

I gaze down the block, looking around for drug dealers or prostitutes or someone who might know where Oscar's mom is. "Um, where are we?"

Instead of checking down more back alleys, Oscar leads me into the store. A bell rings overhead when we walk in, and a husky male voice says, "Drego! Another phone?"

Oscar smirks and gazes over at me. "Someone doesn't know how to take care of her things."

"Ohhhh," the shop owner says. He's a huge, dark-skinned man with a thick mustache and a shining bald head. "This is the girl, huh?"

"This is her," Oscar says.

The guy gazes at the two of us with almost a twinkle in his eye before moving his stare to me. "I never met someone who was so hard on their phone."

I chuckle to myself as he inspects my face. He's probably eating his words right this very second. The bruising surrounding my eyes is very in line with the fact that I'm "so hard on my phone". He must meet a lot of Crew people because he doesn't even bat another eye. "I don't even have any excuses," I tease even though I have a ton of excuses. Explosions. Shootouts. Certainly, one of those could work, but what's the use? He's probably heard it all and then some.

Oscar sets his helmet on the counter in front of the guy. "Can we get another one? Crew tab again."

"Of course. Let's see here." He turns and fiddles with a lower shelf. I move back to find a bunch of displayed phones in the case. He takes the best smartphone there is with a huge screen and sets the box on the counter. He takes it out right in front of us, setting it up and then handing it to me. "All you need to do is input your contacts...again."

I smile. "Thanks. I appreciate it."

"No problem, honey. That's what I'm here for."

Oscar signs a piece of paper the shop owner slides

toward him over the glass countertop. This is the first time I've seen his handwriting. It's tiny and neat. Straight lines except for a swirl in the O's. When he passes the paper back, he asks, "You haven't by any chance seen my mom, have you? She's been gone for a while this time." The way he's talking to the shop owner is decidedly less confrontational than when he was speaking to the drug dealer. "Last time I knew she was hanging out at Candy's with a guy named Gregory."

The man's lips press together. I can tell he instantly feels sorry for Oscar, and I like the guy even more. Sure, he's obviously mixed up somewhat with the Crew if they have an open tab at his shop, but he seems like a good guy. The owner shakes his head. "I haven't seen her for... Well, going on a month now, I think. Last time I saw her, she was a couple of blocks down. I gave her and a redhead there a couple of bottles of water."

Oscar taps the counter. It's hard not to see the disappointment in his gaze. "Thanks, man. I appreciate that. We'll be seeing you."

The guy's lips turn up timidly. "See you. Sooner rather than later, I'm guessing," he adds with a wink to me.

Oscar and I turn to exit the store. To my left on a shelf is a Santa Claus cookie jar I hadn't noticed when we walked in. It's the first Christmassy thing I've seen in a year. Back home, my aunt and uncle would've already had their friends Christmas dinner and gearing up for the big day. I'll have to get my real phone from Brawler and call them. Especially on Christmas. If I don't call them then, they'll freak.

A sudden pang hits me. Regret that I can't be with them this year. It takes me by surprise because as soon as I could leave them, I did. I had such a one-track mind, it never dawned on me I'd miss things like birthdays and holidays. I just wanted out. I wanted this to be over with, so I could get back to my life. In a way, I've realized that this *is* my life. These little moments like right now are what matter. Hanging on to Oscar's hand in the middle of the store, gazing at a fat Santa with chocolate chip cookie crumbs dusted all over his red suit. The thing is kind of garish—ugly, even—but I like it. It's a reminder that it does no good to live in the past or the future. The present is the here and now, and it's the only thing that matters.

Oscar shifts some hair away from my face. "You like that, Princess?"

I bite down on my lip and nod slowly. This is a shitty time to not have Johnny. It's a shitty time to get sentimental about what I do have right here right now.

"How much for the cookie jar, D?" Oscar calls out.

"Nineteen dollars and ninety-nine cents."

Oscar peels my fingers away from him and starts walking back toward the counter.

"You don't have to," I say, realizing what he's about to do. He ignores me, of course. That's Oscar.

He fishes out his wallet and hands D a twenty-dollar bill. "You're a good kid," the guy tells him.

When Oscar turns around, he's smiling, and it's so delicious my face heats up. He reaches out with his right hand and cups the back of my head. "For you, Princess."

I reach up on my tiptoes and kiss him right there in a shop in the middle of the Heights, savoring the moment with just a delicate press of our lips together. It's getting harder and harder to hold back my feelings for each of them. I want to shout it out to the world. Here, in this shop, in this moment, it feels safe to share this with Oscar. This morning, in private, we were needy and feverish. Right now, I want to tattoo this moment into our minds so we can remember it for years to come.

"Let's go, sexy," he says, giving me a swat on the ass. He must obviously trust this guy D, too. "Grab your fat man, we've got a prostitute to talk to."

I laugh, not even stunned out of the moment by Oscar's words because I wouldn't want him any other way.

Like he told me, I grab Santa and carry him like a football under my arm. Oscar stops me, takes his jacket off, and wraps the ceramic up in it and then hands it back to me. I settle it between us on the bike. It's not comfortable, but we make it work.

He pulls away from the curb slowly. We travel only a couple of blocks before he spots a woman walking down the street toward us with a red mini dress on. When she gets closer, her caked-on makeup is apparent in the sunlight. Her tits are small, her rib cage almost showing through. Oscar kills the engine, nodding toward her.

She hurries, her high heels clopping down the sidewalk. When she gets to us, she props her hand on her hip. "It's extra for threesomes."

I almost choke. Then I have the sudden urge to gouge this woman's eyes out of her head.

Oscar grins while the woman sizes me up. I squeeze Oscar's hips, and he starts talking. "Not here for that. Just wondering if you've seen my mom. Cynthia Drego?"

"Cyn? Yeah, I know her." She gazes up and down the street, foot tapping the sidewalk.

"When's the last time you saw her?"

"A week ago. Maybe." Her bored tone is understandable. She knows she's not about to make a sale from us.

"Do you know where she is now?"

She grunts. "Gregory's new place, probably. Prick said I was too skinny." She pins her gaze to Oscar. "Don't you think you could still hold me down and fuck me? I ain't gonna break."

I'd rather Oscar not answer that question, and he wisely doesn't. Instead, he throws another question at her. "Where's Gregory's new place?"

She sighs, blowing hair off her face. "Don't know. Just said he didn't want me. I tried telling him how much money my cunt makes in a week, but he didn't want to hear it. Said something about another class of women needed."

"No clue at all?" I ask. "In the Heights? Out of the Heights? He hasn't seen her in a while, and he's worried."

She gazes at the ground. Pale skin stretches over her sharp cheekbones, and her face falls. "I think...just outside. Maybe."

She's a lost cause. This whole day has been. We're no closer to finding out where Gregory is or Johnny.

"Vi?" a short, crisp voice says.

The prostitute's head snaps up. "Fuck," she grumbles under her breath, and then she immediately turns and starts walking away from us.

"Vi, don't think I didn't just see you."

Vi picks up the pace. She's practically running down the street as the guy yells at her again.

"Christ," Oscar curses.

He gets off the bike and starts to help me off. I don't even hear the footsteps next to us until a hand grabs my arm and hauls me backward. The cookie jar falls from my grip. The sound of porcelain shattering follows putrid breath filtering against my cheek. "You think you can take up my girl's time. Maybe I'll take up your girl's time."

I gag on the smell, but this guy is barely worth it. I can tell just by the way he's holding me that he's all bark with no bite. I grab his arm and use my hips to throw him. He lands on the sidewalk with a thud. A breath gets caught in his throat, and then he starts choking. I place my shoe against his neck, still holding onto his arm. All the while, Oscar only smirks, his arms crossed over his chest.

"You want to say that to me again?" I ask, glaring at the bastard who dared put his hands on me. With one hand, I rip my helmet off and hand it to Oscar.

His eyes widen as he takes me in. "Fuck." *Well, this guy must recognize me.*

"Yeah, you can say that again."

"I'm sorry, but she's my girl, and if she's not out there making me money, I—"

I press harder into his neck, and he coughs again. "You just might have to make your own fucking money?" I sneer at him. "I bet no one's buying you though, are they?"

He grabs hold of my leg with his free hand. "It's just business."

I glance up to find Vi a block away, staring at us in horror. "Call your girl back here."

When he doesn't immediately do as I say, I press even further into his neck. His skin turns red. He grunts out, "Vi. Vi!"

She walks back slowly, working her assets like she has all the time in the world. I'm pretty sure she's enjoying the fuck out of this. I grin at her as she makes her way back, and she gives me a sly smile in return. When she gets to us though, she drops to her knees, asking if he's okay.

I could almost laugh. Almost. Instead, I nod toward

Oscar. "He's going to ask her another question, and you're not going to interrupt them, is that clear?"

I let my foot off, so he can answer better. "Fine."

Oscar turns toward Vi. He holds his hand out to her and helps her to her feet. "Do me a favor?" She nods in response, more attentive than she had been. If I had to guess, we just made her heroes list. "If you hear about where that place could be—or where my mom is—please find me. My name's Oscar Drego. If you ask around, you'll get to me." He releases the girl's hand and glares down at the asshole under my foot. "I'm in the Crew, so I won't be difficult to find."

The guy winces, realizing he's made a terrible fucking mistake.

Oscar reaches for his wallet. Taking out a ten-dollar bill, he hands it to Vi. "Thanks for your time. This is for you and only you. There won't be a problem, will there?" he asks, glaring at her sprawled-out pimp on the sidewalk.

"No," the guy grunts. "No problem at all."

A smile pulls Vi's lips apart. She takes the money from him and nods before stuffing it into her bra. "Thanks, kid. I hope you find her."

"Me too," he says softly, but she's already walking away.

I drop the fucker's arm and he heaves himself to his feet. He avoids our gaze as he walks in the opposite direction of the girl, head hunched between his shoulder blades like the coward he is.

Oscar puts his arm around me as we watch the girl

walk down the street. Her skinny legs barely hold her up. She wobbles on high heels, and I'm not sure I've seen anything sadder than this. "I need to go back to school," I say softly.

"You'll *never* be a prostitute."

"You think she wanted to be a prostitute?" I ask as a car rolls up next to her a block down. No way. Girls don't go to school dreaming about having sex for money, but shit happens.

Oscar bites his lip. He bends to retrieve the broken cookie jar. "You're still taking the online classes, right?"

I bend next to him as he unwraps his leather jacket to find jagged pieces. I frown at the mess. This was the first thing that made it feel like we were actually going to have a holiday. Now, it's gone. "I need to catch up on some assignments," I tell him, realizing it's been a bit since I logged into the system. I've been preoccupied.

Oscar wraps the jar back up and holds it close to him as he stands. "You should finish online. It's probably better than Rawley Heights High, but if you want to, we can all go back to school after Christmas break."

That, right there, is how I know Oscar hasn't given up yet. He'll head back to school after the break. Even though the football season is over, he'll still chase that diploma and the opportunities it gives.

Oscar swings his leg over the bike and helps me onto it. "What now?" I ask.

"Back to my place? I'll text Magnum and Brawler that we'll be there."

I nod, taking the broken Santa and situating it between us again as Oscar sends the text. When we get there, I'll have to add everyone's phone numbers into my new phone again. Once we get out of the Heights, it'll be nice not to have to do that again. Although, I've been spoiled so far. Oscar's been putting my contacts in for me.

He puts his phone away, and we take off again. We drive to the other side of town where we stop near the familiar corner store underneath Oscar's apartment. I get off with the Santa cookie jar and wait for Oscar to put the bike and helmet away in his small garage before we climb the steps to his place.

He's cleaned it a little more since the last time I was here. He must have done it last night or early this morning. On the kitchen bar, I take out all the shards that remain of the Santa and frown down at them. At least they're not in tiny pieces, but still. "Well, this sucks."

"Sorry," Oscar offers, wrapping his arms around me from behind.

Footsteps sound on the steps leading to the apartment, and Oscar moves to the door to open it.

Magnum emerges first, Brawler trailing. As soon as I notice Brawler's blood-splattered face, I move toward him. "What the fuck? Are you okay?" I check him for injuries, but it becomes abundantly clear the red smattering his face isn't Brawler's blood.

"Can I use your shower?" Brawler asks Oscar while pushing my hands away.

Oscar nods, gesturing toward the bathroom.

"Wait, what happened?" I ask.

Brawler's lips thin. "K ordered an initiation task."

11

I gasp.

Brawler turns away. The back of his shirt is even stained with droplets of blood, and I don't even want to know how that happened. He moves to the bathroom while I stand there in a haze for a few moments. I never wanted this for Brawler. He joined to help me, but shit like this is going to whittle him away. I move my gaze to Magnum. "What did he have to do?"

Magnum shifts his stare away. "I'm not going to answer that. He can tell you if he wants you to know." He stares me down. "It's not my place to say anything."

Oscar bounces his gaze between the two of us, but when I turn to look at him, he immediately looks away from me too. It doesn't escape me that Mag probably knew Brawler was going to have to do something like that this morning but didn't inform me of that. "You didn't tell me."

"Brawler wouldn't have wanted you there."

I take a deep breath, letting it out slowly. He's right. I fucking hate that he's right. Actually, I fucking hate that Brawler had to do whatever he had to do. I hate the whole situation. Little by little, what's happening is taking bite-sized pieces out of me. Johnny's gone. Brawler is stuck in the one place I never wanted him. Oscar's mom is missing. And Magnum? He's taking everything on his shoulders, including all our baggage.

I move to the bathroom. Regardless of what happened, Brawler will need me now. He's still in the shower when I close the door behind me. He must hear me come in, but he doesn't say anything. I sit on the closed toilet seat, waiting for him to emerge from the spray. When he does, I hand him a towel and wait for him to wrap himself up in it before putting my arms around him and holding him to me.

With the amount of blood that was on his face, he must have hurt someone bad. That's on Brawler's shoulders now. The only thing I can do is comfort him in this shitty world we live in. "I love you."

He swallows. "I love you, too."

The door opens, and a stack of clothes lands just inside before the door closes again, leaving us alone. I step back, watching the droplets of water cascade down Brawler's impressive chest. "Do you want to talk about it?"

He leans over, gathering the clothes Oscar left him. He unfolds the sweatpants, stretching the waistband out to make sure they'll fit him. He pulls them on and lets the towel drop around his ankles. "I don't know what there is to say." He pulls the shirt on next. The material is so tight around his biceps, he's practically bulging out of them. "K sent us to talk to some of the guys' families that must have sided with Gregory because they were found dead at the scene."

"Magnum told me that part this morning."

"Well, we didn't just talk to some of them," Brawler says. "Me, specifically." Before I can let my mind wander to them beating up wives and kids, he clarifies. "A brother of one of the guys happened to be at the wife's house. We interrogated him, then kicked his ass when he didn't give us anything."

"K wanted you to do that?"

Brawler pulls his shoulders back. "Listen, Kyla, I knew what I was doing when I went to him. I knew eventually he'd have me do something like this. Or worse." He meets my gaze. "And I'd do it all over again, so don't look at me like that. This is just a means to an end."

I bite my lip. "I still wish you didn't have to."

"We're in the Heights. There are a lot of things we don't want to do that we end up having to do." He glares at my still-bruised face to drive the point home.

There's so much truth in his words, but they still don't

make me feel any better. I wind my arms around him again, and we stay there for a while, just hugging and leaning into one another for comfort.

When we finally emerge from the bathroom, Magnum goes around the corner to the local fast food place to get dinner. He returns with a few bags, and we sit down to eat. Oscar and I tell them what happened with our day while Magnum skips over whatever Brawler did and tells them the wife of the ex-Crew member knew nothing. Well, the brother didn't know anything either, so looks like we all struck out today. Brawler is one threatening dude. The guy would've spilled everything if he knew anything. His hands are the size of freaking mallets. I should know. I've been on the receiving end of them.

While we eat, I stick close to Brawler. He's quiet and thoughtful, and even though he says he doesn't, I wonder if he's regretting his decision to join the Crew. No matter his good intentions, whatever he just did had to hurt.

After I finish eating, I get all their phone numbers and put them into my phone. I take the time to try to memorize them in case I'm ever in a position where I don't have my phone—which apparently happens a lot. I also get Finn's number from Oscar and send him a text: **Hey, it's Kyla. Just wanted to let you know that I'm okay. It's going to be a bit before I can get back to training.**

His response: **Girrrrrrrl. WTF. Don't do that to me again.**

Brawler reads over my shoulder as I type out: **I'm so glad you guys weren't there.**

Not going to lie. Me too. Keep safe.

I put my phone away after grabbing Johnny's number from Magnum's phone. I'm half-tempted to call it, but I already know he won't pick up. I just wish we knew where he was already. The video K was sent flickers through my mind, making me queasy. I hope they're still not torturing him.

Magnum's phone lies in the middle of the table from where I left it. It rings. I glance up to find "Cole" scrawling over the screen. My heart jumps in my throat, and Mag immediately picks it up, bringing it to his ear. His one-sided conversation is less than informative. A couple of "yeah's" pass his lips before he hangs up again. He glances up. "He wants to meet."

"Does he know something?"

"He didn't say he did, but I don't think he'd meet up otherwise."

"Let's go," Oscar says, picking up the discarded brown paper bags and throwing them in the trash. I guzzle down some of my water before getting up from the chair. Now, my stomach tightens for a completely different reason. Hope. Fear. Nerves. Basically, anything and everything is going through my mind. All the possible scenarios. All the ways this could end. All the ways this could go wrong.

"What's this?" Mag asks.

I peer over at him to find him standing next to the broken Santa cookie jar. "Oscar bought that for me when we went to the store for my new phone. Then there was a run-in with a pimp."

"Dick broke her Santa cookie jar," Oscar says.

Magnum frowns at it.

"Even broken, it's the only festive thing I've seen," Brawler remarks.

"It doesn't feel festive, does it?" It's hard to celebrate when someone you love is gone, and you don't know if he's hurting or even going to be okay.

If our situations were reversed, he'd be doing everything he could to get me back, so that's what I'm going to do too.

We trek down the stairs and emerge into the crisp night air. In the time that we were inside, the sun has lowered over the horizon. A brush of orange paints the sky in little wisps.

We head right for the car, and I let Oscar take the front while I get in the back with Brawler because he needs me the most right now. Even though he isn't saying much, I know from experience that just having someone nearby who you care about is soothing.

"Where are we headed?" Oscar asks as Mag pulls away from the curb.

"Some place Cole and I both know." Mag moves his

gaze to the rearview mirror, and I catch it. It isn't until we pull up in front of a familiar house that I understand why he caught my gaze. We're at his old house. The one he used to live in with his mom before he joined the Crew. Mag gives Oscar and Brawler a quick rundown of why we're at this particular house before we all get out and head around the side of the house. The porch in the front looks like it's close to falling down, so we don't dare try to get in that way.

The side door opens, and a musty smell greets us. The place is completely empty other than cobwebs and spiders. It's sat untouched, so it has an eerie, un-lived in feel. There's no furniture. No evidence that this place used to be Magnum's or belong to a family at all.

We don't stop on the first floor though. Mag opens a door just off the kitchen. He flicks on a light, and a part of the basement illuminates. Miraculously, there are actually things down here. As we descend the steps, I watch Mag carefully. His movements are a little strained, but nothing how I thought they would be after getting shot. Either he's putting on a damn good show or what he said about K not actually trying to hurt him is correct. Just off the bottom of the stairs is a foosball table. Behind that, there's a couch. On that couch, sits Mag's cousin, Cole.

"I wasn't sure if the electricity still worked," he says as we come into view.

"I keep it on," Mag says.

"But you don't ever come here." Cole says it more like a

statement, and Magnum doesn't bother expanding on his choices. This place must hold bad memories for him. Otherwise, I don't know why he'd choose to live at the tower when he could have this whole house to himself.

"What do you got for us?" Mag asks.

Cole grimaces. "It's not much, but I figured I should tell you guys in case it means something to you. There was some talk today about Gregory's people meeting at the track. I have no idea if that's where Johnny's at, but I don't think the Dragons have him. If they did, I'd have heard about it."

The track? *Shit, the track.*

Mag steps lightly on my sneaker and I take that as a hint to keep my mouth shut. He runs a hand through his copper hair. "I'll have to think about what that might mean."

"I thought he meant the track at the school. I went by there when they were supposed to have the meeting, but I didn't see a thing."

"Thanks, man. I appreciate it," Mag says. "We haven't found much other than it was some of our ex-guys with the guns that night."

Cole whistles. "I bet K blew a gasket."

Magnum's hand drifts to the side where he got shot. "That's a fucking understatement."

Cole brings himself to his full height and peers around the space. "Kind of funny that we're here. This is where everything started."

Cole and Mag both inspect the place. The musty smell

is more predominant down here. A layer of dust coats every-thing. I'm almost afraid to reach out and touch anything. I'm surprised Cole even sat on the couch. A plume of dust parti-cles probably lifted into the air as soon as he did.

"I don't think either one of us knew what we were getting into when we decided to join." Cole shakes his head. "I think if I had to do it over again, I'd pass."

"It's hard to say," Mag says, glancing over at me. "I think it'll all work out in the end though."

"I fucking hope so, dude."

"You're being safe, right?" Mag asks, turning his atten-tion toward his cousin. "Don't stick your neck too far out. You probably shouldn't have even went to the damn track. What if they saw you there? They would've known you were listening in on them."

"I'm being smart, bro. Don't worry. I want Johnny back as much as you guys do." He leans against the foosball table. "When that happens, we won't be able to meet up like this though."

"We'll figure something out," Mag offers half-heartedly.

Johnny's coming around. I know he is. Whether he's willing to let Cole live if he sees him is another thing all together. I guess it depends on how Cole ended things with them.

Cole circles to the back of the sofa. "I'll keep you updated, and you do the same."

He and Mag share a bro hug and then Cole moves to

me. "I'm glad they have you. I wish we were meeting under better circumstances."

"One day," I say, still not forgetting I promised to get Cole out too. Or to at least give him a life. One he never had the chance of having once he joined the Crew.

He gives me a small smile and then claps Brawler on the shoulder. "Mack," he says. "Having you down here is just like having Manning here. I think you might be a little bigger than him though."

Oscar speaks up, telling Cole goodbye so Brawler doesn't need to respond. Evidently, I'm not the only one who's noticed how Brawler reacts when people talk about his brother.

We wait until Cole disappears up the basement steps. Upstairs, the side door opens and closes, and we all turn toward Mag. "Why didn't you want me to say anything?"

Brawler and Oscar both give us dubious looks as Mag answers, "I love my cousin, but he doesn't have the head for all the ins and outs gangs use. The less he knows the better. As long as they don't know he heard anything about the track, he can plead ignorance."

"Wait," Brawler says. "So, you guys know what this track place is?"

"Maybe," Mag says. "A few months ago, Johnny took Kyla to the race track in Doyle. They were scoping out the place to buy. K ultimately decided not to, but maybe

Gregory did. He would've been updated on everything having to do with the potential purchase."

"Oh shit, a race track," Oscar says. "I didn't even think of that."

"We know it was up for sale. We don't know who bought it, or even if Gregory did, we don't know that that's where this meeting was being held." Mag breathes out. "It makes sense though. It's close enough to the Heights without being in the Heights. Gregory wouldn't want to stay here unless he has more followers than we think."

"Even if that is the track the Dragons were talking about, we don't know if Johnny's there," I say, realizing how flimsy this all sounds.

"We can find out who bought it by looking at tax records," Mag says. "Though, he'd be a fool if he bought it under his real name."

"Let's hope he called it Runts Enterprises or something fucking stupid like that."

"At least it's something," Brawler says, finally emerging from his funk. "It's actually something we can act on. We can drive past the track and look to see if it's even being occupied."

"Here's the real question," Oscar says. "Do we tell K what we found out?"

Mag shakes his head. "Who are we going to tell him told us? We can't tell him anything right now. We'll wait until we verify, and then we'll make up a story that keeps Cole's name out of everything." Mag dribbles his hands over the foosball table, then dusts his fingers off on his pants.

We're playing a very dangerous game here.

"What did Cole mean when he said this place is where it all started?" Brawler asks.

Mag's face hardens. His hazel-green eyes shadow over. "He and I were right here when the initiation tasks began. The Crew kidnapped us from this very room, taking us out to the middle of nowhere, and dropping us off. What Cole and I didn't know was that Manning and Johnny were out there too. We thought we had to find our way back home, but eventually, I met up with Manning in the woods after we heard each other. We saw a light in the sky, so we moved toward it. That light brought us to the cabin in the woods. Trust me, it didn't look anything like what it does right now. It was a piece of shit. When we all got there, they ran us for twenty-four straight hours learning gun technique."

"I bet you excelled at that," I say, wondering if that's where he got his nickname.

Brawler runs his hand over his chest. "I asked Manning what he had to do to get into the gang. I remember Mom being worried once when he disappeared for like a day, but Manning was always doing shit like that. It just seemed odd because he said he was going to take a nap in his room, but when I went to get him for dinner, he just wasn't there."

"Honestly, it could've been any number of times," Mag

says. "The Crew was always kidnapping us and making us do shit."

I peek at the muscled fighter next to me. "Will Brawler have to do that?"

Mag shakes his head. "They got rid of that aspect when Mayhem retired. Shit got harder after that. K's techniques are a little more ruthless. A little more real world."

As Brawler knows all too well now. K snapped his fingers, and Brawler had to kick the shit out of a guy.

Mag blows out a breath. "We're not supposed to talk about what we had to do to get into the Crew."

Oscar shifts on his feet. "Agreed. Let's get the fuck out of here and talk about what we're going to do to figure out if Johnny's at this race track."

He's the first to take the stairs, his back ramrod straight. It makes me wonder what he had to do to get into the Crew. He fast-tracked it out of necessity. Does that mean what he had to do was worse than what others do? I can see K making that a thing. Like, if you really want in, you really need to show him. There's no telling what he came up with, but I'm absolutely positive that whatever is going through Oscar's mind about his past isn't good. It's something he doesn't even want to talk about.

We follow him out of the basement, through the side exit, and back to the car. Once we're there, Magnum brings up the tax records on his phone. The race track sold to a

John D. Smith. If that doesn't shout fake name, I don't know what does.

"Fuck," Oscar breathes, rearranging the seat belt over his shoulder. "I say we just do a drive-by. Let's just see what we can see from the road. If it's hopping with sketchy people, then we know at least that's where Gregory is hiding out. We can make up some bullshit story to K, so that he gets all his attention on it. That way, we're not rolling in there blind and making more of a mess of things than what they need to be."

"I agree," Brawler says. "I say we do it tonight. It's dark. It will give us cover. Plus, if it was me in there, I'd want to be found as soon as possible."

"I don't want to sit on this either," Mag finally says. He starts the car, and we begin the trek out to the race track.

My stomach clenches. If we think Johnny's there, I don't know how I'm going to be able to stop myself from just busting in. The video of him replays through my head again and again, and the worst part is, there's no off button.

12

Johnny

I see her again. The tilt of her lips. Her long, dark hair. The fierce gaze in her eyes that struck me the first time I saw her and hasn't left me yet. When I met her, I thought I was strong. It wasn't until after meeting her that I realized all my strength comes from a false place. *Her* power comes from within her soul. Mine has been built up on mudslides and crooked ladders that are two seconds from falling down.

Suddenly, I'm falling through space. Every image of Kyla is erased until I jerk up. I blink, realizing I'd fallen asleep again. Of course, I had. The only time I've seen Kyla in the past couple of days is when my body gives in to sleep despite my surroundings. Otherwise, I see her through a hazy gaze, flames licking up her skin and spreading between us. The heat was real, but I don't know if what my mind is trying to tell me is real, too. Was she on fire? Did Kyla fucking die because of these assholes?

A potent mix of fear and anger barrages me again. I pull at the ties around my wrists, only to find them the same as they were. They're tight. Too tight. These guys aren't messing around. Considering some of them are Crew members, they know our tactics. I'm not getting out of these no matter how much I struggle. I might as well gnaw my arm off. If I could reach it, it would become a very real possibility, just so I could learn the truth.

They told me she died.

They told me my father isn't coming for me.

I don't trust the bastards but try telling my mind that when my last memory is of flames surrounding her. When I get out of here and find out she's dead, I will burn the Heights to the fucking cement it's built on. I won't just stop at where I live. I won't just stop at making sure everyone I've seen here suffers, I'll just kill everybody. Everyone will pay.

The hunger rumbling in my stomach is constant now. I can ignore it for the most part, especially when they come in for my hourly beating where they interrogate me incessantly on how to get into the tower to take my dad out. Gregory wants to usurp him. I haven't seen the asshole once since they shoved me into this small room, but I know it's him. He wants to throw my dad out and put himself in his place.

The thing he doesn't realize is there's a reason why my dad's at the top and he's not. My dad is a ruthless, zero-fucks given psycho. He won't bow to anyone, and he's crazy and smart. A ruthless combination. He won't die. I'd like to see these guys storm the tower. They wouldn't make it inside. They'd be dead before they even started their attempt. Kingston Marx is the nucleus of our group. Everyone in that place will protect him at their own cost.

Even though there are a few Crew guys here who have obviously turned against him, I still believe that. These aren't tower guys. They aren't in the inner circle. They were brainwashed to switch sides, but the core group in that tower will lay down their lives for my dad...and me.

I hope.

Something gnaws at me, but I push it away. My dad's tactics are what they are, but I've always known that deep down he loves me. I'm his only son. The son he wanted more than anything. Since I was a boy, he's talked about us ruling alongside each other in the biggest business in this state. He's smart. He's cunning. He's everything I wished I could be.

Until Kyla. Now I know there's a much bigger world, and not all of it revolves around the Crew. Or business. Or blood. I'd give anything to see her next to me again.

I shake my head, so I don't go down the rabbit hole of believing their lies. I won't believe she's gone until I have proof, and even if it is true, knowing it won't help me get out of here. I need that strength she internally possesses. The strength she needed to bring me around, and I'll be the first to admit I'm a pig-headed fucking asshole. Selfish. Arrogant. Determined beyond belief.

But one thing I do possess is the never give up attitude.

The steel door opens at the end of the room. I'm sitting in a metal chair on the far side of a basement. It's cleaned out, but it smells like motor oil and dankness. I was passed out when they brought me here, so I have no idea where I am, but I have to give them props for their staging. The slow walk of my captor to get to me would make a lesser man pee his pants. For me, it's just another bullet point in the handbook my dad made up. Instill fear. Make sure your hostage knows they have no way out.

Unfortunately for them, the part where the captive starts talking won't happen. When I signed up for the Crew, it wasn't just a good idea, it was the only idea. I've lived and breathed it since I was born. I know no other way.

The fucker finally gets to me. He's in his late twenties. I don't know what exactly he did for the Crew. Our reach is too big to remember everyone's name, and if I hadn't recognized him, he made damn sure to tell me he's an ex-member anyway. He went so far as to ask how I'm going to manage to kill his defected ass. That's what we do to Crew members who leave. They die. He has the upper hand now, the gloating prick, but that doesn't mean he always will.

"We told you he wasn't coming for you."

"And I believe I told you to get fucked."

He smirks. He's playing the prick card right. I'll give him that much. "I know someone who won't be getting fucked anymore. Your pretty little girlfriend is char and you're going to die anyway."

I make no reaction even though I imagine slitting this fucker's throat from ear-to-ear. I told her I'd get her out of the Heights, and I'm the selfish prick that was filled with so much elation when she turned me down. There's something fucking wrong with me. "At least I can die knowing I had the best pussy in the Heights. Your girl's probably raw from overuse and smells like rotten fish."

The guy tilts his head. "You're not wrong, but I get my dick wet and that's all that matters."

I used to think that, too, but not anymore. There's so much more to being with a woman than the carnal pleasure. Not to get too fucking sentimental, but I've never felt more accepted in my life than when I'm with Kyla. What I told him was true. I can die happy knowing I had something real in my life. Even if for a short time. "When does the killing part happen? I have to admit, I'm pretty exhausted." The only parts of my body I can see are my torso and thighs, and I look like shit. The throbbing in my head hasn't stopped since I've been here. The ache in my limbs is something I've never felt before either. Plus, there's the constant pain surging from the bullet in my hip that hasn't been attended to at all. In fact, all they've done is make sure it doesn't heal.

Pushing on it, sticking their fingers inside the hole, ripping my skin. I'm both shocked and proud that we groomed someone like this. He would've been a great asset if he wasn't such a traitor.

"You're next in line. Happy? Any last thoughts?"

I tilt my head to the side. "You would've killed me already if that's what you wanted to do." He opens his mouth to object, but I talk over him. "Not saying you won't because you will. But you obviously want something. My guess is, what you want is for my dad to make a mistake. You—or Gregory I should say because we all know you aren't calling the shots—thinks that by having me here, my dad will do something stupid, which will allow him to swoop into the tower, throw him out, and land in the place of power he's always dreamed of. What you don't understand is that when things get shitty, that's when the best version of my father steps up. No, he's not coming for me. He won't come for me until he knows he can obliterate every last one of you so not even your families will recognize your bodies. It will be the end of you guys. No second chances. No running away. When he hits you, you'll be dead."

His jaw ticks though he tries his best to hide it.

"That's why you're better off just killing me now. If that's the satisfaction you want out of all of this, at least give yourself a few days of having it until he obliterates every last one of you. Then, you can take the memory of killing me to the grave with you while I'll be thinking of my girl." I shrug like the asshole I am. "Whatever gets your rocks off."

I earn a smack to the face which tells me all I need to know. I've gotten to him. This isn't the only time I've gotten to the guy either. He's good, but he's not as good as me. I learned from the best. I saw my first dead body when I was three. Accidentally walked in on my dad cleaning up the mess. It wasn't until I was grown up that I found out it was the mayor of Rawley Heights. Turns out, we didn't like him very much.

I wiggle my jaw around and return his gaze. "You asked for my opinion. If I were you, that's how I'd do it."

"They were right. You are a cocky asshole."

I shrug again because...obviously. "I guess the real question is, how are you going to play it though? What's Gregory instructed? Do you think it's weird he's not here?" I tilt my head for effect. "I don't know. I just think if *I* had someone like me, I'd be all up in his face. I wouldn't be able to help myself."

The guy sighs with a hint of humor. "Who says he's not here?"

"Prove me wrong."

"You're not the one in charge here, Johnny Rocket. In fact, you never were."

"Aren't I, though?"

The unmistakable sounds of muted gunshots fill the room. I sit up straighter. The timing couldn't have been any better, unless this group is way more disorganized than I originally thought and they're currently trying to off each other for no reason other than they just don't like each other, which is exactly why they need a strong leader.

I stifle all my thoughts and peer at the metal door. "You should probably check that out."

The guy glances back and then returns his gaze to me. He's caught between two trains of thought. He's indecisive. Indecision kills people.

When the door opens, a shot rings out, and he falls to the floor with a hole in his head. I'm not surprised. Had he made a decision, he'd still be living. Maybe.

A familiar stature waltzes into the room, gun at the ready. Mag's gaze darts from side-to-side.

"Clear," I say, letting him know there are no other threats in the room with us.

I finally relax, my heart beating like crazy. I knew Dad would come. But when Brawler steps through the metal door next, I bristle. Mag gets to me, working on my ties with a knife from his pocket, but my gaze is glued to the door.

I almost slump forward when Kyla and Oscar come through next. No other guys follow. Not Trey. Not any of the other guards, just—

Kyla runs forward. I clench my jaw together, inspecting her skin for injuries or burn marks or anything, but what I find is just her. Just her perfect self, staring at me with unshed tears. She drops to her knees and starts to untie the ropes around my ankles.

"We have to hurry," Mag barks.

She finally gets them loose, and Brawler pulls me to my feet, propping an arm around me like he did when we tried to make our escape. He was just as lost as I was when we weren't sure what happened to Kyla. I didn't think I'd ever feel bad for the guy after he fucked my girl, but I got it then. I understood the feeling.

Kyla stands, hugging the other side of me. "Get him to the car," Mag demands. "I'm right behind you."

When we start for the door, I already know what Mag's doing. Destroying the evidence that I was ever here. My blood had dripped on the cement floor. He'll be cleaning it. Burning it. Something to make sure that no one knows I was ever here. A top rule of the Crew: Never get caught up in other people's shit.

I hiss in a breath as we move forward. I've been sitting for hours and hours. I've been in that same position since I first got there. Brawler has to basically carry me out of there, and eventually, Oscar takes Kyla's place on my other side. Everything hurts. We hit the steps and come out a door that opens to a race track.

Son of a bitch. We're at the race track. No wonder why it smelled like old gasoline down there. Residual fumes. I suck in the night air like a starved man. My head lolls back.

Now that I don't have to be on, I want nothing more than to just crash. To sleep for ages.

She's alive.

I'm alive.

They carry me to our uniform black car. Sirens sound in the distance, and my heart rate picks up. Luckily, Magnum's footsteps sound behind us, crunching against the gravel at a rapid pace. We hunker down into the car, and Mag takes off like we're still running for our lives. He hits the gas, speeding away from the scene until the sirens get louder. Then, he slows, telling us all to act casual. The police speed past us, and like the good citizen Mag is supposed to be, he pulls over as the five police cars with red and blue lights scream past. Then, he pulls back out like we have every right to drive down this road in the middle of the night.

That's all I can comprehend before sheer exhaustion takes me under.

13

_I_ hold Johnny in the backseat of the car. His clothes have char, black dust, and dirt embedded into the fibers, just like he looked the night of the explosions and fire. A bandage has been placed around his midsection, blood seeping through. It's a half-assed attempt at staunching the blood flow from the injury he received at the hands of one of those fuckers.

We need a doctor.

"Mag..."

"I know," he says.

Johnny's unconscious for the time being but seeing him like this makes my heart hurt. Somehow, everything went wrong the night of the explosion. K left Johnny. We got separated, and even though I should be relieved that we're back together, the pain in my heart I'd been keeping at bay explodes. Right now, I want nothing more than to kill K. He tutored Johnny in this life, and the one time his son needed him, he fucking abandoned his ass.

I've heard people say they'd rather someone rot in jail to atone for their sins, but I'm more of an eye-for-an-eye girl. I want to take K's life. To me, nothing else will make up for what he did other than seeing the light die from his eyes, much like when I watched him kill Fonz and Dunnegan right in front of me. I want to see the moment he passes. I want to see the realization that I did it. I took his life from him because he deserved it. Like, in a literal, now you know not to fuck with me move.

Magnum pulls to a stop at a house on the outskirts of town.

Brawler leans forward, checking out the houses through the side window. "Where are we?"

"A doctor," Mag says, clenching his teeth. He glances at me over his shoulder. "Come in with us, Kyla?"

Oscar's grip tightens on my leg, but I pat his hand, letting him know it's okay. Of course, I want to go in with Johnny. If Mag doesn't want the others in there, it must be for a good reason.

"We'll wait outside," Brawler says. He gives me a nod, and I'm thankful he didn't have to do anything to recover Johnny while we were at the track. Mag and his gun did all the work. Surprisingly, there weren't a lot of people there to stop us from recovering him. Either out of arrogance or just plain dumbassery, I'm not sure. Either way, we used it to our advantage.

Oscar pushes the door open. Helping me crawl over him, he brushes a kiss against my cheek as I go. Mag struggles to get Johnny out of the back seat, so I lend him a hand as soon as I'm out. Johnny comes to a standing position, and the movement wakes him. He squeezes my arm, giving me a half-smile that warms my heart. I've seen his full smiles, the peek of dimples that come out when he's actually trying to be charming. But this half-smile is special. A smile in the face of adversity. A big fuck you to the world. They tried to take us out, but we're fine. We're good. We're all still standing, and that's what matters.

"We'll be quick," Mag says, offering up the info to the guys in the car. He catches all their gazes. "I trust this guy. Everything will be fine."

I don't know if what he says will actually make a difference to the guys, but when I look in the back seat, I can tell it does. Concern is still etched on their faces, but it's not as prominent.

Johnny slides his arm around my shoulders. Mag and I help him up the front sidewalk, climb the stairs, and then Mag knocks on the door. An older man answers. As soon as he sees Johnny, his frown deepens until predominant creases line the edges of his mouth.

He opens the door wide to let us in. "What's wrong with him?"

"Gunshot," I say.

The white-haired guy tsks, making sure to catch Johnny's gaze. "I think you're on to your seventh life, Friend."

Johnny chuckles dreamily as we follow the doctor into a backroom. Oddly enough, past a normal kitchen and bathroom, a room to the right holds everything you see at a regular doctor's office. Sterile bed. That weird paper that always covers it. Mag and I help Johnny onto it, and the doctor immediately finds the source of all the blood. He takes scissors, cutting through Johnny's clothes so he can get a better look without disturbing the wound. He doesn't ask questions. He just treats him, which is probably why Magnum was okay with bringing him here.

The doctor gives him a shot in the side of what I assume is a numbing agent. The doctor's not much for talking, but that's fine with me as long as he's working. He grabs a pair of forceps inside a nearby drawer and digs out the bullet. Johnny's knuckles turn white against the table.

Blood oozes from the wound, and Johnny's doctor uses gauze to wipe it away. It's obvious it's an old wound, and I wonder why he hasn't chastised us for not bringing him here sooner. Though, I suppose since he knows Johnny, he also knows anything can happen in the Crew and there are a million reasons why he wouldn't have been able to come in right away.

I try not to look at the fresh blood coating Johnny's skin. Not that the sight of blood makes me queasy, it's just the fact that it's Johnny's blood. From a gunshot wound that happened days ago. The possibilities of what could've happened are endless, and I don't want to think about it. Not to mention I witnessed actual footage of the fuckers who had him messing with it. Making it worse. Torturing him.

It makes sense that the Crew would have a doctor like this that they would trust to come to and have him not ask any questions. If we'd have taken Johnny to a hospital, it's not as if they wouldn't have figured out there was a bullet inside him. That would open up too many questions. Questions we've tried so hard to stay away from.

"It'll be sore for a while," the guy finally says.

When I peek back, he's stitching Johnny up, and this part, I don't mind watching.

"You didn't hit anything too important," the old doctor muses "Lucky."

I glance up to meet Johnny's gaze. We are, in fact, lucky. Very, very lucky. He's finally back with us.

When will that luck run out though? We're already pushing the cosmic limits of what's possible. You can only throw yourself into the fire so many times without expecting to get burned.

Johnny reaches for me, more coherent now. I put my hand solidly in his, and he slides off the table as soon as he's stitched up fully. "I appreciate it, Doc. I'll wire you the money as soon as I get someplace safe."

He nods, then he finally looks over at me as if he's just realized I'm here with them. He looks me up and down, discerning without judgment. I'm sure this guy has seen it all.

"This is...my Kyla," Johnny says, as if he's unsure of what to label me as. Magnum shuffles from foot-to-foot beside us. He's there with a steadying hand under Johnny's bicep. Miraculously, it didn't take that long to fish out the bullet and stitch him up.

I like his words. I'm his Kyla. Do we need more labels than that? Because I am his, and he's mine.

"Anyone else?" Doc asks, wiggling his bloody fingers in the air like he's ready to take on his next patient.

Mag declines and gives the doc a firm handshake. Then, we head back to the car again. Brawler and Oscar scramble out of the car and into the dark night as soon as they see us walk out. Johnny grimaces at having to walk even though Mag and I are taking the brunt of his weight. At the end of the sidewalk, Johnny plants his feet, and Magnum and I stop next to him. We all stand there looking at one another. Johnny looks worse for wear. He's in days old clothes where we've had a chance to freshen up.

He swallows. "You guys came for me?" The way he asks it is almost accusatory, disbelief coloring his words.

What did he think we were going to do? "We didn't know where you were. We would've come for you sooner," I tell him.

He squeezes me lightly, but I get the feeling it's taking a lot out of him to do and say all of this. Johnny Marx isn't one to show weakness though.

"They cold-cocked me," Brawler says, shaking his head. "I didn't even see them. They came out of nowhere."

Johnny peers at him, almost distrusting. Before I can step in and say anything, though, Johnny says, "I know. We were both worried about Kyla."

"I tried—"

Johnny cuts him off. "We can't stay here all night. Can we have this conversation somewhere where I can take a shower and maybe lie in a bed?" He starts to move forward but doesn't go anywhere because it's Magnum and I who have his puppet strings, practically. Even though he's the worst off out of all of us, he's still trying to pull the strings.

"Take a chill pill, Rocket." Oscar grins. "Kyla's been downright emotional, so give her a moment to take this all in before you start turning into the prickish dick you can be."

I press my lips together. At first, Johnny eyes Oscar with a sneer, but his lips twitch. Eventually. Half-heartedly at first, but then a genuine smile crosses his face. "Are you saying my girl was worried about me?"

"I'm saying *our* girl was worried about you," Oscar retorts.

Mag shakes his head, finally moving Johnny forward. I step in line, keeping up. We help Johnny into the car and then the rest of us get in. Much to Johnny's displeasure, I sit on Brawler's lap to give him enough room, so he doesn't have to sit straight up and down and hurt himself even more. I want to ask him so many questions about what happened while he was there. We checked the place, and Gregory wasn't one of the thugs there, though some of his girls were. Oscar's mom wasn't one of them, and despite the fact that he looks cool about it, I know he's wondering where she is. If she's not at her usual haunts in the Heights and she's not where Gregory's other girls were, where the fuck could she be?

Mag starts the car, but then just sits there, staring out the windshield. His shoulders slump forward. "I don't know where to go," he confesses.

Johnny moves his foot, dragging in a breath. "What do you mean? Go to the tower."

Mag gazes into the rearview mirror, locking eyes with me. None of us think that's a good idea. K is not our friend. He's not our ally. And, he's definitely my foe. Maybe Johnny doesn't remember what happened in the box. Even if he didn't, he certainly doesn't know what happened when we got back to the tower.

"What did he fucking do?" Johnny scowls. His eyes are bloodshot. Streaks of dirt and ash mar every visible piece of skin. It sucks that we have to do this right now, but when else are we going to do it? Johnny and Mag are the ones who know how to deal with Crew shit the best.

"Listen, bro," Oscar says, voice smooth. "Your dad's all

pissed off. He thinks Kyla ruined you." He eyes me, and I give him a quick shake of my head. I'm not telling Johnny why I'm here yet. Fuck that. Not right now. I need to do it eventually, but now is just not the time.

Johnny licks his lips. They're suddenly pinker than they were just a moment ago. He can probably taste ash on his tongue. "Did he hurt you?" he asks me, eyeing my face.

I shake my head. I got the feeling he wanted to, but I also think K is smarter than that. He knew we were on his side about Johnny. He wanted to make sure he had us to get him back. Now that we have, I don't know what he'll do.

"Listen, I can't hide from my dad," Johnny says. He darts his gaze around to the guys, kind of like a skittish pup. He's still wondering if he can trust Brawler and Oscar. "I don't want to," he says finally, lifting his chin. "He'll want to know right away that you found me. How did you find me, anyway?"

"About that," Mag says. "We can't tell your dad how we found you. I'll take us back to the tower." He turns around in the seat and gives Johnny a dark look. "But for right now, that piece of information stays between us." He gives Oscar, Brawler, and I a warning look.

"Fine," Johnny says through clenched teeth. "Listen, I'm so fucking tired, and I hurt too fucking much to come up with an excuse right now. We go to the fucking tower because we have nowhere else to go, and even if we did, I need to see my father."

Oscar sighs and shakes his head, dribbling his fingers over the car door in the front seat. Brawler holds me to him.

Just before Magnum pulls away from the curb, Johnny sighs reluctantly. "Thank you," he says, almost inaudibly. It's tight, like giving thanks isn't something he's used to, but it's genuine. "I'm glad you guys came."

Johnny's gaze is glassy when I look over. I don't know if it's just lethargy or something else, but it's like there's a clear-plated door slamming closed between us. I don't know why. I don't get it. Sometimes, the things Johnny does don't make sense to me. He's in a constant push and pull over his thoughts and emotions. If I had to guess, it's one of those times where he's wondering if what he feels is really real. If it's foreign to him, he rebels against it.

Which probably means we're getting somewhere with Johnny Marx.

We might not all be on the same page, but at least we're all in the same chapter in the same book, reading the same story. Our paths could still divert away from each other, but I'm going down fighting. I'll fight until that last sentence— the last period—that signals The End.

14

Before we get to the tower, Mag drops Oscar and Brawler off at their apartments. We figure the least amount of people implicated in this, the better. K is going to want to know exactly how we found this information, to exploit them for more, I imagine. Hopefully, Johnny being back will distract him for the moment.

Johnny's out cold when we pull into the parking lot. Magnum tells the security guy in the booth to alert K we need to see him right away. It must be late. *Really* fucking late. Even the streets of Rawley Heights are sleepy. I'd rather be going to the cabin with all of them than come back here with just Johnny and Mag considering how awful K has been lately. However, I also know Johnny is right. His dad will want to see him. If we take him somewhere else tonight, it'll just make him suspicious and ask more questions about what's going on.

As soon as Mag parks, I run my hand up Johnny's arm. He still looks bad. Tonight is going to be rough for him. His eyelids flutter open at my touch. A small smile turns his lips up until they drop again. "You're really here?"

I nod, trailing my fingers down his hands. "I'm really here."

He peers over his shoulder out the window of the car. The shadowy underground parking garage greets him. The halos of synthetic light only brighten some sections of the parking area. "I need to ask you something." I slide over the backseat to get closer to him. He lifts himself into more of a sitting position. "At The Ring..."

"Yeah?"

"After I got shot." He licks his dry, blood-stained lips. Looking at him hurts my soul. I never want to see anyone I love look like this again. "And after you guys came in...it was just us at the end, wasn't it?"

My heart ricochets in my chest. I squeeze his fingers. "What do you mean?"

"My dad was there, and then he wasn't. Am I making that up?"

I shake my head slowly, watching his usual blue eyes turn ice cold. "No, you're not making that up. It was just you, me, Brawler, and Magnum until we got separated."

"Where—"

"Your dad left us," Mag says, turning around in his seat. His voice holds a thread of warning I haven't yet heard from him before when it's just us. "He took off with his last guard. Then, the box half collapsed. We're lucky we got out of there."

Johnny sits up even straighter, pulling his feet down to rest on the floorboards at his feet. He shoves the car door open, and it bounces off its hinges until he stops it from closing on him again with his palm. He doesn't say a word, and I share a look with Magnum. He needed to know. He asked. His mind probably wouldn't let him believe what happened, but it did. His dad fucking left him, and I still can't get over it, so I can't imagine what Johnny is going through right now.

Mag and I hurry out of the car to help Johnny to the elevator. His macho bullshit attitude is turned on full strength like he can walk by himself, but he can't. He's had a bullet festering in his hip for two days. He's been beaten and tortured. He needs us, whether he wants to admit it or not.

We still hold onto him as we take the longest elevator ride to the suite level. The doors open, and the guards on duty just stare as we take Rocket past them. They bow their heads in respect until we get to Trey. "Is he awake?" Johnny asks.

"We woke him. He's in the living room."

Trey moves out of the way, and we push past him. Johnny relaxes his hold on us, trying to walk himself, so we take the hint and let him limp his way badly into his father's suite.

Watching Big Daddy K eye Johnny as we approach makes me trigger happy. He's stoic. I mentally plot out grabbing Magnum's gun and putting a bullet in his head. It's just unfortunate for me that there are a shitton of guards outside this fucking room who would just be waiting for me to come barreling out.

Vengeance is one thing. Surviving it is another. I have to survive. They have to survive. Otherwise, all of this will have been for nothing.

Then again, I wish I would've killed K already. If I had, Johnny never would've known the hurt of a parents' betrayal. He didn't say anything, but I don't care who you are. You could be someone who prides yourself on not having any feelings, but when a parent leaves you behind, that's the day you find out there's a spark of humanity left in you and betrayal fucking hurts.

It's okay. Johnny has me. And he has Oscar, Magnum, and Brawler. The sooner he realizes that the four of us will do anything for him, the better. He doesn't need his father. He never did.

K stands when Johnny closes in on him. He inspects him, dragging his gaze from the tip of his head to the soles of his feet. I hope every speck of blood turns his stomach. I hope every bruise reminds him of what he did.

It's not even that K could've stopped what happened. In

fact, that's probably not the case. The thing is, you stick by the ones you love no matter what. There's no survival instinct in cases like this because your survival instinct is also making sure the ones you care about are alive, too. Not just yourself. Because if the person you love dies, a piece of you dies, too. For whatever reason, K doesn't have that inside him, and he probably never will.

They just stare at each other. With each passing second, I glare holes into K's temple, begging him to say something to Johnny, fucking anything about how he's alive. Ask him if he's okay for Christ's sake. Just fucking do something.

"We took him to Doc's before we brought him here. He got the bullet out and cleaned him up."

With Mag's words, K seems to have shaken himself out of whatever was going through his head. "Good to hear. I've always liked that old man." He sits back on the couch now without another word.

Johnny sways on his feet, and I move forward to put my arm around him. Less in a helpful way, and more in a way that just seems like I want to hold him. We move back to sit on the opposite couch, and Mag moves in behind us.

"Tell me everything," K says. The only telltale sign that K was asleep is that the suit he wore earlier is slightly disheveled. He's combed his hair, he's put the suit back on along with his shiny black shoes. Johnny looks like death warmed over, but not his father. His father looks like he's spent two days in the tower while Johnny was getting beaten because that's exactly what happened.

"After Brawler and I went to check out the family of our ex-guy, Kyla and I had the idea to talk to some of the prostitutes in the area. We thought some of them would know where Gregory was, especially if they used to work for him at Candy's. We were in luck. She didn't know much, but she heard something about some of the girls being taken to a track. A few months ago, Johnny checked out the racetrack. We decided to do a drive by since we weren't sure. We figured if someone was there, we might see signs of life, and sure enough, there was. We went in right away."

"Gregory?"

Mag shakes his head. "Wasn't even there. Fewer than ten guys, too. It was an easy in and out. They were banking on us not knowing how to find him, but they bet on the wrong location."

K turns his attention to Johnny who's stiff at my side. Slight tremors shake his body, as if he's barely keeping himself together. K's eyes darken as he looks at his son. "Did you see Gregory at all?"

"No, but the guy who tortured me made it clear who he was working for."

"They sent me a video."

"I know," Johnny says. "They told me they were going to send it to you."

"What's your assessment?" K asks.

I lock my jaw together and lean into Johnny further in case he needs comfort or strength. I would cut myself open and give him anything he needs.

"Hostage situation to send you a message. They tried playing mind games. Mainly that you didn't care and wouldn't be coming for me."

K smirks. "Divide and conquer."

"Classic," Johnny says, lip curling in that "I'm second in line to the Crew" way that turns my stomach.

"What else?" K asks.

"The situation seemed to have no real purpose whatsoever. Just sending a message to you. Trying to get you to back off."

K cocks his head. "Interesting. A few of our guys were part of their shooters."

"Unrest," Johnny says with a simple shrug of his shoulders.

"We'll take care of it."

My stomach rolls. Suddenly, they're a 'we' again. What happened to 'we' when his son needed him?

K stands. "You need to get some sleep and some recovery time. When you're up to it, we'll talk retaliation."

Johnny struggles to his feet, but gets there on his own nonetheless. I stand after him, and it's then when he takes my hand and squeezes it, hanging on to me a little more for support.

K moves his gaze to rest on Magnum and then myself.

"Good work. I'll expect a report, including why you thought it necessary not to involve me when you found out where he could be."

Mag nods, and I have to practically bite off a piece of my tongue to keep my mouth shut. At that, K walks around the couch, retreating to the back. We move slowly toward the door. Everything is catching up with Johnny. Since his suite is the closest, we head just across the hall to remove ourselves from the guards' prying eyes.

As soon as the door is closed behind us, Johnny says, "I need a shower." He gazes at me, questions in his eyes. It's a no-brainer. I'm not going to let him take a shower by himself. Who knows if he can even keep himself upright for that amount of time?

I pin Mag with a look, hoping he knows I want him to stay. I don't know anything about injuries like this. If Johnny were to take a turn for the worse, he would be better off with Magnum right here.

Mag helps us past Johnny's room and into his en suite. He lets himself out as I help Johnny disrobe himself. The amount of ash and blood caked on his skin makes my veins harden just under my skin. The sooner we get out of the Heights, the better.

I turn the shower on and help Johnny in. He braces himself against the wall, the spray hitting him in the chest and turning the water at his feet a murky gray. I take a lot of showers with my guys, but this one has to be the most intimidating yet. Johnny, the one who acts like nothing hurts him, is physically hurt. The evidence washing down the drain right this very moment. Within a couple of minutes, it might not even look like he went through hell. Sure, he'll have the bruises and the patching, but it won't be as fresh.

"Come here," he demands. His voice is guttural, throaty, like it almost pains him to talk.

He watches my every movement as I peel my clothes off. My skin lights with tension. I quickly throw my hair up into a bun piled at the top of my head before moving under the spray. "Do you need me?"

He lifts his hand to cup my face. "I'll always need you. If I could move right now, I'd lift you against the shower and fuck you so good, babe." His hand trembles. "I just need to feel something real right now."

"Do you want to talk about it?"

He shakes his head slowly. A back-and-forth motion that looks like it takes a great amount of effort. I'm sure his mind is reeling from the truth of what happened at The Ring.

I wanted Johnny to see what his father was really like. No, I *needed* him to see what his father was really like. I don't want this push and pull between me and the Crew anymore, but now that he's seen it—or I think he has—pain lances at me. When people I love feel pain, I feel pain. Satisfaction should be rolling through me right now, but that's not the case at all. I just feel sorry for him. Sorry for the parts of Johnny that still thought his dad was his dad.

Someone who would care for him no matter what. Someone who would look out for him no matter what.

Johnny's never known unconditional love. It's been conditional all the way. I'll love you only if you do this. I'll love you only if you're the best little Crew member you can be. I'll love you if...you're just like me. He made Johnny in his image.

Not anymore.

I press against him. Not giving a shit about the dirty drops of water pooling between our chests. "I was so fucking worried about you, Johnny Marx. That footage they sent to your father broke me in two."

"Did you get hurt?" Johnny asks, pulling me closer until we rest our foreheads against one another. "Tell me you didn't get hurt." He eyes the bruising around my eyes suspiciously.

"I'm fine," I say, heat gathering quickly behind my eyes. "I'm more than fine now. I didn't know what they were going to do to you."

"Better me than you."

I swallow my argument. "We came for you as soon as we could. All of us."

"I know," he says, threading his fingers over the back of my neck. He holds me there, his eyes shut tight before he drags his fingers down my skin. He lets his hands roam, as if they're working on their own, moving over every square inch of my body.

While he touches me, I direct him backward under the spray, cleaning the remnants of his ordeal from his skin. He won't be able to forget what happened, but we can start fresh. We can start stronger together.

"I'm so glad you're here, babe. I don't know if I've said this yet. I don't know if I've said half as much as I feel in my heart, but if you weren't here, I'd be lost. As soon as you came here, I found the real person I was meant to be."

I push him against the wall. Carefully, of course. I slant my mouth over his to seal a promise to him. No matter what, I'm getting him out of this. Even if it kills me.

Over the spray of the shower, the door to Johnny's bathroom creaks open. In walks a copper-haired badass, drowning in an emotion that peaks my nipples until they hurt.

<hr>

15

Johnny eyes Mag as he shuts the door behind him. The steam inside the room fades Mag out, like it's possible he could be a figment of my imagination. However, that can't be true because Johnny has a very real reaction to seeing him.

His muscles clench, and his perusal of my lips slow until they're not moving. "What are you doing?"

I glance over to find Mag shrugging his shirt off. His chiseled chest muscles are less defined with all the steam, but I know exactly what he's packing. Mag lifts a brow at him as he pulls his black tactical pants down, revealing a bandage that matches Johnny's.

Johnny swallows hard. "You've never come into my shower before."

"You see this?" Mag asks, pointing to his matching wound. "One guess who did this to me."

Johnny darts his tongue out to lick along the seam of his lips. His fragile body breaks even more. Droplets coat his beautiful, marred skin, but underneath there's a layer of fractured tension. Of boneless resignation. "He shot you?"

Mag nods carefully, keeping his gaze on him. Then, he moves it to me, his thumbs hooking around his boxer briefs, questions dancing in his gaze.

I nod, and Mag lowers his boxers, revealing his cut body.

"So, you think that means I'm okay with sharing her now?"

Mag steps into the shower. "No, I think it means we're brothers more than we already were, and I think it means you know I not only care for you, I care for her, too. You can't keep thinking you deserve her more than the rest of us." Magnum moves up my backside, his thickening cock sliding over the small of my back.

"I never thought I deserved her more than you," Johnny says. He catches my gaze, his stare burning into my own.

"We're all in this together," Mag continues. "Being together—all of us—doesn't mean you're missing out on anything. It means you're gaining something."

Mag cups my ass, and I bite my lip. Johnny must be able to feel my pebbled nipples against his skin because he peeks down at my heaving chest. I'm trying not to think too hard about being in a Magnum-Johnny sandwich because I need to make sure Johnny is comfortable before moving forward, but I can't keep the obvious want from my gasp as Mag's hands settle on my hips, pulling me back against his erection.

He presses kisses to the curve of my neck. "You see this woman? She wants to share herself with us, and I understand maybe more than anyone that you've never had a good damn thing in your life, but neither have we." Mag's fingers dip between my legs briefly before moving to my stomach, using the palm of his hand to press me back against him. Magnum's holding me there for Johnny to peruse. He takes his fill, heated gaze and all. "Sharing doesn't mean losing. Losing will happen if you don't let us share."

He moves his hand to press between my breasts. Spreading his fingers wide, the tip of his fingers just barely grazes the swell of my breasts.

"We came after you because of you, J. Not because of the Crew. Not because you're Rocket. Not because you're Big Daddy K's son. We all fanned out, worked hard, made sure we were the ones to get you back from those cocksuckers. Not because of some obligation to the rank you pull, but because we didn't want anything to happen to *you*."

Johnny's pulse feathers. He keeps darting his gaze between Mag's slow perusal of me and his friend's face.

"This woman right here. I saw her crack when you were gone. I saw her lose a piece of herself, and I don't want to see that shit again, so I'm imploring you, J. Don't make her fucking choose."

Johnny's lip wobbles before he straightens it out again almost immediately. He heaves in a breath. "I really can't fucking stand to see you touch her."

Mag presses his lips against my shoulder. The heat of his touch makes me shiver even under the warm spray. "That's normal. It's something we need to work at. When I walked in here and saw her pressed against you, you didn't think I wanted to rip her from you? You don't think I wanted to claim her as my own? You don't own the rights to jealousy, Rocket." Mag reaches up to completely palm my breast. I close my eyes, my chest heaving naturally into his touch. "Let me ask you a question. Do you think this woman deserves to be loved?"

"Yes," Johnny breathes.

"Do you think this woman deserves what she wants?"

"Yes," he practically growls in answer.

"Who are we to keep her from that?"

I open my eyes to slits when Johnny doesn't respond right away. A tug of war still plays out inside him. It's as if he thinks agreeing will make him weak, and he's been taught that being weak is bad. It isn't. There are times to be tough. There are times when it's okay to be weak. There are times to just search within yourself and feel whatever it is you want to feel regardless of what you've been told your whole life.

That's what Mag is trying to get him to see.

Johnny places his hands on my hips, making me step forward with a quick pull. Mag's fingers slip from my breast, but Johnny presses his lips against mine with fervor. He pushes his hips forward, moving me back into Mag's waiting erection. "Is this what you want?" Johnny asks against my lips. He barely gives me time to respond. He's nipping, biting, devouring my mouth until all I can do is moan.

I grab his shaft, pinning him back against the shower wall. He groans into my mouth. The vibrations sink to my core. I pump his cock, holding him in place. He just got back from the doctor for crying out loud. No matter how much he wants to bury himself inside me right now, he can't. He's barely keeping it together as it is. I'm surprised he's even down for this much physical activity, but by the short thrusts of his cock into my hand, I know he is. Or at least, I know his body is speaking louder than his mind right now.

Magnum trails a hand down my spine, claiming my ass in the palm of his hand again. I lean forward, shoving my ass out for him. I know what he wants, too.

"Our girl wants to be fucked, J. Are you okay with this? I'm going to slide my cock inside her until she's coming all over me. Not because of me, but because of us."

Johnny hisses as my hold on his cock tightens at Mag's words. I slide my hand over his cock greedily. "Fuck yes."

Magnum maneuvers me into position, spreading my legs wider and arching my back, giving Johnny free rein to do what he wants with my chest. He grips my hips. On Mag's first thrust, I match my movement to Johnny's cock, stroking him in sync.

The slow rhythm Mag starts is just a tease. Johnny matches the pace, forcing his cock into my fist. I press a kiss to Johnny's chest. His heart beats like mad underneath his skin. A frantic rhythm that matches my excitement of the moment.

Mag rocks me into Johnny, his movements coming quicker. Johnny cups my breasts, teasing my nipples with sure strokes. "Oh, fuck," I moan. The more turned on I get, the faster I stroke Johnny.

He starts to shake. "Fuck, fuck…" I can tell he wants to hold off, but I'm with him. It's too much.

Mag bends me lower, lining up my mouth with Johnny's dick. He slows until my lips move around his friend, and then he picks up the pace again, moving me right over Johnny's hard ridges.

"Jesus fuck. Yes, Kyla."

I moan and then peer up into his eyes. As soon as he sees me looking at him, his cock jerks in my mouth. Hot cum spills onto my tongue. I grip him, moving him in and out of my wet heat until he's spent. I give him one last suck until he pops free. With a hand under my chin, he raises my head as Magnum grunts, taking possession of my hips.

"That was fucking hot," he groans.

His hand skates down my stomach and flits over my clit.

My mouth opens in a sigh. Immediately, Johnny claims my lips, eating up all my moans. The shower spray only dulls the slap, slap of Magnum's hips against mine.

"I want to feel you clench around me, angel."

I release Johnny's lips, crying out. He pinches my nipples, and a shudder rolls through me. "Yes. More."

Mag grinds against me, his thrusts almost punishing until my body locks up. Johnny cups my face, and I come apart, falling over the blissful edge of pleasure. Magnum strokes inside me a couple more times before he, too, jerks. He slows his movements, pumping every last bit of his climax inside me.

When he finishes, he pulls my shoulders up while staying seated inside me. He steps me forward until I'm literally sandwiched between them. We're a tangle of arms and feet. Of hearts and souls. But at this moment, our hearts are all beating the same beat. We're all experiencing the same reality.

I am in love with these men, and they're in love with me.

"I enjoyed that way too fucking much," Johnny says huskily. He kisses me firmly on the mouth until Mag pulls out and spins me in his arms. He presses me back against Johnny and claims my lips for his own. He holds me there, his tongue parting my lips, kissing me with so much emotion that I'm left breathless. Johnny holds onto my hips, thumbs tracing along the indents of my muscles. "I'm too tired to get hard again," he breathes, "but fuck me if I don't want to."

Mag pulls away, ending the kiss and glancing behind me to Johnny. "That's how you treat someone you love."

Hallelujah. If that's what he has in mind, I want more, more, more.

Mag backs away, leaving the shower. All three of us end up in Johnny's bed. Mag relaxes against the headboard after pulling his boxers on. Johnny lies on his back while I lie facing him, placing my hand on his chest. I'm not ready to drift to sleep yet. I just want to lie here knowing that he's safe. That he's back with us.

Mag's fingers drift over my bare shoulders. "Go to sleep, angel. He'll still be here in the morning."

I close my eyes, my hand lifting and lowering with Johnny's breaths, lulling me into sleep.

My hand moves. My eyelids flutter open, and I find Johnny trying to wiggle out of my grip. I don't know what time it is, but if I had to guess, the room darkening shades are doing their job. "Sorry," Johnny grimaces. "I didn't want to wake you."

"It's okay," I say sleepily.

I bring my hand back to myself, allowing him to get up and hobble to the bathroom. He's only gone for a minute or so before returning and slipping in next to me on the sheets. While he was gone, I noticed Mag was also gone, probably out doing Mag things like making sure we're all safe. Inspecting the suite for bugs. Working on target practice. Lifting weights, so he doesn't lose his ass-kicking muscles. "How are you feeling?" I ask Johnny.

"Surprisingly better," he says on a yawn. He looks

better, too. Color has come back to his cheeks. He's not as pale as he was last night. The sleep and the painkillers have helped him. Hopefully, just being back here without having to worry about the stress of what was going to happen has helped him too. I know having him back helped me. I slept like a rock. I don't even think I tossed and turned once last night.

A knock sounds on the door, and I tense. It's on the suite door, not on the bedroom door. I'm happy just to ignore it, but there must be someone else in the suite—most likely Mag—because a voice rises up.

"Duuude. It's cool. I just want to make sure he's okay."

"They're—"

Before Mag can tell him not to come in because we're lying here naked, Jiko pushes the door open. "Fucker," Johnny yells, using his body to shield mine.

"Oops." He turns away. "Sorry. I was just so fucking excited that your dad said you were alive and back. I came right over."

I slip under the covers, pulling the sheets up to my shoulders. I scowl at Jiko's back. Mag's face mirrors mine.

"She's covered," Johnny finally says.

"Are you covered because...?"

"No, dick. I'm not because it's my goddamn bedroom, and you ran in like you owned the place, so now you can stare at my cock for the intrusion."

He's not kidding either. Jiko turns around, and Johnny

just lies there on the bed, not covering himself or anything. Jiko ignores the morning penis, but I sigh and pull the sheets up over Johnny anyway.

"Thanks," Jiko says. "I'm not into dicks." He gives me a rueful smile, but then it drops off his face. He stares, eyes cast down a little. "I haven't seen you since everything went down. Are you okay?"

"I'm fine," I say, still a little weirded out at the fact that I'm lying here naked under these sheets while Jiko is standing right fucking there. I'm not okay with Jiko. That's for sure. I'm not his number one fan. Hell, I'm not even his hundredth fan.

He sucks his lip in. "I did what I did at the fight for you guys. I hope you know that. I figured if Brawler technically didn't beat you, neither of you could get in trouble, so I made sure to jump him right before he could put the last hit in on you."

He turns his face, and I finally see the discoloration on his orbital bones that must be courtesy of Brawler's fist. Not going to lie. I don't feel bad at all. In fact, I'm happy knowing Brawler got in some really good hits. "Am I supposed to thank you?"

"No," Jiko says with finality. "It was my way of throwing a peace offering your way. What I did was shitty."

"Can we just not fucking discuss this right now?" Mag asks. He looks over-the-top annoyed.

Jiko holds his hands up. "Alright, alright. I see we're out

of the Christmas cheer around here. I just wanted to say hey to my friend and also tell him I'm glad he's back."

It takes me far longer than it should to dissect his usage of Christmas cheer. Holy fuck. It's Christmas. I have nothing to give anyone.

Johnny, too, looks shocked by the information. Jiko lingers, and Johnny stands, letting it all hang out again. He gives Jiko a firm handshake while Jiko glances at the bandage briefly. "I'm glad you're okay, man. I have to go home, obviously, but I was waiting until the last possible moment to see if they needed me to help get you back."

"They didn't get me back. Mag and Kyla did."

Jiko nods slowly, eyeing his friend curiously. "Merry Christmas, man. Keep in touch." He strides from the room, and Mag follows to shut the door behind him. As soon as it's shut, it opens again. Oscar's voice bellows out first, and I can't help the smile that overtakes my face when Brawler's follows shortly afterward.

I jump from the bed and rummage through Johnny's drawers to find something to wear. Johnny chuckles beside me as he grabs a pair of joggers out of my hand. "Do you want to give them a good Christmas present? Walk out of here naked."

"Yeah?" I stifle a chuckle and grab his joggers back. "Maybe later," I wink.

We both end up finding joggers and pull them on at the same time. I have to look for a shirt while Johnny slowly walks out into the main living area. No tense words are spoken like would have happened only a few weeks ago. Oscar even teases Johnny about sleeping the day away. Christmas doesn't matter a lot in the Heights, but I can't help but be excited that we're all together. Sure, this will be a different Christmas than I've ever had, but that doesn't mean it will be worse than the others. In fact, it'll just be the start of Christmas's for the rest of my life. I hope.

I hurry toward the door and pull up short when I see them all out there together. Johnny and Mag are in the kitchen, working in tandem, including favoring the same hip that boasts their matching injuries. Oscar and Brawler are sitting at the bar, talking them up. There are no strained words, only smiles. If I close my eyes, I can imagine that we're living years in the future, and I've just come down from my bedroom to see all of us hanging out in our house. Our own house. Where we all live together. A home. Just the five of us.

I miss that feeling of home. Since my parents died, I've always felt like an imposter. To feel like I really belong somewhere would be a dream come true.

Mag spots me and crooks his head to tell me to get my ass out there. I do as he says. Brawler turns first. His stare devours me from head to toe, distracting me to the point that I almost completely miss the small, ceramic pine tree they've placed on the middle of the coffee table. A few presents dot the surface, making me pull up short again.

Brawler's stool creaks as he slips off and moves toward me. He circles his arms around my neck, pulling me in close. He whispers, "Merry Christmas."

"Merry Christmas," I say back. I dig my nails into his skin, making sure he doesn't move from his position.

He lowers his voice even more. "I brought your phone so you can talk to your aunt and uncle. They've already tried to call you."

I nod into his warm embrace. It would be easier if I could keep my phone on me, but since I'm still holding on tight to the last secret I'm keeping from Johnny, I can't.

"Out of the way, big guy," Oscar jibes.

Brawler gives me one last good hug before moving to the side. Oscar's eyes are big and round. He's holding the Santa ceramic cookie jar he bought me, only it's mostly fixed now. Cracks jag their way across his fat belly and face, but Oscar must've super glued it back together. The smile he's sending my way might take over his face. "You fixed it?"

"Open it..."

I pull Santa's hat off and peer inside. Chocolate chip cookies fill the interior. Homemade, too. Or at least they look like homemade. "Where did you get these?"

"I bribed a neighbor lady."

Avoiding the cookie jar altogether, I give Oscar a huge hug. "I can't wait to try them."

"Hope they're better than my mom's cookies," Brawler jokes. "I almost cracked a tooth on them this morning."

"Morning? What time is it?"

"Two in the afternoon," Oscar says. "We figured if we didn't come over now, we'd never get to see you."

"What did you tell the guys at the front?" Mag asks.

Oscar turns serious. Now that he's slipped into gang mode, I notice the definite change in him from just two seconds ago. I never would've pegged Oscar as a holiday guy. He's positively come alive though. He must be sentimental at heart. Down, way down, underneath all that sarcasm and playfulness. "We told them Johnny summoned us to discuss what happened while he was taken captive."

"Good," Mag says.

He and Johnny load up a plate with toast and push it to the edge of the bar. I move toward it, picking up a slice. Just last year, my aunt and uncle were eating a delicious meal around a pristinely decorated dining room table. We ate, then opened presents. It's been that way since I came to live with them. It was nice, but definitely nothing like when I was a kid. My parents would wake up early just because I couldn't stand to wait to open my presents. We'd open gifts first, then eat breakfast. The whole day was chill, relaxed, filled with love and excitement. My aunt and uncle did what they could, but they just weren't my parents.

Sometimes when I think things like that, guilt swarms me. My aunt and uncle gave up a lot to take me in, and I'm so appreciative. But I can't stop comparing. I can't stop wishing I never had to be in their care at all.

Brawler rubs my back. He's more subdued today, and I wonder if he's thinking the same thoughts as me. Christmas probably hasn't been the same for him since he lost his brother and sister. Losing family members makes holidays difficult, like you're always in juxtaposition between being happy and then guilty and then sad. It's a never-ending cycle that takes what the true meaning of Christmas is supposed to be and throws it out the window along with any chance of finding joy in the day.

That's why I didn't realize Christmas was so close.

That's why I'm not prepared.

But you know what? I'm looking forward to seeing what things could be like in my new life. Oscar bribing old ladies to make chocolate chip cookies for us, so he can put them in this gaudy Santa Claus. Maybe one day, we can forego the ceramic tree and get a real Christmas tree.

Whatever it is, we can learn and implement our traditions together like a true family.

I spot the presents again, and my stomach drops. "I didn't think or have time or..." I shrug as all the excuses push to the surface. "I didn't get you guys anything."

"You've given us plenty," Mag says.

"I told you just to get naked. Gift accomplished," Johnny says in a rare instance where he shows his sense of humor. Maybe it's the pain killers I saw him pop just a few moments ago, but maybe it's that he's finally beginning to see he can be comfortable here, like this.

"I didn't get you anything big," Brawler says.

"I only got you the cookies," Oscar adds.

"And the Santa Claus," I say.

"You bought that thing?" Johnny asks, turning his nose up at it. "It's hideous."

"Princess liked it, so Princess got it."

Johnny gives me a cautious glance.

I almost laugh. "This was the first festive thing I saw in the Heights. I thought we should have it to show it doesn't matter what's going on around us, we can always take moments to be happy."

Oscar sets the cookie jar on the coffee table next to the tree and then takes a seat on the couch. "Yeah, the Heights isn't known for Christmas. I remember watching the parade on TV when I was a kid and wondering where the hell that place was because it's nothing like this shithole."

Brawler nods. "Our Christmases were better when my mom was actually coherent. She always made it special until Manning and my sister died. This morning, she barely got out of bed. She asked me to find my present in her closet and bring it to her. We exchanged presents right on her bed so she could go right back to sleep."

My stomach clenches. I peek at Oscar because I know one thing he didn't say is that he didn't share this morning with anyone. His mother is still God knows where.

"What about you?" I ask Mag. "What were the Cottons like around Christmas?"

"Normal," he says. "Until Dad died, of course. Every-thing went to shit after that."

We stare at Johnny. He bites his lip and looks away. "Listen, I got shit for Christmas, but it was just another day in the gang to Dad. We never got sentimental about it. I would wake up to a huge present every year and then it would be back to business the next moment."

I chew on the inside of my cheek. "Well, we should start new traditions."

"Well, wait a second," Oscar says, leaning over to gaze inside the cookie jar. "You didn't say how your Christmases were."

I take another bite of toast and then sit next to him on the couch. "Christmas when my parents were alive were typical storybook highlights." I shrug. "After that, I didn't necessarily feel up to celebrating. When Mom and Dad died, so did my aspirations to do a lot of things. I'm still trying to get that back." I swallow hard. I wish I could just come right out and say what I want to, but with Johnny here, I'm not sure we're in that space yet. We're getting closer and closer, but the worst thing I could do is tell him at a time when he's not ready to hear it. It's not just me in this anymore either. It's the rest of the guys, too. I have to worry about them as well as myself.

"I like the idea of new traditions," Johnny says, sitting gingerly on the couch next to me and squishing me between him and Oscar. Mag takes a chair and Brawler stays on one of the bar stools but turns it to face us. "Here," Johnny says, grabbing his present and offering it to me.

I wipe my crumby fingers down my joggers and eye the shape of the present I'm about to open. It's a small, rectangular box that makes my belly flip. Despite what he's gone through in the last forty-eight hours, Johnny looks pleased to be right here in this moment. "Open it," he urges.

I take a deep breath and rip at the shiny red packaging. It looks professionally wrapped, complete with a silver bow that I finally slip off and then pick at the tape with my fingernail. Under the wrapping paper is a small, black box.

I open it to reveal a ring.

17

"*F*ucking seriously?" Oscar deadpans.

My heart flutters in my chest as I stare down into the box. It's a silver ring—or possibly white gold. A beautiful, square-cut blue sapphire sits in the middle framed on each side by small white stones. My mind tells me they're diamonds, but I push that thought away.

"Do you like it?" Johnny asks, completely ignoring Oscar and the rising tension in the room.

"It's beautiful," I say. They're the only words that came to mind, and it's the truth. I'm almost too stunned for words.

"Prick," Oscar mutters.

"What?" Johnny asks, finally tearing his attention from me.

"I got her a goddamn cookie jar, that's what. Now, here you come with a fucking ring. A ring. That better be all it is because I think a few of us are going to have something to say to you if you think for one fucking second you're about to propose to our girlfriend."

"Calm down, Drego," Johnny says dismissively. Flares of heat burn in his cheeks, bringing a different color to his bruised face.

I gaze up to find Oscar's nostrils flaring. This is not a good sign. "Hey," I say, reaching for him. "I love my cookie jar."

His intense gaze stares me down. "No one in their right mind takes a cookie jar over a ring."

"It's not a competition," Johnny says, clearly annoyed.

"Says the guy who got her a motherfucking ring. For Christmas. I'll never be able to afford to get her a fucking ring."

I shove the ring box back into Johnny's hands and face Oscar completely. The tension coming off him is probably the worst I've seen. He's upset. I don't blame him. I probably would be too. I cup his gorgeous face. "Listen here, Oscar Drego. I love you. I don't care if you can get me a cookie jar or a ring or fucking nothing. I will always love you the same." I lick my lips and frown. "I didn't get you guys anything. I—"

"We didn't expect anything," Brawler finally speaks up to reassure me. He slides his gaze over to Johnny. "We didn't expect anyone to do anything like that."

"As you said," Johnny says stiffly. "She's *our* girlfriend. I should be able to get her what I want."

Something in his voice is off, so I peek back at him. His eyes are cast to the floor. Dealing with more than one boyfriend is kind of exhausting. Especially when more than one needs you at the same time. Johnny goes to get up, but I grab his wrist. "Don't," I say. I look around the room. "We can all acknowledge that this isn't going to be easy, right? I never thought it would be. Things are going to pop up like this, but we can't run from these problems. Let's talk them out."

"Can we do the talking later?" Brawler asks. "I kind of want you to open my present."

There's another package lying next to the cookie jar. It's wrapped in faded snowmen wrapping paper. The thought that Brawler had to go searching for this old paper makes my heart pinch in pain. I hate that they've all been through real shit.

I reach for the package and gently unwrap it. Inside, are bright purple personalized boxing wraps. Uppercut Princess scrawls across the fabric. I smile at him. "These are awesome. Where did you get them?"

"Finn helped me out," Brawler says. "He special ordered them through this company they have an affiliation with."

"I hope you didn't spend too much," I tell him. I know he makes money through organizing the fights, but it can't be much. Plus, I don't know how he was even paid for the couple months that they didn't have fights.

"Don't worry about it," he says. "I wanted to get something for my girl, and I did."

I start wrapping my hands, seeing where my nickname will land when it comes time to train again. With a smile, I wrap them back up and place them on the coffee table. Even though I just had toast, I lean over and sneak one of the cookies from Oscar's cookie jar and bite into it. "Mmm," I moan. "No offense, Brawler, but these are way better than your mom's."

"Eating cat litter is better than my mom's cookies."

We sit silently for a little while. The tension in the room hovers even though it's died down a little. The box is practically taking up all my attention now, sitting in the middle of Johnny's clenched fingers.

"Do you want to tell us what the ring is for?" Mag asks.

There are no accusations in his tone. Just a question from a friend to a friend in the midst of all their other friends.

I run my palm down Johnny's thigh, and he sighs. "It's not an engagement ring if that's what you guys were thinking."

I take a deep breath and release it. It had been something I thought at first, but since he didn't get down on one knee and all that jazz, I pretty much figured it wasn't. Then again, Oscar interrupted him from the beginning, so if that's what he'd wanted to do, he didn't get the chance. And even if he wanted to, I'm not sure he could actually get to one knee right now with his injuries.

I don't see Johnny as a guy who would ask his girlfriend to marry him in front of a bunch of people though. I mean, I don't know. Since we're in a...a fivesome, does that mean we won't get married one day? Or if we do, will they all ask me? Or do I ask them?

My cheeks heat, so I shake those thoughts away.

"It was just a pretty ring that I wanted to get her."

"I love it," I say, squeezing his thigh.

Some of the tension leaves his shoulders. He looks up at me with hopeful eyes. "Can I put it on you?"

I turn toward him. Oscar immediately runs his fingers down my back. I can feel him looking over my shoulder as Johnny takes the pretty ring from the box and places it on the ring finger of my right hand. It glides down smoothly. "I don't think I want to know how you knew the size of my finger just by looking at it."

He shakes his head. "You're the only girl who's ever meant enough to me to buy something like this for. No one even came close, babe."

I wiggle my finger around, letting the overhead light play off the stones. I don't think I've ever owned something so gorgeous before. My personality might say that I'm not into jewelry. I like to fight. I like to sweat. But apparently, I also like shiny things because whoever wants to pry this off my finger will have to do so over my cold, dead body.

Johnny wraps his fingers in mine.

"It's pretty," Mag says.

I drop my hand to my joggers and start to laugh. "I'm totally wearing the wrong outfit for this ring," I joke.

"You look good in anything," Brawler says. "You look sexy in your training outfits."

"Hot as fuck naked," Oscar adds.

"Beautiful in club clothes," Johnny purrs.

"Black," Mag adds. "You need more black."

We all start laughing, and I'm glad the earlier tension has dissipated. I don't want to have to spend Christmas worried that the guys are unhappy in some way.

A knock sounds on Johnny's door. Magnum gets up to answer it. He opens it only a sliver of the way. Words are exchanged that we can't quite hear until Mag shuts the door. "Your dad is waiting for you, J."

Johnny peeks at me, but before he can say anything, Brawler pipes up. "I was hoping Kyla could come with me somewhere...um, private. Special." He blows out a breath. "I go see my sister's grave on Christmas, and I'd like her to come."

Again, my stomach twists with the knowledge of all the pain my guys have been through. We need a lot of happy times to make up for the past.

"Oh yeah, sure. Of course," Johnny says quickly. "It's

been ages since I've been out to Manning's grave. I should probably head out there sometime soon." Brawler doesn't say anything in response, so Johnny gets to his feet gingerly. "You may as well come with Mag and I, Bat. I'm sure Dad will want you involved in some of this stuff."

Oscar stands, and I stand with him. I wrap my arms around him firmly, holding him close. There's an odd weight on my right hand where the ring sits, but it's a nice feeling. "Later we'll have more cookies," I whisper.

He nods into me, placing a small kiss on the curve of my neck. I wish I'd gotten them something. All of them. Otherwise, I don't know how else to express how much what they do means to me. I press up onto my tiptoes and lean back to get a good look at Oscar. His dark eyes shine back at me. I can't help but get lost in the tragedy of them. There's so much underneath the surface that sometimes I don't think I've even grazed the top of what makes Oscar tick.

I press my mouth to his, inhaling him in. His scent. His persona. With the kiss, I tell him I don't care what he got me for Christmas. He should know it isn't material things that matter. It's this. Losing my parents taught me that. You can replace things like rings and cookie jars, but you can't replace people. I would never want to replace these guys. Never.

Tearing myself away from Oscar is hard, but I'm also sure the other guys are waiting their turn, so I step away. Johnny gives my hand a quick squeeze. He doesn't seem the least bit affected with the ring thing anymore. He's beaming. Magnum dips his head low as he walks to the door. The three of them file out, leaving just Brawler and me.

A small smile filters over my face. "I cannot freaking wait to use those wraps. I'm sorry I didn't get you anything."

"You get us something each and every day," he responds, coming up to me to place his large hands at the small of my back. "Hope."

I swallow and lay my head on his chest. The steady beat of his heart calms me.

"Now," he says. "I also brought your phone, so let's call your aunt and uncle first, and then we'll go to the cemetery."

He slips the nondescript phone from his pocket and hands it to me. It feels like ages since I've spoken to them. Or it's just that so many things have happened, making it seem like a lot of time has passed when in reality it hasn't. The screen lights up, and I go to Contacts and press my aunt's name.

She answers right away. "Merry Christmas!"

"Merry Christmas!" I say back, and for the first time in a long time, I don't even have to fight any of the cheer filling me up. In fact, I have to fight back some sadness from not being around them.

This is what my relationship with them is supposed to be like. Not guardian-ward, but aunt and niece. For so long, something was missing. The kind of love that comes from an immediate family. That comes from having people who will love you unconditionally. I never wanted to feel like I just showed up in their life and made myself an obligation.

I'm no longer their obligation, and I love it.

"God, I miss you guys," I say, allowing the thick emotion to creep up my throat.

My aunt is silent for a moment until she says, "Me too, Joey. Me too. Does that mean you'll come visit soon?"

"Hopefully, soon," I say. I obviously can't promise anything like that because there's a lot to do between then and now. Soon might turn into a long time, but for the first time in forever, I hope it doesn't. "Are you having a dinner later?"

"You know us," she says, clearly enjoying her day. Dishes rattle in the background like she's getting out her special holiday plates. "Everyone's been asking about you. Do you have friends to spend the day with? I've been freaking out that you're all alone."

"I have friends," I say, unable to keep the smile that's currently pulling my lips apart out of my voice.

"Ohhh," my aunt says. "That sounds like it has something to do with a boy. For God's sake, be careful. My sister would turn over in her grave if she found out you were—"

I laugh immediately. "I'm fine. I promise. Mom won't be turning over in her grave anytime soon, and yes, it's about a boy...s." I slur the S, tacking it on at the last moment. I definitely don't want to have the polyamorous relationship conversation with my aunt over the phone. I have no prior knowledge, but I'm pretty sure that's a conversation to have face-to-face.

She tells me all about my uncle's new vegetable garden in the backyard. Then, she runs down the list of everyone who is coming over for dinner and the gossip going around their gated estate community. Back in the day, I could've purchased anything I wanted for the guys. I actually still could do the same thing, but there will be plenty of time to use that money on useless things as soon as we leave the Heights together.

We talk for a while. At least a half hour. My uncle also gets on the phone briefly, asking me all the same questions my aunt just pestered me with, but I'm not even annoyed when I go through it again for a second time. When I realize how long we've been talking, I tell them I need to go. Brawler wants to get to the cemetery, and I can't blame him. I'd be doing the same if I were closer to where my parents are buried.

"Hey," I say, right before I get off the phone. "Next time you go to the graves, make sure you tell them I say hi."

My aunt takes a second to answer. "I do it every time, Joey, you know that. Plus, you can tell them whenever you want."

"I know." That's not the first time my aunt has said those words to me. It's not even the hundredth. Those words have pushed past her lips countless times. And they're true, too.

"Merry Christmas," I say again.

"Merry Christmas. Love you."

"Love you, too."

I hang up the phone, and Brawler smiles at me. "That sounded like it went well."

"Really well," I say.

He reaches his hand out, and I place mine in his. Today was definitely a good day.

18

I hold Brawler's hand tightly as he stares down at the simple gravestone. My own heart breaks because I get this feeling. Helplessness. Yearning.

Why?

There's never been a word that plagued me more than that. Even more than unfair, unjust, wrong or any other adjective I could use to describe what happened. No, it's definitely *why*.

Some things can't be made to make sense. When Big Daddy K's name was spoken all those years ago, I knew he was my why. The reason my parents were taken from me. The reason why I wasn't whole. The reason I now had a goal to work toward, and the reason why I trained so hard. He was the hate in my heart that fueled everything I did.

I'm starting to become whole again. Little by little,

things in my life are changing from abnormal back to my new normal. That doesn't mean my why is different. It's still Big Daddy K. It's still making him pay for the sins he committed against me and countless others. Yes, I walked into a huge pile of shit when I came to the Heights, but it's what I wanted. I'll take all that bad as long as I come out with the dream intact in the end: Me looming over Big Daddy K. Grinning. Telling him why it's me. Why I'm the one who finally got to take him out. Just for a split second, I want the clouds to clear in his mind and realize what he did was wrong. That what he did set off a chain reaction neither one of us could stop.

He thinks he's untouchable. He thinks he's the mother-fucking queen of England. He certainly thinks he's the king of the Heights, but even he's getting a taste of his own misery right now.

The subjects are starting to revolt.

I don't like Gregory. I'd wager I wouldn't like many members of the Dragons either, but they're helping me get to BDK, even if they're nothing but a distraction for him to focus on while I come up from behind.

Not for the first time, I wonder if I'm as bad as him. I don't think so though. He kills for inexplicable reasons. Reasons that in his own deranged mind mean something, but not in reality. Me? I should think about the countless lives I'll save by taking him out. By putting him away far earlier than anyone could imagine, so much death and destruction will be avoided.

After minutes of standing there silently, Brawler shifts on his feet, taking me out of the revenge spiral in my head. I've been going there more and more lately, almost as if I can feel K's demise nearing. It makes butterflies flap in my stomach like crazed insects thirsting for blood. "You okay?" Brawler finally asks, breaking into my thoughts.

I gaze over at him and give him a half smile. It's been a long time since I had the luxury of thoughts that weren't plagued with how the guys and I were going to get out of the shit we got ourselves in. "I'm fine," I say. "Are you? You're not saying much."

He stares back down at the gray stone. His broad shoulders slump forward. The wings of his angel tattoos are even more stark in this place of death and loss than they are at any other time. "I guess it's easy to forget about Manning," he starts. He lets out a breath that says so much without saying anything at all. "But when it's right here in my face, it's difficult not to think about us...as kids...as friends."

I give him a slight tug until he faces me. Then, I wrap my arms around his waist and lay my head on his chest. He encapsulates me in his python grip. While I listen to his heart beat beneath his skin, I tell him, "Have you ever thought about trying to forgive him?"

He stills.

"Manning brought the Crew to your house, but he was also a victim, Brawler. A victim of hate. Of senseless death."

His fingers dig into my sides. "I think I've been trying to forgive him since he died, but it's so damn hard."

I tighten my grip around him until I can't tell where he ends and I begin. We're a mesh of bodies and doubts, of fears and limbs. I don't know much about life, but I know about death. I know about the tragedy of loss. About the ripping anger that threatens to tear at your seams. The *why, why, why* cry of not wanting to believe what happened.

Maybe I'm just searching for the easy target, but it's the guys like Big Daddy K who should reap all the blame. Like Mayhem before him, he promised these guys...these *boys*...a life of brotherhood and prosperity. He promised them things with a double-edged sword of death and fear. Of conditional kinship. He promised them a life that none of them had while the devil sat on the welcome mat to his tower.

"I'll keep trying," Brawler says.

I shake my head into his warmth. "I'm not forcing you into anything. Healing is on you. It's whatever you're comfortable with. I don't care if you hate Manning for the rest of your life, I'm just...talking," I say lamely.

"I guess—to me—Manning is like my K. He brought the Crew into our lives. Yes, he got killed because of them, but he also killed my sister. He didn't pull the trigger. He didn't plan the drive-by, but if we were just the regular people we were supposed to be, none of that would've happened. They wouldn't be here," he says, gesturing toward the earth at our feet.

"But you can't reconcile it with the brother you used to know."

His chest deflates. "Exactly."

"Then mourn him," I say. "Mourn the brother he was before he got into the Crew. Mourn the friend you had before he got into the gang. Mourn that guy."

Brawler steps back and tips my chin in the air. His turquoise blue eyes are striking against the backdrop of the overcast sky. "I hate when you say things like that because I know what you had to go through to come up with that kind of wisdom."

I push up on my tiptoes and press my lips to his. "I'm healing now. That's all that matters."

"It seems that way, doesn't it?" he asks, gazing back down at the place where his siblings will spend forever. "I was lost until you came to the Heights."

"So was I," I choke out. I came to the Heights for one reason and one reason only...then walk out with four boyfriends. Fingers crossed, anyway. So many things could go wrong between now and then.

Brawler slips his hand around my back as we face the gravesite again. "Can I ask you something?"

I stare at the names on the stone while my stomach churns. "Anything."

He passes his finger over my ring. "If this had been an

engagement ring, would you have said yes?"

I tilt my head to look at him, but he avoids my stare. His lips pressed together, he just stares calmly at the overgrown grass around the grave. I can't get a read on him whatsoever. It's almost as if he's taken pointers from Mag. I lick my lips. "No."

His jaw feathers. "Just no?"

My stomach tightens. I love Johnny. I still don't know how he feels about the five of us, but I know how I feel about the five of us. I love the rest of them, too. "No because I don't want just him." Greediness claws at me, but I whip that feeling back. It's not about saying I want as many guys as I can get, it's about just these four. "Maybe one day, it'll be all five of us."

Brawler's lips turn up in the corners. "Weirdest wedding ever."

I chuckle. "Unconventional, for sure."

He chuckles. "I don't even know how to explain this to my mom." He shakes his head a few times. "Half the time, she's not even living in the real world, so it's difficult. Throwing this at her would really be testing her sanity."

"I know what you mean," I tell him. "My aunt asked today if I sounded so happy because of a guy, and I kind of wanted to tell her, but I don't think that's a conversation you have over the phone."

"People won't get it."

"And I think that's okay. The only people who have to

get it is us."

Brawler squeezes my hand and steps back, and I take it as a sign he's ready to leave. Before we do, I gaze down at the stone and promise Brawler's family that I'll do everything I can to make sure no one else ends up like them. I didn't know them. I don't know them now, but I know Brawler enough to figure out the type of people they were. I can give that promise to them freely and without hesitation.

We start a slow walk past trees dotted across the cemetery and rows of different headstones. Some big, some small. Some ornate, some simple. Brawler slows, and I stop staring at the line of stones and lift my gaze. At the end of the row is a man. Brawler grips my side at the same time I realize who it is.

It's fucking Detective Reynolds.

Brawler keeps the pace with his head in the air. I mimic him, but I also know that this isn't a coincidence. Did he follow us? Did he know Brawler would be at the cemetery today?

He doesn't even allow us the respect of leaving the row Brawler's brother and sister are buried in before he steps right into our path.

"Merry Christmas, Detective," Brawler says.

I can only manage a hard stare. The last time I saw Detective Reynolds, things didn't go so well. He thinks I murdered a little girl based on shitty evidence. The thought that he even worked for the Crew's enemies has even popped into my head, but I don't think that's it. He's just an overeager cop and my fingerprints on the murder weapon are low-hanging fruit.

"Mr. Timms. Miss Samson."

"What can we do for you?" Brawler asks.

Reynolds ignores Brawler's question. He eyes me with a snide gaze. The guy totally has it out for me. If he truly thinks I killed that poor little girl, I don't blame him. "Just out for a leisurely stroll," Reynolds says with a shrug.

Brawler's brows rise. "In a cemetery?"

"During Christmas, I come to the graves of the murdered persons' cases I haven't been able to solve yet." He clucks his tongue against his teeth. "Just so happens one you're involved in is also laid to rest in this cemetery."

"I'm not involved in any murder cases."

He completely ignores me. "Imagine my surprise when I saw you here."

I can't tell if he's telling the truth or not. Does this guy ever take time off? Christ. It's Christmas day for crying out loud. "Likewise," I say. "What a crazy coincidence."

"You don't have to talk to him," Brawler says. Empathy bleeds through his blue eyes when I gaze into them. He wants to do something about this, but he knows our hands are tied. "Come on."

We start to walk around Reynolds, but he stays with us like an annoying gnat. "Mind telling me why every time I go to search for you in our files, I get blocked?"

My stomach clenches. A hundred different thoughts filter through my head. I don't want Reynolds looking too much into my past. My background paper trail is solid, but not if he puts boots on the ground and actually goes searching through the fake trail I left. Right now, I have pretend guardians who I don't see. I never imagined I'd be under this much scrutiny though. Reynolds seems like he could be a dog with a bone about things, and I'm worried I might just be that thing.

"Did you know your phone was found at the site of a shooting, bombing, and fire? And yet, when I went to retrieve it from evidence, it wasn't there. Then, of course, there's the witness to the murder that suddenly changed his tune. At least I still have your gun though."

"I don't know what you're talking about," I say out loud while silently cursing. I knew they'd find my phone upstairs in the locker room as long as the rooms weren't completely burnt. "Should I get my lawyer?"

Reynolds smirks. "Fancy lawyer, too." He shakes his head. "I just don't get how you have all these people on your side, little girl."

I bristle at his comment. Fucking sexist prick. Then again, he thinks I actually committed murder. I'd be an asshole to me too. "One of these days, you're going to see we're on the same side."

He scoffs, sneering at my marred face. "I put thugs like you away."

I shrug. He can think what he wants about me. I don't care.

"So, you have nothing to say about who it is that's helping you?"

"No one is helping me, Detective Reynolds. I'm just a little girl walking with her boyfriend on Christmas to visit his family."

My phone pings in my pocket. I do my best not to look at Reynolds as we walk away from him. I close my eyes and pray he won't be able to touch me right now. The last thing I need is to have to worry about more charges being brought against me. Real or fake.

When we're a few feet away, I pull my phone out and glance down at the screen. There's a text from Magnum. **Don't talk to him.**

I show the screen to Brawler, and we continue to walk away until we're out of the cemetery and only a block from the bus stop. A black car pulls around the corner in front of us, and I stop short. I have no idea how Magnum knew Reynolds was talking to us. Unless he was watching us, but why would he do that? Or how could he have is the better question. I'm sure K has him out doing something.

"Something doesn't seem right," Brawler says as Magnum pulls up to the curb.

I glance back at the cemetery to find Detective Reynolds standing just outside the gate with his hands on his hips, watching us get into the Crew's car.

19

Magnum speeds off as soon as we're in the car. He takes the next right a little too fast and the tires squeal. "What did he ask you?" he demands.

I pull my seatbelt on and try to focus on Magnum instead of the way he's driving. When he realizes he's driving way too fast for me, he presses down on the brakes and curses under his breath. I take a few deep breaths and get my thoughts together. Reynolds sought us out on Christmas? "What the hell was that?" I finally ask. "What are the odds Reynolds would be at the cemetery at the same time we were?"

"Do you think he followed you?" Mag asks, keeping his eyes trained on the road.

Brawler leans forward, placing his right hand on the

back of my seat. "He told us he always visits the victims of the murder cases he hasn't been able to solve on Christmas."

Mag snorts out a laugh. "I highly doubt that."

"Something is going on," I say, mimicking Brawler's earlier words. "Reynolds just told us every time he goes to search for me, he gets blocked from within the police department. Also, they found my phone at The Ring, but it's missing from evidence."

Frown lines crease Mag's forehead. "Must be K's inside guy is working on it."

"K doesn't give a fuck about me."

"No, I imagine he doesn't, but Johnny does. And believe it or not, Johnny still means something to K. I know you look at their relationship and think it's unhealthy—"

"Because it is," I interject.

Magnum side-eyes me. "I wasn't going to dispute that. I was just saying in some weird way of K's, he does actually care for Johnny."

"He acted like it was Johnny's own fault he got kidnapped." I'm not convinced K would help me. Or if he did that his reason for doing so would be Johnny. I doubt K does anything that doesn't have to do with protecting his own interests.

Magnum squeezes my thigh. "I know. I'm sorry," he says. He glances over his shoulder. "I'm sorry he ruined your visit, too. It's not fucking right."

"We were done," Brawler says, "but yeah, not fucking right."

Mag taps his fingers against the steering wheel. "Well, get ready for a huge meeting tomorrow. K's got a plan on our retaliation against Gregory."

Wonderful. I glance back at Brawler to see the tight line of his jaw. He's probably wondering what awful thing K is going to make him do next.

It only takes a few more blocks before I realize Magnum isn't taking us back to the tower. Oscar's familiar neighborhood comes into view out the windshield. "Do you have to go back to your place, Brawler? Oscar has something special planned if you want to stick around."

"I'll be okay," Brawler says. He sounds distracted, so I turn to find him texting on his phone. When I peek to try to see who it is, he leans back in the car and angles the phone away from me. When I face forward again, Magnum smirks, and now I know something is up. What the hell is this "special" thing Oscar has planned?

Magnum parks around the block from Oscar's place. We get out and then climb the stairs to his second-floor apartment. I like being able to get away to a place like this. Somewhere that's not associated with the Crew in a lot of ways. Some place with distance from the inner workings of the Crew. It's why I love the cabin, too. Being in places like this makes me feel like we could actually have a life like this.

When we open the door to the apartment, I know we can.

As soon as I step inside, the smell of ham hits me. I blink, coming to a stop until Magnum hits me from behind. Oscar's apartment is in pristine condition. It was never not clean, but right now, we could probably eat off the floor and be fine. Sitting in the middle of a new dining room table tucked away in the corner is a Christmas dinner.

Oscar and Johnny must not have heard us come in because they're arguing in the kitchen like a pair of old maids. Oscar is making his snide, sarcastic comments, and Johnny is letting everything roll off his back with his cock-sure attitude.

"What is this?"

Johnny and Oscar both glance up at the same time. Their sour faces turn to smiles as soon as they see me. "Princess," Oscar beams. "Surprise!"

"Sur—" Johnny glares at Oscar.

"What?" Oscar asks, elbowing him out of the way. "It's my apartment."

"It's my chefs and cleaners."

"The place didn't need to be cleaned," Oscar all but growls.

Johnny grunts in disapproval, but by the time Oscar gets to me, he pulls me in for a hug. I can't help but smile. They're arguing like an old married couple, which is truly hilarious.

"Are you sure you like him?" Oscar whispers in my ear.

"Afraid so, Drego."

"Alright," he says with a mock groan. "If you're sure."

Johnny casually waits his turn, but when he thinks I'm not looking he glares at Oscar before pulling me to him. "We thought you would enjoy this."

"No Christmas dinner at the tower?" I ask, surprised. He said their Christmases weren't traditional, but I figured they'd be spending more time together than just a business meeting about the Crew.

"No, my dad probably has a bunch of escorts right now." He says it with no emotion whatsoever, so I have to replay his words in my head to make sure I heard him correctly. All I can picture is little pre-teen Johnny having to grow up in a place like that. A place where all K did was act out his needs and desires of sex and violence.

"When did you move into your own suite?"

"When I started getting ready for school by myself." He places the tip of his finger on my lips and stares into my eyes. "Let's not talk about that. Let's eat."

"Yes," Oscar says from across the room. "Let's eat this meal that Johnny paid for and made everyone do extra work during this special day of the year instead of spending time with their families."

"Fuck off, Drego."

Brawler moves past me, brows raised as he listens to the two of them bicker. Even Magnum has a smirk on his face. If those two were any more alike, they'd hate each other with a passion. They absolutely, positively would not be able to stand to be in one another's presence.

My guys stand in front of place settings. Oscar practically wrestles Johnny out of the head chair, so he can sit in it himself. I never had a big family, but this makes me think of movies like that. The arguing, the crass remarks. They're expressing their love for each other, but just in a different way.

"Are you coming?" Magnum asks.

I start to walk toward him and finally notice he's got a red bow tie around his neck. All the guys, actually, except for Brawler, are dressed for a holiday dinner. Johnny's wearing his suit with a red handkerchief in the front pocket. Oscar has on jeans, but he's also wearing a deep green V-neck sweater. It's only Brawler and I that look out of place.

I move toward the table and sit between Oscar at the head and Magnum to my right. Johnny is across from me and Brawler is across from Magnum. Warm fuzzies tingle my skin as we start to eat our Christmas dinner together. Maybe one of these days, we can actually cook it together, too, but this, right now, is so special.

Johnny winks at me from across the table and rubs his foot against mine underneath. We pass the meat and sides around to each other until we're concentrated on eating the delicious meal in front of us. None of us breathe a word about the Crew. None of us talk about Detective Reynolds at the cemetery, which only adds to my belief that a normal life isn't that far away. No, it won't be traditional. We'll get strange looks and be whispered about behind our backs, but I don't care. I want to be happy, and these four make me happy.

At the end of dinner, Oscar jogs off to the kitchen and brings back a pie. I rub my stomach because it's so damn full. I haven't eaten like this in a long time.

"We didn't know what kind of pie you liked," Oscar says.

Johnny pierces him with a look, which Oscar dutifully ignores. "Yes, *we*," Johnny emphasizes, "weren't sure so *we—*"

"—knew you liked chocolate, so we did chocolate pie," Oscar finishes.

He flourishes it in front of me, and my mouth waters. "Excellent choice."

"My mom used to make cheesecake," Mag says.

"My mom used to make every pie imaginable," Brawler adds, staring at the impeccably made pie in front of us.

So did mine, but I don't add to the conversation. I don't want to get bogged down with sadness. "I love chocolate pie," I tell all of them. "I just hope I can eat some."

"It's Christmas," Oscar says, smirking. "You're going to put it in your mouth, and you're going to like it."

The guys roll with laughter. All but Johnny, of course. I

give him a soft kick under the table, and he smiles for me even though it looks like it takes a lot of effort.

This is going to take some getting used to for everyone. We'll have to mesh traditions, but that happens in any relationship, right? We just have more people to contend with, but I wouldn't want it any other way.

"What the hell?" I say. "I'll live a little."

Oscar cuts the pie and gives me the first piece. The others hold out their plates while Oscar serves everyone else before himself. I place the first forkful in my mouth and immediately moan.

Four pairs of eyes move to mine.

Heat swamps my cheeks. "This is so damn good."

"I think I could watch you eat pie all damn day, Princess."

This actually gets a chuckle out of Johnny, along with a look of pure sex. He licks his lips while trailing his gaze from my mouth to my eyes. "How would it work?"

"Hmm?" I ask, shoving another bite in my mouth.

"You. Us. Your harem," he says. The old Johnny might have sneered derisively, but not this Johnny. At least not yet.

I wipe my mouth on a napkin. "What do you mean?"

"I mean sleeping arrangements. I mean sex. I mean dates and touching and just spending time together."

I place my fork down and clear my throat. I'm currently the center of attention, which makes me think the rest of the guys are wondering about this, too. "I think that's a group decision," I tell them all.

"I have a feeling we won't all be on the same page at the same time."

"Probably not, but I'm willing to work on everything that comes up. It's not going to be easy. I've never had a real relationship with anyone let alone with four guys. Things will come up that will make you mad. Oscar mad. Me mad. The rest of us... But that doesn't mean we can't work through it. I guess that's the way you'll have to look at it. Are the people sitting around this table worth working things through with?"

"You are," Johnny says immediately.

"You are, too," I say, "But it won't be just us."

"Stop worrying about the logistics," Brawler offers. "Kyla's done great with all that so far. Can't you see that when she thinks one of us needs her, that's who she spends time with? Yesterday when we got you back, you got her. Today, when we went to the cemetery, she went with me no questions asked. Actually, I don't envy her," Brawler tacks on. "I think this is a terrible idea on her part because think of all the work she'll have to go through to keep us happy. There's only one of her and four of us."

I give him a small smile. Joy fills me. I'm glad he thinks that way. It's not even a conscious thought, really. I'm just attuned to them. I get it. I understand.

"What happens when we *all* need her?"

Johnny asking questions is a good thing. It means he's beginning to think instead of being outright dismissive. Hope blooms in my chest.

Oscar rolls his eyes. "I guess you'll have to actually spend time with the rest of us."

Johnny narrows his gaze. He wipes his hand on a napkin and sets it back down again, watching it shift back into a position that isn't crumpled. "Listen, I know I'm hesitant about this, but I also see how good you guys are for her. How good she is for the rest of you, too. I just want to think about every aspect."

"Family," I say. "That's what it would be like."

Johnny swallows. "I would like that, actually."

The room quiets. We all know it took a lot for Johnny to admit that. Especially in front of these guys. He hasn't always had a problem expressing his feelings in front of me, but he has in front of them. I slide my chair back and get up. I pass Oscar and go to Johnny. He accepts me onto his lap, carefully. I definitely don't want to re-injure him. Oscar grumbles something under his breath, but that's just him. He's not really mad. I've seen Oscar mad. If he's still being sarcastic, he's not mad.

"I'd like that, too," I say.

Johnny cups my face, then brings my hand to his mouth to kiss my knuckles. My heart tap dances in my chest. It may be me, but I believe we've just broken another barrier with Johnny Rocket.

By the time the next day rolls around, all of the quiet and sense of belonging we'd found with one another on the previous day slowly fades. We're awoken by Johnny's phone ringing, a shrill alarm in the early morning hours of the peace we were able to achieve. Johnny's muscles tense, and from that first moment, I realize that what we'd all worked for last night is now gone. We're on K's time again. The perimeter of our bubble has burst. Our facade cracked. We'll be together at the end of all of this, but we need to cut off the cancer, and right now, that cancer is Kingston Marx.

Johnny runs his hands through his dark hair and throws the phone down on the bed. Johnny and Oscar slept next to me on Oscar's bed while Magnum and Brawler took the floor. For all of Johnny's talk about it being awkward, everyone just kind of fell into place in those spots like it was as natural as could be. I'm not delusional enough to think it would stay that way if Oscar and Johnny always get to sleep next to me, but at least this first night of cohabitation went well.

Oscar stirs with a grunt. Magnum has been awake for a while, and Brawler and I have been holding one another's hand for the last half an hour, mine dangling off the very edge of the bed and his holding fiercely to mine.

The door to Oscar's room opens, and Magnum appears. He's already dressed in his tactical outfit, ready for the day. I can't see it, but I'm sure he has his gun slid into the waist-band of his pants, ready for anything that might come up.

Johnny yawns, his black hair sticking out in every which way. "We have to get to the tower."

"Meeting?" Magnum asks.

Johnny nods. Then, he gazes around the room, stopping to stare at each one of the guys, including me. "All of us."

This must be the big meeting Magnum alluded to yesterday. We're all in this now, and we're getting pulled deeper in by the day. "Do you know what his plan is?"

"Not exactly," Johnny says.

The taut lines of his jaw says that what he does know, he's not excited about. Yesterday, we were able to put all of this to the side and enjoy the day, but today, it all comes crashing back on us. It's the moment the water recedes just before the huge tsunami devastates cities.

An overwhelming sense of fierce protection surges inside me. I squeeze Brawler's hand one last time and then scoot toward the end of the bed. I start pulling clothes on over the bra and underwear I slept in and then pull my hair up in a ponytail. Around me, the guys start getting ready, too. None of us are going to let anything happen to each other. They couldn't even kick me out of this plan if they wanted to. Whatever they're involved in, I'm involved in.

After grabbing a quick bite to eat in Oscar's kitchen, we head to the car. Johnny, Mag, Brawler, and I get in while Oscar follows on his bike. On the way there, there's no talk at all, let alone the kind of talks we shared yesterday. There's nothing about getting to know each other or telling stories about our holiday traditions. Right now, we're all business, and I'm sure the guys are feeling the same as me. Big Daddy K will want to retaliate swiftly and quickly. He'll use us to do it. Not himself. He used me already when he wanted to kill Roza Fonz. Since Gregory took his people and stole his business, he'll want to take care of him just like Dunnegan. The only problem is, Gregory will be harder to take down because he's already made a move against us. He didn't just show up at a predetermined spot—a dinner or a fight— where K can easily whip his gun out and shoot him. This time, it will have to be a mission. A plan set into motion where the end result is the same, but the risk to get there is much greater.

I've only been involved in the Crew for a short amount

of time, but it's not hard to decipher how things work here. Even if I didn't know anything about their operations, Johnny's mannerisms would clue me into what's about to go down. He's sitting ramrod straight in the passenger seat of the car. He's barely moved since he first got in, and he's staring out the front windshield without seeing anything. I'd love to pick his brain about his father right now, to see if we're any closer to me telling him what I want to do. Part of me thinks I'll never be able to get Johnny Rocket that much on my side. Part of me thinks if I go through with what I've always planned on doing that he'll want nothing to do with me.

That's this life, I guess. One bad decision leads to another bad decision. It's up to me what I want to do if it comes down to that.

Magnum nods at the security personnel in the underground booth of the parking area. We pull into the usual spot by the elevator, and Oscar kills the engine in the spot next to us. All around the area more cars are parked than I've ever seen here before. I swallow hard, realizing this will be big. Bigger than the dinner I was asked to attend when K took Dunnegan's life. Bigger than any other Crew thing I've been involved in before.

Johnny finally turns in his seat as soon as Magnum pulls into the spot. "Don't say anything," he says. "No one. Don't offer up anything. Don't agree or disagree. Just sit there, and only talk if you're directly asked a question." He gazes over at Brawler. "If you're asked to do something, you have to say yes no matter what it is. If you refuse to do something on this level, it's not even your ass on the line, it's your life. You understand?"

Brawler nods, and a new deep-seated fear takes over. This would be the perfect time for K to use Brawler. He still has initiation tasks to get through, so he'll be asked to do something worse. We'll just have to take the wait-and-see approach, which I've never liked. Unfortunately, I'm not the one pulling the strings in this instance, and neither are the rest of the guys.

We get out of the car, and Oscar joins our group. We take the elevator up together, and Johnny and I naturally slip into our boyfriend-girlfriend role. I don't know how K will react if he finds out I'm seeing all of these guys, but I have a feeling it wouldn't end well for Johnny. He'd probably see it as a personal affront. A lack of masculinity on Johnny's part, and a total, complete disrespect on the others.

Johnny holds my hand steadily, pressing the pad of his thumb against my knuckle to help keep me as calm as him. I gaze at his profile, and I can't help but be in awe of him. Here's a guy who's lived through so much stuff, yet he's come so far.

The elevator doors part in front of us, and the guards in front of K's suite open the door so we walk right in. Oddly, the way we trek into the room reminds me of a united front. An us versus them, though they have no idea there's even an us. We're all supposed to be a part of them, but I haven't been with them from the beginning.

"Excellent," K says, standing from the table that's now moved back into a conference room position rather than a dining room table. I guess it doesn't matter what he dresses it up as, the results are usually the same. This room—this suite—should never be mistaken as a home. Nothing but business takes place here.

Johnny and his father shake hands. Johnny takes the seat next to him, while I take the seat right next to Johnny. The others disperse around the room in available seats while Magnum stands behind Johnny and me. I recognize the faces around the room from previous meetings. Jiko and his father are even here. They're the only other party who has security behind them. I guess even though K trusts these other business professionals with the logistics of his business, that doesn't mean they deserve security like he does. They're dispensable in his mind. People he can use and discard at his leisure.

"As you are all well aware, we had a breach in the Crew," K starts out as soon as he sits. He eyes the people around the room like any of them could be another Gregory. "Someone we thought was our ally turned out to be the opposite. He's turned other members against us. You may think it was just my son who was held hostage, and that it won't affect you, but I'd like to remind you that what affects the Crew, affects you. This isn't an attack against me, it's an attack against the whole Crew. Against you. Against your livelihoods. Against the system we've set up."

If this wasn't all about him, I might even feel a little inspired. The guy can talk. That's for sure. That's how you get to be who he is. No one would follow someone who wasn't worth following. If Hitler couldn't get people to listen to him, no one would have followed him into the terrible shit he did. Eloquent speakers rule the world.

"I'm disgusted that someone we called a friend and business partner has retaliated against you," Cardinale says. Jiko nods right along next to him. "How are you doing, Johnny?"

"Better, thank you," Johnny answers beside me. "I wish I had more information on what Gregory wants, but it seems that their intent was just to get my father to make a mistake. They seemed to be unorganized in a way, so whatever we do in retaliation should be swift and devastating."

I swallow. I get wanting revenge on that fucker. He shouldn't have taken Johnny like that, but to listen to him say those things reminds me of his father, and that churns up the bile in my stomach. I have to wonder if he's playing the part, or if that's just who he is.

K nods. He steeples his hands in front of himself. "The first thing I want done is to burn the racetrack to the ground after scouring it for clues. Magnum got rid of any evidence that we were there. The police haven't finished their investigation yet, but I want the place gone as a message to that fucking prick who thinks he can mess with me."

I can't help but drift my gaze to Oscar. We once thought his mother was in that place. She could still end up there with other helpless drug addict women who have turned themselves into prostitutes just to support themselves. We can't let them suffer because K wants to punish Gregory. In response to his words, Oscar shifts on his seat. K knows nothing about Oscar's mom and telling him would be a terrible idea. The less K knows about the rest of our lives, the better.

"I also want everyone looking out for where Gregory is hiding. He has to be somewhere. The sooner we find him, the better. We'll make quick work of getting rid of him and then we can all return to normal."

Except, the problem isn't Gregory, is it? It's K. I glance around the room and realize I'm at the wrong meeting. I should be at the meeting where Gregory is talking about how to get rid of K. As soon as that's done, then "we can all return to normal" just like he said, except I don't want his normal. Neither does Magnum, Oscar, or Brawler.

"We'll do whatever you want us to do," a guy in a sharp, gray suit says. "As you said, an attack against you is an attack against the Crew, and we're a part of that Crew."

K nods, a sinister smile crossing his face. He has all these guys by the balls, and he knows it. I bet he was shocked when he found out Gregory got others to rally against him. I wish I'd been there to witness it. That moment of realization that not everyone is kissing his fucking ass.

"I want Johnny and his guys to focus on finding Gregory. As for the rest of you, I want all your guys with their noses to the ground, asking all the right questions. Someone out there has to know something. They're hiding in plain sight. As soon as you find out anything, report to Johnny who will report to me." He glances around the room until he stops on Brawler. A smile flickers over his face, kind of like old movies where the picture is lost for a few brief seconds. In between those moments, you see exactly the cold ugliness underneath. "Brawler, our initiate." He beams. "I want you to torch the track, and I don't want you to stop until it's charred remains on the ground."

My stomach sinks. I find Brawler across the room. He moves his gaze to K, and in the fashion of someone who wants to impress him, says, "Consider it done."

The knife sticks into my gut even further.

Johnny and I rise to leave the meeting after K dismisses everyone. Just like that, we have a plan in place. It's not a direct plan, but I have a feeling that's not what Big Daddy K wanted to convey with this meeting anyway. He wanted to let everyone know he wasn't going to tolerate people leaving him. If any of the other guys sitting in that room are also in discussions with Gregory, it's pretty clear they can be sure to worry about breathing if they decide to cross him.

"Johnny, Kyla, will you hold back please?"

I stiffen at his words. Sometimes, I'm able to be in his presence and not feel the overwhelming urge to knife his ass, but other times, I don't think I can stand to be so close to him anymore. I want him gone. I want him dead without the ability to hurt people. Us included.

Johnny holds back on my hand, and we wait for everyone else to leave the room. When they do, K moves over to the couches. We follow, sans Magnum. The hairs almost rise on my arms because it's very rare that I'm without Magnum. He's like a sentry always there to watch over me, and I happen to like it that way.

"How are you feeling?" K asks as Johnny and I take a seat opposite him.

Johnny shrugs. "Healing. No real damage. I can still get around. You don't have to worry about me not finding Gregory. I'll find the fucker."

K smirks. It sends a wave of uneasiness through me. "I know that, son. That's not why I wanted to hold you back here. I wanted to actually say something to Kyla."

I swallow, and Johnny moves imperceptibly closer to me.

"I owe you an apology," K clarifies.

My eyes widen. I can't help the shocked look that passes over my face. Though, he hasn't apologized yet, so... "Why's that?"

He leans further into the black leather cushions at his back. "When Johnny was missing, I said some rather unkind things to you. I'm not saying I disagree with everything I said, but I apologize considering you were one of the ones who went after him that night. I wanted to let you know that I appreciate the work you did."

I gaze into his soulless eyes. They're actually not that

soulless. I just imagine them that way because I know the sneaky, dirty things he's hidden inside himself. On the outside, he looks like any other businessman. Well groomed. Slick. Smart. All the classy attributes, he's got. He's just a master of disguise. "I would do anything for Johnny."

"I'm glad to hear it," K says, looking coolly at me. Johnny's remaining quiet through this whole exchange, but his hand in mine is steady and sure, almost like he's waiting for the moment he has to pull me out of the way. Johnny's father's gaze lowers and catches on the ring on my right hand. He doesn't flinch. He doesn't react. His lack of reaction makes me think he's known about it the whole time. "I'd like you to take more of an active role in our Crew, Kyla. If you're going to be Johnny's girl," he says, his stare still lingering on the ring, "...it's only a matter of time."

"Is there something beyond fighting you'd like me to do?" I ask, not sure what he's getting at. I thought I was a part of the Crew.

"Fighting was a good start, but realistically, how long can you do that for?" He shifts on the sofa, uncrossing his leg and crossing it the other way. "As soon as your looks diminish, no one will want to watch you fight anymore."

"Dad—"

K holds up a hand. "I know she has many years left of that. Possibly." He waves his hand like he's not quite sure when I'll get ugly.

Dick.

"However, you know as well as me that if she's with you, she's with you, Johnny. Through everything. You can't keep secrets in this life. You've obviously dragged her into this and won't let her go despite my attempts to get you to see reason, so I have a proposition for you both."

Nerves skitter over my skin like nails dragging over a chalkboard. Everything he says lights an emergency caution light inside me.

"You can have your Kyla...in whatever way you want. First, I want you to find Gregory and put a bullet through his head. Once you do that, you move into second in command. Second, Kyla needs to move back into the tower. You need to be here, and since you won't relax without her near, I have to make this a condition. Third, you tell her about the inner workings of the Crew and ensure her secrecy." K bores his gaze into his son. "You know what happens to people who talk."

Neither Johnny nor myself say anything, and the longer the time draws out, the deeper the flush of anger carves out onto K's skin.

"Is that not worthy of gratitude?"

Johnny shakes himself out of whatever stony silence he was in and stands. "I'm very grateful you finally see how serious I am about her."

"I should think so," K says flippantly. "You gave her your mother's ring after all."

A gasp parts my lips.

K's eyes round. "Oh, you didn't know?" He lifts his gaze to Johnny's. "I should say a great deal of information needs to be shared with Miss Samson, son. We have to make sure she has the stomach for it."

Johnny nods and reaches back for my hand. I place my grip in his and get to my feet. "I'll make sure she's aware," Johnny says with a cool, even voice.

We start to walk from the room. Part of me wonders what all the dramatics were about. I already know the Crew are a bunch of thugs who don't care about human life, but part of me also wonders if it's worse than I even think it is. For the sake of anyone who crosses their paths, I hope not.

"Oh, son," K calls out. "Please do hurry up and find Gregory. This rebellion is getting tedious."

Johnny doesn't bother answering. He holds the door to the suite open for me and then we head across the hall into his own place. No one else is around. Brawler could be torching the race track right now for all I know. Maybe that's why Magnum didn't stick around because he went to deal with that. Oscar, of course, would've wanted to go to make sure his mother wasn't there. Yet, here Johnny and I are, dealing with that traitorous bastard.

Johnny walks into the apartment calmly, locking the door behind his back, but when I turn to face him, his eyes are nothing but calm. Embers burn in the center of his irises until I can almost feel heat wafting off him in treacherous rays. "Do you see what I mean, Kyla? Do you understand why I keep resisting you being with them, too? How are you going to be able to do that, huh? Even if I wanted to, in my father's eyes, you're mine. You're ours. The Crew's. He won't understand. You think it would be hard for Oscar or Brawler to tell their mom's what we're doing? Imagine telling him that. Imagine what he'll do if he thinks I'm in a relationship with three other guys."

"You're not fucking them," I say.

"Do you think he'll care about that?" he grinds out.

I stare down at the ring, suddenly heavy on my finger. "Why didn't you tell me this was your mother's?"

Some of the anger lifts from him. "I wanted to, but as soon as I gave it to you, Oscar jumped in with his nonsense." He peers away. "The moment was lost."

"It wasn't lost," I say, moving closer. He freezes, staring at me with needy eyes. "I want to know about it."

Johnny licks his lips. He lingers over different areas of my body, heating me up until my skin pricks with nervous energy. He reaches for my hand and brings it up, much like he's done a hundred different times. He brings my knuckles right to his lips, kissing the ring. "This was my mother's ring. It was given to her by her parents when she graduated high school. She hadn't met my father yet, and it was the only thing she owned when she came into the Crew."

"It's beautiful, Johnny," I say, eyeing the sparkly stones as he kisses the ring again.

"I'm scared," he says.

I step forward, right into his embrace.

"I don't want what happened to her to happen to you. I couldn't bear it. I'm not sure my father knows what to do with a love like this. Or if he even loves at all. He doesn't understand it. I see that now. If he did, he would want you as far away from here as possible. He would want you far away from the tower. Far away from me. He certainly wouldn't want me telling you the Crew's secrets."

"There's nothing you can say that would make me want to leave you."

"Can I just forget for one moment?" he asks, staring at me like a lost child. "Just for one moment."

I bridge the small gap between us and press my lips to his. He instantly turns it deeper, hotter, scorching my mouth with his commanding lips until I'm putty in his arms. Even before I was sure about Johnny, he could always do this to me. Make me feel things I wasn't sure I should. Make me want things I was sure I shouldn't, but unable to help myself anyway. He still does the same to me. Though, now, I'm sure about Johnny. One hundred percent.

If Johnny's dad thinks he's going to scare me away, it's going to take a lot.

Johnny runs his hands down my ass and cups my thighs, hoisting me into the air. He hisses, but whatever momentary pain lifting me gave him, he pushes through it. Jesus. These guys will suffer through anything just to be with me. I wrap my legs around his hips lazily as he walks me into the bedroom. He promptly lays me on the bed, crawling over top of me until we're clawing our clothes off each other. We practically tear at them until they're in heaps on the floor.

He worships my body, pressing kisses over the back of my knee, my elbow, the dip in my collarbone. The tip of his tongue traces a perimeter around my breasts until I'm slick with want. He lowers over me until his cock is hard against my stomach. I itch to pull out of his grip to stroke him, but he feathers kisses over my neck before nipping at my sensitive skin.

I groan. "Johnny..."

"Did you like that, babe?"

I try to work my way up the bed to align our bodies, but he holds me down. Sticky pre-cum smears over my stomach. "You know you want to be inside me right now," I plead.

"Right now, I want to make sure you know you're mine." He pushes my knees to the bed and leans back on his knees. He strokes up the inside of my legs until I'm practically shaking with need. The taunt of his fingers excites me. He presses the pad of his finger against my entrance and circles again and again.

My heels dig into the mattress. I let him play his games until I can't take it anymore. Then, I rear up, capture his shoulders, and flip him until I'm on top. I move down his body. "You know I can tease, too." I press my lips around just the tip of his cock. I stroke his slit with my tongue until his breathing deepens. When he gazes at the ceiling, I deep throat him once, sucking him until he releases with a pop.

Before I know it, I'm on the bottom again. Johnny has my arms pinned above my head while he eases himself inside me. Just the tip. Short, teasing strokes. I buck forward, wanting all of him. Needing all of him.

He pulls out, lying over me again. His dick, coated in my juices, presses against my stomach. "You're a tease," I breathe.

"I'm going to give it to you, sexy. I'm going to make you come so hard the guards hear you scream."

My nipples peak. I'm so ready for it.

He drifts his gaze down and then lowers his perfect mouth over my breasts. He pulls one nipple into his mouth, kissing it like it's his sole purpose in life. It makes everything fall away. The meeting with K. All our worries. He switches to my other breast, and a low mewl escapes my throat. Johnny starts shifting his hips into me. His cock slides over my skin in full, taunting strokes he knows are driving me crazy. They need to be a few inches lower.

I capture his leg, prepared to flip him again, but he leans back. His open face stares at me. The icy blue of his eyes are heated in molten fire. "I love you, Kyla."

He feels it. I know he does. Real love. Not the shit his father brought him up with. "I love you, too."

He presses my knees back, finally lining us up though that's secondary now. I'm just watching him gazing at me.

And when he lifts his stare to mine, I fall even deeper for him. "Thank you for showing me."

"I—"

He drops to all fours and slides inside me. I gasp as he works his hips against mine.

He groans, dropping his forehead to mine. "I can forget like this," he says. "Fuck, everything is perfect when I'm inside you."

I lift my hips to meet his, urging him to move over me faster. I need him rocking into me like I need a drop of water in a scorching desert.

He dips his head to pull my nipple into his mouth. I buck into him, fire scorching through my veins and heading straight to my core. He stays still, first giving all his attention to one breast and then the other. All the while, he doesn't move inside me. He pins me to the bed until I'm begging for it. "Please," I practically choke.

He pulls out and then plunges inside again. My shoulders come off the mattress on a silent scream as he repeats this movement again and again. "Fuck, Kyla. I always lose myself with you."

All I can do is hold on as he tortures me so deliciously. Every drive of his cock. Every grind of his hips. His movements stroke a fire inside me. Inside, my muscles tense in preparation. I dig my fingers into his ass, holding him there, making sure he won't tease me again. Not like he would, but I might cry if he pulls out now.

He starts to shake. "Are you close, babe?"

"Uh-huh."

"Mmm." His sure movements increase. He ratchets up the heat inside me until I'm spasming around him. His stroke shudders, and a growl passes his lips that makes me smile. "Fuck, fuck."

His cock jerks inside me. I tighten my legs around his ass, pulling him to me as he spills his pleasure deep between my legs.

"Fuck. What you do to me," he breathes. He presses against me, sending a shockwave of pleasure through my sensitive core. "I never want to leave."

"Doing every day activities might become difficult."

"I can't help myself," he says. "I get next to you, and I can't fucking hold it." He holds our hips together before moving to his side. I match him, holding my head up with my hand and using the other to trace over his chiseled chest muscles and down to his bandages where I give them a quick once-over. How he was able to fuck me like that after getting shot and tortured just shows his persistence, confidence, and stubbornness. I fucking love him for it.

"I don't want you to," I say, smiling at him. "It's nice to see that I have the same effect on you that you have on me."

We lie there just staring at one another for a while. I never minded the silence with him, and I still don't. I'm looking forward to doing this a lot when we get out of the Heights, but right now, there are things we need to discuss.

He smirks. "I see that look in your eyes. You have questions."

"I just want to know what's going on, Johnny."

He takes several long seconds to gather his thoughts. He pulls back, his dick slipping out of me. Usually we would clean up at this point, but instead, he pulls the covers up and wraps them around us. When he starts to speak, he meets my gaze and doesn't wander. "I sometimes wonder if my dad is missing basic human emotions. When he says he wants you in the Crew, I know what he means. He wants you in the Crew like my mom was in the Crew. As property. As an asset. Not in the same way that I want you with me."

"Do you want to tell me about her?" I know what happened to his mother already, but I want to hear it from him.

His entire demeanor changes. The easy, post-sex serenity on his face wears off into a hard mask. "My dad wooed her, brought her here, kept her here to have me, and then she was no longer useful." He dips his head. "I worry about that. That he only wants you here so you can do the same for me like she did for him."

I think I know what that means, but I need that shit clarified. "And that would be?"

"It's going to sound crazy," Johnny says.

What part of Crew shit doesn't sound crazy? "You can trust me."

He moves his hand under the sheets and finds my core.

"To have an heir, Kyla. To have a third in line."

I blink, not sure I heard him right, even though that's what I figured. "He wants you and I to have a baby?"

Johnny shakes his head. "He wants me to have a baby. He doesn't give a shit about you. It sounds crazy. It sounds ridiculous, but you haven't lived the life I have, Kyla. The things I grew up seeing. The things he's told me. The plan he's had in place since I was a kid. It wouldn't surprise me if he's ensuring the Marx's future in the Crew and using you to do it. Because, make no mistake about it, as soon as my mom had me, she wasn't useful anymore. She was nobody. She was nothing. Do you see any women around my father's table? Do you see women anywhere?"

My mouth dries, and I shake my head.

"Exactly," he says. "I can't do that to you. I won't. I actually love you." He cups my cheek. "I love you so damn much." He closes his eyes and swallows. "I won't let him do to you what he did to her." The tension in the room thickens until a buzzing nags in my ear. "She found a way out, and when he tracked her down, he killed her."

I let out a whoosh of air as the turmoil in his eyes combat one another. This time, the emotion over his mother is winning, and it's far less a war of good versus evil or wrong versus right. It's the realization of the wrongness that has happened that darkens his gaze.

"I'll kill him," he says. "If he tries to take you from me, I'll kill him."

I don't know what else to do other than hug him. Walking this line with Johnny is fraying my already frail nerves. It all comes down to the fact that I don't want to lose him, and I'm scared to death anything I say might do just that, despite what he just said.

He combs his fingers through my hair. "We'll have to be very careful," he says. "I don't trust him. He wants you back at the tower, which makes me nervous. I moved you out so you wouldn't be around here, and suddenly, he's conceding the fact that we can be together even though I went against his orders. It's not like him."

I turn my head to kiss his bicep. Words are heavy on my tongue. Heavy on my mind. Johnny and I haven't been as close as this moment right now, but still something tells me not to tell him my secret. It's fear. A healthy dose of fear. I don't know what I would do without him, quite honestly.

Throat thick, I ask, "What are you going to do about Gregory?"

He shudders. It's so unlike him that I immediately gaze up into ice-blue eyes. He captures me there, the force of his gaze keeping me still. He licks his lips in an almost tantalizing tease. "I've killed people before, Kyla. I'll have to kill Gregory. As soon as I find him, he's dead."

He waits for me to say something, but I just keep staring. We continue that way for a long time until I tilt my head to the side. "Did you think that was going to scare me off? I'm pretty sure all of us have a screw missing in the morals department. I want to kill Gregory for what he did to you. Just like I'd want to hurt anyone who hurt you or the guys...or anyone else I loved. That's what we do, right? We fight for those we love?"

Johnny grips my hair. "One hundred percent. Nothing is going to happen to you while I'm around."

"You can't promise that. None of us can. Not with things the way they are."

Johnny blinks. I trace my fingertips up his chest. My head is filled with all the words I need to say. They're just sitting on the tip of my tongue, just waiting for the whistle to go off to tell them it's okay to jump, but Johnny's phone rings, and I end up swallowing everything back.

He cringes as he moves to fish his phone out of the

pocket of his pants, so I push him back down on the bed and get it myself. I pass it over to him without looking. He frowns down at it and then answers. "Hey." He meets my gaze as he listens to whatever is being said on the other end of the line and then finishes with, "Yeah, okay," before he hangs up. "That was Oscar. They found his mom, and she might be able to tell us where Gregory is. They're taking her back to his apartment once they're done."

Guilt slams into me. Brawler had to torch the race track. That's probably where they found Oscar's mom. He's fully involved now. Not just fighting in an underground circuit, which plenty of cities have, but now he's done—or will have done very shortly—something illegal. Something that could get tied to his name.

"Magnum will make sure it goes smoothly," Johnny says, guessing what's on my mind.

"I hope so. Brawler's different than the rest of us."

Johnny smirks. "I used to think that about Manning, too. He has a conscience."

"You have a conscience."

He grins. "That's questionable."

So's mine, I think. "So, we're meeting them over there?"

"They'll give us a call when they're on their way back."

I lie back on the bed and stare at the ceiling. "You say you don't know who your dad has on the inside of the Rawley Heights PD, right?"

"Right," Johnny says. "He keeps that information close.

He's alluded to the fact that I'll get the info when I move up, but he's the only one who knows it right now."

"Do you think for some reason whoever he has would be blocking me from the rest of the cops? Reynolds said that he's getting cut off at every turn. My phone was found at The Ring, but when he went to go look for it in evidence, he couldn't find it. I know you guys took care of the bogus eye witness to the murder of that poor little girl, but I wonder if there's something else going on, too. I just find it hard to believe that your dad would have asked that. I guess...I would have found it hard to believe except for the conversation we just had."

"He probably did," Johnny said. "Or the guy was worried about what else they would find on your phone. Something to implicate me or Dad, so he just got rid of it on the off chance something was in there. Shit like that happens all the time, Kyla. That's why none of us do any time."

That actually seems more plausible than what I'd been thinking. I'm sure that's what it is. Get rid of anything that could hurt the Crew, even if it somehow helped me, too.

"You know what I've been thinking about," Johnny says. "It's odd the police showed up around the same time you guys did that night to save me. If no one knew where I was, and Gregory's people were keeping it quiet, why did you all show up at the same time? Enough time to get me out, but not enough to have anyone else escape."

Huh. I hadn't thought of that before. I was shocked when the red and blue lights of the police were barreling down the road toward us, but my concern for Johnny took over, and I hadn't thought about it since.

"Magnum said my dad didn't know, but..." Johnny shakes his head. "I'm not sure."

I'd hope to fuck that K didn't know where Johnny was that whole time. If he did, why would he send the police? Because he didn't know we were on their trail? But still, why want the police to find Johnny? Crew shit is kept secret. Unless having the police find out what was happening at the track suited him better for some reason. "I suppose you just can't ask him."

Johnny shakes his head. "If he did it and wanted me to know, he'd already have told me."

He traces his finger down the center of my chest, between my breasts, and all the way down to my navel. Dipping his fingers between my legs briefly, he moves his fingers back up, tracing another line all the way up my body to circle first one breast then the other. "It's so distracting to talk to you when you're naked, babe."

"You should talk," I say, moving the sheet out of the way and glancing over at his hardening erection. "I wonder if—"

"Never wonder," he says. "It wastes time." He lifts his hips into the air, stroking his hard cock to the base. Water pools in the back of my throat, salivating for a taste. I sit up and crawl toward him. I use the tip of my tongue to lick the side of his cock while he continues to stroke himself. "Let's try..."

I don't even let him get the words out. I push his hands away and grip the base of his cock with my right hand, stroking him into my mouth. The temptation was just too much.

"Mmm, fuck." He flexes his feet and then grabs my hips. I give a slight shriek as he lifts one of my legs over his face until I'm on my knees, straddling his mouth. He moves his hands over my back, clenching my naked ass before yanking down, making my knees spread wide as he spears my pussy with his tongue.

I shudder, releasing my lips from around his cock. "Fuck, Johnny."

He devours me, fingertips clenching my ass as he finds my clit. I let out a long moan then find my hand clenching around his dick, just begging to be sucked. We're in the perfect position. I move my lips down over him. He fucks my mouth, his hips taking over. All I have to do is keep a suction-tight grip on him as he swirls his tongue over my clit. I taste myself on him, but I don't care. It just makes this more erotic. More heady and dangerous. More Johnny. "That's right. Take me all in," he says, still pumping away. I relax my throat, trying to work in time with him, but I keep losing the pace as his wicked tongue delivers all the pleasure.

He pops free from my mouth so I can breathe out a long

moan. I kiss his silky skin, my insides clenching, ready to release the mother of all fucking orgasms.

I explode. Pure pleasure overtakes my body as I ride his face. Wave after wave laps at me. I press my forehead into his abs as I come down, and as soon as I do, I pick my head back up to devour his dick. He moves his hands all over my skin, urging me on as I take control. His cock is mine. I swallow it, moving him in and out of my mouth in long, quick strokes.

"Yes, baby. Fuck," he pants. I continue the motion until his toes curl. In the next moment, his cock jerks, and he comes in my mouth. I swallow every last bit then release him before rolling off, chest heaving. "Could you get any more fucking perfect?" he breathes, seeking out my hand.

I hold onto him, waiting for my heartrate to return to normal. My head is near his feet and vice versa. I place my other hand over my chest, hoping my heart comes back down. We don't say anything until the phone rings again. Knowing it's probably Oscar or one of the others, I sit up, feeling satiated in all the right ways. Johnny can't take his eyes off me as he speaks to the caller on the other end of the line briefly. When he finishes, he swallows. "They're ten minutes out."

I start to get up, but Johnny stops me. He moves his gaze to my face, holding my attention. "I've been distracting myself, but there's one more thing I have to say. My dad wants me to tell you what it means to be in the Crew. It means doing things that you never would for the sake of a bigger cause. It means putting away your own selfish thoughts and focusing on something bigger. He got rid of my mom because she started to gain a conscience. She was no longer the meek girl he used for his purposes." His chest deflates. "I know you're worried about Brawler, and the truth is, it's only going to get worse. Setting fire to something is nothing in the grand scheme of things. My dad tests your boundaries. He warps your brain. He makes you do stuff he can hold over your head because if you ever do grow a conscience and want to get out, there's no fucking way you could. Do you understand what I'm saying, Kyla?"

"I think so?" I answer, but the truth is, I'm completely distracted. Johnny thinks he can't get out. That's what this is about. Right? A surge of hope cascades over me. Does he want to get out? If he does, what I want to do will only help him.

"Everyone who's moved up has had to do things that will turn your stomach. Even my dad..." Johnny shakes his head. "I don't know the whole story, but I know when Mayhem retired and he was going to take over, he killed two people. Just randomly."

My stomach tightens. Wait. What?

"Mayhem took him for a drive. They weren't even in the Heights. They were gone for days. Dad was excited about what it meant. He was chomping at the bit. He'd do anything to move up the ranks. When they came back, there was a huge celebration. They even took photos. All I remember is seeing two dead bodies lying in the middle of an alleyway. A woman and a man. Nameless to me. Nameless to them. I was only fourteen, but they made sure I was a part of it all."

Bile pours up my throat, threatening to spill all over the place.

Johnny is clueless to the storm brewing inside me. He continues telling his story, not realizing how ours interconnect. "Mayhem made him kill a random couple on the street just to prove he'd do anything for the Crew, and my dad carries that tactic to today. If you'll kill for no reason at all, what won't you do for the Crew?"

I scramble off the bed. I run to the bathroom and expel the contents of my stomach into the pristine ceramic bowl. My stomach keeps revolting and revolting until I'm only dry heaving. I already knew the tragic part of his story but picturing a young Johnny at a meeting celebrating the death of my parents makes me sick on a whole new level.

Johnny moves behind me and tries to comfort me, but I pull away from him. I slide across the bathroom tile, wiping my hand over my lips. My throat burns. My eyes burn. A tang in my nostrils makes them flare.

Now I know. Now I know the truly senseless reason why I ended up with no one. Because some heartless bastards chose my parents randomly so Big Daddy K could take over the Crew. So he could rule people with the same senselessness. So he could force people to ruin other people's lives.

I lurch forward for the toilet again, but nothing comes out. I stand on shaky legs and wipe the vomit from my mouth with the back of my hand. "Where's your gun?"

I move away from the toilet and catch Johnny's gaze in the mirror. He looks lost. "What? Kyla…"

"Your gun," I demand, standing there calmly. I bend to wash my face with water. I swish water in my mouth and then spit it out until my mouth doesn't feel like something died in it. Johnny still hasn't answered me by the time I'm done, so I push past him and scour his suite. I look in all the usual places. The end table by the couch. The closet by the main door. I even look behind the TV.

"Kyla…"

"Where's your fucking gun, Johnny?"

"What's going on?"

"I need it!"

He tries to come to me, but I smack his hands away. The hurt that lances his face doesn't even touch my pain. Nowhere near. "Just calm down," he says. "What do you need my gun for? You can have it. You know I'd give you anything."

I stand in the middle of his living room, breaths heaving out of me until I'm gulping in air like a crazy person. "I just need it."

He shakes his head. He comes toward me again. "Are you okay? I'm worried."

I try to wriggle out of his grasp again, but he holds on tight. We wrestle back and forth. I'm scratching and clawing, but Johnny holds me with a protective fierceness I can't get through despite his injuries. Maybe if I was in my right mind, I'd be able to. I'd incorporate my training, but at the moment, all that is lost. All I see is fucking red.

My parents' blood.

Hate.

Anger.

Fear.

I've held off long enough. This shit needs to stop. "Johnny," I roar.

Johnny wrestles me into the bedroom, surprisingly strong though I can tell it's taking a lot out of him. He pins me on the bed. The side of my face smooshes against the mattress. I'm still trying to get out of his grip, so I don't notice he's talking. Not until I hear him shout, "Magnum."

I breathe out hoarsely.

"It's Kyla. I don't know what's wrong. You guys need to get here now."

23

By the time the rest of the guys arrive, I've stopped fighting Johnny. My mind goes blank. Every time what he revealed tries to drill into my brain, I go completely numb.

I knew K killing them was senseless, but to find out that it was as senseless as this? To find out that it was done as almost a sport? To fucking find out that he got his position because he murdered my parents?

I can't even comprehend it. I don't even want to fucking comprehend it. It's sick. It's wrong. It's fucking awful.

The door opens, and I run to the first body who enters. Magnum wraps me in a hug, holding me so close to him. I can barely breathe, which is fine by me because every time I breathe, I know that what Johnny said to me is true. It really happened that way.

"What the fuck did you do?" Oscar growls.

"I didn't do anything," Johnny yells back. He's dressed in boxers now, and he was able to wiggle a shirt over my head when I was just staring into space. "She just kept asking for my gun. She freaked out, she—"

I start to tremble. I'm not cold. I'm not furious. I'm just so...lost.

"Shh, baby girl," Magnum says. "What happened?"

I close my eyes. I don't even know how I can look at Johnny. This isn't his fault. He's as much of a victim as I am, but I just fucking lost it. How can I still hold everything inside after this?

"Kyla, you're killing me," Johnny says, and the anguish in his voice tells me it's true.

My stomach seesaws, threatening to spill again.

Oscar pushes Johnny, and he stumbles into the wall. "You must have done something to her!"

"Don't test me, Drego."

"You've got to tell us what happened, baby, before the guys kill each other." Magnum loosens his hold, and I gaze up into his hazel-green eyes. He nods.

Behind us, there's still shuffling going on before I finally turn. Oscar and Brawler face Johnny down. "It's not Johnny," I choke out, finally finding my words I'd been wanting to say all this time. But how do I say that and then tell him what I know?

All three of them turn to me. Johnny pushes past them

to move closer. I wince when he goes to cup my face, and he drops his hands at his sides. His eyes are turning vacant, and I'm yelling at myself to calm the fuck down, but I just can't. Not right now. Not after this.

"Kyla, I'll do anything," Johnny pleads.

I wiggle my fingers, feeling the weight of his mom's ring on my finger. What happens when I tell him why I'm here? I'm such a fucking chicken shit because I don't want to find out.

The time is now though. I couldn't even explain away this last half an hour without the truth even if I wanted to.

Magnum kisses the back of my head, and I blow out a breath. I've almost gotten myself under control. I swallow the humongous lump of fear in my throat and stare a distraught Johnny down. "Do you remember the story you were telling me? The one about your dad..."

Brawler glances between the two of us warily. Oscar crosses his arms, and Magnum grips my upper arms. Johnny peeks at all of us and then nods. "Yeah, I told you what my dad had to do to become leader of the Crew." His jaw tenses. "He killed two people. A man and a woman."

The second time he says it is not any better than the first. I slap my hand over my mouth and beg my body not to react the way it did the first time. I breathe in through my nose.

"Fuck," Oscar growls.

"What?" Johnny asks, looking around. No one will look him in the eye now.

No one except me. "Johnny." I draw in a shaky breath. "I think those two people you're talking about were my parents."

Time transcends reality. For a moment, I'm caught in a nanosecond, almost wishing I could hold onto it forever. The next second that blips by could change everything. Strike that. It *will* change everything, I just don't know in which way.

Johnny blinks and shakes his head. "No."

I nod. "I'm sure."

"No!" Johnny yells. He turns to the wall and slams his fist through it. Deep breaths flare his nostrils. He punches the wall several more times. A hole appears. Pieces of drywall litter the floor. A tiny droplet of blood from Johnny's knuckles falls to the wreckage, splattering.

"Stop him," I say.

Brawler immediately reaches out and holds Johnny back from hurting himself any further. He squirms until Brawler has to put him in a bear hug from behind.

Johnny fumes in his grip. He looks like a caged bull. His dark hair is wild around his beautiful face. His eyes spark with electricity. "That's it then? That's the last thing you were keeping from me? That's why you came here? You knew my father killed your parents."

Magnum tightens his grip on me, and if you were an

outsider looking in, you'd think Johnny and I were being held back from going at each other. But that's far from the truth. Our lives have been tangled up in each other's for too long for that. I've never blamed Johnny for what his father did. Never. I don't plan on starting to now either. "I knew he killed them, but I didn't know it was because of something so fucking senseless. So thoughtless. So motherfucking wrong. Killing someone just to move up the ranks? The Crew isn't a fucking brotherhood or a damn business. It's not a fucking group that's saving the Heights, it's fucking killing people for sport."

Johnny bites his lip. "Why did you come here? Just to see him? To find him?"

"No, Johnny. I'm the same as you. I fight for the ones I love, remember? I didn't come here just to see the man who killed my parents, I came here to fucking kill him."

Johnny straightens. If Brawler wasn't holding onto him, he would've stumbled back at the force of my words.

The expression on Johnny's face now is startling. Indescribable. Hurt. Anguish. Pain. Fear. Anger. Worry. Love. It's a toxic cocktail of mixed emotions.

He rips his hands from Brawler's grip and starts for the door. Magnum moves to intervene first, but I'm faster than him. I move in front of the door, anger filling me. "No, Johnny Rocket. You do not get to walk out on me right now. Not fucking now."

"You came here to ruin my life."

Dread sours my stomach. This was what I was worried about. "Your life's already ruined. So's mine."

"Damnit, Kyla," he roars. His face is so close to mine, I can feel his pent-up rage in every cell of my body.

I knew he'd fight me on this. Deep down, I knew he would. He's brainwashed. He's jilted. He's been taught to think a certain way all of his life. Those feelings can't easily be erased.

"Do you even love me?"

I blink at him. "Is that a serious question?" He holds my gaze. "Fuck yes, I love you. I love you despite the history between our families. I love you despite the shit you're mixed up in. I love you—"

"Despite the fact that you were going to turn around to do the same thing to me that my dad did to you?"

I flinch but hold my ground. "You're forgetting the one simple difference. Your father is the scum of the earth. My parents were good people. Innocent people."

"I just can't believe you planned this the whole time. You let me love you. You let me fill you, all the while, planning my father's demise."

"Your father left you at the warehouse, Johnny. He knew you were shot, and he left you."

"Magnum had it handled," Johnny says, echoing his father's words.

I'm almost too shell-shocked to respond. "You can't be serious. Your father doesn't care about anyone but himself.

You know he doesn't care about you. Just an hour ago, you were telling me that you'd kill your father if he tried to hurt me. What the fuck, Johnny?"

"An hour ago, I didn't know you were capable of what you just told me."

I flinch so hard the back of my head smacks the door.

"Johnny," Mag says.

"No, fuck all of you," he yells. "I'm guessing you guys knew about this. I'm guessing you all knew what she was planning on doing. You brought this to me like we were going to be a family, and I almost believed you. Almost."

I reach out because I see it in his eyes. I'm losing him to the anger again. "Johnny—"

He smacks my hand away. "Oh, now you want to touch me?"

"Hey," Brawler says, standing up to him. "Don't fucking touch her like that."

Magnum moves forward, and in one swift push, has Brawler pinned against the wall. I gasp. "New plan. You don't fucking talk to Johnny like that."

Disbelief has me swaying on my feet. "Mag..."

Cold eyes meet mine before moving back to Johnny. "What do you want to do with these three?"

"Three?" Johnny's forehead wrinkles in confusion.

"You think I fucking knew what she had planned? Come on."

My stomach twists like someone grabbed a hold of my insides and tugged.

"I took an oath, brother. You fucking know that."

I snap my jaw shut. I can't fight back. Magnum is lying for a reason.

Johnny reaches up to scratch his jaw. He turns toward me, and some of the anger fades. In one fluid motion, he slams his lips against mine, taking, taking, taking until he rips away from me. He grips my hips. "Goodbye, Kyla. Leave the Heights."

My heart shatters in my chest at the vacant expression I'm met with when he steps away. He turns completely around and walks over to the couch in the living room and sits, crossing one ankle over the other and threading his fingers behind his head. He looks so much like his father I might well and truly throw up.

"Leave," Mag says, flashing us a warning.

He doesn't say anything. He doesn't tell me he's playing. He doesn't tell me he has a plan. The only thing his eyes say is that we better fucking listen to them. To both of them.

Magnum marches into the other room and comes back with my clothes. He throws them at my feet, and I clench my jaw while I pull on something that won't get me looked at like a pariah on my way out of here. Confusion and hurt war for the top emotion over me, but when I finish pulling on a pair of joggers, Oscar and Brawler take a stance on both sides of me. Brawler reaches for my hand and tugs me.

Before I know it, we're in the hallway of the tower, walking to the elevator.

We step into the metal box, taking it down until we hit the ground floor. It feels as if I'm playing a part in a movie. It's like my heart and my head aren't even in my body and brain right now. I'm just going through the motions.

Oscar, Brawler, and I walk up the sidewalk past the guard station and out into the Heights free as birds. Or more like birds who have shackles of the past wrapped around their ankles.

"Well, that went well," Oscar says.

A sob rips up my throat until they stop me right there on the sidewalk, cocooned between the two of them. "What the fuck are we going to do?"

"You told us you had a car once, right?" Brawler asks. "I think it's best we do exactly as Johnny says."

"He hates me."

Brawler shakes his head. "If anything, he loves you so much it scares the fucking shit out of him."

"He told me to leave."

"He's hurt, Kyla."

Oscar sighs. "We can have this conversation, but we should have it someplace safe. Brawler's right. We need that car."

I start to walk toward the bus stop only to pull up short. "What about your mom?"

Oscar shakes his head. "She got away. As soon as we had to detour from the apartment, she ran off."

"Fuck."

"What about your mom?" I ask Brawler.

He lifts his shoulders. "I don't think she's in danger. She's too drugged up and..." He swallows. "She won't leave that apartment anyway. She hasn't left since my brother and sister died."

I close my eyes, pain etching my heart at that sad reality. She just fucking shut down after she lost her two children. If anything, this makes me want to fight back even more. How I'm supposed to do that now is beyond me. I just got kicked out of the fucking tower and Johnny hates my ass.

"Come on," Oscar says. He places his arm around my shoulders, and we walk toward the bus station. Thankfully, the bus we need doesn't take long. It stops and takes us to the parking lot where I hid my car. It's sad that my life has become what I have on my body this very fucking second. The stuff that was in my old apartment got trashed. Johnny bought me clothes, but they're not my clothes, they're his. I'm left with just this shirt, underwear, bra, and joggers.

And Brawler and Oscar, of course.

I take them up to the second floor and find the key I'd hidden with a magnet in the tire well. I get in, and Oscar and Brawler climb in after me.

"You guys got your phones on you?" Oscar asks.

"Yeah," Brawler says.

"Toss it."

Oscar and Brawler both lower their windows and toss their phones out. The hard plastic clatters against the cement, and then I pull out of there. No one tells me where to go, so I take the road out of the Heights. I take it to another main road and drive and drive until I find a hotel on one of the exits. It's a chain hotel. Not high class, but not a dump either. I park in the lot and fall back against the seat.

Brawler reaches over and threads his fingers through mine. I nod toward the glove compartment. "Mind opening that and grabbing my wallet?"

Brawler does as I ask, and we walk inside like three children of the Heights kicking it in the real world. The front desk attendant stares at Brawler's tattoos. Another worker comes up behind him to fiddle with a different computer, but keeps his eyes on Oscar, his stare flicking to me like I'm about to give them the universal salute that I've been kidnapped.

Or maybe not. Maybe that hint in their gaze is that they're scared of me, too. Wouldn't that be something?

I'm no longer a pretend thug. I'm no longer the girl who doesn't fit in with the Heights.

I am Heights, baby. And I will fucking fix this.

24

Travel is easy when you don't have any luggage. It's the baggage back in the Heights that has me troubled.

I walk out of the bathroom with wet hair, dressed back in the outfit I left Johnny's suite in. Brawler and Oscar have taken up each of the queen beds in the room. Oscar has the television on with his back pressed against the headboard while Brawler is sitting on the edge of the other mattress, head in his hands.

He flicks his gaze up when I come out. He stares at me for a while until he gives Oscar a double take. He sighs, grabs one of the numerous pillows on the bed he's claimed and throws it at Oscar.

Oscar blinks and looks over at him slowly. "Dude."

"Dude nothing. Turn that shit off." He cocks his chin

toward me, and Oscar reluctantly hits the power button on the TV until the screen goes dark. Brawler looks back at me. "We need to talk about what happened."

It's odd the calm that's taken over my body right now. I'm not freaking out. I'm not worried. I miss the fuck out of Johnny, but I also don't think all is lost with him yet either. No matter how delusional that sounds. "Let's start with Magnum," I say, sitting on Oscar's bed and facing Brawler. "What the hell was that about?"

Oscar sits up. He scoots down the edge of the bed before he maneuvers himself behind me, his legs straddling my hips. "He obviously stayed for a reason. We all know he knew what you were doing here, so he stayed for Johnny. He didn't want Johnny to lose faith in him."

"Or the Crew to lose faith," I say.

Brawler nods. "I wouldn't worry about him. He's completely on our side."

The way he says it makes me think he believes Johnny isn't. I lean back against Oscar. "I don't know why I'm surprised Johnny reacted like that. He was never going to take me killing his dad well."

Oscar almost snorts. "You think? If there's anything that family has going on for them it's self-preservation and thinking they're God's gift to everything."

"I'm not giving up on him," I say softly. My gut tells me I'm right. My gut tells me things are happening for a reason. I wipe my hands down my face, and Oscar pulls me closer.

"The only thing is, now I'm not even anywhere near the Heights. We might even be public enemy number one by now if Johnny went to his father." I hold tight to Oscar's hands and gaze over at Brawler. "You guys might not ever be able to go back." I bite my lip. "I'm sorry."

"Listen, we don't know what's going on," Oscar says. "Johnny just might need to calm down. Part of me thinks he'll go straight to K and tell him what you had planned, but the other part of me knows he would never do that to you." He leans into me, pressing his chin on my shoulder. "We all saw the way he was with you. Maybe he got overwhelmed and reverted back to his old ways, but he'll be begging for you back in no time."

I lift my hand to stare at the ring Johnny gave me. Just two days ago, we all celebrated Christmas together, and I got the glimpse of what life could be like with all four of them. Now, the rug has been pulled from under my feet. "You don't even like Johnny," I say.

Oscar chuckles. "I never said I didn't like him. He's just a dick."

Brawler shakes his head. "I swear you two are fucking long-lost brothers."

Oscar stiffens behind me, but I laugh. "I've been thinking that myself lately."

"Wait," Oscar says. "I'm a dick?"

I collapse backward onto Oscar in a fit of humor as he

holds me close. "Don't worry. I like dicks," I finally manage to get out.

"Obviously," Brawler says, then catches my double entendre and shakes his head with a smirk.

After a while, the laughter fades, and we just sit there not knowing what to do. Oscar glances around the room. "Confession time. I've never stayed in a hotel room before."

"No?"

He shakes his head. "The only time I've been out of the Heights was when I went to Spring Hill, so..."

"Me either," Brawler says. "I've never been out of the Heights before. Mom always talked about taking us on vacation when we were younger, but then the shootout happened. When she fell apart, she never talked about that again."

"When we get out of here, we'll stay at an even better hotel. In someplace nice. Like Hawaii or—"

"Florida."

I glance over my shoulder at Oscar. "Florida?"

He shrugs. "I hear the East Coast is nice."

"We'll all vote," I say, leaning back into him.

"More real talk," Brawler says. "If Magnum and Johnny don't come back, what's the plan?"

My heart squeezes. I don't want to even think about that happening, but he's right. We're not just going to sit around this hotel waiting for them to show up. No, I still have the reason why I came here. Though, the thought of hurting

Johnny makes me queasy. My mind wants to tell me it would've been easier if I hadn't developed feelings for Johnny Marx, but my heart knows better. After feeling what I feel for him, the real tragedy would be never allowing us to explore these feelings. With him. With any of them.

"My plan hasn't changed," I say. I swallow back the guilt that creeps up. "Big Daddy K needs to go down. We can't just let the Crew do what they've been doing. More people like my parents will end up dead. Maybe even worse, people like you, Brawler, might end up doing those things. They take someone as good as you and twist them into people like them. Then the cycle starts all over again into a spiral of death and power."

"Will you be able to do it though?" Oscar asks. "Actually kill K?"

Everything in me screams yes, but if Johnny were right there, watching, I'd have second thoughts. How could I not? "I'm going to leave that decision for the moment I need to make it in, but that doesn't stop the fact that we need to take him down."

"I've been thinking..." Oscar says. "The Dragons, Gregory's people, they want to take K out. There's no reason why we couldn't work with them to do it. Let's get real, the three of us trying to get back into the Crew to take down Big Daddy K and the entire organization is far-fetched to say the least, but if we had those guys on our side." He shrugs. "Instant allies."

"Except they're probably not any better," Brawler interjects. "They already tried to hurt Kyla. They'll just take over the remnants of the Crew and run it just like K."

I worry over my lip. That doesn't sit well with me either. At first, this was just about taking Big Daddy K out. About wanting revenge for my parents. That's still a major part of it, but what kind of hypocrite would I be if I said the problem was just him? It's not. He's the one who directly wronged me, but there are members upon members who would gladly step into K's place and be just as ruthless and tyrannical as him. Yes, the problem is K, but the problem is also the Crew. The entire organization is fucked.

"If we use them to take out K, we'd have to take them out too. In the end."

"By take out, you mean...? Because if you're talking about killing them, the more the bodies pile up, the less chance we have of actually getting out of here to live that life you want to live, Princess," Oscar says.

"I don't know," I say truthfully. "I've never plotted the demise of an entire criminal organization before."

"Alright, I'm just going to say it," Brawler says. "What if Detective Reynolds isn't our enemy?"

The door to the hotel room clicks, and each of us turn just in time to see Magnum strolling through the entry. His jaw is tight. His copper beard almost standing straight out. I eye him warily, but I know he's not my enemy.

"How the hell did you find us?" Oscar asks, clearly impressed.

Good point. The guys gave up their phones. We left them in the parking lot.

"I have a confession to make." Magnum's sure voice spills into the room as he strides straight for me. "I've known who you were since the day after Johnny claimed you at the fight."

"Your name is Joanne Ridley. Your parents called you Joey. Your mom and dad were gunned down in a shitty alleyway by Kingston Marx. You were sent to live with your aunt and uncle after that. You went to a private school where you didn't always have the easiest time. You—"

My mouth opens and closes a few times. "You knew? The whole time?" Fear ripples through me. It's what I'd always been afraid of. Someone realizing who I was. Ending me before I even got the chance to do what I wanted to. And here Mag is, telling me he's known all this time. Even before I told him who I was.

He nods. He darts his tongue out to lick his lips. "As soon as Johnny wanted you, K had me run your background. You did a good job hiding it. You covered all your bases. Whoever you hired did exactly what he needed to do, but I just couldn't stop. There was just something about you that niggled at me. That wormed its way in and wouldn't let go. I stayed up all night, working my different software until I stumbled across it. Even then, I wasn't sure. I had to use your real name to look you up, connect the dots."

"You didn't tell K?"

"If I had, you would've been dead that night."

I breathe out. "So, you knew Johnny's dad killed my parents to take over Mayhem's position?"

Mag takes in a deep breath, letting it simmer for a while before letting it out. "I knew. There wasn't a way to tell you without telling you I knew who you were the whole time. Without also confessing that I deliberately held back information from the Crew that would hurt them in the long run."

I think back to when I told Magnum. It kind of falls into place now. He didn't react when I told him my past. I thought it was because he was just that good at hiding his feelings, but all this time, it's been because he already knew.

"If I'd known Johnny would've let it slip like that, I would've told you sooner. I would've told you in a way that... I don't know. In a way that maybe it would have hurt less. Johnny didn't know, Kyla. He just thought you were some girl that miraculously came into his life to make it better, and then...all that got upended with one story. I had no idea K was going to urge Johnny to tell you Crew secrets. I thought he was leaning toward shoving you out, not bringing you in."

My mouth suddenly dry, I don't say anything for a few

minutes. Oscar speaks up behind me. "But like, how did you get in the door?"

Magnum lifts his gaze to Oscar's. "I stole a housekeeping key card."

"And you found her because you knew her real name?" Brawler asks.

Of course. The fucking bank card I used to pay for the room.

"I wouldn't have let her leave if I wasn't confident I'd be able to find you guys." He moves his gaze to me again. "I'm sorry I didn't tell you I knew. About who you were and about why your parents were killed."

Is this Magnum's secret? The one he said he'd tell me when the time was right? I stand and face him. "It's okay," I tell him. "I'll be glad when we're out of the Heights and we don't have to keep secrets like this anymore."

He spears me with a look that roots me right where I am. "By the time that happens, everything will be out in the open." He pulls me toward him, wrapping me in his arms again and reminding me how quickly and easily he did that when I was freaking out about my parents. Everything about Magnum says he's a safe space. I would walk into a burning building with him and trust that he would get me out safe. I would throw myself off a cliff without a parachute as long as he said it was okay. It's the badass aura he has that says he protects people at all costs.

"What about Johnny?" I ask, talking about the big

missing link in the room. Could I live a happy life with Magnum, Brawler, and Oscar? Yes. But a happier life would be filled with all four, and I'm not letting that get away now that I've seen a glimpse of it.

"Ask him yourself." Magnum takes out his cell phone and presses a button.

For a few tense moments, nothing happens. Magnum turns toward the door, so we all do, too. Then, the same clicking sound happens, and in walks Johnny fucking Marx.

"One more white lie," Magnum says. "I stole *two* house-keeping keys."

The flood of emotions swirling inside my brain rush in and leave me speechless. Thoughtless. Immovable.

Once again, Johnny and I are facing each other down, not knowing where both of us stand, and the hole that rips inside of me will leave a scar I'll have all my life.

25

Johnny, as usual, is a force to be reckoned with. He's dressed in his suit and tie. His piercing light blue eyes smother me in flames that I can barely take a breath from. Even with the hard look in his gaze, I love that he's back here with me. I love that all of us are once again in the same room.

"Don't hate me," I say. My heart hammers inside my chest. My skin crawls with anxiety. I literally told this guy I wanted to kill his father. Of course, he fucking hates me.

His lips curl up in that sinister way a predator looks at its prey. I'm a piece of meat, and Johnny Rocket wants to eat me up.

His face sobers when my mouth parts. "Babe, I fucking love you. I could never hate you."

Heavy bricks of weight lift from my shoulders. "But your dad..."

He raises his hand, filters his fingers through my hair until he reaches the back of my neck and holds me there. "My dad—" He shakes his head quickly. "My dad's been the only family I've known my entire life...until you. And these fuckers. I get it, okay? I get everything you've tried to say to me. I'm in. I'm so fucking in."

I blink at him, still not comprehending everything that's just gone down. "But you told me to leave the Heights."

He smirks. "Of course, babe. I need you to leave the Heights. I need you far away from my father. All of you. He's toxic. I knew Oscar and Brawler would go with you. I thought Magnum would go, too, but he fucking knows me too well." When he still sees the apprehension on my face, he continues, "I told you what he's doing wasn't sitting right with me, and when you finally told me what he did—" He breaks off. "I'm so fucking sorry. I had no idea." He pulls me toward him until our foreheads rest against each other's. "But you telling me just solidified everything in my head. No father of mine would hurt the girl I love like that."

I hear the words he's saying, but they're not measuring up with what he told me just a few hours ago. "Johnny, I don't get it."

"You don't get that I love you? You don't get that I would do anything to protect you?"

I swallow. "Why would you send me away?"

Mag sighs. "Come on. Let's everyone sit down so we can talk this through."

Johnny drops his hand, tracing down my arm until he laces his fingers with mine. Oscar pulls me back into his lap while Johnny sits next to us. Opposite us on the other bed, Magnum takes a seat next to Brawler.

At least Brawler was right. He told me Johnny loved me. I wanted to believe him, and I kind of did, but I was also worried about what I'd done to him. I get that I'll be doing exactly what was done to me to him, but I still stick by the fact that my parents were good people and Kingston Marx is a motherfucker who doesn't deserve to breathe.

Johnny chuckles. It's such a rare sound that I immediately swing my gaze to his. He gives me a big smile. "Joey..."

I cock my head at him. "Hey."

He laughs harder. "I actually really like your name, but we can't be Johnny and Joey, that just sounds weird."

I narrow my gaze at him, seeing the teasing in his ice blue eyes. "Good because I don't like Joey. I'm Kyla. No matter what, I'm Kyla. And stop changing the subject. Why did you send me away?"

He props some pillows behind him and leans casually against them. "So, you have an aunt and uncle?"

I flick my gaze to Magnum, hoping I can find some answers on his face. For whatever reason, Johnny is acting like this is a first date, and he wants to ask me all the questions about my life.

My mouth drops. Of course, he is. It kind of is a first date. The real me is out there now. I'm holding nothing back from Johnny anymore, and he's holding nothing back from me. My skin pricks, and I bite my lip. "Yeah. They took me in after my parents died."

"You can say it, you know," Johnny says. "You should say it. Your aunt and uncle took you in after my father killed your parents." He grips the sheets in his hands, his knuckles turning white. "I can't believe you can even stand to be in my presence. I can't believe you've even let me touch you. I can't believe you can even be near my father without murdering him."

"It's been...something," I say. "The first time I saw him, I almost threw up."

Johnny squeezes my hand. "I'm so sorry, Kyla. If I--" His mouth works, but there are really no other promises or apologies to make.

"It's not your fault."

His face turns hard. "You say that, but I'm not so sure. I've been wrapped up in this shit my whole life." He skims the room with his eyes, landing on both Oscar and Magnum. "We're all culpable in shit like this. Every one of us. I say it ends."

Energy pricks my skin, but I'm also acutely aware of what that means for Johnny. What he's saying. If he's truly in this, he's going to have some stumbles. I don't care if your father is Hitler or a serial killer, you're going to feel something when he gets his comeuppance. "We'll all be here for you when it does."

Oscar shifts behind me. "Alright, can we start somewhere near the beginning because I don't know about the rest of you, but I'm pretty damn confused about what's going on. You love Kyla. Duh. Anyone can see that. You told her to leave the Heights, but then come find her. That sounds like the perfect place to start."

Magnum breathes out. For the first time in a long time, his features aren't so hard. He doesn't have that look of pure concentration like he usually does. He's just him. Just Jacob Cotton. In fact, he looks the most at ease now that everything is out in the open. "Okay, when everything went down in Johnny's suite, I knew something wasn't right. I know him," he says, nodding toward his friend sitting next to me on the bed. "I knew he wouldn't give Kyla up so easily, so I caught on to what he was doing. He got you out of the Heights, away from his father and whatever ridiculous thing he has planned for you. We went to K and told him that you had a change of heart. We told him you left the Heights and that you and Johnny had broken up."

"I knew you wouldn't leave any other way," Johnny says. "You're too damn stubborn."

"Oh, I'm stubborn?" I say, neck pricking.

He winks.

"Okay, well, I'm out of the Heights, but the problem is that K is in the Heights, and now, I'm not."

"You're safer here," Magnum says. I open my mouth to say something, but he continues. "We're not taking you out of this," he promises. "We're not going to make you sit this one out on the sidelines, but we needed to be smart about how we go about this. Having you here so we don't have to worry about you all the time is a good thing. Now, we can all approach this with a level head. We can plan."

"And we're planning to take K out?" I ask, peeking at Johnny. I need to make sure we're all talking about the same thing.

He swallows, his Adam's apple protruding from his corded neck. "We're going to take him down as Crew leader."

"A coup?" Brawler asks.

Uneasiness rolls through me. Taking him down as Crew leader and killing him are two different things. "That's not enough."

"I know," Johnny says, squeezing my hand again. "He'll get what he deserves."

I bite my lip. I've grown in the last few months. I understand there's more to life now. I even have the beginning of a life I want, but I can't have that life if K is still living. "This might be hard to hear, Johnny, but I *am* going to kill your father. I honestly don't care what you or Magnum or anyone else has to say about that. He's dead. You understand?"

Johnny rubs his temple with his free hand. Magnum sighs. "We have a plan for that. We thought that if we got

Gregory and the Dragons involved that maybe they would take care of the problem for us."

The inside of my cheek is raw as I think. It's not worth arguing with them right now over this. I will kill Big Daddy K. I don't care what they say. It's not enough for him just to be dead. I still want him to know who I am and why he's going to rot in hell for what he's done.

"We actually thought of that, too," Oscar says while rubbing his hands up and down my arms. "We thought we could use them, but then we realized that they just want what K has, so we would actually just be replacing the problem with another problem."

"Plus, you're supposed to be killing Gregory," I say to Johnny. "Your dad's going to notice if he doesn't end up dead."

"Well, I'm done being used by him," Johnny says. "I'm just fucking done."

"Maybe you should leave the Heights too." The truth is, I'm worried for him. Worried for all of them. The chances of this ending well are slim. K won't go down without a fight. He has endless resources at his disposal. We're just us.

"Don't look so worried," Johnny says, squeezing my hand again. "I know how to deal with my dad. I know his weaknesses. I know where we can hurt him the most. Trust me, I know what I'm doing."

I worry over my lip. "That still doesn't make me feel

better. If I'm out of the Heights, you guys should be too. None of you are safe there."

"I think you just need a tension release," Johnny says, giving me a half smile. He winks at me, and suddenly the room is charged. In an instant, the somber mood breaks.

Oscar hauls me back to his chest, whispering huskily in my ear. "You missed it earlier. She was telling us how much she loves dicks."

Johnny's brows pop up. "Dicks, huh. How many dicks?"

With all four eyes on me, I lose my breath. The overwhelming force of their gazes would knock me on my ass if Oscar didn't have his arms wound around me with his hands slipping up my thighs. All rational thought leaves my brain. "You guys aren't fair. We were talking about something important."

"And we were just telling you that you don't need to worry about it," Johnny says. "Not right now. Not right this second. I hated saying that stuff to you back there. I've been dying to make you forgive me."

Oscar takes both my hands behind my back and holds them, pinning them between his body and mine. He then moves his hands freely up my thighs. My breath hitches. "I already—"

Johnny ignores me. His heated gaze burns my skin. "I think she likes that."

I peek over at him. Despite the time with him and

Magnum, I'm not sure what his comfort level is with stuff like this, but the look in his gaze says he's enjoying it.

I move my stare to Brawler. He's watching Oscar's hands intensely.

Magnum, too, burns holes through my needy flesh. My face flushes.

"This is the first time we've all been out of the Heights together, and I think we should celebrate," Oscar says. His erection hardens against my back.

"She hasn't told us how many dicks she likes," Magnum reminds everyone.

Just his voice, his tenor, his sure demeanor saying those words sparks a fire in my belly. "Four," I choke out. "Four dicks."

"Oscar, you should spread her legs," Johnny offers. "I bet someone wants a taste."

Oscar runs his hands down my hips, taking my joggers with him. Brawler drops to his knees in front of me, and a chill sweeps through me. Slowly, he helps Oscar remove my joggers, exposing my bare skin to all of them.

If this is what it's like with these guys in a hotel room, I'm all about it. We can stay here forever.

Oscar pulls my shirt over my head until I'm lying against him with just my bra. He cups my breasts, fondling my nipples between his fingers before he reaches around to unclasp my bra and peel the cups off me, discarding the material to the side.

"Not fair," I breathe out, glaring at their hungry gazes. "I need to see dick."

Oscar cups my breasts, stroking my nipples while Brawler reaches behind him to take his shirt off. His muscles flex as he moves closer until his hot breath hits my center. As soon as his tongue presses against me, Johnny groans. "Fuck, that's hot."

I turn my head and catch Johnny stripping his suit jacket off. He unbuckles his belt, shoves his pants down his thighs and rips his button-up open. His cock presses against his boxers. With his shirt wide open, I get a peek of his chiseled physique. He doesn't waste time reaching inside his boxers and gripping his cock. His gaze meets mine, and he starts to pump his hand down his rigid dick confidently.

Brawler flicks his tongue over my clit, and I cry out.

Behind me, Oscar presses his cock into my back as if he's searching for relief.

I can't believe this is happening. All of them. All four of them.

I flick my gaze to Magnum and find him pushing his tactical pants to the floor, his gun beside him on the bed. He peels his boxers off next, then grips his huge cock in his fist and starts jerking off.

"Aw fuck," Oscar says. "Now I'm going to get a complex."

"Fuck you, Drego," Magnum groans. The way he works his cock is intense. I'm stuck staring, lost in his swift, quick motions. Brawler matches his speed until I'm tensing against Oscar. "You like his tongue, Princess?"

"Mmm," I moan. Everywhere I look, there's a hot guy jerking off or the sensual picture of Brawler's lips on my pussy. A quick look at Johnny tells me he's enjoying this as much as me. Cum beads at the tip of his dick. The fierce look of concentration darkening his features spreads to his jerky movements.

"How does she taste, Big Man?"

"Like I could eat it all fucking day." Brawler cups my ass and pulls me close, feasting off me with moans that vibrate straight through my core. Oscar squeezes my nipples, and I buck into Brawler's mouth.

"Fuck yes. Ride his face," Johnny groans.

My toes curl. I watch Brawler devour me until I'm shaking, then I scream out my climax. I'm not even done coming down when Magnum gets to his feet. "Thank fuck." Brawler moves out of the way. The charged stare between us is replaced with Magnum's cock. Oscar scoots us back until Magnum leans between my legs on the bed. He doesn't come to me though. He shifts back, sitting with his legs bent under him. He reaches for my arms and pulls me up, wrapping my own limbs around him before spearing me with his huge dick.

This angle is everything. "Fuuuuck," I breathe, still getting used to him inside me.

"Fuck him, Princess," Oscar encourages. I gaze to my

right to find his hand wrapped firmly over his erection now, too. Brawler is on the opposite bed, fisting his cock while Johnny's still pumping his, too.

They were right. I really do like dick. Lots of dick.

Mag grips my ass, moving me up and then back down over his cock. I let out a breathy sigh before grinding over him. Just over his shoulder, Brawler's thick, corded thighs tense.

"Give it to him, babe," Johnny orders. "I want to see that ass moving up and down."

I do as he demands, riding Magnum's cock. My sighs turn to pants. Behind Mag, Brawler comes. He cups his hand around his cock as it jerks and jerks. He strangles out a cry, and the rest of them speed up their actions.

"So fucking tight," Mag says, accentuating his words on each stroke inside me.

"Make him come inside you, Princess. Make him lose it."

I work him over harder at their request. "Fuck, Jacob," I say. "You feel so good."

Mag stutters. He loves it when I call him by his real name.

"Jacob, oh fuck." The relentless deluge of cock chases away any hesitation on my part. I grip Magnum's shoulders until we're meeting each other stroke for blissful stroke.

Magnum grips my ass, holding me to him. Out of nowhere, he slams into me so hard the second before his cock jerks inside me. He rides out his orgasm with an animalistic growl until he cups my face. I palm his bearded cheek, staring intently into his hazel green hues.

"Fuck, Princess, I need some of that," Oscar pleads. He lifts up onto the bed.

I move away from Magnum and back toward Oscar, waving my ass into the air for him, letting him know exactly what I want. He grips my hips, spreads my legs, and lines us up. He pushes just the head of his dick inside. "Fuck me," he groans. "Goddamn, I'm going to explode." I push back against him, making him slide deep with one swift motion.

He doesn't waste any time. He moves his hips against me, pounding me over and over, so I have to sink my fingers into the sheets for balance. Magnum and Brawler still watch the show with their underwear on, chests heaving like they're still coming down from their own climaxes. A quick check at Johnny shows he's shaking. He's trying to hold off. He wants me.

I lift a beckoning finger until he scoots down the bed. His wound is still raw with a new bandage. I touch it as carefully as I can while still taking Oscar's cock before bending over him. I move his cock into my mouth while he strokes it inside.

Oscar shifts to accommodate the new position, but it's too much for him. Soon, he spills inside me, letting everyone else in the room know in typical Oscar fashion. "Fuck, fuck, fuck." He grips my hips, grinding against me. His excitement ignites my orgasm, making me cry out. Oscar holds me to him, making sure to finish me off. Just as I lower my lips back to Johnny's waiting cock, he jerks. For the second time today, I swallow his cum while he watches in pure satisfaction.

My body practically dissolves afterward. I lie on the bed, breathing in and out, trying to get my heart to stop jumping out of my chest. Brawler slips off the opposite bed to his knees again. He reaches out and holds my hand. Magnum comes over to run his hands through my hair, and I'm not sure I've ever felt so loved.

"Well, fuck," Johnny says. "That was even better than I imagined."

He's not wrong. He's so not fucking wrong.

26

I wake in the morning with bone-deep satisfaction. Not from the orgasms, but the fact that my entire life is spread out over the two beds in this small hotel room. The fact that Johnny entered our world yesterday in a way that I don't think he's ever going to come back from. I mean, you don't have group sex with people and then bounce, right? His participation was the ultimate form of acceptance. I know it more than anything now. Johnny Rocket Marx is all in with us. He showed each and every one of us yesterday that he's not leaving. That he's staying right here. And more than that, he showed that admitting my plan isn't going to break us. And if that can't, I'm not sure anything can.

We're all in this together.

I shift, feeling Mag's strong arms tighten around me.

They were right last night. We all needed what happened between us to happen, but that didn't mean we didn't interrupt a very important conversation about how we were going to deal with Johnny's dad...together. "Stop thinking so much," Mag says, his hot breath warms my neck.

"It's a character flaw," I whisper into the room. In front of me, Brawler is turned away on his side. His massive, muscled back feels like an impenetrable wall, but I know it isn't. Not when it comes to me.

"Won't you just let us take care of you for once?"

I turn on my side to face Mag. His copper stubble sticks out in a stark contrast to the white linens on the bed. His sleepy look is sexy as fuck. I don't ever see him in anything but rigidity. Muscles that are just shy of being able to move at a moment's notice. This part of Magnum is so nice. So welcoming. I bite my lip. "There's one problem with that," I admit.

He gives me a questioning look.

"I'm pretty used to taking care of myself."

He runs his fingers through the strands of hair that frame my face, fingering the ends. "But your aunt and uncle?" There are a hundred different questions in his eyes, and I realize we still haven't told each other everything. Not by a long shot. How can you tell someone your whole life's story in such a short span of time? Sure, surface level is there. I'm an orphan who wants to avenge my parents, but that doesn't really say jack shit about me.

I cringe. I always cringe when I think about my aunt and uncle. It's different. It's weird. "I love them," I say, starting off with the obvious. I always have. That's never changed. Which is why I've never voiced the opinions floating around in my head. Never to them. Of course, never to them. It would hurt them too much. But with these guys, maybe they would understand. Maybe it's important for them to understand this part about me so we can all move forward together.

"I sense a but," Mag says.

I don't know why, but these whispered words in a room full of the sounds of the guys—the family—I've chosen, seem so intimate. It settles me in a warm blanket that I just want to curl up in and apparently, divulge all of my repressed feelings. "I was never meant to be theirs, you know?" I say, starting out. At the same time, I'm trying to work through my own thoughts on the matter. "Don't get me wrong, they did everything they could for me. They went over and above. I'm sure I even had a better life than I was even meant to have when I went to them, but it wasn't my life. Do you know what I mean, Jacob? I'm not their daughter. I'm not their responsibility. When my parents were killed, my life was my own to make of it what I wanted. I didn't want to be anyone's burden."

"I'm sure you weren't—"

I bristle because that's what I imagined everyone's response would be. "I know I wasn't," I say. But even as I say it, I'm not being entirely truthful. I want to hear that I was never a burden but come on. I wasn't theirs. They didn't plan on having kids. Then, all of a sudden, I'm their responsibility. I'm not dumb enough to think there weren't times when they would rather it have just been them.

"I'm sorry," he says automatically. Maybe it was the terseness of my words or the way my body reacted to his last statement that clued him in, but that's what Mag does. He observes. He knows me even if I don't say anything. Even if I'm not pouring my heart out to him. "It doesn't matter that you weren't. You felt that way."

"K didn't just change my life irrevocably when he did what he did. He changed theirs, too. He changed my parents' friends' lives. He changed everyone who knew them. Hell, he changed everything." I nibble on the inside of my cheek.

"Part of you is still worried, isn't it?"

The hair on the back of my neck rises.

He keeps going, shifting his head on the pillow. "That K is going to change your life again. That you won't be able to do this, which is why you're taking everything on yourself. Kyla, we're here for you. We want to help."

I narrow my eyes at him. "You told me you wouldn't help."

"I told you I wouldn't help kill him."

He thinks he's telling me what I need to know, but to me, it's not adding up. "That's going to be hard to do because my aim is to kill him. It's not just a pie in the sky dream, Mag. I've trained for this. I've taken countless boxing and martial arts lessons. I've even had gun training."

"I've noticed," he says. "Don't think I've missed that. I think it's sexy as fuck." He blinks once. "But that's beside the point. You're not alone in this. I don't care what your goals are, we're here for you. I just want to take care of you because of everything you've just told me. Because since your parents died you haven't felt like you've belonged anywhere, and you do. You belong here, and we'll work as a team. Always."

"If we're working as a team, I want to be in on everything. I want to help with the plan. I want to execute it, and I will be the one to pull the trigger, Magnum. I'm not backing down on that, so if you're planning to stop me when the time comes, you can just forget about that right now."

He presses his lips together. He doesn't say another word, and my flesh ripples. His silence has to mean something, and I'm sure it's not that he's agreeing with me. "Angel?"

"Yeah?"

"My goal is to make sure you never have to worry about anything again. I won't apologize for it. I won't take it back either. No matter what." I shift to pull away, but he stops me, tightening his grip. "I won't stop you, but I also don't want that for you. I'm not going to apologize for thinking that either. Every one of us in this room—except for maybe

Brawler—knows what it feels like to do the things we've done." He casts a glance over his shoulder. "You might think that Oscar doesn't carry that shit around, but he does. Why do you think he's given up on football?"

My eyes widen. I hadn't thought of that.

"And the more you fix Johnny? He gets it. He finally fucking gets it. You should have seen him as soon as you left the tower yesterday. He hated every word that came out of his mouth, even if he knew it was the right thing to do. He knows there's more to life than violence now, and it suits him so fucking perfectly. *You* suit him so fucking perfectly, and I want you just the way you are right now. When we're through with this, I don't want you to become damaged. I don't want you hiding a piece of hurt somewhere in that beautiful brain of yours that might not reveal itself for several years until it's festered and decayed a part of you. None of us are any good without you unless you're...just. Like. This." He says, pressing his fingers into my hips with each word.

I rest my head against his chest. It moves with his every breath. It's so nice to be connected to people in this way. All it does is make me that much more determined to do what I came here to do because if K thinks he's going to ruin any of this for me, he's got another thing coming. And I don't want him ruining anyone else's lives either. I shudder to think about the people he's hurt, knowing they're in this same never-ending spiral that I'm in. "I want to go back to the Heights with you," I say.

Magnum stiffens. "You can't."

"I belong in the Heights," I say as calmly as I can. I knew this was going to be a fight, but my dreams were plagued by these thoughts last night. If I'm here, they'll leave me out of everything because they want to protect me. Fine. Great. I want other people in my corner, but who protects them? I wouldn't be able to live with myself if anything happened to them while I was in this fucking hotel room twiddling my thumbs.

"No," Mag says.

I blink at him, almost disbelieving that he's fighting me this much. I don't want to sound like an argumentative brat, but I'm not backing down. "I'm going back."

Magnum shudders out a breath. He shakes his head, and for the first time that I've noticed, sadness envelops him. Almost like it's a cancer taking over him from the inside out. His whole body is rotting with it. "I've learned my lesson, Kyla. I'm not trying to be a dick about this, but the last time someone stayed in the Heights for me, I never saw them again. They don't speak to me. I don't exist to her."

"Your mom?" I ask. I only know a little bit of his backstory. Just a tiny sliver of his whole life encapsulated by the house he showed me. The house he grew up in. The house his family lived in.

He nods. "I was mad at her, you know. I was so mad that

she wanted to get out of the Heights. I knew she was leaving as soon as I graduated, so I made it easy for her. I don't even think I knew that's what I was doing, but I joined the gang because I saw the slow degradation of my mother, and I wanted the same thing you want so badly. A family. A life. Of my own. No one else's. So, I get it, Kyla, and because I get it, I want you to stay as far from the Heights as possible."

I place my palm over his cheek. He's replaced some of his armor, but he's still a different guy to me in that moment, letting the shields come down so I can see him. "And that's the reason why I have to go back, so we're going to agree to disagree here, Jacob. We all have to make our own decisions. You made yours. Your mom made hers. I need to make mine."

His brows furrow. His lips purse. His eyes look as if they're saying a million different things, but he doesn't open his mouth for a long time. I have an inkling I'm only seeing a tenth of the war going on inside himself. Magnum is a strong-willed man. His quiet demeanor belays the storm always waiting underneath where death and destruction are close at hand.

"You're smart for a kid," he says finally, giving me a small, teasing smile.

I break into a grin. His humor is so out-of-place in the moment, but I'm also not naïve enough to think he's just going to agree with me like that. "I'm strong," I offer. "And I have four incredibly hot, incredibly strong, and incredibly smart men looking after me and looking after one another. We'll get through this."

Magnum's steely expression slips back into place. "No matter how prepared you think you are, you're not. Not for the amount of depravity waiting for us back in the Heights."

"Then we'll get through it together."

"I'm serious, Kyla. You haven't even seen K at his worst yet. Why do you think we're trying so hard to keep you out of it? If you're coming back to the Heights, we all have to get our shit together because one misstep can tear all of this apart."

A solid brick lands in my throat. I can't move it. I can't swallow it away or wish it away. In Mag's hazel-green eyes, I see the reality of the situation. He's not saying any of this to frighten me. He's saying it to prepare me.

I let out a breath and steel my shoulders. "I may not be ready, but I'm willing. It's happening, Magnum. K is going down."

27

*J*ohnny's livid.

It's to be expected, but damn. I'm not staying behind while they go in there and do the thing I came here for in the first place. Like, fuck. No. Just fuck no.

We keep staring daggers at each other, which is getting me hot under the collar because Johnny's dangerous look is dangerously fucking sexy. I never could withstand him.

"The problem is..." he says yet again. "I already told him you left. That we broke up."

"You can tell him you dragged my ass back to the Heights because you want me, and you don't give a flying fuck what I want."

He scoffs. He can react that way all he wants, but it's a

good plan, and he knows it. It sounds exactly like something he'd do.

"Listen, I really don't give a shit what you tell him but tell him something because I'm going back. I haven't come all this way to wuss out now. I only left because you told me to. Because you wanted me to." Honestly, that was all a mistake. He lied to get me out of harm's way, but it was his reaction that threw me for a loop. I never should've left the Heights in the first place. I was too stunned to think clearly then come to find out, it was only because he was being overprotective. "I don't care. Tell him you'll make me pay for it and be done with it. Even better, tell him you got Gregory, and he might even forget that you told him you and I had a little fight."

"So, you want me to take Gregory out?"

"Gregory is a fucking pig," I grumble. The way he treated Oscar's mother. Fuck, what he wanted to do with me. "Yes, of course, he can die."

"I'm cool with that," Oscar says, shrugging from the corner of the room with his arms crossed.

Johnny, Mag, and I are the only ones standing in the middle of the room. Brawler and Oscar bounce their stares between Johnny and me while Mag stays silent. Johnny already tried to get him on his side, but he just pressed his lips closed and shrugged. Thankfully. He knows I mean business.

Johnny moves forward. "I don't know what he'll do to you," he says, his temper cooling for the time being.

I hate to see the fear in his eyes, but my fear of letting this go overcomes any of that. Overcomes rational thought. Sensibility. Fucking everything. I want K dead, and that's that. I grab his hands, and he immediately pulls them up to brush a kiss against my knuckles. My words soften. "I know you'll think of something, Johnny. I don't care what you have to say, just get me back there. I'm willing to go through almost anything to get the end game."

"I don't trust him."

"Which is why we're doing what we're doing." I flick my gaze to the stoic Magnum. He already warned me that Big Daddy K is worse than I think he is, but I already know what the fucker is capable of. My imagination can run wild on that all night, which is another reason why I'm going back with them. I have to see it for my own eyes. I want to see the moment we get K. If I don't, I'm not sure I'll ever be calm inside again.

Magnum said he didn't want murdering someone to change me, but I'm scared of the opposite. I'm scared of the steady demise of my sanity if I don't do this. The constant fear and worry that he's out there doing what he did to my family to someone else. That we'll never be rid of him.

If we run away, let's face it. He'll come after us. He certainly isn't letting Johnny leave without a fight, and I'm not living my life constantly looking over my shoulder for the day Kingston Marx decides to get his revenge. No, fuck that.

I press up on my toes and peck his lips. "I love you. I love all of you," I say, swinging my gaze to the others in the room. I have no idea if I've said that to them all individually yet or not, but it's true, and I don't care who hears. "We're just worried about each other, but we'll make it work. We can think of what we're going to do on the way back."

Heavy silence fills the room, almost like it's another intruder. I don't want them all mad at me, but I'm not going to back down from them either. Otherwise, they'll always gang up on me. I flick my gaze to Magnum. He knows why I want this. I'm hoping he'll be on my side because of it.

Magnum sighs. "Let's think about this tactically. Her idea about getting Gregory is pretty good." His eyes light up. "Actually, we could use it to our advantage. We could tell K we used Kyla as bait. He would eat that up. We find Gregory, take him out, and then tell K we planned it that way the whole time."

"Except he's going to wonder why he wasn't involved in the plan from the beginning."

"Tell him you were worried about it getting out. He's got a decent amount of paranoia lately, so it's understandable. People have double-crossed him, so tell him you wanted it to be an inside job, so it didn't get back to Gregory. You can tell him you were always going to tell him as soon as it happened."

Oscar perks up. "I love this idea. Honestly, it's genius. Plus, Kyla will be back in his good favor if he realizes she volunteered to be the bait."

"I would have," I say. I glance around the room. "I don't know why we didn't think of this before. He wants me. We can draw him in, and then you can take him out. Once we take Gregory out, maybe K's defenses will lower and that's when we can take him."

"It won't be that easy."

"It'll be easier," I say.

Johnny glares at me. "All the attitude coming off you is just distracting me, I hope you know that." He squeezes my fingers. "It makes me want to show you something else you can do with that mouth other than sass me."

I give him a wicked grin. "Take me back to the Heights, and you'll be rewarded."

"That's it. I'm taking her back," Oscar says. He comes up behind me, picks me up by the waist, and carries me toward the door. Magnum stands in our way though, and all he has to do is cross his arms over his chest. Oscar places me on my feet with a chuckle. "Just kidding, dude. Lightening the mood a little." He tugs me back against him and kisses the curve of my neck. "I absolutely do want a piece of this though," he whispers.

I reach my hand back to cup the back of his neck. I meet Johnny's greedy eyes as he watches Oscar kiss the side of my throat. "It's just better this way," I tell him, exhaustion taking over. "Brawler and Oscar both need to be in the Heights for their moms."

"About that," Johnny starts. It seems like he's thought of more than a few problems with my plan while he was asleep. "What's your plan after this? Us leaving the Heights, right? What about them?"

Oscar's body deflates behind me. "My mom won't come," he says. "I'll deal with that when I have to."

I tug his arms back around me. I'm not sure if he's saying his mom won't want to come or if he's saying he wouldn't want his mom to come. She's not the mother he had growing up, I know that. I also know it's hard to get off drugs but leaving her here also feels like leaving her here to die.

Brawler clears his throat. "My mom's not with it, obviously, but I'd love to take her with us. Somehow..." He shakes his head and stares down at the carpet.

"She'll come with us then," I say. "We'll figure it out."

Johnny nods as a sadness creeps into his features. He's probably thinking about his own mother. The mother he went to find but ended with her demise.

"Alright," Johnny says, calling our attention to the current problem. He breathes out a sigh. "Let's do this. We'll use Kyla as bait. People seem to like to strike us around her fights, but we can't do that. That defeats the purpose of keeping Dad in the dark. He'll know if we suddenly plan a fight for her."

"We'll go out tonight," Mag says. "We'll go to the clubs

in the Heights. Those places are Gregory's hangouts. I don't know if he'll be there, but we should be able to get a trace of him. Kyla goes in alone. None of us can follow her because we're all tied to the Crew. The chances of her finding out any information while we're standing right next to her are slim."

"I don't like it," Brawler says. "We're sending her in defenseless?"

I cock my head at him. "Seriously? You, out of all of them, are asking that question? Do I need to remind you that I can take care of my damn self?"

He gives me an apologetic look. "I'm sorry. I just don't like the idea of one of us not being with you."

"We'll be with her," Johnny says. "Just not right there next to her. We have bugs and wires and all that shit back at the tower. She won't be too far away, and we'll always know where she is."

A rush of excitement pours through me. We finally have a plan. We're not at the killing K stage yet, but we're getting there. Everything is coming together just like I wanted.

I grab my car keys from the small, round table in the corner and jiggle them. "Let's get this started."

"You look entirely too happy for someone who is about to put themselves in danger," Mag says.

I shrug his comment off. I know he's being moody about all of this because he doesn't want me anywhere near the

Heights just like Johnny doesn't, but it's not their decision to make. It's always been mine.

"I'm dying to see what kind of car you drive, babe," Johnny says, rubbing his hands together.

I smirk and hold back a laugh. "Yeah? I can't wait to see the light die from your eyes when you see my very sensible, tan-colored sedan."

Johnny frowns, and the frown only deepens when we get to the hotel parking lot and I gesture toward the car my aunt and uncle gave me as a present for my sixteenth birthday. It's practically the only thing I own that's of any value. "This is your car?"

I nod.

He shakes his head. "This just won't do. You need something sexy. Red, maybe? Something with sleek lines and a whole lot of power in the engine."

"Is that supposed to be some sort of weird metaphor for my body?"

He grins. "No, I just like women who drive sexy cars. Plus, I kind of want to bend you over one. Thinking of bending you over this isn't giving me the same feelings."

I laugh. He's got a point there. Though, I'd beg him to reconsider that it wouldn't be all kinds of sexy because I'm pretty sure I would fuck Johnny Rocket in a kids' play place and be all kinds of turned on. After hours, of course. We don't need to sour the minds of today's youth.

Magnum leans against his black car. He practically

blends in with the paint job. He looks between our two cars, and I can tell he hates the idea of us being separated. "We'll be fine," I tell him. "The real threats aren't until we get back to the Heights."

"I'll ride with Princess," Oscar says, throwing his arm around my shoulder. "I'll make sure nothing happens."

The black-clad guard blows out a breath. "I'll follow you the *whole* way. Park in the same parking lot you left from," Mag says. "Then we'll ride together to Oscar's house. You'll have to get something to wear to the club tonight. Oscar, can we use your place to get Kyla all wired up?"

"You got it," Oscar says.

"Good. You'll go to the dress shop with Kyla since Johnny can't be seen with her and everyone knows I'm Johnny's guard."

"Go see Lynette again," Johnny says. "She's discreet. She fucking owes us for Glo."

"That wasn't her fault."

Johnny gives me a look that says I shouldn't argue with him, and I don't plan on it either. I'm agreeing with him. We can trust Lynette.

Oscar goes along the back of my car and stands near the passenger's seat. Surprisingly, Brawler heads to the black car, standing at the rear passenger side door. I give him a strange look, but he ignores me.

We all pile in, and I lead us out of the hotel parking lot and back to the Heights.

"That was weird," Oscar says.

"Definitely."

Oscar leans back, lacing his fingers behind his head, cozying up for the drive. "Also, I told you Johnny loved you."

He says it with a lot less bitterness than he usually does while alluding to anything Johnny Rocket. "Oh, are you trying to say you knew he'd show up?"

He grins over at me.

"Shut up," I say. "You did not."

He smiles. "Okay, maybe I didn't know exactly how it was going down, but I knew he wouldn't be able to stay away from you for long. You forget that we've all seen Johnny at his worst. He's different with you. All he needed to realize is that without you, he's a fucking headcase with a questionable background."

"We all have questionable backgrounds," I say, peeking at Oscar. Magnum alluded to Oscar's dirty past. A reason why he wouldn't go after his football goals.

"It's weird, isn't it?" Oscar asks.

"What do you mean?"

"The fact that you brought us all together," he says, voice low and even. "The only two who really knew each other all that well were Johnny and Magnum. They initiated in together, but you brought us all in close."

"What about you and Brawler?"

Oscar's face falls. "Brawler was my fight organizer. That's it."

"And you knew Johnny, too..."

"My boss?" he scoffs like I'm being ridiculous. "I didn't have anyone." He turns to look at me, his hands still laced behind his head like it's a lazy Sunday afternoon instead of the real reason why we're in the car. "It's been a long time since I had anyone I could count on."

"Well, that shit's changed," I say. "For all of us."

He nods and returns to stare at the road in front of us. "I found some tape of me playing, by the way. I'm thinking of sending it out. What's the worst that could happen?"

My mouth drops, but I reign my emotion back in. I don't want to pounce on the idea and scare him off. "I'll help," I tell him. "Whatever you need, I want to be in on it."

He reaches over to squeeze my thigh. "For the first time, I think my dream of actually getting the fuck out of the Heights could happen."

I press my lips together and suppress the emotions welling up inside. Oscar saying that means everything.

28

*J*ust like we knew she would be, Lynette was discreet as we hit up her dress shop. She gave me a huge smile when Oscar and I walked in. None of the girls who were working there the first time I met her are working there now. Not that it should be a surprise. Glo had tried to kill me and the other girl fucked Johnny in a back dressing room.

The image of him doing that only stings in the way you would think of anyone you love being with someone else. Johnny and I definitely weren't a thing then. He was too many kinds of crazy and messed up in the head. He's nothing like that now. Now, he wouldn't dare do that. He wouldn't think of doing anything like that, and that's how I know he's changed.

Which also means I can be in the store and not want to gag either.

Lynette walks me around her shop and almost exactly the opposite of how I acted the first time, I take charge of picking out the dress. I tap my finger on my lips. "I'm looking for something purple," I say, thinking of my boxing attire.

She smiles. "Makes sense."

I raise an eyebrow. "You've been to my fights?"

"Who hasn't?"

My stomach bottoms out from under me. "Tell me you weren't at the last one."

"No, thankfully," she says, giving me a tight-lipped smile. "You've been through so much while you've been here."

I nod, searching through the rack in front of me, going for all the purple fabric.

"This way," Lynette says. "I think I got the perfect one for you. I actually thought of you as soon as it came in." She whisks away to a straight rack along a wall. She pushes up onto her tiptoes and brings down a royal purple dress. Wait, shorts.

My mouth drops as she lays it over her hands so I can see the design. It's a low-cut V-neck, practically dipping to my navel, but that's not the coolest part. The coolest part is that it's literally shorts with long pieces of fabric that go to the floor, giving the illusion that it's a dress when it's really not. "I need it," I say automatically.

She grins. "I was hoping you'd like it. Come on."

She takes me back to the same dressing room I was in before. Just before we disappear around the corner, I glance over my shoulder. Oscar's staying outside, casually walking back and forth down the block. He made sure I was alone in here before I started looking but wanted to keep his distance without leaving me by myself, too.

I take the outfit from Lynette and pull the curtain closed. I shuck off the joggers and shirt I've been living in lately and pull on the beautiful outfit. The long sleeves give it a business sexy look, but I'm not going to lie, I'm fucking in love with it.

I stare at my nipples. Or, at least, the imprint of my nipples in the mirror. "Little problem, Lynette," I say. "I need something for the girls."

"Ah, of course. Be right back." She leaves while I turn to stare at my ass in the mirror. The extra fabric hides the curve of my figure while showing off just enough too. The drapes of royal purple in the front give it the illusion of a dress when I really am wearing pants that I can move around in and not have to worry I'm showing off my privates to anyone. "Here," Lynette says. The curtains part, and she hands me a box.

I take it from her and glance at it. They're bra cups, kind of. Clear, almost flower petal in shape.

Lynette tells me exactly how to put them on while I use the mirror for help. When they're in place, I shift this way and that, making sure no one can tell what I'm wearing underneath. Honestly, these things are fucking amazing.

I whip the curtain open and Lynette's jaw hits the floor. She squeals. "Yassss. I knew you would look amazing in that. You just have to get it."

"Oh, I'm getting it," I say. "I actually need it for tonight, so I'll wear it out of here if that's okay?"

She nods. "Of course. I'll put your other clothes in a bag for you." She brushes past me to pick up my discarded clothes, almost sneering at my lack of fashion taste, I'm sure.

We head to the front of the shop where she bags my clothes and then rings me up. "On Johnny's credit?"

I shake my head and pull the bag of clothes over to me. Johnny took some cash out for me and slipped it into my hand when we got to the parking lot. "I'm paying cash today," I tell her, not trying to give anything away. I don't want to tell her I'm not Johnny's, but I also don't want her to know I'm still with him either. Not if we want everyone to believe this plot we've come up with.

The change gives me a decent amount left over for tonight. I don't know how long I'll have to stay at the club before Gregory makes contact. Or should I say hopefully makes contact? This is all kind of contingent on Gregory still wanting me to enact his revenge on the Crew. I might just be being optimistic, but I think it's going to work perfectly.

I say goodbye to Lynette and head outside. Oscar nearly has a heart attack when he sees me. "Fucking Christ," he says. His lips part, and I wish I could take a picture of his lust-induced stare right now. "We should've kept your car because the only thing I want to do is get you in the backseat."

I walk up to him, recovering from the heels Lynette slipped in at the last minute after she reminded me I couldn't wear sneakers with the outfit I was buying. "Don't lose focus, Drego."

"You tell yourself that when you're looking like heaven." He finally tracks his gaze to my face. "They're all going to lose their minds." He glances around the streets. There's only one guy a few doors down, lips dragging on a cigarette, but he's completely oblivious to us.

Thankfully, Lynette's shop is only a few blocks from Oscar's apartment, so we head back there. There aren't as many people on the streets as there usually are, and I wonder if it has anything to do with The Ring being taken out not too long ago. It's possible everyone is lying low. If they were smart, they'd be doing just that.

Oscar opens up the door to his apartment, and I climb the stairs in heels. When I get to the top, I fling the shoes off, and I accidentally kick them right at someone. When I glance up to see who it is, I gasp. "Finn? What the fuck?"

He stands from the couch where the rest of my guys are and heads toward me. "Fucking hell, girl." He encloses his arms around me, and I breathe into his shoulder. It's so nice to see him. Them, actually. Jax is right behind him, but he's not giving me a smile like Finn is. "I was so worried about you." He backs away, keeping me at arm's length. "Now I see you looking like this?"

"Watch it," Johnny warns.

Finn ignores him, giving me a saucy wink.

"What the hell are you guys doing here?" I gaze at the two of them and immediately notice something is off. Well, maybe not off exactly. It's just that I'm used to seeing Jax and Finn in workout clothes, but tonight, they're dressed in more casual wear. Nice jeans and tight shirts that show off their muscles.

"We hear you're in need of our services," Finn says, giving me a mock bow.

I glance in the living room where Oscar's now joined the rest of my guys. "What's going on?"

Brawler stands. "I didn't want you going in there completely alone, so I talked Johnny and Mag into seeing if we could get Jax and Finn to help."

That's why he rode in their car back to the Heights.

I groan, not loving the idea of Jax and Finn being involved in any of this. Jax is going to have a fucking coronary. That's all I know.

"Before you say anything, don't worry about it,

Princess," Finn says.

Oscar rolls his eyes, but the fact that they're jealous of my trainers at all is hilarious to me.

"We want to help. Well, one of us wants to help. The other just wants to make sure I'm not getting myself into anything."

"Oh, so you're talking for me now?"

"You know you don't want to fucking be here," Finn throws back at his brother.

Jax's jaw tenses. "That's not exactly what's happening," he says carefully.

"You don't have to explain anything to me," I tell him. I absolutely fucking get it. No one wants to get mixed up in Crew business. Least of all them. They shouldn't either.

Damn. I'm really going to miss these guys when we leave the Heights. I'll have to find new trainers, and fuck, I'll just miss them.

"You don't need to look so hurt," Jax snaps. "It's not personal."

"Obviously," I bite back, shaking my thoughts off. We can't let Jax and Finn in on what we're doing, otherwise, they'll be in too deep. I wouldn't be able to live with myself if something happened to one of them. "I'm glad you guys are here. I missed you, too, but you really don't have to come if you don't want to. You both know I can take care of myself, which I thought is what I explained to Brawler."

"They're just a contingency plan," Johnny says, sticking

up for Brawler. "It's a good idea. They're not going in there with you either, but they're going to keep an eye on you from the inside, which we won't be able to do."

I don't want to admit it, but it actually is a good idea. But it's not if it's at the expense of one of them. I turn to Jax and Finn. "Be careful."

They both give me dubious looks. Look, I know they can defend themselves, but— And now I know exactly why Brawler said the same thing to me. Fuck. I turn toward him and give him a small smile, letting him know I'm not mad. Having backup is always a good idea, especially when you're in the Heights.

"Okay, Princess," Oscar says, giving Finn a death glare. I guess someone is over Finn using his nickname for me. "My mom has a bunch of makeup in the bathroom. I don't know if you want to use any of it to do whatever girls do when they get ready for the club but it's there."

"Are you saying I need makeup, Drego?"

His mouth falls, and his eyes widen. "No."

Johnny snickers in the background. Oscar turns to flip him off, and I chuckle to myself all the way to the bathroom. I'm not sure what I can use of hers because the thought of using someone else's makeup grosses me out. Once I gaze into the mirror, I see Oscar's point. My bruising is fading, but it's still apparent. Unfortunately, Cynthia Drego and I do not have the same skin color, so using her foundation is out of the question. I use my fingers to apply a little blush and some eye shadow. Mascara would be nice, but I'm not using a used one, that's for sure.

I do, however, find a shade of lipstick that hasn't been open yet and use that, smacking my lips together to distribute the color. I shrug in the mirror. It'll have to do. Everyone in the Heights knows I was in a fight less than a week ago and it's not like I'm trying to pick anyone up at the club either. I just have to look the part, and I just have to be available for Gregory or one of his goons to swoop in and try to get me.

I walk out and place my hands on my hips. The guys all swing their gazes over, but the only ones I care about are the four of mine. They all look me over appreciatively, and I decide I can get used to being looked at like this every day for the rest of my life.

Magnum stands, beckoning me forward. "I guess I should have told you to get a dress with a little more fabric to it," he says as he looks me over, trying to decide how they're going to rig me up with a listening device.

I frown. I hadn't thought of that. I actually just kind of lost my mind when I saw this outfit and had to have it.

He finishes attaching the tech to me, explaining that one is a bug so they can listen in to what I'm saying and that the other is a GPS in case they try to take me to another location before the rest of them can intervene.

My stomach twists a little, but I steel my shoulders. Gregory's a piece of shit. He's already tried to take me and kill me. Plus, what he's done to the poor women like Oscar's mom. He can drown in his own blood for all I care. The Heights will be better off without him, too.

Ha. It sounds like I'm some sort of vigilante. I'm not, I promise. This is just a means to the end I've always wanted.

We test the equipment to make sure it works. Then, Oscar once again hands me a new phone. I smile down at it. "Do you just have a stash of these somewhere now?"

"I figure it's a safe bet if we always have backups." He swipes at the screen and points out the ride share app. "Use this to get there. We're right here with you."

"Jax and I are going to do the same, so we won't be far behind you either."

Magnum stands tall and goes over the plan one more time, so we all know our parts to play. If I get desperate, I can start asking for Gregory, but they're hoping it won't take long at all. They've tried to get me when I was surrounded by the Crew, so they're hoping showing up by myself will seem like a gift that they won't think twice about.

I take a deep breath and put the heels back on. I wish they were boots, but Lynette seems to have something against sensible clothing.

Jax and Finn watch as the guys all come up to me to say their goodbyes. They don't outright ask, but it doesn't take a fucking rocket scientist to figure out that I'm with them all, and I wouldn't have it any other way.

Let's do this.

Despite the fact that I'm wearing this rocking outfit, my stomach churns as I'm let inside the club. The bouncer at the front door nods at me, giving me a show of respect before letting me through. Perhaps it's because of what the guys are always saying, I do have a reputation in the Heights.

Much to my surprise, the moment I walk through the crowd, other club goers stare, nudging their friends as I make my way through. This is the first time I've been on my own since I came to the Heights, and I'm not too proud to admit I'm a little lost. Literally, ever since the night when Johnny claimed me after the fight with Cherry, I haven't been alone since. I've been the Crew's property. Johnny's property. I don't much care for the word property, but I'm not going to lie and say I'm mad about always having someone around.

Without anyone nearby, it feels as if my right arm is gone. I can't just turn and see one of my guys lingering somewhere close.

As I move further in, I search for a spot to sit. It doesn't take me long, mainly because a guy with a suit comes up to me. "Uppercut Princess..." He gazes around, his face falling a little when he most likely sees I'm without Johnny Rocket. Knowing how the Heights works, it wasn't just me that was bringing a lot of business into Dunnegan/Gregory's strip joint, it was Johnny and the rest of the guys. Everyone wants to hang out where they're hanging out. I was just an added bonus. "Can I help you find a seat?"

"I'd love that, thank you."

He gestures toward an open path, his hand hovering over my back without actually touching me. Smart move on his part, considering how domineering Johnny got when Finn wrapped me up in a hug. My escort nods toward a table in the front. "Is this acceptable?" We stop in front of it, and he moves a rope out of the way to allow me to sit in one of the chairs. "Or are you having a bigger party?"

"This will be fine," I assure him. "Thank you."

He nods. "I'll get a waitress to come right over."

I smile at him and settle back. If I were here with the guys, Oscar would probably be dragging me out onto the dance floor. Johnny would be sitting back drinking an expensive cognac or something like that. Magnum would just be watching over everything, and Brawler...well, I don't know. He doesn't seem like the dancing type, but I could be way off base. Actually, he doesn't seem like a club guy at all.

A waitress wearing a skimpy outfit makes her way over to me. She brings me a tray of pre-made drinks, angling so I can see them all while she tells me what's in each one. I pick out a few because why the hell not and sit back. Out of the corner of my eye, Jax and Finn move into view. They stay at the edge of the dance floor, and it literally takes all of two seconds before they each have a girl dancing on them.

Shockingly, Jax is a phenomenal dancer. My mouth almost unhinges, even though I shouldn't be all that surprised. They're fighters, which means they're light on their feet. Plus, they have game, so duh. The girls play right into their cover for the night, and they definitely don't let dancing stop them from keeping an eye on me.

I stay in my seat and sip on my drink. The longer this draws out, the more out of place I feel. I'm just sitting here, drinking, watching people look at me. I act cool about it though, kicking back, pretending I'm having a good time by nodding my head to the house music with the hard bass.

Before long, Jax approaches the table. He's handsome in his clubbing outfit, and judging by the looks he's getting from females surrounding us, I'm not the only person who thinks so. He has that hint of danger, too, with the tattoos on his knuckles. He holds his hand out, and I stare at it. "Come on, Princess," he says. "You don't want to waste that dress, do you?"

Hesitantly, I put my hand in his. When I gaze to where they were dancing, Finn is gone. I look up at Jax curiously, but he only has the usual frown on his face that he wears around me. He edges his hand around my back and pulls me close enough, yet far enough away that one of the guys isn't going to chop his dick off for touching me. Smart move, honestly. I move my face toward his ear. "You don't want to get involved in this, Jax. Trust me."

"I'm already involved," he says. "Finn doesn't know when to say no, and I go where Finn goes. Plus, I couldn't stand to see you just sitting there all by yourself the whole night. It looks strange, and if you're going for casual, this is casual. You better call off your boyfriends when they realize we danced though. I really don't want to have to fight four dudes at once."

I smirk. Jax is badass. Strong with a ton of power, but my money would be on my guys. Strength in numbers.

Not that it would ever get to that.

"I don't want either of you involved," I say instead. We're basically just standing in a sea of people now. The writhing bodies next to us make us sway together, but that's it.

He completely ignores me. "I've been meaning to tell you I don't think it's a good idea that you fight anymore." My lips purse, but he just chuckles. "Every time you fight, something terrible happens. You got in an accident and accused of murder." He looks at me pointedly. "Then, the venue you're fighting at gets shot up and bombed. I think that's some terrible luck."

"The Heights is terrible luck," I grumble.

"Don't I know it," he breathes.

Jax slices a guy a look who starts dancing behind me. The dude doesn't stick around. Hell, neither would I, not with that glare. I meet Jax's gaze when he looks back at me. I sigh. "I wonder how long I have to stay here."

"They didn't tell us much. Which is fine by me," he tacks on. "The less we know the better."

A-fucking-men. "So, where did you make Finn go?"

Jax smirks. "Why do you think I made him go somewhere?"

I drop my head to the side. "Seriously? He was right here, and now he's not. I'm guessing since you decided to rescue me from my lonely, pity party of one, you didn't want him anywhere near here...which...is actually really cool of you."

Jax's face turns sour. "If only Finn got that I'm trying to help."

"He's a good guy," I say. "You both are." The song changes after another minute, and Jax and I step away from one another. "Thanks for the dance."

"I'll be around," he says. "If you decide you're going to leave, just give me a signal or something, and I'll be out right behind you."

I give him a nod and slip back to my table. Except, when

I get there, another body is sitting casually across from the seat I was occupying. I try not to start when I realize it's Cole. I don't think any of us thought he'd be out at the club tonight. "Hey," I say, strutting back in my too high heels to sit across from him.

"Out by yourself?"

I shrug noncommittally. "Something like that."

He leans in, gaze flickering with danger underneath. Maybe it's the low lighting in here and the fact that I can see his dragon tattoo sticking out of his shirt. "Does my cousin know? Seems like something he wouldn't want you doing."

"Can't a girl have a night off?" I say, edging the drinks that I'd been drinking to the end of the table. No way will I be drinking from them again. I've heard too many horror stories about roofies slipped into drinks.

"Who was the guy you were dancing with?"

My stomach tightens. He's asking way too many questions. "A friend."

Cole leans back in his chair and side-eyes me. "You better not be breaking my cousin's heart."

I look away before my face reveals anything. "So, how many of your guys are in here right now?" We're in a neutral club, one we picked out because we didn't want to go into a Crew-owned club because we figured that would be a place less likely to be frequented by Gregory or anyone else.

"A fair few."

"Is that what your guys do when they're not blowing up buildings?"

Cole's lips press together. "It's a dog eat dog world."

I never understood the history behind that expression, but I get the meaning of it all too well. That's all the Heights is. A food chain. You definitely don't want to be on the bottom rung of their chain. I lean over the table. "Is the only reason why you're here because you're worried about what I'm doing? If it is, trust me, I'm good. Also, trust that you know your cousin well enough to understand what he's about," I say cryptically. Jesus. If he asks any more fucking questions, he'll get even more suspicious. Plus, he can't be around. Not when I'm trying to lure another gang asshole in. I stand. This whole thing has been a bust. We'll just have to figure out another way to draw Gregory out. The whole gang system needs to die a slow, painful death. "I'll see you around, Cole."

I get up to leave, but Cole stays right with me. He grips my arm and starts walking me through the crowd.

I growl. "Seriously. I've got this."

"Shh," he murmurs in my ear. "Just go with it."

"You need to let go of me, Cole." When he doesn't let go, frustration builds inside me. I slam the heel of my shoe down on his toes and elbow him in the gut. I don't care who he's related to, he doesn't get to manhandle me like that. Behind us, I catch Jax's eye while he trails us. I motion toward the front door and start out.

At that moment, the fire alarm buzzes above us. The house music cuts out and the blaring, wretched sound fills the room. Groans from surrounding mouths edge out, and some people who are too drunk to understand what's going on put their hands over their ears but continue to dance anyway.

I brush past them, joining in with the people who are making their way outside. I'm soon separated from Cole and Jax, just going with the general shove of the crowd. The flow of the people I'm following breaks off toward a side exit door where a red neon light announces we can get out that way. All around me, people are lamenting the fact that their night has ended. I would be too if I was out here for fun. I'm a little more than annoyed that nothing fucking happened. I thought we had such a solid plan in place, too.

A girl accidentally stumbles into me. I have to pick up the extra fabric of my outfit, so I don't get scuff marks on it and someone uses the opportunity to thread their arm through mine. "I'm good," I say, thinking someone just grabbed on to me when the girl accidentally nudged me, but the hold on me tightens. My hackles raise, and a solid object gets shoved into my hip. "Keep struggling and you'll get a matching bullet hole right where your boyfriend's is."

Fear sends an ice-cold chill through my body, but then I remember that this is what we wanted. I came here for this exact reason. I clear my throat, speaking a little louder to make sure my guys can hear on the other end. It'll be hard for them to hear anything over the blare of the alarm, but hopefully Jax has eyes on me too. Then again, right now, it just looks like I'm walking next to this asshole. "Threats don't usually work on me."

"I'm unimpressed," the guy says. Cold air blasts us as we make it outside. He tugs on my arm, and as the crowd starts to disperse down the alleyway in different directions, leaving us out in the open, it's clear he has a hold of me now if Jax is watching. I can only hope he's on the phone with the guys telling them what's going on.

"Good thing I don't look to thugs for validation."

The guy huffs a laugh. "You made a big mistake today, girlie."

Girlie? Seriously?

He pulls me around the corner, and then we both come to an abrupt stop. Magnum and Johnny are there. Magnum has the driver of a silver car at gunpoint while Johnny's gun is aimed right at the guy who has me.

I snicker. "Yep. Big mistake."

30

The guy presses the barrel of the gun into my side again, making sure Johnny and Magnum are aware he has his own weapon and it's aimed at me right now.

Johnny doesn't even flinch. He pulls the trigger, and all of a sudden, the guy is no longer standing next to me. I blink a few times while my ears ring. I peek at the ground and find him sprawled out, blood leaking from a hole in his head.

Johnny jogs toward us. He spits on the guy as he makes his way to me. "Pull a gun on my girl, you piece of shit."

I just stare in awe. Well, shock and awe. I'm perfectly aware of what Johnny is capable of but Jesus fuck. I was right there.

"Call the cleanup crew," Magnum calls out.

Johnny pulls me into his side. He holsters his gun and then retrieves his cell phone one-handed. I keep eyeing him as he makes his phone call, giving whoever is on the other side of the call directions as to where we are—where the clean-up needs to take place. They might not have bothered if he hadn't spit on the body. If the wrong people—like the cops—found out what Johnny just did, we'd be fucked.

"You okay?" Johnny finally asks.

All I can do is nod because I haven't found my voice yet. I'm not upset about what happened. I think it just hit a little too close to home. We are in an alleyway after all.

Magnum drags the other guy out of the car. He hauls him to his feet and then pushes him to his knees in front of the bloody dead body of his friend. "If you don't want the same thing to happen to you, I suggest you tell us where the fuck Gregory is hanging out."

The guy shivers. "You know I can't tell you. I'm dead if I fucking tell you, man."

"You're fucking dead anyway," Johnny crows. "Coming after my girl. If Gregory wants retaliation on the Crew or my dad, he can leave Kyla right the fuck out of it."

The guy holds his hands up. "I'm just a peon. Fuck. I don't know. I was told to drive this car, wait for that guy who was going to come out with a girl, and then drive them back."

"Drive them back where?" Mag urges, thrusting the

barrel of the gun to the guy's temple. "If you tell us, we'll think about letting you live."

"I don't know anything!" the guy pleads. "Really."

"All you have to know is where to find Gregory."

"Fuck," the guy screams. He's shaky and white, like he's coming down off a high. I don't think it's that at all. It's the fucking adrenaline tearing up his insides. The sad reality is, he doesn't have a choice in the matter. Well, he does, but none of the choices are good.

"If I were you," I say, my voice shaky. "I'd pick the one where you might end up alive. And then if you do live, I'd leave the Heights for good. Don't turn back. Don't wait. Just leave because nothing good can come from being here."

The guy locks gazes with me, and the fear in his eyes is so overpoweringly strong that my stomach tightens. I can't save everyone in the Heights. Also, some of these fuckers don't deserve to be saved. This guy is pleading now, but what shit has he done? What did he think was going to happen when they told him to drive a getaway car for a dude that was going into a club to get a girl? That doesn't sound like any kind of shit I would want to be mixed up in.

"Talk. Now."

The guy clenches his jaw, breathing in and out deep like a feral animal. "He's at the old saw mill just outside of town."

"How many guys?"

"Shit, I don't know."

"Think goddammit," Mag yells. He pushes the barrel of the gun to his forehead, and I try not to cringe. It might get messy here really quick, but I'm the one who wanted to come back. I can't make the guys regret it.

The guy cowers. "I think there were ten when we left, but I don't fucking know. I didn't count."

Mag sweeps his gaze to Johnny and me. He nods at us then motions behind him. "Johnny, get her in the car. I'll take care of this."

I avoid any more eye contact with the guy. I don't think they'll let him live, but those might have been the old rules. These are the new rules. I just don't know what they are.

Just as I'm thinking that, a gunshot rings out. I wobble on my feet but keep my chin in the air.

We can't have him telling Gregory we know where to find him. If he gets a heads up, he'll slip out of our grasp again and our plan won't work. Getting to K was always going to get messy. I close my eyes and breathe out. When this is all over, I won't have to do any of this again.

Self-preservation. It's the Heights' motto.

"Did you see Jax make it out?"

Johnny shakes his head. "No, but I hear you had a wonderful dance."

I roll my eyes at him. What a time to be jealous. In a minute, we're about to head out of town to take someone out and he wants to talk about how I danced with another guy. "It was nothing, and you know it."

"Don't care," he says. "I can't stand the thought of other people's hands on you."

I glance over at him with a teasing smile. "You didn't seem to have a problem last night."

"That's different," he bites out.

I'm sick, but a thrill runs through me. He's accepted this. All of this.

Johnny pulls the door to the backseat open, and I brush a kiss across his cheek as I get in. "Jax was just trying to help, babe. He thought it looked suspicious that I was just sitting there."

"Next time, he can leave the thinking to me."

Johnny hauls himself inside, forcing me to slide over in the seat. Somehow, Magnum's already in the driver's seat, waiting for us. "Where are Brawler and Oscar?"

"Just waiting to hear from us," Mag says. He meets Johnny's gaze in the rearview mirror, and Johnny takes his phone out for the second time tonight and dials a number. "We got her. Safe." He pauses for a few moments. "Yes, meet you at the location?"

Mag pulls away from the curb. Through the heavily tinted windows, I notice two men dressed in black approach the area where the dead bodies lie. I tell myself not to look, so I just watch as they bend over to retrieve them and then I immediately meet Johnny's gaze. He's smiling at me. "You did so good tonight."

I shrug. "I didn't think anyone was going to come."

"They were slick with the fire alarm. I'll give them that. Good thing we had guys posted at each of the exits, but when we saw those two dumb fucks loitering around, we knew they had to be Gregory's men. We tried to get the asshole before he even went into the club, but they parked, and he made a straight shot for the side door."

"I wonder how they knew I was in the club..."

"My dad has more enemies than he believes," Johnny says, running his hands down his suit pants. "Over confidence has always been his weak point."

That's the understatement of the goddamn century. I'm right under his fucking nose, and there has to be more like me. "Things like this have happened in the past. Fights over territory. Business. Roza Fonz," I say, letting the two words slip out like a dead weight. That was my second clue as to what I was getting myself into. The first was knowing my parents were murdered in cold blood.

"The threats are constant," Johnny agrees, worrying over his lip. "But usually people aren't so bold about it. They've made it clear at this point that they want a war. My dad can't just stand by. That's where I come in with killing Gregory. If I take him out, it sends a message to everyone else that we're still a force to be reckoned with. If I don't kill Gregory, then they all start to feel like they can do whatever they want. The restlessness is already there. I can feel it. People are wondering which way it's going to go."

Magnum turns down another street and stops. Brawler gets in the front seat and Oscar comes around to the back, slipping across the seat to sit next to me. "Thank God you're okay."

I give him a small smile. "Did anyone check on Jax and Finn?"

"They're good," Brawler says over his shoulder. "They just texted me. I told them to go home and to pretend like this night never happened."

I blow out a breath of relief. Thank goodness they're okay. "Oh..." I start, almost forgetting that I saw someone else in there. "Cole."

"Cole?" Mag asks, meeting my stare in the rearview mirror.

"He was there. He tried to get me out, acting like I shouldn't have been in the club on my own."

"Well, you shouldn't have been," Mag states simply.

"I got rid of him." I cringe a little, hoping Mag doesn't get mad that I took his cousin down.

He meets my gaze. "What does that mean?"

"I may have broken his toe, I'm not sure." I wiggle my heel into the floor of the car. I'm pretty sure these suckers could do just that.

Magnum returns his attention out the front windshield. "I'll make sure he's fine after we get this shit done."

"So, what's the plan?" I ask, darting my gaze around to the car full of guys.

"The act of surprise," Mag answers. "He's expecting you to be there, but he won't be expecting you to be accompanied by the rest of us."

"Just whatever happens, make sure I get Gregory," Johnny says matter-of-factly.

"Whoever gets the shot should take it," Oscar says. I bet he gives less than zero fucks about giving Johnny the shot. He's got beef with Gregory, too. Fucking his mother just so he can keep her fucked up on drugs. It's just disgusting.

"Fine," Johnny says, relenting. I lift a brow at him, and he frowns. "What?"

"You just seem so accommodating."

"I'm trying to remember that I don't have to do everything on my own. Scratch that. I'm trying to remember that *Magnum* and I don't have to do everything anymore. Plus, I'm eager to just get this job done."

I can see it now. The troubled look on his face and the way his leg jumps up and down. Johnny's nervous. I press my hand on his thigh, swirling circles into the material there to try to soothe him. I'm not sure what's going through his head. Maybe it's just the layer of unease over the whole night. I'd be freaking out if we used one of them as bait, but since it worked out really well, I'm not sure what's still bothering him, other than worry over the upcoming issue at the mill.

Several long minutes later, Mag creeps up the road where the old mill is. Oscar whispers its location to me because it's hard to see in the faint light of the moon. Soon, though, the outline of the structure comes into view. A few cars line the road and a short, gravel driveway. A bunch of farm land off to the right of the structure stretches out with overgrown grass and weeds, which makes me wonder what this place used to look like in its heyday. Right now, it looks like a dump. Hardly a respectable hangout for a guy who's trying to take over the Crew.

"Do you think he fucked us?" I ask. If he did, Johnny's going to want to revive him just to put a bullet in his head again.

Magnum points to a circle of light glowing at the side of the structure. "I don't think so. They're back there."

I strain to see what he's talking about and finally catch the tiny circle of light he's pointing out. If I wasn't looking for it, I'd miss it. I guess maybe they are being kind of smart by using the back instead of lighting up the front.

Mag keeps driving down the road until he pulls off onto a dirt side street that's not really a street at all. It's just a section off the side of the road where a Private Property sign dangles between two posts, stopping us from going any further. We don't need to though. We're just enough out of the way so that the darkness swallows us.

Magnum loads his gun, and the rest of the guys do the

same. Well, all except Brawler. He stares at his large hands, smirking. "I think I'm good."

I can't help but chuckle because yeah, he definitely knows how to use those.

Magnum turns in his seat. "I want Brawler and Kyla to take up the rear. Johnny, Bat, and I have the firepower."

I give him a look.

"Listen, I'd rather you stay in the car, but since you won't do that, just do this for me, okay? Stay behind us. It'll be just as easy as it was when we went to get J. They have no idea we're coming."

I give him a nod. My hackles rise at not being included in the main arsenal, but the way Magnum's planned it makes logical sense. "I'm still going to need that gun I asked you for before," I say to Mag. It seems like forever ago, but I told him I needed a gun once the cops had mine.

"I'll get you a gun. I promise."

With that, we all push our car doors open and get out of the vehicle. We stay in the shadows as we work our way around to the back side of the mill. Gearing up for coming face-to-face with Gregory worries me. Both Magnum and Johnny have been shot recently, and although they seem to be recovering well, I still can't help but be concerned that if things get really bad, they may not be able to fight back. I have the urge to call this off, but at the same time, it's now or never. If we can just get through this step, then the next, then the next, everything will be fine.

I push all those thoughts aside and move forward. We keep to the structure itself in case they have cameras, but unless he's been here for a while, I doubt he's had time to put that much tech in. Gregory seemed to be fine biding his time to take over the Crew. It wasn't until K killed Dunnegan that he decided to make his move. It might just be me, but I don't think they're organized. They had to call in the Dragons for help with The Ring.

We make it all the way to the back of the building, Brawler and I taking up the rear, when a guy comes around the corner. Magnum immediately raises his gun and shoots him. The poor guy never even saw what was coming.

As soon as he hits the ground, all hell breaks loose.

Our cover is blown. Brawler grabs my hand and pulls me close. Magnum and Johnny forge ahead with Oscar hot on their heels.

More gunshots ring out. Brawler and I come around the corner and are immediately blindsided by a running body. The force of his tackle sends me to the floor, and I skid across the cracked concrete. My skin tears, and my beautiful new outfit rips. The guy immediately covers me with his body weight. He rears back and punches me in the side of the face. Pain whips through me, which only pisses me off. I roar, then kick out and struggle against his hands until his weight lifts from me in an instant.

I blink. Brawler's dragged the dude off me. He punches him several times with his big, meaty fists until the fucker loses consciousness. He gives him a small push, and he slumps to the floor.

The rest of the guys are already inside, so we cautiously make our way through a barn door to find Johnny aiming a gun at Gregory...

...and Gregory holding up Oscar's doped up mom as a shield.

31

All of my thoughts skid to a grinding halt. Oscar freezes just behind Johnny and Magnum, who have Gregory cornered with Oscar's mom. She's not even aware of what's happening. Her eyes are slits, and her head drops from one side to the other. She can't even hold herself upright let alone realize she's being held hostage right now. Not that I needed the reminder, but I will never ever fucking do drugs. Just fucking no.

Magnum's gaze darts around the room. As usual, he's searching out the next threat. Brawler takes off—probably to make sure Gregory is the only one left—while I walk toward Oscar. He stiffens as I near him. "It's me," I whisper, afraid to talk louder for fear of upsetting the delicate balance everyone is in.

Gregory tugs on Oscar's mom, holding her closer. He

forces the barrel of the gun into the side of her forehead while keeping his own body shielded, so Johnny can't fucking just shoot him like he did to the guy earlier.

"I was wondering when I'd be seeing you, Rocket," Gregory calls out with a sniveling sneer. "It took you long enough."

Johnny gives him one of his threatening smiles. "I wouldn't have had to find you if you weren't hiding like a fucking pussy."

"Who's hiding?" he bites back. "It was me who got you at The Ring. You figured that out, right? My guys had you."

Johnny laughs, and it's dark and dangerous. I sneak a glance over to him, hoping he doesn't fall into old patterns. "You didn't get me. Your guys did. You've been hanging out here, I guess. Or the race track. Letting your guys—or should I say *our* guys—do all the work."

"Yet, I still managed to get you."

Johnny shrugs like he doesn't care to comment. He's standing up straight, trying not to show he's still bothered by the fact that he got shot a few days ago. "I guess whoever has the last word wins."

"I'll kill her," Gregory roars.

Oscar's mom blinks, shooting Gregory a look over her shoulder as if he's ruined her midday nap. She sure looks worse for wear.

"Go ahead," Johnny says. "Like I give a shit about some whore."

Oscar makes no reaction whatsoever, and I pray Johnny knows it's Oscar's mom he's holding. Magnum does. I can see his eyes desperately trying to put a plan together that saves her and kills the asshole holding her.

Brawler reappears from the back room, striding across the rotting boards at our feet calmly. It's just Gregory left now. He must know he's fucked. It's five against one. Though, I admit, the hostage throws things in his favor. He'll be desperate now though, and desperation is never good.

"Aww, just like your father. No appreciation for human life. Just those of the Crew. You know that's why I was able to get so many of your guys to hear me out, right? The Crew used to be something good. Something people would fight for, but K hasn't given a shit about his grunts for a long time."

"And you've talked them into believing you do?" Johnny asks with a smirk.

"What can I say? I've been quite forthcoming with my plan for the Crew's future. All I've had to do is point out certain things you and your dad are doing, and they practically beg me to take them away."

"Too bad you chose your guys poorly. We've been able to steamroll right through all of them."

"They're in need of training, sure, but shouldn't the Crew have done that already? Mayhem used to say the Crew was only as strong as the weakest link. In your father's haste to grow his group, he accepted a shitton of guys who aren't good for anything. They're the weak links, Rocket. They were all too easily talked into joining my side." Oscar's mom starts to slip, so he hauls her up his body again.

The movement jars her awake, and she blinks. "Gre—"

"Shut the fuck up," he grinds out. The more alert she becomes, the more difficult it is for him to hold the gun to her and use her as a shield.

"But you said—"

He digs his nails into her upper arm to hold her steady, and she sucks in a breath. Looking at her now, that's not the first time he, or someone else, has done that to her. She's marked up all over the place, and they're not just needle markings either. She's bruised and frail. She looks far worse than when I saw her at Candy's before.

"Let her go," Magnum demands. He steps forward, ready to put an end to this shit.

Gregory makes a clicking sound and steps back. "The infamous Magnum. Your reputation precedes you."

Oscar's mom giggles, a phony sound that dies on her lips as soon as Gregory sinks his nails into her again.

"Fuck this," Oscar growls. He darts forward, slipping from my grasp. Gregory turns, swinging the gun toward him. The movement jostles Oscar's mom awake, and for a moment, recognition slams into her.

"Wait!" Gregory yells, eyes wide.

A shot fires, and my heart catapults into my throat. For a

moment, Oscar's mom and I are mirrors of each other. Horror stretches across our faces. Disbelief. Fear. Love. The split second of gunfire freezes me in place. I stand there, unable to breathe until the scene ahead of me comes into sharp focus.

Oscar's still moving, running forward. Gregory and his mom drop in a heap to the cement floor. I start after them, praying Oscar didn't just see his mom get murdered right in front of him. He leans over the tangle of limbs and pulls her away just as a fresh coat of crimson stains Gregory's shirt.

I let out a sigh of relief, closing my eyes for a brief moment of reprieve from all the craziness. My guys are okay. Oscar's mom is okay. And Gregory is dead. Finally.

Magnum bends to one knee in front of Oscar and his mom. "Is she good?"

Now that I'm this close, splatters of blood coat her hair. Magnum's a damn good shot. Oscar gave him the perfect distraction he needed. Just one opening.

Johnny stands in front of Gregory, taking pictures with his cell phone. He's no doubt going to send them to his father as proof.

As inhuman as it sounds, the calm serenity I feel at Gregory being dead could almost bring a smile to my face. He deserved what he got. Not because he was going against the Crew, but because he was just like them. Using women as trade. Using innocent people to make others suffer. He wasn't going to overhaul the Crew to make it better. It would've ended the same, and anyone who tried to follow him for promises of a better future was just delusional. Well, now they're mostly dead, but they were delusional.

I switch places with Magnum and kneel beside Oscar. His mother shakes uncontrollably on the floor. Her red-rimmed eyes search for her son as she clings to him like tomorrow isn't promised. It's not. Not for anyone.

I take a seat right next to him, and he unceremoniously drops his head to my shoulder. He's stiff at first, but then his muscles relax until his breathing becomes shaky and uneven. My Oscar is close to crying or is crying. I scoot closer, putting my arm around him to let him know I'm here. I comfort him while he comforts his mother.

Johnny's fancy shoes move into view. He clears his throat. "I know she's your mom, Drego. I wasn't going to let anything happen to her."

Oscar can't even make words. I've seen bits and pieces of his relationship with his mother, but I've never seen him as raw as this. Trying to take care of her and himself is too much. He can act as blasé as he wants, but he cares for her deeply, despite her addiction.

Johnny places his hand on Oscar's shoulder for a moment, and my heart nearly cracks in half at the emotion that conjures. These guys are just too much for me sometimes. To have gone through so much and still have the capacity to care, to grow. Fuck.

He squeezes and lets Oscar go. He brings his phone to

his ear again, and I'm sure he's calling in people to clean up the mess we just made. Or, maybe he's calling his father to let him know it's done. Either way, both calls will get made and life moves on.

This is why the Heights is bad. You're not supposed to move on easily from scenes like this.

Brawler kneels next to us. "We should probably get her to a hospital, man," he says softly.

Oscar strokes his hands through his mother's hair, and they come back red. "We'll get the blood off her first," he says.

She doesn't just need a hospital, she needs rehab. She needs a place to go to that will help her get off the fucking drugs. If only for Oscar's sake. I don't think I could bear to see him like this again.

When we were talking about who would come with us when we left the Heights, Oscar stated his mom would never leave. But what if she could? What if she got better, and he could have his mom in his life again? That would be the best-case scenario.

Mag, who'd followed Johnny out of the room, strides back inside. "We've got guys coming in. We need to leave."

Brawler helps me up, and then steadies Oscar as he gets to his feet with his mother in his arms. He holds her with one hand around her shoulders and the other under her knees. It's a tight squeeze in the car, but no one is going to complain. We use napkins and a water bottle to wash the blood from her hair. At some point, she passes out again, and Oscar sighs in relief. "She hates the hospital. If she's passed out, she won't even know that's where she's headed."

Brawler grabs another water bottle from the back and wets another napkin. I don't understand what he's doing until he runs it down the inside of my arm. I hiss a little, then turn my arm over to see a long scrape. "You got hurt," he whispers.

Johnny turns around in his seat. His eyes darken when he sees my injury, but he leans forward for a moment before handing Brawler back a box of tissues. From there, Brawler cleans my scrapes as best as he can that lead all the way down my arm. They go farther than that, too. Brawler notices the tear in my outfit and uses the napkins to clean my bloody thigh. "It's just a scratch," I say, steadying his hand.

He gives me a look like he knows I'm just trying to be brave. Maybe I am, but I have to put the injuries aside. We all do.

Magnum drives straight to the hospital. I offer to get out with Oscar, but he waves me away. "There's nothing you can do here. You're better off going to see K."

I frown at him, but Brawler squeezes my leg. "I'll go with him. I'll make sure he's good."

It's probably for the best, anyway. Going into the hospital like this would only arouse suspicions.

"Call us when you hear anything," Johnny orders. "And

I got the financials covered. Tell Oscar not to even worry about it."

Brawler claps him on the shoulder and then hurries to catch up with Oscar as the automatic doors open for him while he carries his druggie mother. I'm sure Oscar has had a hundred different moments like this with his mom, but I'm hoping this one sticks. That this could be the start of a good life for her again. Away from the Heights, she might even be able to breathe. To live.

I lean forward, now the only one in the backseat, and Johnny takes my hand. He tugs on it and then helps me maneuver through the tight space to sit on his lap. He holds me tightly, feathering kisses over my neck while Magnum reaches over and places his hand on my thigh, carefully avoiding my new injury. I place my hand right over his, and we give each other a squeeze.

It feels like we're ticking things off a list at this point. Gregory's down, and I'm already thinking about what's next on the agenda. We have to tell K our hatched-up plan—that was never really a plan from the beginning—though we're pretending it was. That will get me back to the Heights, and that will get me close enough to do what should have been done a long time ago.

People like Kingston Marx don't deserve to live. They certainly don't deserve to have power over so many human beings.

"Is what Gregory said true?" I ask Johnny. "About your father growing the Crew?"

Johnny shrugs. "He believes in strength in numbers. An army is better than a club."

"Loyalty, though, is even more important."

"It took me up until The Ring to get it, but the only person my father is loyal to is himself. I'm not sure how he got that way. Maybe he's always been that way, and it just took me way too fucking long to figure it out. Either way, I get it now. The only thing is, I'm not sure I shouldn't be brought to justice right alongside him."

I suck in a breath. "Don't say that."

"Why?" The force of his stare clenches the muscles in my stomach. "You saw what I did today. Gregory was right. Before you, I'm not sure I thought about anyone else but myself."

I don't know how to make him feel better because I don't know the extent of what he's done. I'm not sure I need to know either. I know the Johnny now, and that guy deserves to have what he wants in life.

"It was always your dad," Mag says, speaking up. "If you want to lay the blame for all the guilt you're feeling right now, put it where it's supposed to be. Your dad did this to you. You're only now realizing it because you got someone in your life who finally sees the real you, not just a pawn to place where you're needed in a plan for taking complete power and monetary control over people."

"I still did what I did."

"And what would've happened if you didn't?" Magnum asks, voice hard. I glance between the two of them. I almost feel like this is a conversation I shouldn't be here for, but at the same time, I'm glad I am.

Johnny clears his throat. "What if when we get out of here..." He finally turns toward me. "What if when we leave and you get everything you want— What if I'm not good enough for you then? What if I can't be saved? What if—?"

I place my finger over his lips. I'd kiss him, but I really want him to hear these next words out of my mouth because they're so fucking important, and I can't talk and kiss at the same time. "You're better than your surroundings. You just never knew that because your surroundings happened to live in the same house as you. Just like Brawler and Oscar and Mag, you all grew up in a place no one should. The fact that you overcame something like that tells me how special you are. What I can say for certain is that when we do get out of the Heights, you're going to thrive. Not because you know how to shoot people. Not because you're constantly thinking about the devious way to get shit done, but because you'll finally be able to see there's a whole other world out there, and they're waiting for Johnny Marx to show them what he has."

He shakes his head. A smear of blood on his forehead catches the moonlight. It could've been from any number of guys he saved us from tonight, but to me, it's just a scar from this life. When we get out, no more blood. No more death. No more anything other than long nights in bed.

Well, at least for the first few months.

I snicker to myself. Who am I kidding? It's going to take me my whole life to fuck these guys out of my system.

With Johnny's hand solidly in mine and Magnum at our backs, we approach K's suite. Exhaustion whips through me, but I hold my head high because I'm about to go back into the snake's den. The predator. The baddie to end all baddies.

I steel my stomach as I always do as the guard next to the door swings the doors open for us. He eyes me, and I wonder how fast word got around that Johnny and I broke up. Judging by the way Johnny holds my hand, everyone can see that wasn't the case.

The smell of sweet pasta sauce greets us as we walk in. K moves his gaze to our entrance, peering at our little trio as we make our way to the table. He makes no outward acknowledgment that I'm here, though there was a slight widening of his eyes when he first saw me.

Good. Asshole. I like to think that things can still surprise him, even with him being the almighty figure in the Heights.

He wipes his mouth and hands casually with an ivory cloth napkin and sets it aside. He leans back in his chair, his half-eaten spaghetti in front of him. "Well, this is...interesting." He darts his gaze between Johnny and me, a smirk playing over his lips. "I see you have Miss Kyla back. Care to tell me what's going on?"

One of the chefs emerges from the back and walks up to K. She gives him a curtsy, and I have to refrain from rolling my eyes. "Sir, should I get Mr. Rocket and his girlfriend a plate?"

K steeples his fingers in front of his chest, bouncing his pointer fingers off one another. His gaze turns to slits, staring at us as if he's trying to figure us out already. "Yes, please do. I'm sure this will be an entertaining story."

The woman nods gracefully and then disappears again.

Johnny and I take our seats at the table. Johnny immediately leans forward, placing his elbows on the silver table. "Did you receive my texts?"

"I did," he says, smiling. His gleaming white teeth remind me of shark's incisors. "Excellent job, Son. I knew you could do it."

Johnny turns an adoring look to me. At first, I refuse to peer into his eyes because I think the look he's giving me will be fake, but when I peek at him, his eyes are soft and genuine. A warmer blue than his usually icy eyes stare back at me. "We have Kyla to thank for that."

K's brows wrinkle in confusion. "Really." He barks out a laugh, leaning further back in his chair like he's getting ready for a movie to start playing and he's looking for the most comfortable spot. The whole thing seems forced and disingenuous. My stomach rolls over, but I tighten my stomach muscles and force a smile to my face. K shifts his gaze between us. "I'm looking forward to hearing this because the last I was aware, Kyla decided she didn't want the Crew life. She ran away, or so you said."

Johnny leans back now too, mirroring his father's position. "It was all part of a plan Mag and I concocted to get Gregory." Johnny's devilish smile comes out to play, which is uber sexy and disconcerting at the same time. "We're pretty sure we have a leak in the Crew, right?" Johnny says, laying it on thick. "I thought I'd put it out there that Kyla and I were no longer a thing so we could use her as bait."

K's gaze flicks to me. "I'm intrigued."

"Earlier, we took Kyla to the club, hoping it would draw Gregory's goons out. We mic'd her up, tracked her, and everything. Gregory did exactly what we thought he would do. He sent his guys to pick her up, and when they did, we coerced..." he says with a grin. "...his guy into telling us where he's been hiding out. The rest I'm sure you can guess from the photos I sent."

"Quite a devious plan," K says, looking proud and astonished at the same time. He scratches his jaw. "Couldn't have worked it better myself."

Johnny beams under his scrutiny.

"How many guys did he have there with him?"

"A dozen."

"And?"

"Being taken care of," Johnny says. "We called in the clean up team for them as well as the driver and the guy who picked Kyla up at the club."

"All ex-Crew guys?"

"Yep, all of them. As far as I'm aware."

The cook returns from the back with a rolling cart. She brings over steaming plates of pasta and places them in front of Johnny and me. The food actually smells delicious, but I couldn't trust K any less than I already do.

Johnny takes a few bites while I move the pasta around with my fork.

"The dinner not to your liking?" K asks. He lifts a brow at my plate.

I smile at him. "I've just had a long day, I guess. I don't really have an appetite."

"Who could blame you? Being used as bait. Storming a rival gang member's lair," he says flippantly. "So, all this about you not having the stomach for a Crew life was just...a story?"

Johnny clears his throat, using the cloth napkin the cook left next to his plate to wipe his face. "We wanted to keep the plan a secret because of the number of guys we've had defect lately. We thought it would work perfectly, and it did."

"So, Kyla's in?" K asks, keeping his glare firmly on me. "She's all on board?"

I twirl a piece of pasta around my fork and eat it slowly before answering. "I'm all in."

K rocks back in his chair again. He looks entirely too happy for someone who doesn't like me. "Gosh, this is fun, isn't it? This life? This...everything?" A shiver must go through him because he visibly shakes like he's having a moment of profound joy. It sends an icy ball of dread down my spine with how uncaring and ruthless he is. "There's just one thing, guys. Just one thing. Gregory's guys that you killed? They weren't Gregory's guys. They were Crew."

Johnny sits back. "Used to be Crew, you mean. They defected to go to Gregory."

K shrugs. "Nope, they were Crew, I'm afraid. Them, and Gregory. All Crew."

Johnny's fingers tighten on the fork in his hand. He sets it down lightly. "Gregory's guys shot up The Ring. They took me hostage and have plans to overthrow you, Dad. They're not part of the Crew, they're our enemies."

"Except they're not," K says. When Johnny's jaw slackens, K laughs. "Don't look so upset over killing innocent people, Son." He leans over and playfully punches him in the knee.

My back stiffens as I watch the scene play out. With the way K is getting so much satisfaction from this, it looks like he's had this revelation planned for a long time.

"What are you saying?" Johnny growls out.

"I'm saying," K says, still all teeth as he works up to his big reveal. "With as much as you strung your plan together, I've been stringing my own. You knew you'd have to do something big to be my right-hand man. Well, here it is. You did it. You're in."

"Killing Gregory?" Johnny shakes his head, and I'm with him. I have no idea what K is getting at. "One of our own Crew members?" Johnny questions softly as if he still can't believe it.

Warning bells go off in my head, but there's nothing I can do about any of this except to wait for it to play itself out.

K's gaze flicks to me. "You were getting soft. Your tight cunt here had you pussy-whipped, and I wanted to make sure you still had it in you. You proved me wrong on that fact, Johnny. I thought you were just going to let him go. I thought you didn't care about the Crew anymore, your true family."

"Of course, I—"

"Stop right there," K growls, a threat that curls my toes with its authenticity. "If you're about to make some pledge to the Crew, you can fucking save it, Son." He bites his last word out like a curse. His eyes turn glassy with anger, with sadness, with a contempt I haven't witnessed before. The stone-cold color of his eyes is liable to freeze anyone on the spot. "I know what you're plotting. You think you're steps ahead of me, but you're wrong." He pushes his chair back, and the legs scrape against the tile. He stands in one fluid motion, coming up behind Johnny.

I go to move, but a hand falls on my shoulder. I start, expecting to see Magnum, but it's not him. It's a guard who came in from the hallway. He holds me in place as K puts his fingers on Johnny's shoulders. "You're no son of mine anymore."

The pulse in Johnny's neck feathers, and his jaw tenses. "I can explain."

"No need to. I know, Johnny. I know you and your little girlfriend's plan to take me out." He slides his fingers around Johnny's throat and squeezes.

It escalates so quickly I don't immediately react until Johnny starts clawing at his father's fingers.

I try to stand, but the guard pushes my shoulders back down. The chair backs are so fucking high, I don't have any leverage, so I punch back wildly until I connect with something hard. His grip loosens, and I'm able to stand enough so that when he grabs for me again, I throw him in a move I learned in a Judo class several years ago. He ends up with his back on the table, a groan filling the air and several broken dishes under him.

I pull the gun off his hip and point it at K. My hands

shake. Excitement, panic, everything, just pours into me that I'm finally at this moment. I'm at the point where I can pull the trigger.

K loosens his grip on his son, and Johnny chokes, falling forward to the table, gripping the side as he breathes life back into himself. K doesn't even give him a second glance. "Dearest Kyla. What's this? Defending my traitorous son? I thought you wanted to be a part of the Crew?"

"I hate you," I spit. I never exactly practiced the words I wanted to say to K when this moment happened, but they slide easily from my tongue. "I've hated you for so long." I step forward, and he takes a step back, moving around the table to shield himself.

"You women are always so dramatic. I've barely known you a few months."

I laugh, the sound wild and erratic. "I've known your name for a long time, Kingston Marx. They were uttered by a cop in the middle of a dining room." I lick my lips, my heart beating frantically inside my chest. "You killed my parents when I was twelve."

K's gaze darts behind him, but I don't look. I don't know where Mag is, but I know he'll let me do this. This has been the plan all along. He's scared. I can see it.

It makes this so much sweeter.

"My parents were Kyle and Anna Ridley. You—" His eyes round, stopping my planned speech. I hadn't planned on him knowing who they were. "You killed them in an alleyway. You killed them so you could get this spot in the Crew that you don't fucking deserve. You killed them for nothing."

K laughs. He laughs so loud, a chill runs through me. He turns gleaming eyes my way. "You're her daughter. Ha." The cackling sound of his laughter settles into my bones with a hardness that I fear will make me crack from the inside out. He grips the back of a chair, leaning over to laugh. "This can't be happening."

I want to pull the trigger. Just fucking pull it, but his words eat at me. Instead, I steady the barrel of the gun at his chest. "You knew my mother?"

K grins at Johnny. "I understand why you're so obsessed with her now." He puffs his cheeks out. "She has good DNA."

"What the fuck are you saying?"

"Let me guess, you think I just killed your parents randomly? You've concocted this whole plan to get back at me for murdering your innocent parents. That's rich. I like it. I'm kind of impressed right now."

I step closer to him, and he sobers up.

"You don't know the whole story, Kyla. Neither does Johnny. We should all sit so we can talk about it."

I shake my head. I've already wasted too much time. Kill him. Leave. The same words echo through my brain. No matter how much he's trying to worm something else in there, it won't do. "Talk now."

The guard on the table lunges for me. I turn and pull the trigger. I step just out of the way while he lands lifeless at my feet before I return my attention to K. "You're next."

A sheen of perspiration dots his forehead. I doubt K has ever been in a position like this. He straightens. "I met your mother before I met Johnny's mom. When that bitch escaped, I went looking for my Anna, and I found her alright. New life. A husband. I was so angry with Johnny's mother that I fucking killed Anna, right there in the alley while she hung onto her husband with adoration. I'm so sick of women thinking they can get away from me. It felt so good, I went and found Johnny's mother and killed her too."

K turns a grin to his son, but Johnny smiles right back, rubbing his throat at the same time. "Joke's on you. I already knew you killed her."

K glares across the table, but we have him now. He breathes out a sigh. "Alright, I'm done with this. Magnum." He runs a hand through his hair like this is any other day. He gestures toward Johnny. "Take him to jail. Or something. Spending his life getting ass fucked in prison is good enough penalty for me."

My gaze flicks to Magnum, who, so far, has stayed out of this. I thought it was because he still didn't want me to kill K, but...

"Today, Mag," K bellows. "I'm sure you can think of something." His eyes light up. "I know. He can go down for Gregory's murder."

Johnny sucks in a breath, whirling on the copper-haired bodyguard. "You're the dirty cop?"

Mag swallows. As resolute as he always is, he just nods.

My stomach falls to my feet. I glare at him as he moves forward and yanks Johnny's arms, putting them behind his back like he's actually going to cuff him.

"Make the charges stick," K says.

"What about her?" Mag asks, gesturing toward me.

My hand falls to my side in shock, the gun resting against my thigh. Magnum's doing this. He's actually doing this. The door behind the suite bursts open and more guards move into the room. We're fucked now. I've lost my chance.

K comes to my side. He takes a piece of my hair and twirls it around my finger. "I used to like her mother. I think I'll keep her."

33

I move just out of K's reach, my stomach rolling. My mother and...him?

K tugs my hair back, making me look forward again. I catch Johnny's gaze as Magnum hauls him backward. "Say goodbye to your boyfriend, Kyla. He'll never see the light of day again."

Mag avoids my stare, but it wouldn't matter, anyway. Johnny and I stare at one another for as long as we can, holding each other's gazes. I swear, in this moment, I can even read his thoughts. They're dark and angry...and scared. A lump forms in my throat the size of a whole continent. A sob works its way around it, but I refuse to let it out.

K has been a step ahead of us this whole time. Gregory's still in the Crew? But fucking how?

And Magnum?

My chest expands until my confusion and anger is too big to contain. A tear leaks from my cheek. As soon as Johnny sees it, he fights free from Magnum's grip and lunges forward. He runs toward me. I ram my elbow into K's side to get some space, but in the next instant, a guard wraps his hands around Johnny's mid-section and tackles him to the floor. He cries out in pain. I step forward as the guard cold-cocks him. Strong hands haul me back again though. Another set of hands grab me too, so it doesn't matter how much I struggle, their grips are strong and immovable.

Trey yanks Johnny to his feet. His head lulls forward, but he blinks his eyes open slowly.

"Nice try, Son. Don't worry," K says, his disgusting, hot breath hitting the curve of my neck. "I'll take care of your little bitch." He cups my breast, stroking my nipple.

I go numb again. The light from Johnny's eyes fades as Magnum and Trey force him back. Helplessness mars Johnny's handsome face as he struggles against the two, fully stacked guards. The door closes, and I'm left there with the man who's plagued my nightmares since I was twelve.

He cups my breast again, and my stomach rolls. He's not doing it as a show for Johnny. "Your mom's were bigger."

"Fuck. You."

"She didn't have a mouth on her, though. I quite like a girl who fights back if you know what I'm saying. They make it so much more fun to break."

Pain twists my stomach. The thought of him and my

mom together makes me dizzy. It makes me revolt. How in the fuck did she get mixed up with someone like him?

He gives my nipple one last squeeze and pushes me forward. I stumble the first few steps but catch my balance before whirling to face him. I back up against a wall, and he waves his only guard left away. "You showed a lot of fight back there." He tilts his head as if he's finally taking stock of me. Not like I haven't been around for these past few months. Suddenly, I'm new and shiny to him, and being new and shiny to someone like Big Daddy K isn't a good thing. "I see the questions in your eyes, too. Let's sit back down at the table, and we'll talk. My dinner was so rudely interrupted by my son conspiring against me."

"Conspiring against you? You tricked him into killing someone, just so he could move up."

"I only felt like I had to trick him because of you. So, it's only fair." He turns and moves back to his seat at the metal dining room table. It's a mess now. The guard I threw on top of it smashed some dishes. He frowns and then yells out for the maid. She comes bustling in, and all he has to do is point at the shit he wants taken care of, and she gets to work. When she leaves, he gazes over at me. "Sit," he orders, gesturing toward where Johnny was sitting only a few minutes ago.

Loneliness hits me in the gut. Just fuck. Here I am where I thought I would be. Facing down K by myself, but since I've met the guys, I honestly never thought I'd be alone again. I never wanted to be alone again. I got the taste of what I never even knew I wanted, and I don't want to let it go.

What if that was the last time I'll see Johnny? Or Brawler or Oscar? Magnum... When he pops into my head, I'm so confused I grab the wall for support.

"I won't ask you again, Kyla."

"I'm not sitting with you at a table like nothing just happened."

K wraps spaghetti around his fork and peeks over at the guard. He doesn't wait for audible orders, he marches toward me and grabs my hands. My feet, my limbs, everything feels so heavy and weighted down. I try to struggle against him, but my training has been kissed goodbye.

The guard forces me to sit in Johnny's place. He pushes my shoulders down so hard, I'm almost positive he cracks my tailbone, but I squeeze my lips shut. The maid walks pleasantly out of the rear of K's suite and switches my plate for Johnny's and then takes his into the back with her.

"There," K says. "Now we can have a polite conversation. Perhaps you have questions about your mom?"

I have a billion questions, but I won't give him the satisfaction. A burning hole of curiosity tempts me, but I sit straight in the chair. I'm outnumbered right now. I don't know where any guns are. I lost track of them in all of the commotion, so it's best to play this by ear for the time being. Brawler and Oscar will come for me when they figure out what's happening. Then, we can save Johnny. We can tell the police...

Except, Johnny might've killed Gregory. He certainly isn't innocent by any means. He and Magnum annihilated people today. Took them out without warning because we had a goal. If K's guys never picked up the scene, it would be so easy to put Johnny away for life when the real culprit is sitting to my right. He might not have killed anyone today, but he's the puppet master with everyone. He orders, they act. To me, he's just as culpable as the rest of these guys. Maybe even more so because if he didn't tell them what to think, maybe they'd think differently. Johnny's already proven that.

"I don't know how I didn't see it before. Your eyes remind me of hers."

"Don't fucking talk about her," I growl. The fucker acts as if he loved her—liked her. It's sick. His reasoning for murdering her is absolute bullshit. Because she was happy? And he wasn't? That shit happens all the fucking time.

"She was surprised to see me. I was just grateful she even recognized me. I knew her when I was about your age." He looks away as if these are fond memories for him.

I almost gag.

"Our relationship was short and intense. Just a summer fling, really, but the thought of her never left me."

"I bet she never thought of you again."

Pain radiates from my hand. It happened so fast, I didn't

see him move. I try to move my hand from the point of pain, but it sticks, and another wave of pure agony radiates up my arm. I glance over to find a knife handle sticking out of my hand. The blade wedged just below my middle knuckle. I gasp in a breath. *Fuuuuuck.*

"She loved me."

I close my eyes and fight through the pain. Dots blur my vision. Wetness creeps over my skin, but I don't dare look at what I'm sure is blood seeping everywhere. Dirtying his pristinely laid table. His whole life is a greeting card with ugly words inside it. Looks beautiful from the outside, but the inside is where the true story lies.

We're silent for a few moments as he peacefully returns to eating his meal. Light-headedness hits me, so I reach out with my free hand and take a sip of Johnny's water glass, making sure to keep my other hand as still as can be.

K laughs into his napkin, and I peek at him before I can stop myself. He shakes his head like he's about to tell a funny joke. "Aw, my son. He knows better than what he did today. I still maintain you ruined him because he let his feelings get in the way of his work. I learned not to do that a long time ago." He chuckles again, and a sliver of ice worms its way up my spine. "He didn't check the car for bugs. The minute he told me you left the Heights, I knew something was up. We Marx's don't just give up our toys like that. I had Trey install the bug in the backseat, and it turns out I was right. You know what I heard coming out of his mouth?"

I lick my lips. My mouth won't stay wet, and I'm feeling woozy. I concentrate on his question though. He must have heard them in the car talking...on the way back to the Heights with Brawler in the car. That's when we'd solidified the plan. Brawler rode back to ask them if Jax and Finn could go into the club with me. "You heard a plan to trap Gregory," I say.

K reaches out to grab his water. He holds it to his lips for a second. "That's what I heard at first." He takes a long swallow, and I envy the fucking free movement of his hand. Meanwhile, I'm turning cold all over. He sets the cup back down. "Then I heard him say, 'Do you really think Kyla will do it? Will she kill my dad?'" He flings the glass across the room, and it shatters against the wall. I flinch, and another round of pain shoots through my palm. "I knew right then he was compromised because the son I raised would've killed you the moment you spoke out against me. No questions. No second chances. A bullet to your forehead, Kyla Samson." He turns to glare at me and laughs. "That's not your real name, is it? You're good. I'll hand it to you. You got past my guys, and they're very thorough."

I bite the inside of my cheek. I never got past Magnum. Magnum knew all along. What is he doing? I can't help but think that he's playing a part again. Just like he did when Johnny told me to leave the Heights.

No fucking wonder the little things I saw didn't sit right with me. Magnum's a cop. A dirty cop. He's been K's informant this whole time, and fucking shit. K did know that Gregory was holding Johnny. What in the actual fuck? Does that mean he sent the cops there that night too? Or was that Magnum?

"You shouldn't frown. The only thing a woman is good for is her looks, and the moment you get wrinkles, you'll cease to be of use to me. If you're smart, you'll do anything to stay under my good graces, Kyla. I think I've made it clear what happens when women don't."

The smirk that crosses his face makes me look away. He can talk so casually about killing my mother, someone he claimed to care for. Johnny was right. Women are property in the Crew. I didn't see it because I was doing them a service. I made them look good, but all along, I was also their property to do with what they wanted. If I decided I didn't want to fight, I'm sure they wouldn't have needed me. If I hadn't been Johnny's girlfriend—or even if I was—that probably meant I didn't deserve to breathe anymore.

This whole world is sick.

K reaches over to move a strand of hair off my face. I can't even flinch away. He literally has me pinned right where I am. "I think I might have another use for you, too. Other than to keep me sated, anyway." He licks his lips. "That's why I kept you when I could've killed you. The truth is, I've been salivating for a taste of your cunt for a while, and now that I know you're Anna's daughter, I need a taste. I'll feel eighteen again, balls deep in the beautiful girl from out-of-town." He rubs his hand down the crotch of his pants. "I'll warn you right now, fighting only makes me even more turned on." His lips turn up even higher. "I have a feeling you're going to do it anyway, which just makes me that much more excited. I hired a dark-haired slut the night Johnny gave me the pictures of you and Jiko, but now I'm about to have the real thing. Anna number two. Not the original, but you'll do." He trails his hand down my arm, getting closer and closer to the knife. "I hope you're excited about experiencing the original Marx. I'm much more experienced than my son. I'm looking forward to the moment your eyes change from hate to bliss because I've fucked you so good you can't fucking help it."

The need to throw up is overpowering, but I can't move. His hand hovers near the knife, and I have a feeling the next wrong thing I say will only mean more pain for me. He's already injured my hand. My strong, uppercut hand. If he's fucking ruined me for fighting, I'm going to rip his balls off and shove them down his goddamn throat.

He tilts his head to the side. "I hope that sassy mouth comes back later." He yanks the knife from my hand, and my other hand digs into my thigh to keep from screaming. "I have business to take care of. While you guys were worried about Gregory, I was putting my plan into motion." He stands from the table, and I just stare straight ahead. "I'm guessing you know about the Dragons being in town." He sighs happily. "Well, they're about to be Crew, and the

Crew's boundaries will increase tenfold. My empire is finally falling into place." He tsks as he walks away. "It's a shame Johnny turned out defective. We could've ruled the tri-state area as one." Just before a door closes, K orders the guard to take me to Johnny's suite and to make sure I don't leave.

As soon as he's gone, I take the closest napkin on the table and hold it to my hand. Blood leeches out. I bite back a cry as I pull the makeshift bandage between my teeth and free hand to tie the knot around it tighter to stop the bleeding. Hopefully.

"Come on, bitch," the guard says, pulling me to my feet. The world tilts as I stand, but I make it to Johnny's suite on unsteady legs. The guard pushes me inside, and I fall to my knees. Without the strength to get up, I just lie there, letting my cheek rest against the cool tile.

I don't have time to think about how trapped I am. Or about how alone I am. Or about how I fucked up everything. The blackness takes me under, and I'm out.

34

My head throbs. My eyelids peel open like they're made of sandpaper. A swish-swish sound increases my curiosity. The last I remembered, I was on the floor just inside Johnny's door. I'm definitely lying on something more comfortable than tile though.

Finally, I force my eyes the rest of the way open and climb out of the fog. My hand is at my hip, resting on a pair of clean joggers. Despite having fallen asleep using a stark white cloth napkin as dressing, there's a real bandage there now. Beyond the stretchy gauze is a dark square of blood.

The swish-swish sound returns again. I glance over to find Magnum with his back to me, a mop in his hand. He's cleaning the floor where I passed out. The taut muscles in his back move as I watch. Fortunately for me, I'm not in any pain other than the overall exhaustion begging to drag me under again. I'm almost relieved. I was pretty certain I was going to wake up and want to saw my own arm off from the pain.

Magnum places the sponge mop in a bucket and bends to pick it up. He peeks over at me and does a double-take. The bucket slips from his hand and falls to the floor, the bloody water sloshing over the sides.

His eyes latch to mine, burning into me. I try to sit up, but he rushes to my side. "Don't move. I gave you something for the pain, and I don't think you could get up right now even if you wanted to."

"Planning on taking me to jail too? Or sticking a knife in my back?"

His lips purse. The freckles that dot his nose are stark against his much paler skin. Actually, a different Magnum than I've seen yet sits on the sofa beside me. He rubs his hands through his copper hair before looking over at me again. "I told you I had a secret."

"I don't give a fuck about that." I groan because I actually do give a fuck about that, but that's not why I'm mad. "That's nothing compared to what you did to Johnny. Where the fuck is he?"

"You think I'd do something to him? Come on, Kyla. You're so much smarter than this."

I lift my good hand up and slap him with all I can muster. Unfortunately, it's not much. It's about as annoying to him as a buzzing fly. His eyes spark, and I follow right after him. He has no right to be pissed at me. "You know my weaknesses, Magnum. You took Johnny. You left me alone in there with *him*." I spit out, conjuring up Big Daddy K's ruthless grin as he stabbed me through the hand. Glaring down at my new wound, I finish my sentence. "What the fuck am I supposed to think?"

He grabs my free hand and kisses it. He holds it to his forehead, bowing over it like he's saying a prayer of forgiveness over and over. "Johnny's fine. I didn't take him to the police. Well, I did, but—"

I gasp. "You took him in?"

"He's not being charged with anything. He's being held there in case Kingston checks up on me, which he most certainly will. Fuck! I can't fucking believe I didn't check the car for bugs." He growls but reverts back to the stricken look I've noticed since I woke up. "We just wanted to get to you. We knew you'd be freaking out over what we said, how we made you leave the Heights, so we just got in the car and left." His mouth works, but nothing comes out at first. "I guess I just didn't fucking check."

I don't blame him for K finding out what we were plotting. Anyone can make a mistake, and he can't expect to be perfect all the time. Shit fucking happens.

I groan inwardly. I need to listen to my own inner voice and give Magnum the benefit of the doubt. Despite his dirty looks, I pull myself up to a sitting position. My hand skims a bandage on my thigh, and there's another one on my arm, too. I guess Magnum patched me up everywhere. I wrap my arms around my knees and try not to glare at him but fail. "If anything happens to him…"

"I would never forgive myself. If anything happens to any of you, I'll never forgive myself. Damnit, Kyla. I've never said an empty word to you, I swear. I've meant every single thing I've ever said. I love you. You captivated me from the very beginning. None of that was a lie. What I want with you in the future, isn't a lie. Everything is the same as when we walked into Marx's suite earlier. I swear to you."

"Oscar and Brawler?"

"I heard from Oscar a little while ago. His mom is being held at the hospital. He and Brawler just left there."

"And what did you happen to tell them about what was going on?"

"I told them there were some developments…"

I roll my eyes. It seems like such a high-schooler thing to do in this moment, but oddly, also fitting. "Developments is an understatement. You're a fucking cop, Magnum."

The things I've seen that should've been major clues filter through my head. I should've figured it out sooner. The way the cop at The Ring was so familiar with him. He told me he had a secret. Other little things like the police being called when we got Johnny, though to be honest, I'm not sure if that was K's doing or Mag's.

"I told you I had a secret."

"I thought the secret was that you knew who I fucking was this whole time. You did my background check. You found my real name. You knew about my other life."

"And that information has been safe with me this whole time. No one knows who you are because of me. They only found out when you told them."

Nausea laps at me. My mouth is still dry as fuck. I lick my lips and swallow.

"Hungry? Thirsty? It could be a side effect of the pain reliever I gave you."

I eye him warily. "If you're playing the dirty cop, why are you even here right now? I doubt Kingston approved this visit."

"Kingston sent me in here to deal with your injury." He gnashes his teeth together and peers down at it. "I can't be in here for long, but I just wanted to explain what was going on." He pushes up from the sofa and retrieves a package of cookies from the cupboard along with a bottle of water. He sets them on the coffee table in front of us and offers me one. When I don't immediately take it, he says, "Sugar will do your body good. Come on."

I snatch it from him. "I'll eat as long as you keep talking."

He flinches at my harsh words, but I stick my chin in the air. If shit was going to go down like this, a heads up would've been nice. Didn't we make a promise recently that we hoped not to have to lie to each other again? Maybe that's why I'm so hurt. Plus, it wasn't just me that was caught up in this. It was Johnny, too. I don't want to be a hypocrite. I've lied throughout this. I've kept some devious shit to myself, but with what the five of us just shared in that hotel room? Calling Magnum out for backstabbing us isn't too far off.

"I'll tell you everything," he says, voice full and even. "It started when I first joined the Crew. Mayhem brought me on board. You remember me telling you that part, right? I was Security from the beginning. Exactly where I wanted to be. I was slowly moving up the ranks all throughout Mayhem's last year and Kingston's first year. One day, Marx pulls me aside and tells me he wants me to join the Rawley Heights police force. They were giving us a hard time back then about...something." He shakes his head. "He was sick of the inside guys we thought we had in our pockets demanding more money—more everything—in order to give him the information he needed and to keep his businesses safe. So, he had the brilliant idea of making one of his guys from the inside go in. So, I did. In the Crew's eyes, I went to do a job for him that took me about a year and a half. In reality, I went to a police academy in another state. Once I got in, I approached the Rawley Heights police force and told them a redemption story about how I wanted to make a better life. They all knew who I was, of course. They decided they were going to up the ante. I wasn't just going to be a beat cop. With my knowledge of the gang's workings, they decided I'd be going in undercover to try to take them down."

Magnum stops to take a drink of water before handing the bottle to me. I brush the cookie crumbs from my fingers and take a drink. I hand him back the bottle, and he sets it back on the table. "I thought at first Kingston was going to be super pissed about this new development. I wasn't only on the force, I was supposed to be working to take them down. I thought I somehow fucked up his idea, but he loved the idea. He just loved that I was right under their noses and they didn't even know it. It made him feel all-powerful. By controlling me, he had control over the police, let alone the tower and the streets and the people. He felt indestructible."

"So, you're a dirty cop? Just like K said you were."

Mag leans over me. He drops his hand to my arm, tracing lines over my skin. "I never had any intention of turning in the Crew, no. I've done everything I could to help K out."

"And the cops? They've never been suspicious?"

"K's smart. I feed them information that's just enough. That whets their appetite so they think I'm getting closer and closer. K and I work on it together. Alone. No one else knows about me."

I nod. Not even Johnny knew. He knew K had someone, but he never dreamed it was Magnum.

"I'm not a good person, Kyla. When I think about the things I've done..." He shakes his head. "...I don't even know.

And to think I joined the Crew so my father would be proud of me. The more I got into it, the harder it was to get out. I'm wrapped up in two systems right now. If either one finds out I've been screwing them over, I'm either dead or in jail for the rest of my life."

I cock my head. "Wait, but—"

Magnum runs his fingers through my hair, and I'm not going to lie, it feels amazing. Part of me wants to save this conversation for later and cuddle up on the couch and hopefully wake up in a different time and place. A time where all of my guys are still right here, and we literally don't have to deal with this bullshit anymore.

Mag gives me a small smile. "When you came, you intrigued me. I didn't see someone who wanted to hide from the Crew like the rest of us were doing. For a little while, I'd begun to grow a conscience. I saw so much shit go down. I participated in so much, and when you showed up with your determination and fearlessness.... You have to remember, I figured out your plan from the beginning. Here was this little girl coming in here to fuck shit up when I'd been bemoaning my life choices for too long. As hokey as it sounds, you empowered me. I'll never be able to make up for the shit I've done, but I've started to actually work for the people I'm supposed to be helping. I'm not feeding them misinformation anymore. I've decided if you can stick to your values, so can I, whether they're new or not."

My anger for Mag is slipping away like sand through an

hourglass, and that's okay with me. "So, you've been playing both sides?"

"I'm fucked is what I am, Kyla. I've been able to hold Kingston off because of our history. He's not suspicious of me. That's why I didn't check for the fucking bug, and that's why I had to take Johnny. It killed me to do it, and to leave you alone, but I had to. If I didn't, we all would've ended up dead right there. I told you we were playing a dangerous game."

I grab his arm. He stops talking, and for the first time, there's a flicker of hope in his gaze. Great. Now I really do feel like shit. I'm supposed to love these guys, and I was so quick to think badly of him. "I'm sorry."

He grinds his teeth together. "Don't apologize to me. I don't deserve it."

"You're going to get my apologies, Jacob Cotton, because I'm going to tell you the same thing I tell Johnny. You couldn't have helped who you were." I choke back a sob as feelings overwhelm me. It's not that I feel bad for them. It's that I'm so fucking proud to know them. The shit they endured. The paths they were made to take. The fact that they have any shred of human decency in them whatsoever gives me hope for everything. "You rose up from the garbage that is the Heights, that is the Crew, and you turned it around. You're not perfect. I'm not perfect. Johnny sure as fuck isn't perfect and neither are Brawler and Oscar, but we're so much more than just Heights trash.

I don't care what we have to do to get out of this, we're doing it."

"It's not going to be easy."

I'm transported back to a time when I was a kid. Dad was helping me with my homework, and I was crying over science. It was always my worst subject. He took my hand and smiled. "Honey, I know it's hard. But the hard things are always worth it."

I tell that to Mag now, even knowing I sound like a coddling parent, but not giving a fuck anyway. The look he gives me afterward tells me he doesn't care either. He leans over, pressing his lips to mine. He savors me. It's the kind of kiss that lingers for a long time. The kind I can recall later because it just means something.

In this moment, it means so very much.

"We'll get through this," Mag promises. "I'm going to figure it out." He peeks at the door, and I know he's thinking that our time should be up.

I hate letting him go, but we don't need to arouse any more suspicion. "I have one demand, Jacob."

He swallows and glances back, awaiting my words.

"I kill Big Daddy K. In the end, it's still me. I don't care what else you have to do, but in the end, it's me and him. Promise?"

He kisses the inside of my palm. "Promise." He bows his head over my hand again. "I'll hold him off tonight. I'll keep him in meetings about our next step. I—"

I swallow and cup his cheek. "You'll do exactly what you need to do to not get us all killed, Jacob. You understand? Even if that is letting him stab me in the hand again. I don't care. You. Me. Johnny, Brawler, and Oscar. That's all that fucking matters. You will not sacrifice them for me. Promise me."

His jaw clenches. "I—" He breaks off with a groan.

"Just this once, let go of your need to take care of me first and foremost. The bigger picture is at stake, and that means more to me than anything. Promise me, Jacob."

His hazel green eyes spark. I see a future in them. I see the need he carries to have exactly what I wish for all of us. "I promise."

With that, he stands and leaves, and even though I'm alone again, I don't feel that way. I'm trusting Jacob to do what I asked. That's what love is, sometimes. Setting aside your own needs for the one—well, in this case, *ones* —you love.

35

Rough hands shake me awake. When an unfamiliar pair of eyes stares at me out of the darkness, flight mode kicks in. I kick away, but hands grab for my own until they have me under control. A body pins me to the couch. "Shh, Kyla," a sinister voice says. The more the sleep wears off, I figure out it's Trey. Man, I never liked this asshole. "Big Daddy wants you."

A nugget of fear roots itself in my stomach. It almost feels like bad cramps.

His eyes practically laugh at me. He knows as well as I do that getting summoned by K in the middle of the night is bad. Really bad. With all the talk he gave me earlier, I was hoping he was... Well, I don't know because all that hope seems ridiculous now that I'm being forced off Johnny's couch and dragged to K's suite. Another guard joins

Trey, and they bypass the living areas, the areas I've been to already, and take me right to an open door. A humongous bed looms in the center of it. They throw me to the edge and then stand back, arms crossed while flanking the door.

In the bathroom, the sound of the shower shutting off turns my stomach. I'm outnumbered. Surrounded by enemies.

I'm about to get raped.

The sobering thought ignites indignation in the center of my chest. I didn't take hundreds upon hundreds of martial arts classes to end up like this. I didn't perfect my fighting technique to become the victim of a deranged, narcissistic psychopath who thinks I'm my mother.

Before I can hype myself up even more, the bathroom door opens. K steps out in a dark blue bathrobe tied loosely around his waist. The top falls open, showing off a chest that might be called defined if I hadn't been able to compare it to my guys. Looking at him, all I see is dad-bod.

"Leave us," K says. "But stay close."

The two guards who brought me here leave and shut the door behind them. I imagine them standing just on the other side. How often do they do this? How often does K rape women?

"You're disappointing me already, Kyla. I was hoping for that smart mouth of yours."

There are a few thousand things I want to shout at him,

but I'm stubborn as fuck. If that's what he wants, he's going to get a silent fight.

"Take your clothes off."

"No."

K bores holes into my skin as if he has x-ray vision and can see right through the material now covering me. "I never understood why Johnny let you wear these garish clothes. Then when I saw you at the club after your fight, I understood. He doesn't want anyone else looking at his toy."

"Or he just lets me wear what I want because he's not a fucking asshole."

He drops his head back and laughs. "Now I know your feelings for him have blinded you. My son is an asshole. He's just like me. I made him who he is."

It's my turn to laugh. "He used to be, but he's nothing like you anymore. I'd tell you what you are, but I think you'd like it. You don't see it for the insult it is."

"You got a point there." He loosens the belt on his robe and pulls it off his shoulders.

I swallow. He's full on naked. Erect, too. It's clear what he thinks he's going to do.

"Undress, lie down, and part those legs for me."

"No."

He grins. "I already told you I like a fight."

"More like you want your son's seconds. That's disgusting."

"What's funny is you think I care. I see a pretty thing. I

want a pretty thing. I take a pretty thing. It's as simple as that." He cups his cock and starts moving his hand up and down his shaft. "He didn't hide you away well enough, and now that I know you're Anna's daughter... Oh fuck." He closes his eyes and squeezes his cock until it looks painful.

I look away.

As soon as I do, he's in my face. "Watch me." He stands to his full height, which puts his dick pretty much in my face. He strokes himself slowly, and my stomach churns again. I haven't felt right all day, and who could blame me?

"Take your shirt off. Let me see those titties."

"Fuck you."

He moans, and a sadistic smile covers his face. He licks his lips. "I'm trying to decide if my cock in your mouth or your pussy would be best. I guess if I was in your mouth, I won't be able to hear your screams."

He moves closer, and I try to push past him. He grabs me. He pulls my arms down by my sides, igniting the scrape on my arms, but I refuse to cry out. His cock brushes my upper thighs. I struggle against him. It's time. This isn't going to just end. I have to fight my way out of here. It seems like a fool's attempt because there are guys just outside this door, but I can't just sit here and let him do whatever he wants to me.

"Deep down you want it, Kyla. Remember I said I'd fuck you so much better than my son?"

His words give me the burst of energy I need to free

myself from his grip even though the pain in my hand is almost unbearable. I move around the side of the bed, trying to put as much distance between us as I can. "Not possible because I love Johnny."

His eyes widen, and then he laughs. "Now you just made this an even better game. Now I can think about what I'm taking away from my traitorous son while also getting my rocks off."

"You're sick."

He stops and cocks his head to the side. "You're right. Nothing you throw at me will hurt me. I'm just proud of the fact that I make you sick. You weaklings will never make it in the world. Trust me, I'm doing you a favor."

"Raping me is a favor?"

He works his way around the bed and grabs my throat. The back of my legs hit his bedside table. "I like that. Yes, I'm going to rape you, but that's not what I was referring to, Kyla." With his free hand, he trails a hand down my body. Every inch he passes over, I erase the feel of him the very next second. I numb myself to what's going on. He squeezes harder, constricting my air. "I was talking about when I hand you over to the Dragons tomorrow. Well, actually, you're just bait. You liked being bait so much for Gregory, you guys gave me the idea."

He loosens his hold, and I take a deep breath. My throat burns. Pain radiates from where his fingers dug into me.

"The Dragons are trying to take you down. Why would you use me as bait?"

Big Daddy K laughs. "I had Gregory working on them this whole time. He brought them here, looking for an alliance to get rid of me, but what the Dragons don't know is that I was pulling Gregory's strings this whole time. I have a knack at pulling the wool over people's eyes. I do whatever it takes to do it. Even telling Gregory to start a rebellion that was never going to go anywhere."

"You didn't care whether he lived or died."

"I don't care whether anyone lives or dies. The guys who Gregory was able to tempt to his side would've been killed. You guys have already gone and done that for me, so now it only leaves the Dragons."

"But Gregory is dead."

"They don't know that."

I swallow, and the rawness in my throat scratches like steel wool. "This all worked out perfectly for you then, didn't it?"

"It did," K says, tightening his fingers around my throat again. "I found out the leader of the Dragons likes young girls, so after I'm through with you, you're theirs. Well, at least he thinks so. He won't live to get you."

"Once you kill him, you'll own the Dragons, too."

K nods. "Strength in numbers, Kyla. Speaking of..." He whistles, and the doors open behind him. The two guards come in, and I start to shake. K throws me on the bed. "Hold her down."

I kick at them. I thrash around. K leans his weight directly on the bandage on my thigh, then pries open my other thigh forcing my knees to the bed while the other two grab each hand. A cry works its way up my throat because Jesus fuck, my fucking hand. I force the scream down. His stare roams over my body greedily while I try to move. Tears spill from my eyes. He grabs the hem of my shirt and rips it. He keeps tearing until I'm in my bra, the sides of my shirt cast aside.

"I'm going to enjoy this so fucking much."

"No!" I cry out. I think of every move I know. I twist and turn. I buck my hips. I struggle. I fight like I've never fought before. I rebel against the pain radiating from my hand and the scrapes on my thigh. Every class I took comes down to this. Every tear I shed from the pain comes down to this. Every win in the ring means nothing if this happens to me.

"Look at her go, boys."

Humiliation slaps me. I have nowhere to go. I have nothing else to give. I'll never stop, but it's useless. There are three of them, and I'm only me.

Only me.

I sob. Choked breaths burst from my chest.

"Now I'm really disappointed," K says. "I wanted that smart mouth."

I yank at my hands. I move my feet. They've done this

before. They know exactly where to hold me so I won't move, but more to their advantage, where K can do his thing and there's nothing I can fucking do about it.

K rubs his thumb over the apex of my thighs. I stare up at the ceiling. I'm still thrashing. I'm still trying. I'll never fucking stop, but I allow myself not to feel. I retreat within.

K moves off me, yanking at the top of my joggers. I kick out, hitting him solidly in the gut. He roars and lunges for me. He punches me square in the jaw, but I keep kicking despite the new shock of pain. I know for sure I hit him in the dick at least once because he punches me again and again. The two guards tag team to help. They hold my hips down as K tears my joggers down, taking skin with it.

I whimper when the fresh air hits me. I know it's done. It's over. The last barrier between this not happening and it definitely happening was just removed.

"Fuck!" K screams.

Everything stops. I blink. The guards stare down at K, so I slowly move my gaze that way.

"You bitch!"

He throws my feet to the side, but not before I see what made him so angry. I got my period. Blood stains the crotch of my panties.

He punches me again, and my head lulls to the side, and my vision darkens. He drags me off the bed, and I drop unceremoniously to my ass. My joggers are around my ankles, and my shirt is wide open, still revealing my bra.

"Fucking women," K fumes. "Get her sorry ass out of my sight and bring me Victoria."

The two guards come around the side of the bed and haul me to my feet. They drag me from the room. All I can manage are tiny, agonizing footsteps with my clothes around my ankles, so they end up taking all my weight. Pain blooms over my face in different areas, and I can't help but be grateful. I'd rather have gotten the shit kicked out of me than been raped by that fucking— Scratch that. Than raped at all.

"Take her to the fucking cells," K roars after us. "And I want Victoria now!"

I've never been happier to be a menstruating woman than this very moment.

And what a fucking bastard. Scared of a little period blood. It's no wonder Johnny's mom left him.

The guard on my left opens K's suite door and they drag me out. Other guards line the hall who don't mind taking their fill of my bare ass, bloody underwear, and bruised face. None of them make a sound, and I've never wanted to burn down the Crew's world more than I do right now.

Magnum had better come up with a plan.

$\mathcal{I}$ wake on the floor of the cell in the basement with stiff bones and a sore face. Last night when they brought me down, it was dark, and I was too emotional to look around. This morning—or whatever time it is—a single light blinks on and off, revealing where I spent the night.

Outside the cell I'm in, it looks like a regular basement. Cement block walls. The furnace is off to the right. There are tubs of brightly colored storage containers stacked ceiling high next to it. I pull myself off the stone floor and scramble back when I notice the stains. Bleach has definitely been poured on these floors over and over again, but the ring right in front of me is unmistakable. They probably brought Glo here, and this is probably where she died, too.

Now, I'm here.

I look around to gather my surroundings because at one point, I'd been interested in where they were taking Glo, but not anymore. Literal metal, cylindrical bars are spaced six inches apart from ceiling to floor all around me, giving me a six by six-foot space. There's no bed. No toilet. No sink. In the corner though, I spy a package of sanitary napkins, a fresh pair of underwear, and two pills.

My heart warms. Magnum did this.

I can only imagine what kind of mess I've made of my clothes, but I swear as long as I live, I'll never fucking bitch about my period again. It's a fucking gift.

I crawl to the package and lower my black joggers. Thankfully, they're a dark color. Yanking them off, I quickly pull on the new underwear, place a pad on top, and then pull the joggers back up. I stare at the two pills before popping them one-by-one into my mouth and swallowing them with a mouthful of spit. I can only hope the pain reliever kicks in soon because I feel like I've been through a garbage compactor.

It's been a whole day since I've seen Brawler or Oscar. Magnum will have told them what's going on by now. Hopefully, they got Johnny out of jail and they're figuring something out together. Something with the Dragons maybe? K plans on double-crossing them. Maybe Magnum can use the Dragons to do the same, and then double-cross both their asses by throwing everyone in jail.

Well, not everyone. K's going to hell. That's a fact.

The sound of footsteps on stairs makes its way to me. I scramble up the cell bars, using them as leverage to pull myself to my feet while my body screams at me. I've never fought so hard for myself. Never felt so powerless or wracked with fear.

And I never want to feel that way again.

Trey comes into view. I kick the package of pads under the bars, hoping they're out of his view. I don't know what he'll do or say if he thinks someone is giving me such a basic necessity. Since K seemed so grossed out by it, you'd think he'd have brought down the appropriate products himself.

"You look like shit."

"Fuck off," I say, still gripping the cell bars while my injured hand throbs. I sneer at him.

"You're supposed to be a prize for the Dragons, but they might take one look at you and forget the whole thing."

"I guess K can let me take a shower then."

Trey chuckles. He opens the cell door with a key and then stands in front of me. His eyes narrow at my face. "I really want to punch you for that one time you got me in trouble, but you look so pathetic."

"Don't let that stop you."

He doesn't. He hauls off and gives me a right hook. His knuckles crash against my cheek, but all-in-all, I've been hit by worse.

I don't give him the satisfaction of making a reaction. Instead, I turn to face him again. "Am I up?"

"Hopefully, the leader of the Dragons gives you what you deserve."

"A horse? I always wanted a horse."

Damn. I'm way too mouthy for someone who's currently being held captive. Meh. If this is my last hurrah, I better make it a good one.

Trey yanks my arm, and we walk toward the steps. It turns out this is a sub-sub basement, only reachable by a set of metal steps. The elevator doesn't even go down this far, which I found out last night. We climb to the next level, and Trey shoves a rusty metal door open, revealing the parking area. Trey keeps his tight hold as he marches me across the length of the lot, stopping in front of a black Escalade limo.

"He's waiting for you." Trey yanks the limo door open and shoves me in.

I sprawl out on the seat but recover quickly. I pull my feet in and face the surrounding leather couches. K's drinking a glass full of amber liquid against one side. No one else is in sight. "New ride?"

K isn't in a friendly mood anymore. I almost miss his Satan-esque laughter. "We bring this one out for special occasions."

"Like taking over new territory?"

"Exactly like taking over new territory." This brings a smile to his lips. "I've waited a long time for this," K drawls on, turning the glass in his hands and watching the lights play over the liquid. "Unlike my predecessor, I was never happy with just the Heights. Growth. Expansion. You'd be surprised at the underground world living just on the edges of society. I was enthralled as soon as I was introduced to it. Sex. Drugs. Money. That's the core. On the outside though, you have gambling rings, prostitution, and drug trafficking. It's a shame the sheep living their uptight lives don't see the freedom that's right under their noses. The things that are right there for the taking."

"I guess that's a good thing for you," I deadpan. "You don't seem like you like to share."

"Sharing is for the weak."

Or the kind-hearted, I think. The caring. The people who have more values in their little toe than this fucker has in his whole being. "Any plan I should know about? Just stand there and be quiet, I assume?"

"You're finally learning. It's a shame my Johnny couldn't wrangle you under control before you ruined him."

"He's not your Johnny."

Pure anger radiates from K. He slams his glass down. "Now he's neither of ours."

"I'd rather give him up than have him still be stuck with you. I'd rather him spend his life in prison than spend his time with an abusive father figure who doesn't even care about him. Besides, you're wrong. I didn't ruin Johnny. I didn't take him from you. You pushed him away."

"I gave him everything he ever wanted."

"But nothing he needed. Like love. Like companionship.

Like the knowledge that the person you love most in the world would do anything for you."

Laughter returns to K's eyes. "You're just a silly, little girl. You came here to kill me but look at you now. Trust me, Kyla, you won't make it out of this alive. As soon as I don't need you as bait anymore, you're gone. I'll make sure Johnny never finds out what happened to you because you don't deserve to be mourned. You're nothing, Kyla Samson."

His words hit me like an explosion to the chest. I have a love-hate relationship with the mourning process. I hated the fact that my parents were dead but mourning them gave me some semblance of peace. A time I could come to terms with the fact that they were gone. Just like Brawler visits his brother and sister on Christmas. Like Johnny and Jacob yearn for their mothers. Grieving is a facet of life. A cog in the cycle of love and death. If things go down like K wants them to, if he gets his way like he always does, the guys will never know what happened to me, and for some reason, that devastates me to my very core.

I deserve to be loved even when I'm dead.

The gravity of the situation falls on my shoulders. I might not make it out of here alive. Even if Magnum does have a plan, it might not work. Everything always seems to swing in K's favor, and no matter how much I'd like to break that cycle, what if it just doesn't happen?

I'll lose everything.

The thought of death being a very real possibility sobers

me up. K picks his glass up again, not even aware his words did more damage than his fists did last night. That's the thing with words. They leave everlasting marks that actions never could.

The limo comes to a stop, and K puts down his glass. He glares at me as he slides toward the door. "You stay with me. If you try anything, you'll be dead before you know it." He pushes back his suit coat and reveals a small handgun.

The door opens, and K steps from the car. The guards reach back in and yank me out with more force than necessary. I know I can't hide in the limo forever. I stay just behind and to the left of K as he walks over the uneven terrain. Stone mixes with cracked cement. Weeds poke up through fissures in the broken foundation. Around us are the charred remains of the race track.

Guards stick close to us as we move toward a pile of ash. I don't understand K's plan here. If he got the Dragons to meet him under the guise that he's Gregory, they're definitely going to figure out he's not Gregory as soon as they see him.

Then again, K is just that fucking cocky.

I close my eyes. *One Kyle and Anna. Two Kyle and Anna. For God's sake, if you can hear me, keep me and my guys alive.*

In the distance, three figures come into view. I take stock of who we have with us and am startled when I spy

Magnum to our right. That makes Trey, Magnum, K, and me. And I'm just here for bait.

At least that's what they think.

Magnum doesn't meet my eye, but I doubt he'd show up here without a plan. Unless we're all just fucked.

Clearly, I'm the only one who doesn't know the plan. When we get within twenty feet of the Dragons, I scan their faces. My jaw almost unhinges when I find Cole as part of the team. Actually, he's not just part of the team. He's standing directly in the middle. His head drops back, a laugh escaping his mouth that is not nearly as crazy as K's can be, but it has the same force. "You've got to be shitting me."

K nearly smiles. "Surprise."

"Surprise my ass. Where's Gregory?"

I glance between Cole and K. It's obvious K doesn't recognize him. I guess having all those little Crew members means you forget faces. Or just plain don't give a fuck enough to remember them. Trey must be new because he isn't saying shit either. I don't dare look at Magnum. Is he surprised? Did he know about this?

"Gregory was always my little bitch. He never acted without my command, but he's surprisingly found himself not breathing recently."

Cole's face darkens. The earlier mirth is completely stricken from his face. They must be nervous, but they don't show it. In fact, they look pretty calm for just finding out they were double-crossed.

"Give up."

"Give up or die, you mean?" Cole asks.

K smirks. "Come on. You know I don't play like that. It's give up and die."

Cole darts his gaze to me then back to K. Uneasiness crawls through me. I was literally here for just this. Just to keep them rooted in this spot. The carrot dangling in front of them.

"If we all die, you don't get shit, and you know it."

"It's a hostile takeover," K gleams. "Your underlings will see reason."

"Like I haven't prepared for something like this. You don't get to be a leader without being smart." This time, Cole moves his gaze to Magnum. Holy shit. He's actually the leader of the Dragons. He's been the leader this whole time.

They can sort their shit out later, if there is a later. We have more pressing concerns.

"Trust me, I know what I'm doing," K says. "I took out Roza. Her merry clan of assholes never recovered. If your guys still want to make it, they'll gladly fall under my wing. If not, the Dragons will be nothing but a memory."

"You forget we're bigger than you."

K chuckles. "In size. Your holdings are nothing compared to ours."

His guard moves first. He reaches in his pocket, but movement to my left catches my attention. Trey goes for his gun. I react. I slam my body into his, knocking his gun from his hand. The gun clatters against the uneven terrain.

The roar of an engine breaks the tension. A speeding car barrels into view headed straight for us. Before it gets too close, I'm slammed from the side. I go down hard. Trey bashes my head against the ground. Around me, gunshots ring out, and suddenly, Trey slumps over me.

The weight of his body presses down against me. I push him off and scramble out from underneath him only to hit something solid.

"Kyla, watch out!"

That voice. I roll out of the way and stand to find Johnny staring down the barrel of a gun, aimed right at his father.

Cole and his two men come out from around the car. Brawler and Oscar flank Johnny. Magnum joins them, and then I sneak on the other side of the invisible line, too. I'm on the right side. I always have been. It's not about morals, really. It's about right and wrong, and to me, I see nothing wrong with doing what I'm about to do. I'm not taking one person from the world. I'm saving the world from him.

"Christ," Cole stutters out. "I almost had a heart attack."

Oscar puts a finger under my chin and makes me look at him. He frowns at my face. "Are you okay?"

"Fine," I tell him. I go down the line, squeezing my guys, letting myself believe that we're all here again.

Magnum nods when I get to him. He then reaches in his waistband and pulls out a royal purple gun. It's sleek and shiny. It gives me goosebumps. He told me he'd get me a gun, and he fucking did.

"I bet you never thought it would end like this," Johnny says to his dad.

I take the gun from Magnum and move into place next to Johnny. His father glances down the line at us, and I let him. I want him to take all our faces to the grave with him. This is the moment K didn't get his way. This is the moment his best-laid plans never came to fruition. In fact, I'd say they blew up in his face.

"You're going to kill your own father?"

"I don't have a father."

I steady my hand on Johnny's, lowering his gun while raising my own. This has always been my task to complete. I know I've had doubts in the past. Could I really pull the trigger? Could I really take someone's life? The truth is, K's not a person. He's a living, breathing monster whose reign of terror was never going to stop. Women. Johnny. Roza. Dunnegan. Gregory. His complete lack of empathy for human life is jarring. My mom and dad. Johnny's mom. The countless others I'll never know all the names and faces of.

I level the barrel at his forehead. "You know my name."

He glares at me. He doesn't say a word, and I still see the tick of defiance in his dead eyes.

"You know their names." I thought all along that I had to

say something important. Something that would make him think about what he's done. Something to make him know that it was me that got the better of him. But right now, I understand that none of that matters. One pull of a muscle, and I can have the rest of my life. I'll have the life I should have had. "As soon as I pull this trigger, I vow to never think of you again."

His eyes widen. His reaction is like a magnet that pulls my finger backward.

The purple gun discharges.

The bullet flies through the air.

It hits Big Daddy K, leader of the Crew, dead center in the forehead.

And just like that, I'm free.

Sirens sound in the distance. Magnum places his hand on my arm, lowering it to my side as I stare into the void. I smile. I smile so fucking huge that I think it's going to break my face. Then, the tears start coming. Make no mistake, I'm not sad. I'm fucking happy. I'm fucking proud.

"You guys need to go," Magnum says.

"Remind me never to fuck with her," Cole says to one of his guys, and I start to laugh, which I think freaks him out even more. He nods at his guys, and they take off. He and Magnum share a look, and I know this probably isn't the last I've seen of Jacob's cousin.

Oscar takes my face in his hands. His dark eyes sear into mine like a brand. He wipes the happy tears from my cheeks. "God, I love you," he breathes. "I don't know what it says about me that I have a stiff one right now, but I could literally lay you down right here and—"

"Drego..." Magnum chastises. "You guys need to go."

Oscar gives me a smirk, then pulls me close, pressing his lips against mine hungrily before stepping away.

Brawler's next. He runs his fingers through my hair. I stare at the angel wings peeking out of his t-shirt and smile before meeting his turquoise eyes. "New life," he says.

"Together," I promise.

He steps closer and kisses my forehead, lingering there while his hands work up and down my arms. "We have to go."

"Go," I tell him. "It's fine. We have our whole lives."

He pulls back and gives me a tentative smile before he and Oscar take off running toward the woods surrounding the race track. I'd bet anything somewhere in there, a getaway vehicle waits for them. Oscar's bike perhaps. They must have had all this set up. For me.

I turn to find Johnny rooted in his spot. He's glaring down at his father's body. A chill runs through me. "I'm—"

"Don't even say you're sorry," Johnny says. The dark-haired, stony-faced angel turns to me. There isn't a shred of sympathy in his eyes. Of sadness. There's nothing but his love for me that shines back in his icy blue gaze.

I nod, taking in what that must mean. "Shouldn't you be going?" I ask as the sirens get closer.

He shakes his head and smiles. "No, I'm not leaving you. This is part of the plan, babe."

"Should I know the plan?" I ask.

The sirens are the sounds of reckoning. They're echoing all around us now.

Magnum steps next to Johnny. "It's simple," he says. "We lured Big Daddy K to get him to admit to kidnapping you among the other heinous things he's done." He touches his chest. "Unfortunately, our wires malfunctioned, so they haven't been able to hear anything, and when they do get here, it won't matter because there was a fight. You killed K in self-defense...." He trails off. "Unless you want one of us to say we did it. If so, give us the gun now, and we'll wipe your prints and replace our own."

I blink at him. "Am I going to get into trouble?" The plan was always not to get in trouble. Not that I would let either of them go down for what I did. That's not how this relationship works, but I need to know.

Magnum shakes his head. "Lucky for you, you have two eyewitnesses that can attest to the fact that you killed K in self-defense. One of them is a cop, so no, you won't be getting into trouble, angel."

The gun's getting warm in my hands, but I'm not giving it up. "I got this," I tell them both.

Dirt kicks up as the cop cars come screaming up the barely used road to get here. Magnum gives me a smile. "There was a struggle. You don't remember much, but you were able to get away, and you shot blindly. Kingston Marx fell. That's it."

"That's it?"

"That, and I fucking love you more than life itself, Kyla Samson."

The tears are coming again. I don't hide them. I don't push them back. I use them as part of the act we're about to put on.

The cop cars skid to a halt. There's a line of three of them in front of us. The first cop gets out of the car and uses his door as a shield while pulling a gun on me. "Drop your weapon!"

I do as he says, though a part of me hopes it doesn't get scuffed. I've only had that gun for a total of a few minutes, but I'm pretty attached.

"Kick it away from you!" he orders.

Again, I do as he says. His next order is for us to put our hands in the air, and we all do. Johnny and I are separated from Jacob, and while we wait to get spoken to, he weaves his tale. They take out the wires and inspect them to see why they didn't work. Not that it matters. Big Daddy K is dead. His reign of terror is over. We got our justice.

A few policemen head over to K's body and check for a pulse. A second later, they use their radios to call for an ambulance.

The next hour or so goes by in a blur. The medics who come to take K's body look at my hand. Besides giving me a tetanus shot, they flush the wound to stave off infection. Which hurt like a fucking bitch. After bandaging it, they make me promise to see a regular doctor. They don't think there was any damage to tendons, but if I want to have not only regular use of my hands, but punching power, I can't let it go unchecked.

You better fucking believe I'm following through on that. K's taken so much from me. If he takes my fight career away, I'll revive him just to kill his ass again.

Afterward, Johnny and I are taken separately to the Rawley Heights police station where they let me clean up and give me new clothes, taking the ones I had on as evidence. I recount the physical abuse by Big Daddy K. I tell them about the almost rape and about spending the night in the basement cells. When they ask about gang stuff, I tell them I don't know anything.

When it comes time to recount what happened at the burnt down race track, I say it exactly like Magnum instructed. Everything happened so fast. K tried to kill me. I wrestled for the gun. I got away. I shot him.

"Whose gun was it?"

This hurts to say, but I shrug anyway. "I have no idea."

My hands shake, and the policemen in the interrogation room bring me water and granola bars. To them, I'm Johnny Rocket's little girlfriend who got herself in too deep.

They're not wrong, but I will punch anyone who actually dares say something like *little girlfriend.*

The police let me go, and Johnny waits for me with open arms. As soon as I spy him near the door, I pick up the pace, throwing my arms around him. I close my eyes and take in the moment. Neither one of us has anything dangling over our heads. We could literally do nothing right now. We could go to dinner. We could skip town. No one's going to be calling Johnny back for an important meeting. He's all mine.

"You okay?" he asks.

"Better than okay," I whisper against his chest.

He squeezes me tighter, but a man clearing their throat pierces my Crew-free bubble. I turn to find Detective Reynolds staring back at us. His jaw clenches as he looks me up and down. I'm not sure what my face looks like, but people have been doing that to me all day, so it must be bad. "I hear I was wrong about you killing that little girl."

Jesus. I almost forgot about that. Johnny winds his arms around me from behind, and I lean back against him for support. "I tried to tell you."

He nods to the far side of the room where Jacob emerges from a doorway laughing with uniformed cops. "And I know why your evidence went missing and why I was blocked from looking into you."

I just stare at him. If he's trying to apologize... Well, one, I don't care, and two, he's doing a terrible job of it.

Johnny kisses my temple. When Reynolds doesn't say anything for a while, he asks, "You ready to go, babe?"

"Yeah," I croak out. Right before I leave, Reynolds nods at me, and I guess that's as good as I'm going to get. It's a relief only because that's one more thing I don't have to take with me into my new life.

Johnny steers me toward the door. We walk outside, and I swear I've never breathed air as sweet as this even if it does smell like the Heights. I smile up at him. "What do two people do who're starting a new life?"

He chuckles. "They go see your other boyfriends before one boyfriend gets his dick chopped off." I laugh, but he gives me a look. "Seriously. I'm not kidding." He brings his phone out and gives it to me. I scroll through the latest texts.

Brawler: What's happening?

Brawler: Is she okay?

Drego: Why is it taking so long?

Brawler: A response would be nice.

Drego: I swear to fuck, we're going to be eating fillet o' dick if I don't get a response in .2 seconds.

I hand it back to him, trying to stifle the laugh bubbling up my throat. "You didn't respond back?"

"I'm not his bitch." He shoves his phone back in his pocket, and I shake my head. These guys are going to be a handful.

Nothing I can't handle though.

We walk around the side of the building and out onto the sidewalk. I'm about to ask Johnny where we're going, but

up ahead, I spy the familiar black car with two perfect speci-
mens of men leaning against it. It seems like ages since I've
seen Oscar and Brawler, and even when I did see them, we
were a little busy. I squeeze Johnny's hip and take off at a
run. My face hurts again from smiling so much, but I barrel
right into Brawler who picks me up and twirls me around
like a princess. It's some actual fairy tale shit, but I love
every moment.

As soon as Brawler sets me down, Oscar hugs me from
behind. For a blissful few moments, I'm in an Oscar-Brawler
sandwich. Oscar nips at my ear. "I'm glad you came out, I
was about to march my ass in there."

"Great idea. Then we'd have to explain why the hell you
knew we were all there."

"If someone had just thought to send a short text," Oscar
throws at Johnny. "I wouldn't have had to make such
desperate plans."

I cup Oscar's cheek and give him a loud, smacking kiss
on his jawline. "No need to worry. I'm right here."

Brawler glances between Oscar and Johnny. "You're
sure you're signing up for this shit?"

I give him a smirk. "Are you kidding me? We just fought
the greatest fight and won. What's waiting for us on the
other side is...our prize."

"You've always been my prize."

Oscar and Johnny glare at each other after saying the
same thing at the exact same time. I must be on happy

pills because it makes me laugh. Brawler chuckles, shaking his head while Oscar and Johnny continue to stare each other down like they don't like one another. When push comes to shove though, we'll always have each other's backs.

I wouldn't have it any other way.

Footsteps sound, and we all turn to find Magnum walking up the sidewalk toward us. The street lamp above us flashes on as the sun starts to set. The horizon is a beautiful orange color, silhouetting Magnum's movements. The closer he gets, the more at ease I feel.

We're all together again.

Magnum with his fierce protection. Johnny with his fierce everything. Brawler with his unending love. And Oscar...well, Oscar with his aptitude for saying the wrong thing at the wrong time.

"Anyone hungry?"

Or maybe that's the right thing at the wrong time. I smile and lift up on my toes to kiss the cheek of one of the most loyal and devoted men I've ever known but who can also make me smile when I most need it. "Starving."

"Well, there you have it," Johnny says. "When five people are starting the rest of their lives, they apparently start it with food."

The guys turn to head to the car. Jacob steps up to me and runs his hands through my hair. "You okay, angel?"

"Couldn't be better." I lower my voice to a whisper.

"Did you tell them...?" I ask, finishing the thought with my eyes. He knows what Big Daddy K almost did to me.

He shakes his head. "I figured that was your decision to make."

I already know my decision. I vowed to never think about K again and that includes taking everything he did to me and releasing it.

I reach up on my tiptoes and give him a kiss. "I love you."

He takes my hand while I get in the car. Before I sit, I peer up at the beautiful sunset.

I've made a lot of plans while staring up at the sky. A lot of promises to the people I love that I can't see or hear anymore.

Right now, though, I just smile and admire the beauty. I don't need to make plans or promise myself anything because my life is all around me. It's in the hearts of the four men who've been through this shitshow with me, and despite the setbacks and danger and the fear that threatened our lives, we're walking out of here together. Stronger. And with more love than I could've ever imagined.

I wipe sweaty palms down my jeans. My own jeans. Jeans bought with my money because I liked them and that was enough.

"He'll be fine, Princess," Oscar says. Brawler, Oscar, and I walked out of Rawley Heights High a half hour ago with our transcripts in hand. I've already been enrolled in online learning, but Oscar and Brawler are signing up for the program I'm in right away.

I give him a look. He knows I don't like being singled out when my anxiety is getting the better of me.

Today's *the* day. Jacob has his meeting with the Internal Review Board of the Rawley Heights Police Department. They're going to go over his undercover assignment with a fine-tooth comb.

All of us were completely shocked about his involvement with the police, but maybe Johnny most of all. That was a lot of time for Magnum to be keeping that secret of which only one other person in the world knew.

Imagine being the devil's puppet.

I shudder to even think about it now. None of us got out of the Crew unscathed. The guys have scars they'll hold forever, and maybe that's why when all was said and done, forgiveness was easier.

"If this—" I break off and clear the sudden ball of emotion clogging my throat. The thing is, if this review goes badly, everything we worked so hard for could be for nothing. Magnum could be found at fault and—

"Quick. Distract her," Johnny says.

Oscar lifts his brow. "Dude. We're in public. The only way I know to distract Princess can't be done on the streets outside of the police department."

Brawler rolls his eyes. "He just means to change the subject. How's your mom?"

Damn. Brawler is smart. I peer at Oscar, waiting for his answer. A week ago, she was moved into a drug rehabilitation center a few hours away. They were supposed to have their first therapy phone call this morning. "Well...?" I ask.

Oscar grins. "She's...good. I don't know. I'm hopeful this time." He shrugs like it's no big deal, but it's a huge fucking deal. If Oscar's mom can work her shit out on her own, Oscar will be able to move on with his life like he should. He won't have to be her parent. Maybe she can even be his for the first time in a long time. "I told her about homeschooling, and she was fine with it."

"Did you tell her about—?"

Oscar shakes his head. "No, not yet. I figured it didn't make a difference right now because she's in rehab anyway."

I reach out to squeeze his hand. It's not my imagination that he seems lighter, like a huge responsibility has lifted from his shoulders. "She's going to do great."

He crosses his fingers and brings them up to show them off. He drops them to his side again and turns toward Brawler. "What about your mom?"

Brawler heaves out a breath. "You know she fought me at first, but I actually think she loves the new place."

He can't bring himself to say the words. He acts like Yellowfield is some sort of new condo his mom had the opportunity to move into, but in fact, it's an assisted living facility. The tenants there get as much or as little help as they need. His mom doesn't need much assistance, but he's hoping the scheduled activities and social mixers will get his mother out of her bedroom and into real life. The change of scenery should do wonders for her, too. She's way outside the Heights now. Away from the tragedy and loss she was stuck in. Brawler and I drove her three hours north four days ago to get her settled. That was the first time she'd been out of the apartment since her children died.

No wonder she's so depressed.

Now, she can get mental health monitoring right on site.

There are dozens of tenants around her age only a few steps away. She has her own things. She can come and go as she pleases. Honestly, when we were there, I kind of wanted to stay.

"When I talked to her this morning, she said she went to the communal dining room to eat dinner."

I gasp. "No…"

He nods, a smile slipping over his lips. Eating around other people seems like such a little thing, but this is huge for her.

My heart swells. "That's awesome, Brawler. I'm so excited for her."

Brawler rubs the back of his neck and then glances at Johnny.

Johnny puts his hand up. "I swear to God if you say thank you one more time, I'm going to kill you. We should all be thankful I have *one* account that wasn't tied to the Crew's and not currently frozen in litigation."

I move toward him and wrap my arms around his hips. "That's because you're smart."

Despite my words, the frown line between his eyes deepens. When he told me how much money was currently frozen in all of the Crew's accounts, I almost had a heart attack, but we don't need that money. It's dirty. It's gross. It's Crew-stained, and that's all I need to know to keep away from it.

"We can make more money," I tell him.

He gives me a dubious look. "How?"

So, assimilating into real life isn't going all that well for Johnny, but he'll get used to it. He just has to shake off all his illegal tendencies. I give him the biggest grin I can. "Are you kidding me?" I point to Oscar. "NFL quarterback right there." I turn my huge smile on Brawler next. "UFC champ."

"Right back at you, knockout," Brawler says teasingly.

I place my hands on my hips and face him. "That's Knockout *Queen* to you guys."

"Well, well," Oscar says. "So, you're moving up the line of royalty now? Princess no longer good enough for you?"

I shrug. "New life, new nickname." I glare at him. "But if you stop calling me Princess, I'll castrate you."

Oscar fights off a smile. "You guys notice how she goes right for the goods now? She doesn't even pretend we're not pussy-whipped."

I laugh, giving Oscar a playful shove. I'd like to see any of these guys be pussy-whipped. Please. If anything, I'm the one who turns into a puddle of arousal nearly every hour on the hour.

The back door to the police station creaks open. We all turn to find Jacob making his way out. He has his hands shoved into a pair of actual suit pants. They're a little tight on him because he borrowed Johnny's. He refused to wear a button-up shirt, but a black polo stretches over his muscles as he walks down the ramp toward us. It isn't until he's close enough to touch that he lifts his head.

He's all smiles.

My stomach drops. In a good way. I almost forgot what a good stomach drop could feel like. The hair on my arms raises with goosebumps. I'm so carefree I could almost get swept away at this very moment by the tiniest breeze.

"Seriously, man?" Johnny asks, brows pulling together in hope.

Ha. He could fake it all he wanted, but I knew he was worried too. We all were. Throughout the multiple discussions we've had after the fact, we all came to realize the pressure Jacob was under. Playing both sides. Trying to keep us all alive while also not tipping either side off. When I think about what he was able to maneuver us through...I owe him my life. Several times over.

He won't accept that type of praise because of the guilt he still holds, but I plan on making it up to him for the rest of my life.

A surprised smile turns Jacob's lips up at the corners. "I check out. Everything checks out."

"Fuck..." Oscar shakes his head, disbelieving. It's what we're all thinking. Somehow, the planets aligned, and everything seems to be going our way lately.

"I was offered a new assignment."

I peek up at Jacob who even trimmed his beard for this.

"I turned it down and put in my resignation."

Johnny slaps him on the back. "Good because I'm not sure you'd hack it if you had to go clean." They both laugh, and the simple fact they're able to push past the hurt and lies says everything. "According to Kyla, Brawler and Oscar are going to need security when they get famous, so I guess you have that to look forward to."

"Mock me all you want, but it's happening," I tell them. I have all the confidence in the world.

In my bag that's currently sitting in the front seat of the car, I have a flash drive filled with footage of Oscar playing football. Some of the many highlights of his career that I was able to get from his coach. When we get settled, I fully intend on making copies and sending it to every college in the tri-state area. Or wherever. East coast. West coast. Doesn't matter. As long as I'm there.

As for Brawler, he doesn't need the extra push. We'll both find a gym to train at eventually.

Magnum gazes at me with those hazel-green eyes. I step toward him to wrap my arms around his solid hips. "I'm so happy," I whisper.

Resigning from his job was the last thing we needed to fall into place. We already have my car filled with our stuff, but we also hired a moving company to pack up and take the rest of our shit wherever we end up. But bottom line, we're getting the hell out of here.

Us leaving the Heights is what Oscar is keeping from his mom. I don't know why. Maybe it's because he's worried it will get ruined somehow, but so help me, nothing is stopping us from leaving this fucking city.

"I have one more thing that's going to make you extremely happy," Mag says. He reaches into the back of his pants, and I eye him suspiciously until he brings out a gun. *The* gun. He places the purple handgun in his open palms and offers it to me.

I reach for it, admiring the color just like I did when I originally saw it the night our new life started. Wrapping my hand around the grip, I test the weight. My ring glitters almost in tandem with the gun, immediately making my heart pound. A glow starts from my chest and pours warmth through my limbs. Where we're headed, I hope I don't need it, but I sure as fuck want it as a souvenir. Of the actual reason we were able to get the fuck out of the Heights.

Honestly? Things couldn't be any more perfect than they are right now.

"This is it?" Johnny asks, looking around him to the rest of us.

"That's it," Magnum says.

We turn toward my car, but Johnny just can't help himself. He groans. "I really wish you would've let me buy you something...sportier." He slides a pair of sunglasses over his face like he doesn't want to be seen near my totally sensible, totally boring car.

"We all agreed we'd rather spend the money on...vacation!" Oscar runs up to the car and bangs his hand on the roof. "Come on, let's go!"

Excitement blossoms in my chest. This is really happening. We're driving to the coast where we've rented a beach house for an indefinite amount of time. It's our new start. Our gift to one another.

I slip the gun into the waistband of my joggers and climb in behind the wheel as the rest of the guys try to get comfortable inside my moderately roomy, mid-sized vehicle. I peer in the rearview mirror, meeting three sets of eyes, and then glance to my right to a pair of hazel green ones. You couldn't pry the smile from my face right now. What I wanted is actually coming true.

I pull away from the curb. We don't even make it a block when Oscar rolls his window down and starts to scream. He punches the roof of the car with excited pumps of his fist. The energy coming off him makes the rest of us roll our windows down, too.

We all scream as we leave the streets of the Heights behind. We scream for our losses. We scream for our wins. But most of all, we scream for the excitement of our new lives...together.

Lots of people don't get the chance to leave the Heights. Not us. We're out of here, and we're not looking back.

E. M. Moore is a USA Today Bestselling author of Contemporary and Paranormal Romance. She's drawn to write within the teen and college-aged years where her characters get knocked on their asses, torn inside out, and put back together again by their first loves. Whether it's in a fantastical setting where human guards protect the creatures of the night or a realistic high school backdrop where social cliques rule the halls, the emotions are the same. Dark. Twisty. Angsty. Raw.

When Erin's not writing, you can find her dreaming up vacations for her family, watching murder mystery shows, or dancing in her kitchen while she pretends to cook.